A Letter From Mrs. Robert A. Heinlein:

Amidst all of the fan mail coming in on EXPANDED UNIVERSE, I find that I must pause to advise you of what is happening.

The mail on this book has been coming in in quantities we had never dreamed of. Almost every day, we receive about half a dozen to a dozen letters, telling Robert how much people have enjoyed this book. It seems strange to us, because fan mail has a tendency to drift in slowly when a new book is out, but this has been coming in a flood. Never has any book of Robert's had this amazing response . . . Some of it is from people who are, or have been, in the military. More is just from people who have read the book. All of it is friendly, and much of it heart-warming.

For over thirty years I have been reading fan mail, and answering much of it, but this response has amazed me.

—*Virginia Heinlein*

EXPANDED UNIVERSE

ROBERT A. HEINLEIN

ACE SCIENCE FICTION BOOKS
NEW YORK

EXPANDED UNIVERSE

An Ace Science Fiction Book / published by arrangement with
the author

PRINTING HISTORY
First hardcover edition / October 1980
First trade paperback edition / February 1981
First mass market edition / March 1982
Eighth printing / March 1986

ISBN: 0-441-21891-1

Library of Congress Catalog Card number: 80-67367

Ace Science Fiction Books are published by The Berkley Publishing Group,
200 Madison Avenue, New York, New York 10016.
PRINTED IN THE UNITED STATES OF AMERICA

Table of Contents

To William Targ

FOREWORD

Warning! Truth in advertising requires me to tell
you that this volume contains THE WORLDS OF
ROBERT A. HEINLEIN, published 1966. But this new
volume is about three times as long. It contains fiction
stories that have never before appeared in book form,
nonfiction articles not available elsewhere, a 30-year
updating on my 1950 prognostications (as well as the
15-year updating that appeared in THE WORLDS OF
R.A.H.), with the usual weasel-worded excuses as to
why I guessed wrong—and (ruffles & flourishes) not
one but *two* scenarios for the year 2000, one for people
who like happy endings and another for people who
can take bad news without a quiver—as long as it happens to somebody else.

On these I will do a really free-swinging job as the
probability (by a formula I just now derived) that
either I or this soi-disant civilization will be extinct by
2000 A.D. approaches 99.92+%. This makes it unlikely that I will again have to explain my mistakes.

But do not assume that *I* will be the one extinct. My
great-great-great-grandfather Lawrence Heinlein died
prematurely at the age of ninety-seven, through having carelessly left his cabin one winter morning without his gun ·— and found a buck deer on the ice of

his pond. Lack of his gun did not stop my triple-great-grandfather; this skinful of meat must *not* be allowed to escape. He went out on the ice and bulldogged the buck, quite successfully.

But in throwing the deer my ancestor slipped on the ice, went down, and a point of the buck's rack stabbed between his ribs and pierced his heart.

No doubt it taught him a lesson—it certainly taught *me* one. So far I've beaten the odds three times: continued to live when the official prognosis called for something less active. So I intend to be careful—not chopped down in my prime the way my ancestor was. I shan't bulldog any buck deer, or cross against the lights, or reach barehanded into dark places favored by black widow spiders, or—most especially!—leave my quarters without being adequately armed.

Perhaps the warmest pleasure in life is the knowledge that one has no enemies. The easiest way to achieve this is by outliving them. No action is necessary; time wounds all heels.

In this peaceful crusade I have been surprisingly successful; most of those rascals are dead . . . and three of the survivors are in very poor health. The curve seems to indicate that by late 1984 I won't have an enemy anywhere in the world.

Of course someone else may appoint himself my enemy (all my enemies are self-appointed) but I would not expect such an unlikely event to affect the curve much. There appears to be some unnamed ESP force at work here; the record shows that it is not healthy to hate me.

I don't have anything to do with this. The character can be more than a thousand miles away, with me doing my utter best to follow Sergeant Dogberry's advice; nevertheless it happens: He starts losing weight, suffering from insomnia and from nightmares, headaches, stomach trouble, and, after a bit, he starts hearing voices.

The terminal stages vary greatly. Anyhow, they are

unpleasant and I should not be writing about such things as I am supposed to be writing a blurb that will persuade you to buy this book despite the fact that nearly a third of it is copy you may have seen before.

Aside from this foreword the items in this book are arranged in the order in which written, each with a comment as to how and why it was written (money, usually, but also— Well, money)—then a bridging comment telling what I was writing or doing between that item and the next.

The span is forty years. But these are not my memoirs of those four decades. The writing business is not such as to evoke amusing memoirs (yes, I do mean you and you and you and especially *you*). A writer spends his professional time in solitary confinement, refusing to accept telephone calls and declining to see visitors, surrounded by a dreary forest of reference books and somewhat-organized papers. The high point of his day is the breathless excitement of waiting for the postman. (The low point is usually immediately thereafter.)

How can one write entertaining memoirs about such an occupation? Answer: By writing about what this scrivener did when *not* writing, or by resorting to fiction, or both. Usually both.

I could write entertaining memoirs about things I did when not writing. I shan't do so because a) I hope those incidents have been forgotten, or b) I hope that any not forgotten are covered by the statute of limitations.

Meanwhile I hope you enjoy this. The fiction is plainly marked fiction; the nonfiction is as truthful as I can make it—and here and there, tucked into space that would otherwise be blank are anecdotes and trivia ranging from edifying to outrageous.

Each copy is guaranteed—or double your money back—to be printed on genuine paper of enough pages to hold the covers apart.

—R.A.H.

FOREWORD

The beginning of 1939 found me flat broke following a disastrous political campaign (I ran a strong second best, but in politics there are no prizes for place or show). I was highly skilled in ordnance, gunnery, and fire control for Naval vessels, a skill for which there was no demand ashore—and I had a piece of paper from the Secretary of the Navy telling me that I was a waste of space—"totally and permanently disabled" was the phraseology. I "owned" a heavily-mortgaged house.

About then THRILLING WONDER STORIES ran a house ad reading (more or less):

GIANT PRIZE CONTEST—Amateur Writers!!!!!!
First Prize $50 Fifty Dollars $50

In 1939 one could fill three station wagons with fifty dollars worth of groceries. Today I can pick up fifty dollars in groceries unassisted—perhaps I've grown stronger. So I wrote the story LIFE-LINE. It took me four days—I am a slow typist. But I did not send it to THRILLING WONDER; I sent it to ASTOUNDING, figuring they would not be so swamped with amateur short stories.

ASTOUNDING bought it . . . for $70, or $20 more than that "Grand Prize"—and there was never a chance that I would ever again look for honest work.

LIFE-LINE

The chairman rapped loudly for order. Gradually the catcalls and boos died away as several self-appointed sergeants-at-arms persuaded a few hot-headed individuals to sit down. The speaker on the rostrum by the chairman seemed unaware of the disturbance. His bland, faintly insolent face was impassive. The chairman turned to the speaker and addressed him in a voice in which anger and annoyance were barely restrained.

"Dr. Pinero"—the "Doctor" was faintly stressed—"I must apologize to you for the unseemly outburst during your remarks. I am surprised that my colleagues should so far forget the dignity proper to men of science as to interrupt a speaker, no matter"—he paused and set his mouth—"no matter how great the provocation." Pinero smiled in his face, a smile that was in some way an open insult. The chairman visibly controlled his temper and continued: "I am anxious that the program be concluded decently and in order. I want you to finish your remarks. Nevertheless, I must ask you to refrain from affronting our intelligence with ideas that any educated man knows to be fallacious. Please confine yourself to your discovery—if you have made one."

Pinero spread his fat, white hands, palms down. "How can I possibly put a new idea into your heads, if I do not first remove your delusions?"

The audience stirred and muttered. Someone shouted from the rear of the hall: "Throw the charlatan out! We've had enough."

The chairman pounded his gavel.

"Gentlemen! Please!"

Then to Pinero, "Must I remind you that you are not a member of this body, and that we did not invite you?"

Pinero's eyebrows lifted. "So? I seem to remember an invitation on the letterhead of the Academy."

The chairman chewed his lower lip before replying. "True, I wrote that invitation myself. But it was at the request of one of the trustees—a fine, public-spirited gentleman, but not a scientist, not a member of the Academy."

Pinero smiled his irritating smile. "So? I should have guessed. Old Bidwell, not so, of Amalgamated Life Insurance? And he wanted his trained seals to expose me as a fraud, yes? For if I can tell a man the day of his own death, no one will buy his pretty policies. But how can you expose me, if you will not listen to me first? Even supposing you had the wit to understand me? Bah! He has sent jackals to tear down a lion." He deliberately turned his back on them.

The muttering of the crowd swelled and took on a vicious tone. The chairman cried vainly for order. There arose a figure in the front row.

"Mr. Chairman!"

The chairman grasped the opening and shouted: "Gentlemen! Dr. Van Rhein-Smitt has the floor." The commotion died away.

The doctor cleared his throat, smoothed the forelock of his beautiful white hair, and thrust one hand into a side pocket of his smartly tailored trousers. He assumed his women's-club manner.

"Mr. Chairman, fellow members of the Academy of Science, let us have tolerance. Even a murderer has the right to say his say before the State exacts its tribute. Shall we do less? Even though one may be intellectually certain of the verdict? I grant Dr. Pinero every consideration that should be given by this august body to any unaffiliated colleague, even though" —he bowed slightly in Pinero's direction— "we may not be familiar with the university which bestowed his degree. If what he has to say is false, it cannot harm us. If what he has to say is true, we should know it." His mellow, cultivated voice rolled on, soothing and calming. "If the eminent doctor's manner appears a trifle inurbane for our tastes, we must bear in mind that the doctor may be from a place, or a stratum, not so meticulous in these matters. Now our good friend and benefactor has asked us to hear this person and carefully assess the merit of his claims. Let us do so with dignity and decorum."

He sat down to a rumble of applause, comfortably aware that he had enhanced his reputation as an intellectual leader. Tomorrow the papers would again mention the good sense and persuasive personality of "America's Handsomest University President." Who knows; maybe now old Bidwell would come through with that swimming-pool donation.

When the applause had ceased, the chairman turned to where the center of the disturbance sat, hands folded over his little round belly, face serene.

"Will you continue, Dr. Pinero?"

"Why should I?"

The chairman shrugged his shoulders. "You came for that purpose."

Pinero arose. "So true. So very true. But was I wise to come? Is there anyone here who has an open mind, who can stare a bare fact in the face without blushing? I think not. Even that so-beautiful gentleman who asked you to hear me out has already judged me and condemned me. He seeks order, not truth. Suppose truth defies order, will he accept it? Will you? I think not. Still, if I do not speak, you will win your point by default. The little man in the street will think that you little men have exposed me, Pinero, as a hoaxer, a pretender.

"I will repeat my discovery. In simple language, I have invented a technique to tell how long a man will live. I can give you advance billing of the Angel of Death. I can tell you when the Black Camel will kneel at your door. In five minutes' time, with my apparatus, I can tell any of you how many grains of sand are still left in your hourglass." He paused and folded his arms across his chest. For a moment no one spoke. The audience grew restless.

Finally the chairman intervened. "You aren't finished, Dr. Pinero?"

"What more is there to say?"

"You haven't told us how your discovery works."

Pinero's eyebrows shot up. "You suggest that I should turn over the fruits of my work for children to play with? This is dangerous knowledge, my friend. I keep it for the man who understands it, myself." He tapped his chest.

"How are we to know that you have anything back of your wild claims?"

"So simple. You send a committee to watch me demonstrate. If it works, fine. You admit it and tell the world so. If it does not work, I am discredited, and will apologize. Even I, Pinero, will apologize."

A slender, stoop-shouldered man stood up in the back of the hall. The chair recognized him and he spoke.

"Mr. Chairman, how can the eminent doctor seriously propose such a course? Does he expect us to wait around for twenty or thirty years for someone to die and prove his claims?"

Pinero ignored the chair and answered directly.

"*Pfui!* Such nonsense! Are you so ignorant of statistics that you do not know that in any large group there is at least one who will die in the immediate future? I make you a proposition. Let me test each one of you in this room, and I will name the man who will die within the fortnight, yes, and the day and hour of his death." He glanced fiercely around the room. "Do you accept?"

Another figure got to his feet, a portly man who spoke in measured syllables. "I, for one, cannot countenance such an experiment. As a medical man, I have noted with sorrow the plain marks of serious heart trouble in many of our older colleagues. If Dr. Pinero knows those symptoms, as he may, and were he to select as his victim one of their number, the man so selected would be likely to die on schedule, whether the distinguished speaker's mechanical egg timer works or not."

Another speaker backed him up at once. "Dr. Shepard is right. Why should we waste time on voodoo tricks? It is my belief that this person who calls himself *Dr.* Pinero wants to use this body to give his statements authority. If we participate in this farce, we play into his hands. I don't know what his racket is, but you can bet that he has figured out some way to use us for advertising his schemes. I move, Mr. Chairman, that we proceed with our regular business."

The motion carried by acclamation, but Pinero did not sit down. Amidst cries of "Order! Order!" he shook his untidy head at them, and had his say.

"Barbarians! Imbeciles! Stupid dolts! Your kind have blocked the recognition of every great discovery since time began. Such ignorant canaille are enough to start Galileo spinning in his grave. That fat fool down there twiddling his elk's tooth calls himself a medical man. Witch doctor would be a better term! That little bald-headed runt over there— You! You style yourself a philosopher, and prate about life and time in your neat categories. What do you know of either one? How can you ever learn when you won't examine the truth when you have a chance? Bah!" He spat upon the stage. "You call this an Academy of Science. I call it an undertakers' convention, interested only in embalming the ideas of your red-blooded predecessors."

He paused for breath and was grasped on each side by two members of the platform committee and rushed out the wings. Several reporters arose hastily from the press table and followed him. The chairman declared the meeting adjourned.

The newspapermen caught up with Pinero as he was going out by the stage door. He walked with a light, springy step, and whistled a little tune. There was no trace of the belligerence he had shown a moment before. They crowded about him. "How about an interview, doc?" "What d'yuh think of modern education?" "You certainly told 'em. What are your views on life after death?" "Take off your hat, doc, and look at the birdie."

He grinned at them all. "One at a time, boys, and not so fast. I used to be a newspaperman myself. How about coming up to my place?"

A few minutes later they were trying to find places to sit down in Pinero's messy bed-living room, and lighting his cigars. Pinero looked around and beamed. "What'll it be, boys? Scotch or Bourbon?" When that was taken care of he got down to business. "Now, boys, what do you want to know?"

"Lay it on the line, doc. Have you got something, or haven't you?"

"Most assuredly I have something, my young friend."

"Then tell us how it works. That guff you handed the profs won't get you anywhere now."

"Please, my dear fellow. It is my invention. I expect

to make money with it. Would you have me give it away to the first person who asks for it?"

"See here, doc, you've got to give us something if you expect to get a break in the morning papers. What do you use? A crystal ball?"

"No, not quite. Would you like to see my apparatus?"

"Sure. Now we're getting somewhere."

He ushered them into an adjoining room, and waved his hand. "There it is, boys." The mass of equipment that met their eyes vaguely resembled a medico's office X-ray gear. Beyond the obvious fact that it used electrical power, and that some of the dials were calibrated in familiar terms, a casual inspection gave no clue to its actual use.

"What's the principle, doc?"

Pinero pursed his lips and considered. "No doubt you are all familiar with the truism that life is electrical in nature. Well, that truism isn't worth a damn, but it will help to give you an idea of the principle. You have also been told that time is a fourth dimension. Maybe you believe it, perhaps not. It has been said so many times that it has ceased to have any meaning. It is simply a cliché that windbags use to impress fools. But I want you to try to visualize it now, and try to feel it emotionally."

He stepped up to one of the reporters. "Suppose we take you as an example. Your name is Rogers, is it not? Very well, Rogers, you are a space-time event having duration four ways. You are not quite six feet tall, you are about twenty inches wide and perhaps ten inches thick. In time, there stretches behind you more of this space-time event, reaching to, perhaps, 1905, of which we see a cross section here at right angles to the time axis, and as thick as the present. At the far end is a baby, smelling of sour milk and drooling its breakfast on its bib. At the other end lies, perhaps, an old man some place in the 1980s. Imagine this space-time event, which we call Rogers, as a long pink worm, continuous through the years. It stretches past us here in 1939, and the cross section we see appears as a single, discrete body. But that is illusion. There is physical continuity to this pink worm, enduring through the years. As a matter of fact, there is physical continuity in this concept to the entire race, for these pink worms branch off from other pink worms. In this fashion the race is like a vine whose branches intertwine and send out shoots. Only by taking a cross section of the vine would we fall into the error of believing that the shootlets were discrete individuals."

He paused and looked around at their faces. One of them, a dour, hard-bitten chap, put in a word.

"That's all very pretty, Pinero, if true, but where does that get you?"

Pinero favored him with an unresentful smile. "Patience, my friend. I asked you to think of life as electrical. Now think of our long, pink worm as a conductor of electricity. You have heard, perhaps, of the fact that electrical engineers can, by certain measurements, predict the exact location of a break in a transatlantic cable without ever leaving the shore. I do the same with our pink worms. By applying my instruments to the cross section here in this room I can tell where the break occurs; that is to say, where death takes place. Or, if you like, I can reverse the connections and tell you the date of your birth. But that is uninteresting; you already know it."

The dour individual sneered. "I've caught you, doc. If what you say about the race being like a vine of pink worms is true, you can't tell birthdays, because the connection with the race is continuous at birth. Your electrical conductor reaches on back through the mother into a man's remotest ancestors."

Pinero beamed. "True, and clever, my friend. But you have pushed the analogy too far. It is not done in the precise manner in which one measures the length of an electrical conductor. In some ways it is more like measuring the length of a long corridor by bouncing an echo off the far end. At birth there is a sort of twist in the corridor, and, by proper calibration, I can detect the echo from that twist."

"Let's see you prove it!"

"Certainly, my dear friend. Will you be a subject?"

One of the others spoke up. "He's called your bluff, Luke. Put up or shut up."

"I'm game. What do I do?"

"First write the date of your birth on a sheet of paper, and hand it to one of your colleagues."

Luke complied. "Now what?"

"Remove your outer clothing and step upon these scales. Now tell me, were you ever very much thinner, or very much fatter, than you are now? No? What did you weigh at birth? Ten pounds? A fine bouncing baby boy. They don't come so big anymore."

"What is all this flubdubbery?"

"I am trying to approximate the average cross section of our long pink conductor, my dear Luke. Now will you seat yourself here? Then place this electrode in your mouth. No, it will not hurt you; the voltage is quite low, less than one microvolt, but I must have a good connection." The doctor left him and went behind his apparatus, where he lowered a hood over his head before touching his controls. Some of the exposed dials came to life and a low humming came from the machine. It stopped and the doctor popped out of his little hideaway.

"I get sometime in February, 1902. Who has the piece of paper with the date?"

It was produced and unfolded. The custodian read, "February 22, 1902."

The stillness that followed was broken by a voice from the edge of the little group. "Doc, can I have another drink?"

The tension relaxed, and several spoke at once: "Try

it on me, doc." "Me first, doc; I'm an orphan and really want to know." "How about it, doc? Give us all a little loose play."

He smilingly complied, ducking in and out of the hood like a gopher from its hole. When they all had twin slips of paper to prove the doctor's skill, Luke broke a long silence.

"How about showing how you predict death, Pinero?"

No one answered. Several of them nudged Luke forward. "Go ahead, smart guy. You asked for it." He allowed himself to be seated in the chair. Pinero changed some of the switches, then entered the hood. When the humming ceased he came out, rubbing his hands briskly together.

"Well, that's all there is to see, boys. Got enough for a story?"

"Hey, what about the prediction? When does Luke get his 'thirty'?"

Luke faced him. "Yes, how about it?"

Pinero looked pained. "Gentlemen, I am surprised at you. I give that information for a fee. Besides, it is a professional confidence. I never tell anyone but the client who consults me."

"I don't mind. Go ahead and tell them."

"I am very sorry. I really must refuse. I only agreed to show you how; not to give the results."

Luke ground the butt of his cigarette into the floor. "It's a hoax, boys. He probably looked up the age of every reporter in town just to be ready to pull this. It won't wash, Pinero."

Pinero gazed at him sadly. "Are you married, my friend?"

"No."

"Do you have anyone dependent on you? Any close relatives?"

"No. Why? Do you want to adopt me?"

Pinero shook his head. "I am very sorry for you, my dear Luke. You will die before tomorrow."

DEATH PUNCHES TIME CLOCK
... within twenty minutes of Pinero's strange prediction, Timons was struck by a falling sign while walking down Broadway toward the offices of the *Daily Herald* where he was employed.

Dr. Pinero declined to comment but confirmed the story that he had predicted Timons' death by means of his so-called chronovitameter. Chief of Police Roy . . .

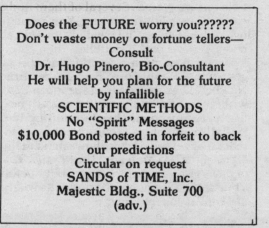

Does the FUTURE worry you??????
Don't waste money on fortune tellers—
Consult
Dr. Hugo Pinero, Bio-Consultant
He will help you plan for the future
by infallible
SCIENTIFIC METHODS
No "Spirit" Messages
$10,000 Bond posted in forfeit to back
our predictions
Circular on request
SANDS of TIME, Inc.
Majestic Bldg., Suite 700
(adv.)

Legal Notice
To whom it may concern, greetings; I, John Cabot Winthrop III, of the firm of Winthrop, Winthrop, Ditmars and Winthrop, Attorneys-at-law, do affirm that Hugo Pinero of this city did hand to me ten thousand dollars in lawful money of the United States, and did instruct me to place it in escrow with a chartered bank of my selection with escrow instructions as follows:

The entire bond shall be forfeit, and shall forthwith be paid to the first client of Hugo Pinero and/or Sands of Time, Inc., who shall exceed his life tenure as predicted by Hugo Pinero

by one per centum, or the estate of the first
client who shall fail of such predicted tenure in
a like amount, whichever occurs first in point
of time.

> Subscribed and sworn,
> John Cabot Winthrop III.

Subscribed and sworn to before
me this 2nd day of April, 1939.
Albert M. Swanson
Notary Public in and for this
county and State. My commission
expires June 17, 1939.

"Good evening, Mr. and Mrs. Radio Audience, let's
go to press! Flash! Hugo Pinero, the Miracle Man from
Nowhere, has made his thousandth death prediction
without anyone claiming the reward he offered to the
first person who catches him failing to call the turn.
With thirteen of his clients already dead, it is mathematically certain that he has a private line to the main
office of the Old Man with the Scythe. That is one piece
of news I don't want to know about before it happens.
Your coast-to-coast correspondent will *not* be a client
of Prophet Pinero—"

The judge's watery baritone cut through the stale
air of the courtroom. "Please, Mr. Weems, let us return
to our subject. This court granted your prayer for a
temporary restraining order, and now you ask that it
be made permanent. In rebuttal, Dr. Pinero claims
that you have presented no cause and asks that the
injunction be lifted, and that I order your client to
cease from attempts to interfere with what Pinero describes as a simple, lawful business. As you are not ad-
dressing a jury, please omit the rhetoric and tell me in
plain language why I should not grant his prayer."

Mr. Weems jerked his chin nervously, making his
flabby gray dewlap drag across his high stiff collar,
and resumed:

"May it please the honorable court, I represent the public—"

"Just a moment. I thought you were appearing for Amalgamated Life Insurance."

"I am, your honor, in a formal sense. In a wider sense I represent several other of the major assurance, fiduciary and financial institutions, their stockholders and policy holders, who constitute a majority of the citizenry. In addition we feel that we protect the interests of the entire population, unorganized, inarticulate and otherwise unprotected."

"I thought that I represented the public," observed the judge dryly. "I am afraid I must regard you as appearing for your client of record. But continue. What is your thesis?"

The elderly barrister attempted to swallow his Adam's apple, then began again: "Your honor, we contend that there are two separate reasons why this injunction should be made permanent, and, further, that each reason is sufficient alone.

"In the first place, this person is engaged in the practice of soothsaying, an occupation proscribed both in common law and in statute. He is a common fortune-teller, a vagabond charlatan who preys on the gullibility of the public. He is cleverer than the ordinary gypsy palm reader, astrologer, or table tipper, and to the same extent more dangerous. He makes false claims of modern scientific methods to give a spurious dignity to the thaumaturgy. We have here in court leading representatives of the Academy of Science to give expert witness as to the absurdity of his claims.

"In the second place, even if this person's claims were true—granting for the sake of argument such an absurdity—" Mr. Weems permitted himself a thin-lipped smile— "we contend that his activities are contrary to the public interest in general, and unlawfully injurious to the interests of my client in particular. We are prepared to produce numerous exhibits with the legal custodians to prove that this person did publish, or cause to have published, utterances urging the public to dispense with the priceless boon of life insurance to the great detriment of their welfare and to the financial damage of my client."

Pinero arose in his place. "Your honor, may I say a few words?"

"What is it?"

"I believe I can simplify the situation if permitted to make a brief analysis."

"Your honor," put in Weems, "this is most irregular."

"Patience, Mr. Weems. Your interests will be protected. It seems to me that we need more light and less noise in this matter. If Dr. Pinero can shorten the proceedings by speaking at this time, I am inclined to let him. Proceed, Dr. Pinero."

"Thank you, your honor. Taking the last of Mr. Weems' points first. I am prepared to stipulate that I published the utterances he speaks of—"

"One moment, doctor. You have chosen to act as your own attorney. Are you sure you are competent to protect your own interests?"

"I am prepared to chance it, your honor. Our friends here can easily prove what I stipulate."

"Very well. You may proceed."

"I will stipulate that many persons have canceled life-insurance policies as a result thereof, but I challenge them to show that anyone so doing has suffered any loss or damage therefrom. It is true that the Amalgamated has lost business through my activities, but that is the natural result of my discovery, which has made their policies as obsolete as the bow and arrow. If an injunction is granted on that ground, I shall set up a coal-oil-lamp factory, and then ask for an injunction against the Edison and General Electric companies to forbid them to manufacture incandescent bulbs.

"I will stipulate that I am engaged in the business of making predictions of death, but I deny that I am practicing magic, black, white or rainbow-colored. If to make predictions by methods of scientific accuracy is illegal, then the actuaries of the Amalgamated have been guilty for years, in that they predict the exact percentage that will die each year in any given large group. I predict death retail; the Amalgamated predicts it wholesale. If their actions are legal, how can mine be illegal?

"I admit that it makes a difference whether I can do what I claim, or not; and I will stipulate that the so-called expert witnesses from the Academy of Science will testify that I cannot. But they know nothing of my method and cannot give truly expert testimony on it—"

"Just a moment, doctor. Mr. Weems, is it true that your expert witnesses are not conversant with Dr. Pinero's theory and methods?"

Mr. Weems looked worried. He drummed on the table top, then answered. "Will the court grant me a few moments' indulgence?"

"Certainly."

Mr. Weems held a hurried whispered consultation with his cohorts, then faced the bench. "We have a procedure to suggest, your honor. If Dr. Pinero will take the stand and explain the theory and practice of his alleged method, then these distinguished scientists will be able to advise the court as to the validity of his claims."

The judge looked inquiringly at Pinero, who responded: "I will not willingly agree to that. Whether my process is true or false, it would be dangerous to let it fall into the hands of fools and quacks"— he waved his hand at the group of professors seated in the front row, paused and smiled maliciously— "as these gentlemen know quite well. Furthermore, it is not necessary to know the process in order to prove that it will work. Is it necessary to understand the complex miracle of biological reproduction in order to observe that a hen lays eggs? Is it necessary for me to re-educate this entire body of self-appointed custodians of wisdom—cure them of their ingrown superstitions—in order to prove that my predictions are correct?

"There are but two ways of forming an opinion in science. One is the scientific method; the other, the scholastic. One can judge from experiment, or one can blindly accept authority. To the scientific mind, experimental proof is all-important, and theory is merely a convenience in description, to be junked when it no longer fits. To the academic mind, authority is everything, and facts are junked when they do not fit theory laid down by authority.

"It is this point of view—academic minds clinging like oysters to disproved theories—that has blocked every advance of knowledge in history. I am prepared to prove my method by experiment, and, like Galileo in another court, I insist, 'It still moves!'

"Once before I offered such proof to this same body of self-styled experts, and they rejected it. I renew my offer; let me measure the life length of the members of the Academy of Science. Let them appoint a committee to judge the results. I will seal my findings in two sets of envelopes; on the outside of each envelope in one set will appear the name of a member; on the inside, the date of his death. In the other envelopes I will place names; on the outside I will place dates. Let the committee place the envelopes in a vault, then meet from time to time to open the appropriate envelopes. In such a large body of men some deaths may be expected, if Amalgamated actuaries can be trusted, every week or two. In such a fashion they will accumulate data very rapidly to prove that Pinero is a liar, or no."

He stopped, and thrust out his chest until it almost caught up with his little round belly. He glared at the sweating savants. "Well?"

The judge raised his eyebrows, and caught Mr. Weems' eye. "Do you accept?"

"Your honor, I think the proposal highly improper—"

The judge cut him short. "I warn you that I shall rule against you if you do not accept, or propose an equally reasonable method of arriving at the truth."

Weems opened his mouth, changed his mind, looked up and down the faces of the learned witnesses, and faced the bench. "We accept, your honor."

"Very well. Arrange the details between you. The temporary injunction is lifted, and Dr. Pinero must not be molested in the pursuit of his business. Decision on the petition for permanent injunction is reserved without prejudice pending the accumulation of evidence. Before we leave this matter I wish to comment on the theory implied by you, Mr. Weems, when you claimed damage to your client. There has grown up in the minds of certain groups in this country the notion that because a man or corporation has made a profit out of the public for a number of years, the government and the courts are charged with the duty of guaranteeing such profit in the future, even in the face of changing circumstances and contrary to public interest. This strange doctrine is not supported by statute nor common law. Neither individuals nor corporations have any right to come into court and ask that the clock of history be stopped, or turned back."

Bidwell grunted in annoyance. "Weems, if you can't think up anything better than that, Amalgamated is going to need a new chief attorney. It's been ten weeks since you lost the injunction, and that little wart is coining money hand over fist. Meantime, every insurance firm in the country's going broke. Hoskins, what's our loss ratio?"

"It's hard to say, Mr. Bidwell. It gets worse every day. We've paid off thirteen big policies this week; all of them taken out since Pinero started operations."

A spare little man spoke up. "I say, Bidwell, we

aren't accepting any new applicants for United, until we have time to check and be sure that they have not consulted Pinero. Can't we afford to wait until the scientists show him up?"

Bidwell snorted. "You blasted optimist! They won't show him up. Aldrich, can't you face a fact? The fat little pest has something; how, I don't know. This is a fight to the finish. If we wait, we're licked." He threw his cigar into a cuspidor, and bit savagely into a fresh one. "Clear out of here, all of you! I'll handle this my way. You, too, Aldrich. United may wait, but Amalgamated won't."

Weems cleared his throat apprehensively. "Mr. Bidwell, I trust you will consult me before embarking on any major change in policy?"

Bidwell grunted. They filed out. When they were all gone and the door closed, Bidwell snapped the switch of the interoffice announcer. "O.K.; send him in."

The outer door opened. A slight, dapper figure stood for a moment at the threshold. His small, dark eyes glanced quickly about the room before he entered, then he moved up to Bidwell with a quick, soft tread. He spoke to Bidwell in a flat, emotionless voice. His face remained impassive except for the live, animal eyes. "You wanted to talk to me?"

"Yes."

"What's the proposition?"

"Sit down, and we'll talk."

Pinero met the young couple at the door of his inner office.

"Come in, my dears, come in. Sit down. Make yourselves at home. Now tell me, what do you want of Pinero? Surely such young people are not anxious about the final roll call?"

The boy's pleasant young face showed slight confusion. "Well, you see, Dr. Pinero, I'm Ed Hartley and this is my wife, Betty. We're going to have . . . that is, Betty is expecting a baby and, well—"

Pinero smiled benignly. "I understand. You want to know how long you will live in order to make the best possible provision for the youngster. Quite wise. Do you both want readings, or just yourself?"

The girl answered, "Both of us, we think."

Pinero beamed at her. "Quite so. I agree. Your reading presents certain technical difficulties at this time, but I can give you some information now. Now come into my laboratory, my dears, and we'll commence."

He rang for their case histories, then showed them into his workshop. "Mrs. Hartley first, please. If you will go behind that screen and remove your shoes and your outer clothing, please."

He turned away and made some minor adjustments of his apparatus. Ed nodded to his wife, who slipped behind the screen and reappeared almost at once, dressed in a slip. Pinero glanced up.

"This way, my dear. First we must weigh you. There. Now take your place on the stand. This electrode in your mouth. No, Ed, you mustn't touch her while she is in the circuit. It won't take a minute. Remain quiet."

He dove under the machine's hood and the dials sprang into life. Very shortly he came out, with a perturbed look on his face. "Ed, did you touch her?"

"No, doctor." Pinero ducked back again and remained a little longer. When he came out this time, he told the girl to get down and dress. He turned to her husband.

"Ed, make yourself ready."

"What's Betty's reading, doctor?"

"There is a little difficulty. I want to test you first."

When he came out from taking the youth's reading, his face was more troubled than ever. Ed inquired as to his trouble. Pinero shrugged his shoulders and brought a smile to his lips.

"Nothing to concern you, my boy. A little mechanical misadjustment, I think. But I shan't be able to give you two your readings today. I shall need to overhaul my machine. Can you come back tomorrow?"

"Why, I think so. Say, I'm sorry about your machine. I hope it isn't serious."

"It isn't, I'm sure. Will you come back into my office and visit for a bit?"

"Thank you, doctor. You are very kind."

"But, Ed, I've got to meet Ellen."

Pinero turned the full force of his personality on her. "Won't you grant me a few moments, my dear young lady? I am old, and like the sparkle of young folks' company. I get very little of it. Please." He nudged them gently into his office and seated them. Then he ordered lemonade and cookies sent in, offered them cigarettes and lit a cigar.

Forty minutes later Ed listened entranced, while Betty was quite evidently acutely nervous and anxious to leave, as the doctor spun out a story concerning his adventures as a young man in Tierra del Fuego. When the doctor stopped to relight his cigar, she stood up.

"Doctor, we really must leave. Couldn't we hear the rest tomorrow?"

"Tomorrow? There will not be time tomorrow."

"But you haven't time today, either. Your secretary has rung five times."

"Couldn't you spare me just a few more minutes?"

"I really can't today, doctor. I have an appointment. There is someone waiting for me."

"There is no way to induce you?"

"I'm afraid not. Come, Ed."

After they had gone, the doctor stepped to the window and stared out over the city. Presently he picked out two tiny figures as they left the office building. He watched them hurry to the corner, wait for the lights to change, then start across the street. When they were part way across, there came the scream of a siren. The two little figures hesitated, started back, stopped and turned. Then a car was upon them. As the car slammed to a stop, they showed up from beneath it, no longer two figures, but simply a limp, unorganized heap of clothing.

Presently the doctor turned away from the window. Then he picked up his phone and spoke to his secretary.

"Cancel my appointments for the rest of the day.... No.... No one.... I don't care; cancel them."

Then he sat down in his chair. His cigar went out. Long after dark he held it, still unlighted.

Pinero sat down at his dining table and contemplated the gourmet's luncheon spread before him. He had ordered this meal with particular care, and had come home a little early in order to enjoy it fully.

Somewhat later he let a few drops of Fiori D'Alpini roll down his throat. The heavy, fragrant syrup warmed his mouth and reminded him of the little mountain flowers for which it was named. He sighed. It had been a good meal, an exquisite meal, and had justified the exotic liqueur.

His musing was interrupted by a disturbance at the front door. The voice of his elderly maidservant was raised in remonstrance. A heavy male voice interrupted her. The commotion moved down the hall and the dining-room door was pushed open.

"*Madonna mia! Non si puo' entrare!* The master is eating!"

"Never mind, Angela. I have time to see these gentlemen. You may go."

Pinero faced the surly-faced spokesman of the intruders. "You have business with me; yes?"

"You bet we have. Decent people have had enough of your damned nonsense."

"And so?"

The caller did not answer at once. A smaller, dapper individual moved out from behind him and faced Pinero.

"We might as well begin." The chairman of the committee placed a key in the lock box and opened it. "Wenzell, will you help me pick out today's envelopes?" He was interrupted by a touch on his arm.

"Dr. Baird, you are wanted on the telephone."

"Very well. Bring the instrument here."

When it was fetched he placed the receiver to his ear. "Hello.... Yes; speaking.... What?... No, we have heard nothing.... Destroyed the machine, you say.... Dead! How?... No! No statement. None at all.... Call me later."

He slammed the instrument down and pushed it from him.

"What's up?"

"Who's dead now?"

Baird held up one hand. "Quiet, gentlemen, please! Pinero was murdered a few moments ago at his home."

"Murdered!"

"That isn't all. About the same time vandals broke into his office and smashed his apparatus."

No one spoke at first. The committee members glanced around at each other. No one seemed anxious to be the first to comment.

Finally one spoke up. "Get it out."

"Get what out?"

"Pinero's envelope. It's in there, too. I've seen it."

Baird located it, and slowly tore it open. He unfolded the single sheet of paper and scanned it.

"Well? Out with it!"

"One thirteen P.M.... today."

They took this in silence.

Their dynamic calm was broken by a member across the table from Baird reaching for the lock box. Baird interposed a hand.

"What do you want?"

"My prediction. It's in there—we're all in there."

"Yes, yes."

"We're all in there."

"Let's have them."

Baird placed both hands over the box. He held the eye of the man opposite him, but did not speak. He licked his lips. The corner of his mouth twitched. His hands shook. Still he did not speak. The man opposite relaxed back into his chair.

"You're right, of course," he said.

"Bring me that wastebasket." Baird's voice was low and strained, but steady.

He accepted it and dumped the litter on the rug. He placed the tin basket on the table before him. He tore half a dozen envelopes across, set a match to them, and dropped them in the basket. Then he started tearing a double handful at a time, and fed the fire steadily. The smoke made him cough, and tears ran out of his smarting eyes. Someone got up and opened a window. When Baird was through, he pushed the basket away from him, looked down and spoke.

"I'm afraid I've ruined this table top."

For any wordsmith the most valuable word in the English language is that short, ugly, Anglo-Saxon monosyllable: No!!! It is one of the peculiarities in the attitude of the public toward the writing profession that a person who would never expect a free ride from a taxi driver, or free groceries from a market, or free gilkwoks from a gilkwok dealer, will without the slightest embarrassment ask a professional writer for free gifts of his stock in trade.

This chutzpah is endemic in science fiction fans, acute in organized SF fans, and at its virulent worst in organized fans-who-publish-fan-magazines.

The following story came into existence shortly after I sold my first story—and resulted from my having not yet learned to say No!

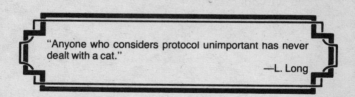

"Anyone who considers protocol unimportant has never dealt with a cat."

—L. Long

SUCCESSFUL OPERATION

"How dare you make such a suggestion!"

The State Physician doggedly stuck by his position. "I would not make it, sire, if your life were not at stake. There is no other surgeon in the Fatherland who can transplant a pituitary gland but Doctor Lans."

"You will operate!"

The medico shook his head. "You would die, Leader. My skill is not adequate."

The Leader stormed about the apartment. He seemed about to give way to one of the girlish bursts of anger that even the inner state clique feared so much. Surprisingly he capitulated.

"Bring him here!" he ordered.

Doctor Lans faced the Leader with inherent dignity, a dignity and presence that three years of "protective custody" had been unable to shake. The pallor and gauntness of the concentration camp lay upon him, but his race was used to oppression. "I see," he said. "Yes, I see . . . I can perform that operation. What are your terms?"

"Terms?" The Leader was aghast. "Terms, you filthy swine? You are being given a chance to redeem in part the sins of your race!"

The surgeon raised his brows. "Do you not think that I *know* that you would not have sent for me had

29

there been any other course available to you? Obviously, my services have become valuable."

"You'll do as you are told! You and your kind are lucky to be alive."

"Nevertheless I shall not operate without my fee."

"I said you are lucky to be alive—" The tone was an open threat.

Lans spread his hands, did not answer.

"Well—I am informed that you have a family . . ."

The surgeon moistened his lips. His Emma—they would hurt his Emma . . . and his little Rose. But he must be brave, as Emma would have him be. He was playing for high stakes—for all of them. "They cannot be worse off dead," he answered firmly, "than they are now."

It was many hours before the Leader was convinced that Lans could not be budged. He should have known—the surgeon had learned fortitude at his mother's breast.

"What is your fee?"

"A passport for myself and my family."

"Good riddance!"

"My personal fortune restored to me—"

"Very well."

"—to be paid in gold before I operate!"

The Leader started to object automatically, then checked himself. Let the presumptuous fool think so! It could be corrected after the operation.

"And the operation to take place in a hospital on foreign soil."

"Preposterous!"

"I must insist."

"You do not trust me?"

Lans stared straight back into his eyes without replying. The Leader struck him, hard, across the mouth. The surgeon made no effort to avoid the blow, but took it, with no change of expression. . . .

"You are willing to go through with it, Samuel?"
The younger man looked at Doctor Lans without fear
as he answered,

"Certainly, Doctor."

"I can not guarantee that you will recover. The
Leader's pituitary gland is diseased; your younger
body may or may not be able to stand up under it—
that is the chance you take."

"I know it—but I am out of the concentration
camp!"

"Yes. Yes, that is true. And if you do recover, you are
free. And I will attend you myself, until you are well
enough to travel."

Samuel smiled. "It will be a positive joy to be sick in
a country where there are no concentration camps!"

"Very well, then. Let us commence."

They returned to the silent, nervous group at the
other end of the room. Grimly, the money was counted
out, every penny that the famous surgeon had laid
claim to before the Leader had decided that men of his
religion had no need for money. Lans placed half of the
gold in a money belt and strapped it around his waist.
His wife concealed the other half somewhere about
her ample person.

It was an hour and twenty minutes later that Lans
put down the last instrument, nodded to the surgeons
assisting him, and commenced to strip off operating
gloves. He took one last look at his two patients before
he left the room. They were anonymous under the ster-
ile gowns and dressings. Had he not known, he could
not have told dictator from oppressed. Come to think
about it, with the exchange of those two tiny glands
there was something of the dictator in his victim, and
something of the victim in the dictator.

Doctor Lans returned to the hospital later in the
day, after seeing his wife and daughter settled in a first
class hotel. It was an extravagance, in view of his un-

certain prospects as a refugee, but they had enjoyed no luxuries for years back *there*—he did not think of it as his home country—and it was justified this once.

He enquired at the office of the hospital for his second patient. The clerk looked puzzled. "But he is not here."

"Not here?"

"Why, no. He was moved at the same time as His Excellency—back to your country."

Lans did not argue. The trick was obvious; it was too late to do anything for poor Samuel. He thanked his God that he had had the foresight to place himself and his family beyond the reach of such brutal injustice before operating. He thanked the clerk and left.

The Leader recovered consciousness at last. His brain was confused—then he recalled the events before he had gone to sleep. The operation!—it must be over! And he was alive! He had never admitted to anyone how terribly frightened he had been at the prospect. But he had lived—he had lived!

He groped around for the bell cord, and, failing to find it, gradually forced his eyes to focus on the room. What outrageous nonsense was this? This was no sort of a room for the Leader to convalesce in. He took in the dirty white-washed ceiling, and the bare wooden floor with distaste. And the bed! It was no more than a cot!

He shouted. Someone came in, a man wearing the uniform of a trooper in his favorite corps. He started to give him the tongue-lashing of his life, before having him arrested. But he was cut short.

"Cut out that racket, you unholy pig!"

At first he was too astounded to answer, then he shrieked, "Stand at attention when you address your Leader! Salute!"

The man looked dumbfounded, then guffawed. "Like this, maybe?" He stepped to the side of the cot, struck a pose with his right arm raised in salute. He carried a rubber truncheon in it. "Hail to the Leader!" he shouted, and brought his arm down smartly. The truncheon crashed into the Leader's cheekbone.

Another trooper came in to see what the noise was while the first was still laughing at his witticism. "What's up, Jon? Say, you'd better not handle that monkey too rough—he's still carried on the hospital list." He glanced casually at the Leader's bloody face.

"Him? Didn't you know?" He pulled him to one side and whispered.

The second's eyes widened; he grinned. "So? They don't want him to get well, eh? Well, I could use some exercise this morning—"

"Let's get Fats," the other suggested. "He always has such amusing ideas."

"Good idea." He stepped to the door, and bellowed, "Hey, Fats!"

They didn't really start in on him until Fats was there to help.

FOREWORD

LIFE-LINE, MISFIT, LET THERE BE LIGHT, ELSEWHEN, PIED PIPER, IF THIS GOES ON—, REQUIEM, THE ROADS MUST ROLL, COVENTRY, BLOWUPS HAPPEN—for eleven months, mid March 1939 through mid February 1940, I wrote every day . . . and that ended my bondage; BLOWUPS HAPPEN paid off the last of that pesky mortgage—eight years ahead of time.

BLOWUPS HAPPEN was the first of my stories to be published in hard covers, in Groff Conklin's first anthology, THE BEST OF SCIENCE FICTION, 1946. In the meantime there had been World War II, Hiroshima, The Smyth Report—so I went over my 1940 manuscript most carefully, correcting some figures I had merely guessed at in early 1940.

This week I have compared the two versions, 1940 and 1946, word by word—there isn't a dime's worth of difference between them . . . and I now see, as a result of the enormous increase in the art in 33 years, more errors in the '46 version than I spotted in the '40 version when I checked it in '46.

I do not intend ever again to try to update a story to make it fit new art. Such updating can't save a poor story and isn't necessary for a good story. All of H. G. Wells' SF stories are hopelessly dated . . . and they remain the best, the most gripping science fiction stories to be found anywhere. My BEYOND THIS HORIZON (1941) states that H. sapiens has forty-eight chromosomes, a "fact" that "everybody knew" in 1941. Now "everybody knows" that the "correct" number is forty-six. I shan't change it.

The version of BLOWUPS HAPPEN here following is exactly, word for word, the way it was first written in February 1940.

34

BLOWUPS HAPPEN

"Put down that wrench!"

The man addressed turned slowly around and faced the speaker. His expression was hidden by a grotesque helmet, part of a heavy, leaden armor which shielded his entire body, but the tone of voice in which he answered showed nervous exasperation.

"What the hell's eating on you, Doc?" He made no move to replace the tool in question.

They faced each other like two helmeted, arrayed fencers, watching for an opening. The first speaker's voice came from behind his mask a shade higher in key and more peremptory in tone. "You heard me, Harper. Put down that wrench at once, and come away from that 'trigger.' Erickson!"

A third armored figure came around the shield which separated the uranium bomb proper from the control room in which the first two stood. "Whatcha want, Doc?"

"Harper is relieved from watch. You take over as engineer-of-the-watch. Send for the standby engineer."

"Very well." His voice and manner were phlegmatic as he accepted the situation without comment. The atomic engineer whom he had just relieved glanced from one to the other, then carefully replaced the wrench in its rack.

"Just as you say, Dr. Silard—but send for your relief,

too. I shall demand an immediate hearing!'' Harper
swept indignantly out, his lead-sheathed boots clump-
ing on the floor plates.

Dr. Silard waited unhappily for the ensuing twenty
minutes until his own relief arrived. Perhaps he had
been hasty. Maybe he was wrong in thinking that Harper had at last broken under the strain of tending the
most dangerous machine in the world—an atomic
power plant. But if he had made a mistake, it had to be
on the safe side—slips *must not happen* in this business; not when a slip might result in the atomic deto-
nation of two and a half tons of uranium.

He tried to visualize what that would mean, and
failed. He had been told that uranium was potentially
forty million times as explosive as TNT. The figure
was meaningless that way. He thought of it, instead,
as a hundred million tons of high explosive, two
hundred million aircraft bombs as big as the biggest
ever used. It still did not mean anything. He had once
seen such a bomb dropped, when he had been serving
as a temperament analyst for army aircraft pilots. The
bomb had left a hole big enough to hide an apartment
house. He could not imagine the explosion of a thousand such bombs, much less a hundred million of
them.

Perhaps these atomic engineers could. Perhaps,
with their greater mathematical ability and closer
comprehension of what actually went on inside the
nuclear fission chamber—the "bomb"—they had
some vivid glimpse of the mind-shattering horror
locked up beyond that shield. If so, no wonder they
tended to blow up—

He sighed. Erickson looked up from the linear resonant accelerator on which he had been making some
adjustment. "What's the trouble, Doc?"

"Nothing. I'm sorry I had to relieve Harper."

Silard could feel the shrewd glance of the big Scandinavian. "Not getting the jitters yourself, are you,
Doc? Sometimes you squirrel sleuths blow up, too—''

"Me? I don't think so. I'm scared of that thing in there—I'd be crazy if I weren't."

"So am I," Erickson told him soberly, and went back to his work.

The accelerator's snout disappeared in the shield between them and the bomb, where it fed a steady stream of terrifically speeded up subatomic bullets to the beryllium target located within the bomb itself. The tortured beryllium yielded up neutrons, which shot out in all directions through the uranium mass. Some of these neutrons struck uranium atoms squarely on their nuclei and split them in two. The fragments were new elements, barium, xenon, rubidium—depending on the proportions in which each atom split. The new elements were usually unstable isotopes and broke down into a dozen more elements by radioactive disintegration in a progressive chain reaction.

But these chain reactions were comparatively unimportant; it was the original splitting of the uranium nucleus, with the release of the awe-inspiring energy that bound it together—an incredible two hundred million electron-volts—that was important—and perilous.

For, while uranium isotope 235 may be split by bombarding it with neutrons from an outside source, the splitting itself gives up more neutrons which, in turn, may land in other uranium nuclei and split them. If conditions are favorable to a progressively increasing reaction of this sort, it may get out of hand, build up in an unmeasurable fraction of a microsecond into a complete atomic explosion—an explosion which would dwarf the eruption of Krakatoa to popgun size; an explosion so far beyond all human experience as to be as completely incomprehensible as the idea of personal death. It could be feared, but not understood.

But a self-perpetuating sequence of nuclear splitting *just under the level of complete explosion* was necessary to the operation of the power plant. To split the first uranium nucleus by bombarding it with neutrons from the beryllium target took more power than the death of the atom gave up. In order that the output of power from the system should exceed the power input in useful proportion it was imperative that each atom split by a neutron from the beryllium target should cause the splitting of many more.

It was equally imperative that this chain of reactions should always tend to dampen, to die out. It must not build up, or the entire mass would explode within a time interval too short to be measured by any means whatsoever.

Nor would there be anyone left to measure it.

The atomic engineer on duty at the bomb could control this reaction by means of the "trigger," a term the engineers used to include the linear resonant accelerator, the beryllium target, and the adjacent controls, instrument board, and power sources. That is to say, he could vary the bombardment on the beryllium target to increase or decrease the power output of the plant, and he could tell from his instruments that the internal reaction was dampened—or, rather, that it had been dampened the split second before. He could not possibly know what was actually happening *now* within the bomb—subatomic speeds are too great and the time intervals too small. He was like the bird that flew backward; he could see where he had been, but he never knew where he was going.

Nevertheless, it was his responsibility, and his alone, not only to maintain the bomb at a high input-output efficiency, but to see that the reaction never passed the critical point and progressed into mass explosion.

But that was impossible. He could not be sure; he could never be sure.

He could bring to the job all of the skill and learning

of the finest technical education, and use it to reduce the hazard to the lowest mathematical probability, but the blind laws of chance which appear to rule in subatomic action might turn up a royal flush against him and defeat his most skillful play.

And each atomic engineer knew it, knew that he gambled not only with his own life, but with the lives of countless others, perhaps with the lives of every human being on the planet. Nobody knew quite what such an explosion would do. The most conservative estimate assumed that, in addition to destroying the plant and its personnel completely, it would tear a chunk out of the populous and heavily traveled Los Angeles-Oklahoma Road City a hundred miles to the north.

That was the official, optimistic viewpoint on which the plant had been authorized, and based on mathematics which predicted that a mass of uranium would itself be disrupted on a molar scale, and thereby rendered comparatively harmless, before progressive and accelerated atomic explosion could infect the entire mass.

The atomic engineers, by and large, did not place faith in the official theory. They judged theoretical mathematical prediction for what it was worth—precisely nothing, until confirmed by experiment.

But even from the official viewpoint, each atomic engineer while on watch carried not only his own life in his hands, but the lives of many others—how many, it was better not to think about. No pilot, no general, no surgeon ever carried such a daily, inescapable, ever-present weight of responsibility for the lives of other people as these men carried every time they went on watch, every time they touched a vernier screw or read a dial.

They were selected not alone for their intelligence and technical training, but quite as much for their characters and sense of social responsibility. Sensitive men were needed—men who could fully appreciate the importance of the charge intrusted to them; no other sort would do. But the burden of responsibility was too great to be borne indefinitely by a sensitive man.

It was, of necessity, a psychologically unstable condition. Insanity was an occupational disease.

Dr. Cummings appeared, still buckling the straps of the armor worn to guard against stray radiation. "What's up?" he asked Silard.

"I had to relieve Harper."

"So I guessed. I met him coming up. He was sore as hell—just glared at me."

"I know. He wants an immediate hearing. That's why I had to send for you."

Cummings grunted, then nodded toward the engineer, anonymous in all-inclosing armor. "Who'd I draw?"

"Erickson."

"Good enough. Squareheads can't go crazy—eh, Gus?"

Erickson looked up momentarily and answered, "That's your problem," and returned to his work.

Cummings turned back to Silard and commented: "Psychiatrists don't seem very popular around here. O.K.—I relieve you, sir."

"Very well, sir."

Silard threaded his way through the zigzag in the tanks of water which surrounded the disintegration room. Once outside this outer shield, he divested himself of the cumbersome armor, disposed of it in the locker room provided, and hurried to a lift. He left the lift at the tube station, underground, and looked around for an unoccupied capsule. Finding one, he strapped himself in, sealed the gasketed door, and settled the back of his head into the rest against the expected surge of acceleration.

Five minutes later he knocked at the door of the office of the general superintendent, twenty miles away.

The power plant proper was located in a bowl of desert hills on the Arizona plateau. Everything not necessary to the immediate operation of the plant—administrative offices, television station and so forth—lay beyond the hills. The buildings housing these auxiliary functions were of the most durable construction technical ingenuity could devise. It was hoped that, if *Der Tag* ever came, occupants would stand approximately the chance of survival of a man going over Niagara Falls in a barrel.

Silard knocked again. He was greeted by a male secretary. Steinke. Silard recalled reading his case history. Formerly one of the most brilliant of the young engineers, he had suffered a blanking out of the ability to handle mathematical operations. A plain case of *fugue*, but there had been nothing that the poor devil could do about it—he had been anxious enough with his conscious mind to stay on duty. He had been rehabilitated as an office worker.

Steinke ushered him into the superintendent's private office. Harper was there before him, and returned his greeting with icy politeness. The superintendent was cordial, but Silard thought he looked tired, as if the twenty-four-hour-a-day strain was too much for him.

"Come in, Doctor, come in. Sit down. Now tell me about this. I'm a little surprised. I thought Harper was one of my steadiest men."

"I don't say he isn't, sir."

"Well?"

"He may be perfectly all right, but your instructions to me are not to take any chances."

"Quite right." The superintendent gave the engineer, silent and tense in his chair, a troubled glance, then returned his attention to Silard. "Suppose you tell me about it."

Silard took a deep breath. "While on watch as psychological observer at the control station I noticed that the engineer of the watch seemed preoccupied and less responsive to stimuli than usual. During my off-watch observation of this case, over a period of the past several days, I have suspected an increasing lack of attention. For example, while playing contract bridge, he now occasionally asks for a review of the bidding, which is contrary to his former behavior pattern.

"Other similar data are available. To cut it short, at 3:11 today, while on watch, I saw Harper, with no apparent reasonable purpose in mind, pick up a wrench used only for operating the valves of the water shield and approach the trigger. I relieved him of duty and sent him out of the control room."

"Chief!" Harper calmed himself somewhat and continued: "If this witch doctor knew a wrench from an oscillator, he'd know what I was doing. The wrench was on the wrong rack. I noticed it, and picked it up to return it to its proper place. On the way, I stopped to check the readings!"

The superintendent turned inquiringly to Dr. Silard.

"That may be true. Granting that it is true," answered the psychiatrist doggedly, "my diagnosis still stands. Your behavior pattern has altered; your present actions are unpredictable, and I can't approve you for responsible work without a complete checkup."

General Superintendent King drummed on the desk top and sighed. Then he spoke slowly to Harper: "Cal, you're a good boy, and, believe me, I know how you feel. But there is no way to avoid it—you've got to go up for the psychometricals, and accept whatever disposition the board makes of you." He paused, but Harper maintained an expressionless silence. "Tell you what, son—why don't you take a few days leave? Then, when you come back, you can go up before the board, or transfer to another department away from the bomb, whichever you prefer." He looked to Silard for approval, and received a nod.

But Harper was not mollified. "No, chief," he protested. "It won't do. Can't you see what's wrong? It's this constant supervision. Somebody always watching the back of your neck, *expecting* you to go crazy. A man can't even shave in private. We're jumpy about the most innocent acts, for fear some head doctor, half batty himself, will see it and decide it's a sign we're slipping. Good grief, what do you expect?" His outburst having run its course, he subsided into a flippant cynicism that did not quite jell. "O.K—never mind the straitjacket; I'll go quietly. You're a good Joe in spite of it, chief," he added, "and I'm glad to have worked under you. Good-bye."

King kept the pain in his eyes out of his voice. "Wait a minute, Cal—you're not through here. Let's forget about the vacation. I'm transferring you to the radiation laboratory. You belong in research, anyhow; I'd never have spared you from it to stand watches if I hadn't been short on Number One men.

"As for the constant psychological observation, I hate it as much as you do. I don't suppose you know that they watch me about twice as hard as they watch you duty engineers." Harper showed his surprise, but Silard nodded in sober confirmation. "But we have to have this supervision. Do you remember Manning? No, he was before your time. We didn't have psychological observers then. Manning was able and brilliant. Furthermore, he was always cheerful; nothing seemed to bother him.

"I was glad to have him on the bomb, for he was always alert, and never seemed nervous about working with it—in fact, he grew more buoyant and cheerful the longer he stood control watches. I should have known that was a very bad sign, but I didn't, and there was no observer to tell me so.

"His technician had to slug him one night. He found him dismounting the safety interlocks on the trigger. Poor old Manning never pulled out of it—he's been violently insane ever since. After Manning cracked up we worked out the present system of two qualified engineers and an observer for every watch. It seemed the only thing to do."

"I suppose so, chief," Harper mused, his face no longer sullen, but still unhappy. "It's a hell of a situation just the same."

"That's putting it mildly." King rose and put out his hand. "Cal, unless you're dead set on leaving us, I'll expect to see you at the radiation laboratory tomorrow. Another thing—I don't often recommend this, but it might do you good to get drunk tonight."

King had signed to Silard to remain after the young man left. Once the door was closed he turned back to the psychiatrist. "There goes another one—and one of the best. Doctor, what am I going to do?"

Silard pulled at his cheek. "I don't know," he admitted. "The hell of it is, Harper's absolutely right. It does increase the strain on them to know that they are being watched—and yet they have to be watched. Your psychiatric staff isn't doing too well, either. It makes us nervous to be around the bomb—the more so because we don't understand it. And it's a strain on us to be hated and despised as we are. Scientific detachment is difficult under such conditions; I'm getting jumpy myself."

King ceased pacing the floor and faced the doctor. "But there must be *some* solution—" he insisted.

Silard shook his head. "It's beyond me, Superintendent. I see no solution from the standpoint of psychology."

"No? Hm-m-m. Doctor, who is the top man in your field?"

"Eh?"

"Who is the recognized Number One man in handling this sort of thing?"

"Why, that's hard to say. Naturally, there isn't any one leading psychiatrist in the world; we specialize too much. I know what you mean, though. You don't want the best industrial-temperament psychometrician; you want the best all-around man for psychoses nonlesional and situational. That would be Lentz."

"Go on."

"Well—he covers the whole field of environmental adjustment. He's the man who correlated the theory of optimum tonicity with the relaxation technique that Korzybski had developed empirically. He actually worked under Korzybski himself, when he was a young student—it's the only thing he's vain about."

"He did? Then he must be pretty old; Korzybski died in— What year did he die?"

"I started to say that you must know his work in symbology—theory of abstraction and calculus of statement, all that sort of thing—because of its applications to engineering and mathematical physics."

"*That* Lentz—yes, of course. But I had never thought of him as a psychiatrist."

"No, you wouldn't, in your field. Nevertheless, we are inclined to credit him with having done as much to check and reduce the pandemic neuroses of the Crazy Years as any other man, and more than any man left alive."

"Where is he?"

"Why, Chicago, I suppose. At the Institute."

"Get him here."

"Eh?"

"Get him down here. Get on that visiphone and locate him. Then have Steinke call the port of Chicago, and hire a stratocar to stand by for him. I want to see him as soon as possible—before the day is out." King sat up in his chair with the air of a man who is once more master of himself and the situation. His spirit knew that warming replenishment that comes only with reaching a decision. The harassed expression was gone.

Silard looked dumfounded. "But, Superintendent," he expostulated, "You can't ring for Dr. Lentz as if he were a junior clerk. He's . . . he's *Lentz*."

"Certainly—that's why I want him. But I'm not a

neurotic clubwoman looking for sympathy, either.
He'll come. If necessary, turn on the heat from Washington. Have the White House call him. But get him
here at once. Move!" King strode out of the office.

When Erickson came off watch he inquired around
and found that Harper had left for town. Accordingly,
he dispensed with dinner at the base, shifted into
"drinkin' clothes," and allowed himself to be dispatched via tube to Paradise.

Paradise, Arizona, was a hard little boom town,
which owed its existence to the power plant. It was
dedicated exclusively to the serious business of detaching the personnel of the plant from their inordinate salaries. In this worthy project they received
much cooperation from the plant personnel themselves, each of whom was receiving from twice to ten
times as much money each pay day as he had ever received in any other job, and none of whom was certain
of living long enough to justify saving for old age. Besides, the company carried a sinking fund in Manhattan for their dependents; why be stingy?

It was said, with some truth, that any entertainment
or luxury obtainable in New York City could be purchased in Paradise. The local chamber of commerce
had appropriated the slogan of Reno, Nevada, "Biggest Little City in the World." The Reno boosters retaliated by claiming that, while any town that close to
the atomic power plant undeniably brought thoughts
of death and the hereafter, Hell's Gates would be a
more appropriate name than Paradise.

Erickson started making the rounds. There were
twenty-seven places licensed to sell liquor in the six
blocks of the main street of Paradise. He expected to
find Harper in one of them, and, knowing the man's
habits and tastes, he expected to find him in the first
two or three he tried.

He was not mistaken. He found Harper sitting alone

at a table in the rear of DeLancey's Sans Souci Bar. DeLancey's was a favorite of both of them. There was an old-fashioned comfort about its chrome-plated bar and red leather furniture that appealed to them more than did the spectacular fittings of the up-to-the-minute places. DeLancey was conservative; he stuck to indirect lighting and soft music; his hostesses were required to be fully clothed, even in the evening.

The fifth of Scotch in front of Harper was about two thirds full. Erickson shoved three fingers in front of Harper's face and demanded, "Count!"

"Three," announced Harper. "Sit down, Gus."

"That's correct," Erickson agreed, sliding his big frame into a low-slung chair. "You'll do—for now. What was the outcome?"

"Have a drink. Not," he went on, "that this Scotch is any good. I think Lance has taken to watering it. I surrendered, horse and foot."

"Lance wouldn't do that—stick to that theory and you'll sink in the sidewalk up to your knees. How come you capitulated? I thought you planned to beat 'em about the head and shoulders, at least."

"I did," mourned Harper, "but, cripes, Gus, the chief is right. If a brain mechanic says you're punchy, he has *got* to back him up and take you off the bomb. The chief can't afford to take a chance."

"Yeah, the chief's all right, but I can't learn to love our dear psychiatrists. Tell you what—let's find us one, and see if he can feel pain. I'll hold him while you slug 'im."

"Oh, forget it, Gus. Have a drink."

"A pious thought—but not Scotch. I'm going to have a martini; we ought to eat pretty soon."

"I'll have one, too."

"Do you good." Erickson lifted his blond head and bellowed, "Israfel!"

A large, black person appeared at his elbow. "Mistuh Erickson! Yes, suh!"

"Izzy, fetch two martinis. Make mine with Italian."
He turned back to Harper. "What are you going to do
now, Cal?"

"Radiation laboratory."

"Well, that's not so bad. I'd like to have a go at the
matter of rocket fuels myself. I've got some ideas."

Harper looked mildly amused. "You mean atomic
fuel for interplanetary flight? The problem's pretty
well exhausted. No, son, the stratosphere is the ceiling
until we think up something better than rockets. Of
course, you *could* mount the bomb in a ship, and figure
out some jury rig to convert its radiant output into
push, but where does that get you? One bomb, one
ship—and twenty years of mining in Little America
has only produced enough pitchblende to make one
bomb. That's disregarding the question of getting the
company to lend you their one bomb for anything that
doesn't pay dividends."

Erickson looked balky. "I don't concede that you've
covered all the alternatives. What have we got? The
early rocket boys went right ahead trying to build better rockets, serene in the belief that, by the time they
could build rockets good enough to fly to the Moon, a
fuel would be perfected that would do the trick. And
they did build ships that were good enough—you
could take any ship that makes the antipodes run, and
refit it for the Moon—*if* you had a fuel that was sufficiently concentrated to maintain the necessary push
for the whole run. But they haven't got it.

"And why not? Because we let 'em down, that's why.
Because they're still depending on molecular energy,
on chemical reactions, with atomic power sitting right
here in our laps. It's not their fault—old D. D. Harri-
man had Rockets Consolidated underwrite the whole
first issue of Antarctic Pitchblende, and took a big slice
of it himself, in the expectation that we would produce
something usable in the way of a concentrated rocket
fuel. Did we do it? Like hell! The company went hog-

wild for immediate commercial exploitation, and there's no fuel yet."

"But you haven't stated it properly," Harper objected. "There are just two forms of atomic power available—radioactivity and atomic disintegration. The first is too slow; the energy is there, but you can't wait years for it to come out—not in a rocketship. The second we can only manage in a large mass of uranium. There you are—stymied."

Erickson's Scandinavian stubbornness was just gathering for another try at the argument when the waiter arrived with the drinks. He set them down with a triumphant flourish. "There you are, suh!"

"Want to roll for them, Izzy?" Harper inquired.

"Don' mind if I do."

The Negro produced a leather dice cup, and Harper rolled. He selected his combinations with care and managed to get four aces and a jack in three rolls. Israfel took the cup. He rolled in the grand manner with a backward twist to his wrist. His score finished at five kings, and he courteously accepted the price of six drinks. Harper stirred the engraved cubes with his forefinger.

"Izzy," he asked, "are these the same dice I rolled with?"

"Why, Mistuh Harper!" The Negro's expression was pained.

"Skip it," Harper conceded. "I should know better than to gamble with you. I haven't won a roll from you in six weeks. What did you start to say, Gus?"

"I was just going to say that there ought to be a better way to get energy out of—"

But they were joined again, this time by something very seductive in an evening gown that appeared to have been sprayed on her lush figure. She was young, perhaps nineteen or twenty. "You boys lonely?" she asked as she flowed into a chair.

"Nice of you to ask, but we're not," Erickson denied

with patient politeness. He jerked a thumb at a solitary figure seated across the room. "Go talk to Hannigan; he's not busy."

She followed his gesture with her eyes, and answered with faint scorn: "Him? He's no use. He's been like that for three weeks—hasn't spoken to a soul. If you ask me, I'd say that he was cracking up."

"That so?" he observed noncommittally. "Here"— he fished out a five-dollar bill and handed it to her— "buy yourself a drink. Maybe we'll look you up later."

"Thanks, boys." The money disappeared under her clothing, and she stood up. "Just ask for Edith."

"Hannigan does look bad," Harper considered, noting the brooding stare and apathetic attitude, "and he has been awfully standoffish lately, for him. Do you suppose we're obliged to report him?"

"Don't let it worry you," advised Erickson. "There's a spotter on the job now. Look." Harper followed his companion's eyes and recognized Dr. Mott of the psychological staff. He was leaning against the far end of the bar, and nursing a tall glass, which gave him protective coloration. But his stance was such that his field of vision included not only Hannigan, but Erickson and Harper as well.

"Yeah, and he's studying us as well," Harper added. "Damn it to hell, why does it make my back hair rise just to lay eyes on one of them?"

The question was rhetorical; Erickson ignored it. "Let's get out of here," he suggested, "and have dinner somewhere else."

"O.K."

DeLancey himself waited on them as they left. "Going so soon, gentlemen?" he asked, in a voice that implied that their departure would leave him no reason to stay open. "Beautiful lobster thermidor tonight. If you do not like it, you need not pay." He smiled brightly.

"Not sea food, Lance," Harper told him, "not tonight. Tell me—why do you stick around here when you know that the bomb is bound to get you in the long run? Aren't you afraid of it?"

The tavernkeeper's eyebrows shot up. "Afraid of the bomb? But it is my friend!"

"Makes you money, eh?"

"Oh, I do not mean that." He leaned toward them confidentially. "Five years ago I come here to make some money quickly for my family before my cancer of the stomach, it kills me. At the clinic, with the wonderful new radiants you gentlemen make with the aid of the bomb, I am cured—I live again. No, I am not afraid of the bomb, it is my good friend."

"Suppose it blows up?"

"When the good Lord needs me, He will take me." He crossed himself quickly.

As they turned away, Erickson commented in a low voice to Harper, "There's your answer, Cal—if all us engineers had his faith, the bomb wouldn't get us down."

Harper was unconvinced. "I don't know," he mused. "I don't think it's faith; I think it's lack of imagination—and knowledge."

Notwithstanding King's confidence, Lentz did not show up until the next day. The superintendent was subconsciously a little surprised at his visitor's appearance. He had pictured a master psychologist as wearing flowing hair, an imperial, and having piercing black eyes. But this man was not very tall, was heavy in his framework, and fat—almost gross. He might have been a butcher. Little, piggy, faded-blue eyes peered merrily out from beneath shaggy blond brows. There was no hair anywhere else on the enormous skull, and the apelike jaw was smooth and pink. He was dressed in mussed pajamas of unbleached linen. A long cigarette holder jutted permanently from one corner of a wide mouth, widened still more by a smile with suggested unmalicious amusement at the worst that life, or men, could do. He had gusto.

King found him remarkably easy to talk to.

At Lentz's suggestion the superintendent went first into the history of the atomic power plant, how the fission of the uranium atom by Dr. Otto Hahn in December, 1938, had opened up the way to atomic power. The door was opened just a crack; the process to be self-perpetuating and commercially usable required an enormously greater mass of uranium than there was available in the entire civilized world at that time.

But the discovery, fifteen years later, of enormous deposits of pitchblende in the old rock underlying Little America removed that obstacle. The deposits were similar to those previously worked at Great Bear Lake in the arctic north of Canada, but so much more extensive that the eventual possibility of accumulating enough uranium to build an atomic power plant became evident.

The demand for commercially usable, cheap power had never been satiated. Even the Douglas-Martin sunpower screens, used to drive the roaring road cities of the period and for a myriad other industrial purposes, were not sufficient to fill the ever-growing demand. They had saved the country from impending famine of oil and coal, but their maximum output of approximately one horsepower per square yard of sun-illuminated surface put a definite limit to the power from that source available in any given geographical area.

Atomic power was needed—was demanded.

But theoretical atomic physics predicted that a uranium mass sufficiently large to assist in its own disintegration might assist too well—blow up instantaneously, with such force that it would probably wreck every man-made structure on the globe and conceivably destroy the entire human race as well. They dared not build the bomb, even though the uranium was available.

"It was Destry's mechanics of infinitesimals that showed a way out of the dilemma," King went on. "His equations appeared to predict that an atomic explosion, once started, would disrupt the molar mass inclosing it so rapidly that neutron loss through the outer surface of the fragments would dampen the progression of the atomic explosion to zero before complete explosion could be reached.

"For the mass we use in the bomb, his equations predict a possible force of explosion one seventh of one percent of the force of complete explosion. That alone, of course, would be incomprehensibly destructive—about the equivalent of a hundred and forty thousand tons of TNT—enough to wreck this end of the State. Personally, I've never been sure that is all that would happen."

"Then why did you accept this job?" inquired Lentz.

King fiddled with items on his desk before replying. "I couldn't turn it down, Doctor—I *couldn't*. If I had refused, they would have gotten someone else—and it was an opportunity that comes to a physicist once in history."

Lentz nodded. "And probably they would have gotten someone not as competent. I understand, Dr. King—you were compelled by the 'truth-tropism' of the scientist. He must go where the data is to be found, even if it kills him. But about this fellow Destry, I've never liked his mathematics; he postulates too much."

King looked up in quick surprise, then recalled that this was the man who had refined and given rigor to the calculus of statement. "That's just the hitch," he agreed. "His work is brilliant, but I've never been sure that his predictions were worth the paper they were written on. Nor, apparently," he added bitterly, "do my junior engineers."

He told the psychiatrist of the difficulties they had had with personnel, of how the most carefully selected men would, sooner or later, crack under the strain. "At first I thought it might be some degenerating effect from the hard radiation that leaks out of the bomb, so we improved the screening and the personal armor. But it didn't help. One young fellow who had joined us after the new screening was installed became violent at dinner one night, and insisted that a pork chop was about to explode. I hate to think of what might have happened if he had been on duty at the bomb when he blew up."

The inauguration of the system of constant psychological observation had greatly reduced the probability of acute danger resulting from a watch engineer cracking up, but King was forced to admit that the system was not a success; there had actually been a marked increase in psychoneuroses, dating from that time.

"And that's the picture, Dr. Lentz. It gets worse all the time. It's getting me now. The strain is telling on me; I can't sleep, and I don't think my judgment is as good as it used to be—I have trouble making up my mind, of coming to a decision. Do you think you can do anything for us?"

But Lentz had no immediate relief for his anxiety. "Not so fast, superintendent," he countered. "You have given me the background, but I have no real data as yet. I must look around for a while, smell out the situation for myself, talk to your engineers, perhaps have a few drinks with them, and get acquainted. That is possible, is it not? Then in a few days, maybe, we'll know where we stand."

King had no alternative but to agree.

"And it is well that your young men do not know what I am here for. Suppose I am your old friend, a visiting physicist, eh?"

"Why, yes—of course. I can see to it that the idea gets around. But say—" King was reminded again of something that had bothered him from the time Silard had first suggested Lentz's name— "may I ask a personal question?"

The merry eyes were undisturbed.

"Go ahead."

"I can't help but be surprised that one man should attain eminence in two such widely differing fields as psychology and mathematics. And right now I'm perfectly convinced of your ability to pass yourself off as a physicist. I don't understand it."

The smile was more amused, without being in the least patronizing, nor offensive. "Same subject, symbology. You are a specialist; it would not necessarily come to your attention."

"I still don't follow you."

"No? Man lives in a world of ideas. Any phenomenon is so complex that he cannot possibly grasp the whole of it. He abstracts certain characteristics of a given phenomenon as an idea, then represents that idea as a symbol, be it a word or a mathematical sign. Human reaction is almost entirely reaction to symbols, and only negligibly to phenomena. As a matter of fact," he continued, removing the cigarette holder from his mouth and settling into his subject, "it can be demonstrated that the human mind can think only in terms of symbols.

"When we think, we let symbols operate on other symbols in certain, set fashions—rules of logic, or rules of mathematics. If the symbols have been abstracted so that they are structurally similar to the phenomena they stand for, and if the symbol operations are similar in structure and order to the operations of phenomena in the real world, we think sanely. If our logic-mathematics, or our word-symbols, have been poorly chosen, we do not think sanely.

"In mathematical physics you are concerned with making your symbology fit physical phenomena. In psychiatry I am concerned with precisely the same thing, except that I am more immediately concerned with the man who does the thinking than with the phenomena he is thinking about. But the same subject, always the same subject."

"We're not getting anyplace, . . . Gus." Harper put down his slide rule and frowned.

"Seems like it, Cal," Erickson grudgingly admitted. "Damn it, though—there ought to be some reasonable way of tackling the problem. What do we need? Some form of concentrated, controllable power for rocket fuel. What have we got? Power galore in the bomb. There must be some way to bottle that power, and serve it out when we need it—and the answer is someplace in one of the radioactive series. I *know* it." He stared glumly around the laboratory as if expecting to find the answer written somewhere on the lead-sheathed walls.

"Don't be so down in the mouth about it. You've got me convinced there is an answer; let's figure out how to find it. In the first place the three natural radioactive series are out, aren't they?"

"Yes—at least we had agreed that all that ground had been fully covered before."

"O. K.; we have to assume that previous investigators have done what their notes show they have done—otherwise we might as well not believe anything, and start checking on everybody from Archimedes to date. Maybe that is indicated, but Methuselah himself couldn't carry out such an assignment. What have we got left?"

"Artificial radioactives."

"All right. Let's set up a list of them, both those that have been made up to now, and those that might possibly be made in the future. Call that our group—or rather, field, if you want to be pedantic about definitions. There are a limited number of operations that can be performed on each member of the group, and on the members taken in combination. Set it up."

Erickson did so, using the curious curlicues of the calculus of statement. Harper nodded. "All right—expand it."

Erickson looked up after a few moments, and asked,

"Cal, have you any idea how many terms there are in the expansion?"

"No—hundreds, maybe thousands, I suppose."

"You're conservative. It reaches four figures without considering possible new radioactives. We couldn't finish such a research in a century." He chucked his pencil down and looked morose.

Cal Harper looked at him curiously, but with sympathy. "Gus," he said gently, "the bomb isn't getting you, too, is it?"

"I don't think so. Why?"

"I never saw you so willing to give up anything before. Naturally you and I will never finish any such job, but at the very worst we will have eliminated a lot of wrong answers for somebody else. Look at Edison— sixty years of experimenting, twenty hours a day, yet he never found out the one thing he was most interested in knowing. I guess if he could take it, we can."

Erickson pulled out of his funk to some extent. "I suppose so," he agreed. "Anyhow, maybe we could work out some techniques for carrying on a lot of experiments simultaneously."

Harper slapped him on the shoulder. "That's the ol' fight. Besides—we may not need to finish the research, or anything like it, to find a satisfactory fuel. The way I see it, there are probably a dozen, maybe a hundred, right answers. We may run across one of them any day. Anyhow, since you're willing to give me a hand with it in your off-watch time, I'm game to peck away at it till hell freezes."

Lentz puttered around the plant and the administration center for several days, until he was known to everyone by sight. He made himself pleasant and asked questions. He was soon regarded as a harmless nuisance, to be tolerated because he was a friend of the superintendent. He even poked his nose into the commercial power end of the plant, and had the mercury-steam-turbogenerator sequence explained to him in detail. This alone would have been sufficient to disarm any suspicion that he might be a psychiatrist, for the staff psychiatrists paid no attention to the hard-bitten technicians of the power-conversion unit. There was no need to; mental instability on their part could not affect the bomb, nor were they subject to the man-killing strain of social responsibility. Theirs was simply a job personally dangerous, a type of strain strong men have been inured to since the jungle.

In due course he got around to the unit of the radiation laboratory set aside for Calvin Harper's use. He rang the bell and waited. Harper answered the door, his antiradiation helmet shoved back from his face like a grotesque sunbonnet. "What is it?" he asked. "Oh—it's you, Dr. Lentz. Did you want to see me?"

"Why, yes and no," the older man answered. "I was just looking around the experimental station, and wondered what you do in here. Will I be in the way?"

"Not at all. Come in. Gus!"

Erickson got up from where he had been fussing over the power leads to their trigger—a modified cyclotron rather than a resonant accelerator. "Hello."

"Gus, this is Dr. Lentz—Gus Erickson."

"We've met," said Erickson, pulling off his gauntlet to shake hands. He had had a couple of drinks with Lentz in town and considered him a "nice old duck." "You're just between shows, but stick around and we'll start another run—not that there is much to see."

While Erickson continued with the setup, Harper conducted Lentz around the laboratory, explaining the line of research they were conducting, as happy as a father showing off twins. The psychiatrist listened with one ear and made appropriate comments while he studied the young scientist for signs of the instability he had noted to be recorded against him.

"You see," Harper explained, oblivious to the interest in himself, "we are testing radioactive materials to see if we can produce disintegration of the sort that takes place in the bomb, but in a minute, almost microscopic, mass. If we are successful, we can use the power of the bomb to make a safe, convenient, atomic fuel for rockets." He went on to explain their schedule of experimentation.

"I see," Lentz observed politely. "What metal are you examining now?"

Harper told him. "But it's not a case of examining one element—we've finished Isotope II with negative results. Our schedule calls next for running the same test on Isotope V. Like this." He hauled out a lead capsule, and showed the label to Lentz, who saw that it was, indeed, marked with the symbol of the fifth isotope. He hurried away to the shield around the target of the cyclotron, left open by Erickson. Lentz saw that he had opened the capsule, and was performing some operation on it in a gingerly manner, having first lowered his helmet. Then he closed and clamped the target shield.

"O.K., Gus?" he called out. "Ready to roll?"

"Yeah, I guess so," Erickson assured him, coming around them. They crowded behind a thick metal shield that cut them off from direct sight of the setup.

"Will I need to put on armor?" inquired Lentz.

"No," Erickson reassured him, "we wear it because we are around the stuff day in and day out. You just stay behind the shield and you'll be all right. It's lead—backed up by eight inches of case-hardened armor plate."

Erickson glanced at Harper, who nodded, and fixed his eyes on a panel of instruments mounted behind the shield. Lentz saw Erickson press a push button at the top of the board, then heard a series of relays click on the far side of the shield. There was a short moment of silence.

The floor slapped his feet like some incredible bastinado. The concussion that beat on his ears was so intense that it paralyzed the auditory nerve almost before it could be recorded as sound. The air-conducted concussion wave flailed every inch of his body with a single, stinging, numbing blow. As he picked himself up, he found he was trembling uncontrollably and realized, for the first time, that he was getting old.

Harper was seated on the floor and had commenced to bleed from the nose. Erickson had gotten up; his cheek was cut. He touched a hand to the wound, then stood there, regarding the blood on his fingers with a puzzled expression on his face.

"Are you hurt?" Lentz inquired inanely. "What happened?"

Harper cut in. "Gus, we've done it! We've done it! Isotope V's turned the trick!"

Erickson looked still more bemused. "Five?" he said stupidly. "But that wasn't Five; that was Isotope II. I put it in myself."

"*You* put it in? *I* put it in! It was Five, I tell you!"

They stood staring at each other, still confused by the explosion, and each a little annoyed at the boneheaded stupidity the other displayed in the face of the obvious. Lentz diffidently interceded.

"Wait a minute, boys," he suggested. "Maybe there's a reason—Gus, you placed a quantity of the second isotope in the receiver?"

"Why, yes, certainly. I wasn't satisfied with the last run, and I wanted to check it."

Lentz nodded. "It's my fault, gentlemen," he admitted ruefully. "I came in and disturbed your routine, and both of you charged the receiver. I know Harper did, for I saw him do it—with Isotope V. I'm sorry."

Understanding broke over Harper's face, and he slapped the older man on the shoulder. "Don't be sorry," he laughed; "you can come around to our lab and help us make mistakes any time you feel in the mood. Can't he, Gus? This is the answer, Dr. Lentz; this is it!"

"But," the psychiatrist pointed out, "you don't know which isotope blew up."

"Nor care," Harper supplemented. "Maybe it was

both, taken together. But we *will* know—this business is cracked now; we'll soon have it open." He gazed happily around at the wreckage.

In spite of Superintendent King's anxiety, Lentz refused to be hurried in passing judgment on the situation. Consequently, when he did present himself at King's office, and announced that he was ready to report, King was pleasantly surprised as well as relieved. "Well, I'm delighted," he said. "Sit down, Doctor, sit down. Have a cigar. What do we do about it?"

But Lentz stuck to his perennial cigarette and refused to be hurried. "I must have some information first. How important," he demanded, "is the power from your plant?"

King understood the implication at once. "If you are thinking about shutting down the bomb for more than a limited period, it can't be done."

"Why not? If the figures supplied me are correct, your output is less than thirteen percent of the total power used in the country."

"Yes, that is true, but you haven't considered the items that go into making up the total. A lot of it is domestic power, which householders get from sunscreens located on their own roofs. Another big slice is power for the moving roadways—that's sunpower again. The portion we provide here is the main power source for most of the heavy industries—steel, plastics, lithics, all kinds of manufacturing and processing. You might as well cut the heart out of a man—"

"But the food industry isn't basically dependent on you?" Lentz persisted.

"No. Food isn't basically a power industry—although we do supply a certain percentage of the power used in processing. I see your point, and will go on and concede that transportation—that is to say, distribution of food—could get along without us. But, good heavens, Doctor, you can't stop atomic power without causing the biggest panic this country has ever seen. It's the keystone of our whole industrial system."

"The country has lived through panics before, and we got past the oil shortage safely."

"Yes—because atomic power came along to take the place of oil. You don't realize what this would mean, Doctor. It would be worse than a war; in a system like ours, one thing depends on another. If you cut off the heavy industries all at once, everything else stops, too."

"Nevertheless, you had better dump the bomb." The uranium in the bomb was molten, its temperature being greater than twenty-four hundred degrees centigrade. The bomb could be dumped into a group of small containers, when it was desired to shut it down. The mass in any one container was too small to maintain progressive atomic disintegration.

King glanced involuntarily at the glass-inclosed relay mounted on his office wall, by which he, as well as the engineer on duty, could dump the bomb, if need be. "But I couldn't do that—or rather, if I did, the plant wouldn't stay shut down. The Directors would simply replace me with someone who *would* operate the bomb."

"You're right, of course." Lentz silently considered the situation for some time, then said, "Superintendent, will you order a car to fly me back to Chicago?"

"You're going, Doctor?"

"Yes." He took the cigarette holder from his face, and, for once, the smile of Olympian detachment was gone completely. His entire manner was sober, even tragic. "Short of shutting down the bomb, there is no solution to your problem—none whatsoever!

"I owe you a full explanation." Lentz continued, at length. "You are confronted here with recurring instances of situational psychoneurosis. Roughly, the symptoms manifest themselves as anxiety neurosis or some form of hysteria. The partial amnesia of your secretary, Steinke, is a good example of the latter. He might be cured with shock technique, but it would hardly be a kindness, as he has achieved a stable adjustment which puts him beyond the reach of the strain he could not stand.

"That other young fellow, Harper, whose blowup was the immediate cause of your sending for me, is an anxiety case. When the cause of the anxiety was eliminated from his matrix, he at once regained full sanity. But keep a close watch on his friend, Erickson—

"However, it is the cause, and prevention, of situational psychoneurosis we are concerned with here, rather than the forms in which it is manifested. In plain language, psychoneurosis situational simply refers to the common fact that, if you put a man in a situation that worries him more than he can stand, in time he blows up, one way or another.

"That is precisely the situation here. You take sensitive, intelligent young men, impress them with the fact that a single slip on their part, or even some fortuitous circumstance beyond their control, will result in the death of God knows how many other people, and then expect them to remain sane. It's ridiculous—impossible!"

"But, good heavens, Doctor, there must be some answer! There must!" He got up and paced around the room. Lentz noted, with pity, that King himself was riding the ragged edge of the very condition they were discussing.

"No," he said slowly. "No. Let me explain. You don't dare intrust the bomb to less sensitive, less socially conscious men. You might as well turn the controls over to a mindless idiot. And to psychoneurosis situational there are but two cures. The first obtains when the psychosis results from a misevaluation of environment. That cure calls for semantic readjustment. One assists the patient to evaluate correctly his environment. The worry disappears because there never was a real reason for worry in the situation itself, but simply in the wrong meaning the patient's mind had assigned to it.

"The second case is when the patient has correctly evaluated the situation, and rightly finds in it cause for extreme worry. His worry is perfectly sane and proper, but he cannot stand up under it indefinitely; it drives him crazy. The only possible cure is to change the situation. I have stayed here long enough to assure myself that such is the condition here. Your engineers have correctly evaluated the public danger of this bomb, and it will, with dreadful certainty, drive all of you crazy!

"The only possible solution is to dump the bomb—and leave it dumped."

King had continued his nervous pacing of the floor, as if the walls of the room itself were the cage of his dilemma. Now he stopped and appealed once more to the psychiatrist. "Isn't there *anything* I can do?"

"Nothing to cure. To alleviate—well, possibly."

"How?"

"Situational psychosis results from adrenalin exhaustion. When a man is placed under a nervous strain, his adrenal glands increase their secretion to help compensate for the strain. If the strain is too great and lasts too long, the adrenals aren't equal to the task, and he cracks. That is what you have here. Adrenalin therapy might stave off a mental breakdown, but it most assuredly would hasten a physical breakdown. But that would be safer from a viewpoint of public welfare—even though it assumes that physicists are expendable!

"Another thing occurs to me: If you selected any new watch engineers from the membership of churches that practice the confessional, it would increase the length of their usefulness."

King was plainly surprised. "I don't follow you."

"The patient unloads most of his worry on his confessor, who is not himself actually confronted by the

situation, and can stand it. That is simply an amelio-
rative, however. I am convinced that, in this situation,
eventual insanity is inevitable. But there is a lot of
good sense in the confessional," he added. "It fills a
basic human need. I think that is why the early psy-
choanalysts were so surprisingly successful, for all
their limited knowledge." He fell silent for a while,
then added, "If you will be so kind as to order a stra-
tocab for me—"

"You've nothing more to suggest?"

"No. You had better turn your psychological staff
loose on means of alleviation; they're able men, all of
them."

King pressed a switch and spoke briefly to Steinke.
Turning back to Lentz, he said, "You'll wait here until
your car is ready?"

Lentz judged correctly that King desired it and
agreed. Presently the tube delivery on King's desk
went *ping!* The Superintendent removed a small white
pasteboard, a calling card. He studied it with surprise
and passed it over to Lentz. "I can't imagine why he
should be calling on me," he observed, and added,
"Would you like to meet him?"

Lentz read:

THOMAS P. HARRINGTON
CAPTAIN (MATHEMATICS)
UNITED STATES NAVY

DIRECTOR
U.S. NAVAL OBSERVATORY

"But I do know him," he said. "I'd be very pleased to
see him."

Harrington was a man with something on his mind.
He seemed relieved when Steinke had finished usher-
ing him in, and had returned to the outer office. He
commenced to speak at once, turning to Lentz, who
was nearer to him than King. "You're King? . . . Why,
Dr. Lentz! What are you doing here?"

"Visiting," answered Lentz, accurately but incompletely, as he shook hands. "This is Superintendent King over here. Superintendent King—Captain Harrington."

"How do you do, Captain—it's a pleasure to have you here."

"It's an honor to be here, sir."

"Sit down?"

"Thanks." He accepted a chair and laid a briefcase on a corner of King's desk. "Superintendent, you are entitled to an explanation as to why I have broken in on you like this—"

"Glad to have you." In fact, the routine of formal politeness was an anodyne to King's frayed nerves.

"That's kind of you, but— That secretary chap, the one that brought me in here, would it be too much to ask you to tell him to forget my name? I know it seems strange—"

"Not at all." King was mystified, but willing to grant any reasonable request of a distinguished colleague in science. He summoned Steinke to the interoffice visiphone and gave him his orders.

Lentz stood up and indicated that he was about to leave. He caught Harrington's eye. "I think you want a private palaver, Captain."

King looked from Harrington to Lentz and back to Harrington. The astronomer showed momentary indecision, then protested: "I have no objection at all myself; it's up to Dr. King. As a matter of fact," he added, "It might be a very good thing if you did sit in on it."

"I don't know what it is, Captain," observed King, "that you want to see me about, but Dr. Lentz is already here in a confidential capacity."

"Good! Then that's settled. I'll get right down to business. Dr. King, you know Destry's mechanics of infinitesimals?"

"Naturally." Lentz cocked a brow at King, who chose to ignore it.

"Yes, of course. Do you remember theorem six and the transformation between equations thirteen and fourteen?"

"I think so, but I'd want to see them." King got up and went over to a bookcase. Harrington stayed him with a hand.

"Don't bother. I have them here." He hauled out a key, unlocked his briefcase, and drew out a large, much-thumbed, loose-leaf notebook. "Here. You, too, Dr. Lentz. Are you familiar with this development?"

Lentz nodded. "I've had occasion to look into them."

"Good—I think it's agreed that the step between thirteen and fourteen is the key to the whole matter. Now, the change from thirteen to fourteen looks perfectly valid—and would be, in some fields. But suppose we expand it to show every possible phase of the matter, every link in the chain of reasoning."

He turned a page and showed them the same two equations broken down into nine intermediate equations. He placed a finger under an associated group of mathematical symbols. "Do you see that? Do you see what that implies?" He peered anxiously at their faces.

King studied it, his lips moving. "Yes . . . I believe I do see. Odd . . . I never looked at it just that way before—yet I've studied those equations until I've dreamed about them." He turned to Lentz. "Do you agree, Doctor?"

Lentz nodded slowly. "I believe so . . . . Yes, I think I may say so."

Harrington should have been pleased; he wasn't. "I had hoped you could tell me I was wrong," he said, almost petulantly, "but I'm afraid there is no further doubt about it. Dr. Destry included an assumption valid in molar physics, but for which we have absolutely no assurance in atomic physics. I suppose you realize what this means to you, Dr. King?"

King's voice was dry whisper. "Yes," he said, "yes— It means that if that bomb out there ever blows up, we must assume that it will go up all at once, rather than the way Destry predicted—and God help the human race!"

Captain Harrington cleared his throat to break the silence that followed. "Superintendent," he said, "I would not have ventured to call had it been simply a matter of disagreement as to interpretation of theoretical predictions—"

"You have something more to go on?"

"Yes and no. Probably you gentlemen think of the Naval Observatory as being exclusively preoccupied with ephemerides and tide tables. In a way you would be right—but we still have some time to devote to research as long as it doesn't cut into the appropriation. My special interest has always been lunar theory.

"I don't mean lunar ballistics," he continued. "I mean the much more interesting problem of its origin and history, the problem the younger Darwin struggled with, as well as my illustrious predecessor, Captain T. J. J. See. I think that it is obvious that any theory of lunar origin and history must take into account the surface features of the Moon—especially the mountains, the craters, that mark its face so prominently."

He paused momentarily, and Superintendent King put in: "Just a minute, Captain—I may be stupid, or perhaps I missed something, but—is there a connection between what we were discussing before and lunar theory?"

"Bear with me for a few moments, Dr. King," Harrington apologized. "There is a connection—at least, I'm *afraid* there is a connection—but I would rather present my points in their proper order before making my conclusions." They granted him an alert silence; he went on:

"Although we are in the habit of referring to the 'craters' of the Moon, we know they are not volcanic craters. Superficially, they follow none of the rules of terrestrial volcanoes in appearance or distribution, but when Rutter came out in 1952 with his monograph on the dynamics of vulcanology, he proved rather conclusively that the lunar craters could not be caused by anything that we know as volcanic action.

"That left the bombardment theory as the simplest hypothesis. It looks good, on the face of it, and a few minutes spent throwing pebbles into a patch of mud will convince anyone that the lunar craters could have been formed by falling meteors.

"But there are difficulties. If the Moon was struck so repeatedly, why not the Earth? It hardly seems necessary to mention that the Earth's atmosphere would be no protection against masses big enough to form craters like Endymion or Plato. And if they fell after the Moon was a dead world while the Earth was still young enough to change its face and erase the marks of bombardment, why did the meteors avoid so nearly completely the great dry basins we call lunar seas?

"I want to cut this short; you'll find the data and the mathematical investigations from the data here in my notes. There is one other major objection to the meteor-bombardment theory: the great rays that spread from Tycho across almost the entire surface of the Moon. It makes the Moon look like a crystal ball that had been struck with a hammer, and impact from outside seems evident, but there are difficulties. The striking mass, our hypothetical meteor, must be small enough to have formed the crater of Tycho, but it must have the mass and speed to crack an entire planet.

"Work it out for yourself—you must either postulate a chunk out of the core of a dwarf star, or speeds such as we have never observed within the system. It's conceivable but a farfetched explanation."

He turned to King. "Doctor, does anything occur to you that might account for a phenomenon like Tycho?"

The Superintendent grasped the arms of his chair, then glanced at his palms. He fumbled for a handkerchief, and wiped them. "Go ahead," he said, almost inaudibly.

"Very well then." Harrington drew out of his briefcase a large photograph of the Moon—a beautiful full-Moon portrait made at Lick. "I want you to imagine the Moon as she might have been sometime in the past. The dark areas we call the 'seas' are actual oceans. It has an atmosphere, perhaps a heavier gas than oxygen and nitrogen, but an active gas, capable of supporting some conceivable form of life.

"For this is an inhabited planet, inhabited by intelligent beings, beings capable of discovering atomic power and exploiting it!"

He pointed out on the photograph, near the southern limb, the lime-white circle of Tycho, with its shining, incredible, thousand-mile-long rays spreading, thrusting, jutting out from it. "Here . . . here at Tycho was located their main power plant." He moved his fingers to a point near the equator and somewhat east of meridian—the point where three great dark areas merged, *Mare Nubium*, *Mare Imbrium*, *Oceanus Procellarum*—and picked out two bright splotches surrounded, also, by rays, but shorter, less distinct, and wavy. "And here at Copernicus and at Kepler, on islands at the middle of a great ocean, were secondary power stations."

He paused, and interpolated soberly: "Perhaps they knew the danger they ran, but wanted power so badly that they were willing to gamble the life of their race. Perhaps they were ignorant of the ruinous possibilities of their little machines, or perhaps their mathematicians assured them that it could not happen.

"But we will never know—no one can ever know. For it blew up and killed them—and it killed their planet.

"It whisked off the gassy envelope and blew it into outer space. It blasted great chunks off the planet's crust. Perhaps some of that escaped completely, too, but all that did not reach the speed of escape fell back down in time and splashed great ring-shaped craters in the land.

"The oceans cushioned the shock; only the more massive fragments formed craters through the water.

Perhaps some life still remained in those ocean depths. If so, it was doomed to die—for the water, unprotected by atmospheric pressure, could not remain liquid and must inevitably escape in time to outer space. Its life-blood drained away. The planet was dead—dead by suicide!"

He met the grave eyes of his two silent listeners with an expression almost of appeal. "Gentlemen . . . this is only a theory, I realize . . . only a theory, a dream, a nightmare . . . but it has kept me awake so many nights that I had to come tell you about it, and see if you saw it the same way I do. As for the mechanics of it, it's all in there in my notes. You can check it—and I pray that you find some error! But it is the only lunar theory I have examined which included all of the known data and accounted for all of them."

He appeared to have finished. Lentz spoke up. "Suppose, Captain, suppose we check your mathematics and find no flaw—what then?"

Harrington flung out his hands. "That's what I came here to find out!"

Although Lentz had asked the question, Harrington directed the appeal to King. The Superintendent looked up; his eyes met the astronomer's, wavered and dropped again. "There's nothing to be done," he said dully, "nothing at all."

Harrington stared at him in open amazement. "But good God, man!" he burst out. "Don't you see it? That bomb has *got* to be disassembled—at once!"

"Take it easy, Captain." Lentz's calm voice was a spray of cold water. "And don't be too harsh on poor King—this worries him even more than it does you. What he means is this: We're not faced with a problem in physics, but with a political and economic situation. Let's put it this way: King can no more dump the bomb than a peasant with a vineyard on the slopes of Mount Vesuvius can abandon his holdings and pauperize his family simply because there will be an eruption some day.

"King doesn't own that bomb out there; he's only

the custodian. If he dumps it against the wishes of the legal owners, they'll simply oust him and put in someone more amenable. No, we have to convince the owners."

"The President could do it," suggested Harrington. "I could get to the President—"

"No doubt you could, through the Navy Department. And you might even convince him. But could he help much?"

"Why, of course he could. He's the *President*!"

"Wait a minute. You're Director of the Naval Observatory; suppose you took a sledge hammer and tried to smash the big telescope—how far would you get?"

"Not very far," Harrington conceded. "We guard the big fellow pretty closely."

"Nor can the President act in an arbitrary manner," Lentz persisted. "He's not an unlimited monarch. If he shuts down this plant without due process of law, the Federal courts will tie him in knots. I admit that Congress isn't helpless but—would you like to try to give a congressional committee a course in the mechanics of infinitesimals?"

Harrington readily stipulated the point. "But there is another way," he pointed out. "Congress is responsive to public opinion. What we need to do is to convince the public that the bomb is a menace to everybody. That could be done without ever trying to explain things in terms of higher mathematics."

"Certainly it could," Lentz agreed. "You could go on the air with it and scare everybody half to death. You could create the damnedest panic this slightly slug-nutty country has ever seen. No, thank you. I, for one, would rather have us all take the chance of being quietly killed than bring on a mass psychosis that would destroy the culture we are building up. I think one taste of the Crazy Years is enough."

"Well, then, what do *you* suggest?"

Lentz considered shortly, then answered: "All I see is a forlorn hope. We've got to work on the Board of

Directors and try to beat some sense into their heads."

King, who had been following the discussion with attention in spite of his tired despondence, interjected a remark: "How would you go about that?"

"I don't know," Lentz admitted. "It will take some thinking. But it seems the most fruitful line of approach. If it doesn't work, we can always fall back on Harrington's notion of publicity—I don't insist that the world commit suicide to satisfy my criteria of evaluation."

Harrington glanced at his wristwatch—a bulky affair—and whistled. "Good heavens!" he exclaimed. "I forgot the time! I'm supposed officially to be at the Flagstaff Observatory."

King had automatically noted the time shown by the Captain's watch as it was displayed. "But it can't be that late," he had objected. Harrington looked puzzled, then laughed.

"It isn't—not by two hours. We are in zone plus-seven; this shows zone plus-five—it's radio-synchronized with the master clock at Washington."

"Did you say radio-synchronized?"

"Yes. Clever, isn't it?" He held it out for inspection. "I call it a telechronometer; it's the only one of its sort to date. My nephew designed it for me. He's a bright one, that boy. He'll go far. That is"—his face clouded, as if the little interlude had only served to emphasize the tragedy that hung over them— "if any of us live that long!"

A signal light glowed at King's desk, and Steinke's face showed on the communicator screen. King answered him, then said, "Your car is ready, Dr. Lentz."

"Let Captain Harrington have it."

"Then you're not going back to Chicago?"

"No. The situation has changed. If you want me, I'm stringing along."

The following Friday, Steinke ushered Lentz into King's office. King looked almost happy as he shook hands. "When did you ground, Doctor? I didn't expect you back for another hour or so."

"Just now. I hired a cab instead of waiting for the shuttle."

"Any luck?"

"None. The same answer they gave you: 'The Company is assured by independent experts that Destry's mechanics is valid, and sees no reason to encourage an hysterical attitude among its employees.' "

King tapped on his desk top, his eyes unfocused. Then, hitching himself around to face Lentz directly, he said, "Do you suppose the Chairman is right?"

"How?"

"Could the three of us—you, me and Harrington—have gone off the deep end—slipped mentally?"

"No."

"You're sure?"

"Certainly. I looked up some independent experts of my own, not retained by the Company, and had them check Harrington's work. It checks." Lentz purposely neglected to mention that he had done so partly because he was none too sure of King's present mental stability.

King sat up briskly, reached out and stabbed a push button. "I am going to make one more try," he explained, "to see if I can't throw a scare into Dixon's thick head. Steinke," he said to the communicator, "get me Mr. Dixon on the screen."

"Yes, sir."

In about two minutes the visiphone screen came to life and showed the features of Chairman Dixon. He was transmitting, not from his office, but from the board room of the Company in Jersey City. "Yes?" he said. "What is it, Superintendent?" His manner was somehow both querulous and affable.

"Mr. Dixon," King began, "I've called to try to impress on you the seriousness of the Company's action. I stake my scientific reputation that Harrington has proved completely that—"

"Oh, that? Mr. King, I thought you understood that that was a closed matter."

"But, Mr. Dixon—"

"Superintendent, please! If there were any possible legitimate cause to fear, do you think I would hesitate? I have children, you know, and grandchildren."

"That is just why—"

"We try to conduct the affairs of the company with reasonable wisdom and in the public interest. But we have other responsibilities, too. There are hundreds of thousands of little stockholders who expect us to show a reasonable return on their investment. You must not expect us to jettison a billion-dollar corporation just because you've taken up astrology! Moon theory!" He sniffed.

"Very well, Mr. Chairman." King's tone was stiff.

"Don't take it that way, Mr. King. I'm glad you called—the Board has just adjourned a special meeting. They have decided to accept you for retirement—with full pay, of course."

"I did not apply for retirement!"

"I know, Mr. King, but the Board feels that—"

"I understand. Good-by!"

"Mr. King—"

"Good-by!" He switched him off, and turned to Lentz. " '—with full pay,' " he quoted, "which I can enjoy in any way that I like for the rest of my life—just as happy as a man in the death house!"

"Exactly," Lentz agreed. "Well, we've tried our way. I suppose we should call up Harrington now and let him try the political and publicity method."

"I suppose so," King seconded absentmindedly. "Will you be leaving for Chicago now?"

"No," said Lentz. "No . . . I think I will catch the shuttle for Los Angeles and take the evening rocket for the antipodes."

King looked surprised, but said nothing. Lentz answered the unspoken comment. "Perhaps some of us on the other side of the Earth will survive. I've done all that I can here. I would rather be a live sheepherder in Australia than a dead psychiatrist in Chicago."

King nodded vigorously. "That shows horse sense. For two cents, I'd dump the bomb now and go with you."

"Not horse sense, my friend—a horse will run back into a burning barn, which is exactly *not* what I plan to do. Why don't you do it and come along? If you did, it would help Harrington to scare 'em to death."

"I believe I will!"

Steinke's face appeared again on the screen. "Harper and Erickson are here, chief."

"I'm busy."

"They are pretty urgent about seeing you."

"Oh . . . all right," King said in a tired voice, "Show them in. It doesn't matter."

They breezed in, Harper in the van. He commenced talking at once, oblivious to the Superintendent's morose preoccupation. "We've got it, chief, we've got it—and it all checks out to the umpteenth decimal!"

"You've got what? Speak English."

Harper grinned. He was enjoying his moment of triumph, and was stretching it out to savor it. "Chief, do you remember a few weeks back when I asked for an additional allotment—a special one without specifying how I was going to spend it?"

"Yes. Come on—get to the point."

"You kicked at first, but finally granted it. Remember? Well, we've got something to show for it, all tied up in pink ribbon. It's the greatest advance in radioactivity since Hahn split the nucleus. Atomic fuel, chief, atomic fuel, safe, concentrated, and controllable. Suitable for rockets, for power plants, for any damn thing you care to use it for."

King showed alert interest for the first time. "You mean a power source that doesn't require the bomb?"

"The bomb? Oh, no. I didn't say that. You use the

bomb to make the fuel, then you use the fuel anywhere and anyhow you like, with something like ninety-two percent recovery of the energy of the bomb. But you could junk the mercury-steam sequence, if you wanted to."

King's first wild hope of a way out of his dilemma was dashed; he subsided. "Go ahead. Tell me about it."

"Well—it's a matter of artificial radioactives. Just before I asked for that special research allotment, Erickson and I—Dr. Lentz had a finger in it, too—found two isotopes of a radioactive that seemed to be mutually antagonistic. That is, when we goosed 'em in the presence of each other they gave up their latent energy all at once—blew all to hell. The important point is, we were using just a gnat's whisker of mass of each— the reaction didn't require a big mass like the bomb to maintain it."

"I don't see," objected King, "how that could—"

"Neither do we, quite—but it works. We've kept it quiet until we were sure. We checked on what we had, and we found a dozen other fuels. Probably we'll be able to tailormake fuels for any desired purpose. But here it is." Harper handed King a bound sheaf of type-written notes which he had been carrying under the arm. "That's your copy. Look it over."

King started to do so. Lentz joined him, after a look that was a silent request for permission, which Erickson had answered with his only verbal contribution, "Sure, Doc."

As King read, the troubled feeling of an acutely harassed executive left him. His dominant personality took charge, that of the scientist. He enjoyed the controlled and cerebral ecstasy of the impersonal seeker for the elusive truth. The emotions felt in the throbbing thalamus were permitted only to form a sensuous obbligato for the cold flame of cortical activity. For the time being, he was sane, more nearly completely sane than most men ever achieve at any time.

For a long period there was only an occasional grunt, the clatter of turned pages, a nod of approval. At last he put it down.

"It's the stuff," he said. "You've done it, boys. It's great; I'm proud of you."

Erickson glowed a bright pink and swallowed. Harper's small, tense figure gave the ghost of a wriggle, reminiscent of a wire-haired terrier receiving approval. "That's fine, chief. We'd rather hear you say that than get the Nobel Prize."

"I think you'll probably get it. However"—the proud light in his eyes died down—"I'm not going to take any action in this matter."

"Why not, chief?" Harper's tone was bewildered.

"I'm being retired. My successor will take over in the near future; this is too big a matter to start just before a change in administration."

"*You* being retired! What the hell! *Why?*"

"About the same reason I took you off the bomb—at least, the Directors think so."

"But that's nonsense! You were right to take me off the bomb; I *was* getting jumpy. But you're another matter—we all depend on you."

"Thanks, Cal—but that's how it is; there's nothing to be done about it." He turned to Lentz. "I think this is the last ironical touch needed to make the whole thing pure farce," he observed bitterly. "This thing is big, bigger than we can guess at this stage—and I have to give it a miss."

"Well," Harper burst out, "I can think of something to do about it!" He strode over to King's desk and snatched up the manuscript. "Either you superintend the exploitation or the company will damn well get along without our discovery!" Erickson concurred belligerently.

"Wait a minute." Lentz had the floor. "Dr. Harper, have you already achieved a practical rocket fuel?"

"I said so. We've got it on hand now."

"An escape-speed fuel?" They understood his verbal

shorthand—a fuel that would lift a rocket free of the Earth's gravitational pull.

"Sure. Why, you could take any of the Clipper rockets, refit them a trifle, and have breakfast on the Moon."

"Very well. Bear with me—" He obtained a sheet of paper from King and commenced to write. They watched in mystified impatience. He continued briskly for some minutes, hesitating only momentarily. Presently he stopped and spun the paper over to King. "Solve it!" he demanded.

King studied the paper. Lentz had assigned symbols to a great number of factors, some social, some psychological, some physical, some economical. He had thrown them together into a structural relationship, using the symbols of calculus of statement. King understood the paramathematical operations indicated by the symbols, but he was not as used to them as he was to the symbols and operations of mathematical physics. He plowed through the equations, moving his lips slightly in unconscious subvocalization.

He accepted a pencil from Lentz and completed the solution. It required several more lines, a few more equations, before the elements canceled out, or rearranged themselves, into a definite answer.

He stared at this answer while puzzlement gave way to dawning comprehension and delight.

He looked up. "Erickson! Harper!" he rapped out. "We will take your new fuel, refit a large rocket, install the bomb in it, and throw it into an orbit around the Earth, far out in space. There we will use it to make more fuel, safe fuel, for use on Earth, with the danger from the bomb itself limited to the operators actually on watch!"

There was no applause. It was not that sort of an idea; their minds were still struggling with the complex implications.

"But, chief," Harper finally managed, "how about your retirement? We're still not going to stand for it."

"Don't worry," King assured him. "It's all in there, implicit in those equations, you two, me, Lentz, the Board of Directors—and just what we all have to do to accomplish it."

"All except the matter of time," Lentz cautioned.

"Eh?"

"You'll note that elapsed time appears in your answer as an undetermined unknown."

"Yes . . . yes, of course. That's the chance we have to take. Let's get busy!"

Chairman Dixon called the Board of Directors to order. "This being a special meeting, we'll dispense with minutes and reports," he announced. "As set forth in the call we have agreed to give the retiring superintendent three hours of our time."

"Mr. Chairman—"

"Yes, Mr. Thornton?"

"I thought we had settled that matter."

"We have, Mr. Thornton, but in view of Superintendent King's long and distinguished service, if he asks a hearing, we are honor bound to grant it. You have the floor, Dr. King."

King got up and stated briefly, "Dr. Lentz will speak for me." He sat down.

Lentz had to wait till coughing, throat clearing and scraping of chairs subsided. It was evident that the board resented the outsider.

Lentz ran quickly over the main points in the argument which contended that the bomb presented an intolerable danger anywhere on the face of the Earth. He moved on at once to the alternative proposal that the bomb should be located in a rocketship, an artificial moonlet flying in a free orbit around the Earth at a convenient distance—say, fifteen thousand miles—while secondary power stations on earth burned a safe fuel manufactured by the bomb.

He announced the discovery of the Harper-Erickson technique and dwelt on what it meant to them com-

mercially. Each point was presented as persuasively
as possible, with the full power of his engaging personality. Then he paused and waited for them to blow off
steam.

They did. "Visionary—" "Unproved—" "No essential change in the situation—" The substance of it was
that they were very happy to hear of the new fuel, but
not particularly impressed by it. Perhaps in another
twenty years, after it had been thoroughly tested and
proved commercially, and provided enough uranium
had been mined to build another bomb, they might
consider setting up another power station outside the
atmosphere. In the meantime there was no hurry.

Lentz patiently and politely dealt with their objec-
tions. He emphasized the increasing incidence of occupational psychoneurosis among the engineers and
grave danger to everyone near the bomb even under
the orthodox theory. He reminded them of their insurance and indemnity-bond costs, and of the "squeeze"
they paid State politicians.

Then he changed his tone and let them have it directly and brutally. "Gentlemen," he said, "we believe
that we are fighting for our lives—our own lives, our
families and every life on the globe. If you refuse this
compromise, we will fight as fiercely and with as little
regard for fair play as any cornered animal." With that
he made his first move in attack.

It was quite simple. He offered for their inspection
the outline of a propaganda campaign on a national
scale, such as any major advertising firm should carry
out as matter of routine. It was complete to the last
detail, television broadcasts, spot plugs, newspaper
and magazine coverage and—most important—a supporting whispering campaign and a letters-to-Con-
gress organization. Every businessman there knew
from experience how such things worked.

But its object was to stir up fear of the bomb and to
direct that fear, not into panic, but into rage against
the Board of Directors personally, and into a demand

that the government take action to have the bomb removed to outer space.

"This is blackmail! We'll stop you!"

"I think not," Lentz replied gently. "You may be
able to keep us out of some of the newspapers, but you
can't stop the rest of it. You can't even keep us off the
air—ask the Federal Communications Commission."
It was true. Harrington had handled the political end
and had performed his assignment well; the President
was convinced.

Tempers were snapping on all sides; Dixon had to
pound for order. "Dr. Lentz," he said, his own temper
under taut control, "you plan to make every one of us
appear a blackhearted scoundrel with no other
thought than personal profit, even at the expense of
the lives of others. You know that is not true; this is a
simple difference of opinion as to what is wise."

"I did not say it was true," Lentz admitted blandly,
"but you will admit that I can convince the public that
you are deliberate villains. As to it being a difference
of opinion—you are none of you atomic physicists; you
are not entitled to hold opinions in this matter.

"As a matter of fact," he went on callously, "the only
doubt in my mind is whether or not an enraged public
will destroy your precious power plant before Congress has time to exercise eminent domain and take it
away from you!"

Before they had time to think up arguments in answer and ways of circumventing him, before their hot
indignation had cooled and set as stubborn resistance,
he offered his gambit. He produced another layout for
a propaganda campaign—an entirely different sort.

This time the Board of Directors was to be built up,
not torn down. All of the same techniques were to be
used; behind-the-scenes feature articles with plenty of
human interest would describe the functions of the
company, describe it as a great public trust, adminis-
tered by patriotic, unselfish statesmen of the business
world. At the proper point in the campaign, the Har-

per-Erickson fuel would be announced, not as a semi-accidental result of the initiative of two employees, but as the long-expected end product of years of systematic research conducted under a fixed policy growing naturally out of their humane determination to remove forever the menace of explosion from even the sparsely settled Arizona desert.

No mention was to be made of the danger of complete, planet-embracing catastrophe.

Lentz discussed it. He dwelt on the appreciation that would be due them from a grateful world. He invited them to make a noble sacrifice and, with subtle misdirection, tempted them to think of themselves as heroes. He deliberately played on one of the most deep-rooted of simian instincts, the desire for approval from one's kind, deserved or not.

All the while he was playing for time, as he directed his attention from one hard case, one resistant mind, to another. He soothed and he tickled and he played on personal foibles. For the benefit of the timorous and the devoted family men, he again painted a picture of the suffering, death and destruction that might result from their well-meant reliance on the unproved and highly questionable predictions of Destry's mathematics. Then he described in glowing detail a picture of a world free from worry but granted almost unlimited power, safe power from an invention which was theirs for this one small concession.

It worked. They did not reverse themselves all at once, but a committee was appointed to investigate the feasibility of the proposed spaceship power plant. By sheer brass Lentz suggested names for the committee and Dixon confirmed his nominations, not because he wished to, particularly, but because he was caught off guard and could not think of a reason to refuse without affronting the colleagues.

The impending retirement of King was not mentioned by either side. Privately, Lentz felt sure that it never would be mentioned.

It worked, but there was left much to do. For the first few days after the victory in committee, King felt much elated by the prospect of an early release from the soul-killing worry. He was buoyed up by pleasant demands of manifold new administrative duties. Harper and Erickson were detached to Goddard Field to collaborate with the rocket engineers there in design of firing chambers, nozzles, fuel stowage, fuel metering and the like. A schedule had to be worked out with the business office to permit as much power of the bomb as possible to be diverted to making atomic fuel, and a giant combustion chamber for atomic fuel had to be designed and ordered to replace the bomb itself during the interim between the time it was shut down on Earth and the later time when sufficient local, smaller plants could be built to carry the commercial load. He was busy.

When the first activity had died down and they were settled in a new routine, pending the shutting down of the bomb and its removal to outer space, King suffered an emotional reaction. There was, by then, nothing to do but wait, and tend the bomb, until the crew at Goddard Field smoothed out the bugs and produced a space-worthy rocketship.

They ran into difficulties, overcame them, and came across more difficulties. They had never used such high reaction velocities; it took many trials to find a nozzle shape that would give reasonably high efficiency. When that was solved, and success seemed in sight, the jets burned out on a time-trial ground test. They were stalemated for weeks over that hitch.

Back at the power plant Superintendent King could do nothing but chew his nails and wait. He had not even the release of running over to Goddard Field to watch the progress of the research, for, urgently as he desired to, he felt an even stronger, an overpowering compulsion to watch over the bomb lest it—heart-breakingly!—blow up at the last minute.

He took to hanging around the control room. He had

to stop that; his unease communicated itself to his watch engineers; two of them cracked up in a single day—one of them on watch.

He must face the fact—there had been a grave upswing in psychoneurosis among his engineers since the period of watchful waiting had commenced. At first, they had tried to keep the essential facts of the plan a close secret, but it had leaked out, perhaps through some member of the investigating committee. He admitted to himself now that it had been a mistake ever to try to keep it secret—Lentz had advised against it, and the engineers not actually engaged in the changeover were bound to know that something was up.

He took all of the engineers into confidence at last, under oath of secrecy. That had helped for a week or more, a week in which they were all given a spiritual lift by the knowledge, as he had been. Then it had worn off, the reaction had set in, and psychological observers had started disqualifying engineers for duty almost daily. They were even reporting each other as mentally unstable with great frequency; he might even be faced with a shortage of psychiatrists if that kept up, he thought to himself with bitter amusement. His engineers were already standing four hours in every sixteen. If one more dropped out, he'd put himself on watch. That would be a relief, to tell himself the truth.

Somehow, some of the civilians around about and the nontechnical employees were catching on to the secret. That mustn't go on—if it spread any farther there might be a nationwide panic. But how the hell could he stop it? He couldn't.

He turned over in bed, rearranged his pillow, and tried once more to get to sleep. No soap. His head ached, his eyes were balls of pain, and his brain was a ceaseless grind of useless, repetitive activity, like a disk recording stuck in one groove.

God! This was unbearable! He wondered if he were

cracking up—if he already had cracked up. This was worse, many times worse, than the old routine when he had simply acknowledged the danger and tried to forget it as much as possible. Not that the bomb was any different—it was this five-minutes-to-armistice feeling, this waiting for the curtain to go up, this race against time with nothing to do to help.

He sat up, switched on his bed lamp, and looked at the clock. Three thirty. Not so good. He got up, went into his bathroom, and dissolved a sleeping powder in a glass of whiskey and water, half and half. He gulped it down and went back to bed. Presently he dozed off.

He was running, fleeing down a long corridor. At the end lay safety—he knew that, but he was so utterly exhausted that he doubted his ability to finish the race. The thing pursuing him was catching up; he forced his leaden, aching legs into greater activity. The thing behind him increased its pace, and actually touched him. His heart stopped, then pounded again. He became aware that he was screaming, shrieking in mortal terror.

But he had to reach the end of that corridor; more depended on it than just himself. He had to. He had to! *He had to!*

Then the sound hit him, and he realized that he had lost, realized it with utter despair and utter, bitter defeat. He had failed; the bomb had blown up.

The sound was the alarm going off; it was seven o'clock. His pajamas were soaked, dripping with sweat, and his heart still pounded. Every ragged nerve throughout his body screamed for release. It would take more than a cold shower to cure this case of the shakes.

He got to the office before the janitor was out of it. He sat there, doing nothing, until Lentz walked in on him, two hours later. The psychiatrist came in just as he was taking two small tablets from a box in his desk.

"Easy . . . easy, old man," Lentz said in a slow voice. "What have you there?" He came around and gently took possession of the box.

"Just a sedative."

Lentz studied the inscription on the cover. "How many have you had today?"

"Just two, so far."

"You don't need a sedative; you need a walk in the fresh air. Come, take one with me."

"You're a fine one to talk—you're smoking a cigarette that isn't lighted!"

"Me? Why, so I am! We both need that walk. Come."

Harper arrived less than ten minutes after they had left the office. Steinke was not in the outer office. He walked on through and pounded on the door of King's private office, then waited with the man who accompanied him—a hard young chap with an easy confidence to his bearing. Steinke let them in.

Harper brushed on past him with a casual greeting, then checked himself when he saw that there was no one else inside.

"Where's the chief?" he demanded.

"Gone out. Should be back soon."

"I'll wait. Oh—Steinke, this is Greene. Greene—Steinke."

The two shook hands. "What brings you back, Cal?" Steinke asked, turning back to Harper.

"Well . . . I guess it's all right to tell you—"

The communicator screen flashed into sudden activity, and cut him short. A face filled most of the frame. It was apparently too close to the pickup, as it was badly out of focus. "Superintendent!" it yelled in an agonized voice. "The bomb—"

A shadow flashed across the screen, they heard a dull *smack*, and the face slid out of the screen. As it fell it revealed the control room behind it. Someone was down on the floor plates, a nameless heap. Another figure ran across the field of pickup and disappeared.

Harper snapped into action first. "That was Silard!"

he shouted, "In the control room! Come on, Steinke!"
He was already in motion himself.

Steinke went dead-white, but hesitated only an unmeasurable instant. He pounded sharp on Harper's
heels. Greene followed without invitation, in a steady
run that kept easy pace with them.

They had to wait for a capsule to unload at the tube
station. Then all three of them tried to crowd into a
two-passenger capsule. It refused to start, and moments were lost before Greene piled out and claimed
another car.

The four-minute trip at heavy acceleration seemed
an interminable crawl. Harper was convinced that the
system had broken down, when the familiar click and
sigh announced their arrival at the station under the
bomb. They jammed each other trying to get out at the
same time.

The lift was up; they did not wait for it. That was
unwise; they gained no time by it, and arrived at the
control level out of breath. Nevertheless, they speeded
up when they reached the top, zigzagged frantically
around the outer shield, and burst into the control
room.

The limp figure was still on the floor, and another,
also inert, was near it. The second's helmet was missing.

The third figure was bending over the trigger. He
looked up as they came in, and charged them. They hit
him together, and all three went down. It was two to
one, but they got in each other's way. The man's heavy
armor protected him from the force of their blows. He
fought with senseless, savage violence.

Harper felt a bright, sharp pain; his right arm went
limp and useless. The armored figure was struggling
free of them.

There was a shout from somewhere behind them,
"Hold still!"

Harper saw a flash with the corner of one eye, a deafening crack hurried on top of it, and re-echoed painfully in the restricted space.

The armored figure dropped back to his knees, balanced there, and then fell heavily on his face. Greene stood in the entrance, a service pistol balanced in his hand.

Harper got up and went over to the trigger. He tried to reduce the dampening adjustment, but his right hand wouldn't carry out his orders, and his left was too clumsy. "Steinke," he called, "come here! Take over."

Steinke hurried up, nodded as he glanced at the readings, and set busily to work.

It was thus that King found them when he bolted in a very few minutes later.

"Harper!" he shouted, while his quick glance was still taking in the situation. "What's happened?"

Harper told him briefly. He nodded. "I saw the tail end of the fight from my office—Steinke!" He seemed to grasp for the first time who was on the trigger. "He can't manage the controls—" He hurried toward him.

Steinke looked up at his approach. "Chief!" he called out. "Chief! *I've got my mathematics back!*"

King looked bewildered, then nodded vaguely, and let him be. He turned back to Harper. "How does it happen you're here?"

"Me? I'm here to report—we've done it, chief!"

"Eh?"

"We've finished; it's all done. Erickson stayed behind to complete the power-plant installation on the big ship. I came over in the ship we'll use to shuttle between Earth and the big ship, the power plant. Four minutes from Goddard Field to here in her. That's the pilot over there." He pointed to the door, where Greene's solid form partially hid Lentz.

"Wait a minute. You say that everything is ready to install the bomb in the ship? You're sure?"

"Positive. The big ship has already flown with our fuel—longer and faster than she will have to fly to reach station in her orbit; I was in it—out in space, chief! We're all set, six ways from zero."

King stared at the dumping switch, mounted behind glass at the top of the instrument board. "There's fuel enough," he said softly, as if he were alone and speaking only to himself; "there's been fuel enough for weeks."

He walked swiftly over to the switch, smashed the glass with his fist, and pulled it.

The room rumbled and shivered as two and a half tons of molten, massive metal, heavier than gold, coursed down channels, struck against baffles, split into a dozen streams, and plunged to rest in leaden receivers—to rest, safe and harmless, until it could be reassembled far out in space.

AFTERWORD

December 1979, exactly 40 years after I researched BLOWUPS HAPPEN (Dec. '39): I had some doubt about republishing this because of the current ignorant fear of fission power, recently enhanced by the harmless flap at Three Mile Island. When I wrote this, there was not a full gram of purified U-235 on this planet, and no one knew its hazards in detail, most especially the mass and geometry and speed of assembly necessary to make "blow-ups happen." But we now know from long experience and endless tests that the "tons" used in this story could never be assembled—no explosion, melt-down possible, melt-down being the worst that can happen at a power plant; to cause U-235 to explode is very difficult and requires very different design. Yes, radiation is hazardous BUT —

RADIATION EXPOSURE

*Half a mile from Three-Mile plant
  during the flap* ....*83 millirems*
At the power plant ....*1,100 millirems*
*During heart catheterization for
  angiogram* ....*45,000 millirems*
  *–which I underwent 18 months ago. I feel fine.
R.A.H.*

FOREWORD

I had always planned to quit the writing business as soon as that mortgage was paid off. I had never had any literary ambitions, no training for it, no interest in it—backed into it by accident and stuck with it to pay off debt, I being always firmly resolved to quit the silly business once I had my chart squared away.

At a meeting of the Mañana Literary Society—an amorphous disorganization having as its avowed purpose "to permit young writers to talk out their stories to each other in order to get them off their minds and thereby save themselves the trouble of writing them down"—at a gathering of this noble group I was expounding my determination to retire from writing once my bills were paid—in a few weeks, during 1940, if the tripe continued to sell.

William A. P. White ("Anthony Boucher") gave me a sour look. "Do you know any retired writers?"

"How could I? All the writers I've ever met are in this room."

"Irrelevant. You know retired school teachers, retired naval officers, retired policemen, retired farmers. Why don't you know at least one retired writer?"

"What are you driving at?"

"Robert, there are no retired writers. There are writers who have stopped selling . . . but they have not stopped writing."

I pooh-poohed Bill's remarks—possibly what he said applied to writers in general . . . but I wasn't really a writer; I was just a chap who needed money and happened to discover that pulp writing offered an easy way to grab some without stealing and without honest work. ("Honest work"—a euphemism for underpaid bodily exertion, done standing up or on your knees, often in bad weather or other nasty circumstances, and frequently involving shovels, picks, hoes, assembly lines, tractors, and unsympathetic supervisors. It has never appealed to me.

Sitting at a typewriter in a nice warm room, with no boss, cannot possibly be described as "honest work.")

BLOWUPS HAPPEN *sold and I gave a mortgage-burning party. But I did not quit writing at once (24 Feb 1940) because, while I had the Old Man of the Sea (that damned mortgage) off my back, there were still some other items. I needed a new car; the house needed paint and some repairs; I wanted to make a trip to New York; and it would not hurt to have a couple of hundred extra in the bank as a cushion—and I had a dozen-odd stories in file, planned and ready to write.*

So I wrote MAGIC, INCORPORATED *and started east on the proceeds, and wrote* THEY *and* SIXTH COLUMN *while I was on that trip. The latter was the only story of mine ever influenced to any marked degree by John W. Campbell, Jr. He had in file an unsold story he had written some years earlier. JWC did not show me his manuscript; instead he told me the story line orally and stated that, if I would write it, he would buy it.*

He needed a serial; I needed an automobile. I took the brass check.

Writing SIXTH COLUMN *was a job I sweated over. I had to reslant it to remove racist aspects of the original story line. And I didn't really believe the pseudoscientific rationale of Campbell's three spectra—so I worked especially hard to make it sound realistic.*

It worked out all right. The check for the serial, plus 35¢ in cash, bought me that new car . . . and the book editions continue to sell and sell and sell, and have earned more than forty times as much as I was paid for the serial. So it was a financial success . . . but I do not consider it to be an artistic success.

While I was back east I told Campbell of my plans to quit writing later that year. He was not pleased as I was then his largest supplier of copy. I finally said, "John, I am not going to write any more stories against deadlines. But I do have a few more stories on tap that I could write. I'll send you a story from time to time . . . until the day

*comes when you bounce one. At that point we're
through. Now that I know you personally, having a story
rejected by you would be too traumatic."*

So I went back to California and sold him CROOKED
HOUSE and LOGIC OF EMPIRE and UNIVERSE and
SOLUTION UNSATISFACTORY and METHUSELAH'S
CHILDREN and BY HIS BOOTSTRAPS and COMMON
SENSE and GOLDFISH BOWL and BEYOND THIS
HORIZON and WALDO and THE UNPLEASANT
PROFESSION OF JONATHAN HOAG—which brings
us smack up against World War II.

Campbell did bounce one of the above (and I shan't
say which one) and I promptly retired—put in a new irrigation system—built a garden terrace—resumed serious photography, etc. This went on for about a month
when I found that I was beginning to be vaguely ill: poor
appetite, loss of weight, insomnia, jittery, absent-
minded—much like the early symptoms of pulmonary
tuberculosis, and I thought, "Damn it, am I going to
have still a third attack?"

Campbell dropped me a note and asked why he hadn't
heard from me?—I reminded him of our conversation
months past: He had rejected one of my stories and that
marked my retirement from an occupation that I had
never planned to pursue permanently.

He wrote back and asked for another look at the story
he had bounced. I sent it to him, he returned it promptly
with the recommendation that I take out this comma,
speed up the 1st half of page umpteen, delete that adjective—fiddle changes that Katie Tarrant would have done
if told to.

I sat down at my typewriter to make the suggested
changes . . . and suddenly realized that I felt good for the
first time in weeks.

Bill "Tony Boucher" White had been dead right. Once
you get the monkey on your back there is no cure short of
the grave. I can leave the typewriter alone for weeks, even
months, by going to sea. I can hold off for any necessary
time if I am strenuously engaged in some other full-time,

worthwhile occupation such as a construction job, a political campaign, or (damn it!) recovering from illness.

But if I simply loaf for more than two or three days, that monkey starts niggling at me. Then nothing short of a few thousand words will soothe my nerves. And as I get older the attacks get worse; it is beginning to take 300,000 words and up to produce that feeling of warm satiation. At that I don't have it in its most virulent form; two of my colleagues are reliably reported not to have missed their daily fix in more than forty years.

The best that can be said for SOLUTION UNSATISFACTORY is that the solution is still unsatisfactory and the dangers are greater than ever. There is little satisfaction in having called the turn forty years ago; being a real-life Cassandra is not happy-making.

SOLUTION UNSATISFACTORY

In 1903 the Wright brothers flew at Kitty Hawk.

In December, 1938, in Berlin, Dr. Hahn split the uranium atom.

In April, 1943, Dr. Estelle Karst, working under the Federal Emergency Defense Authority, perfected the Karst-Obre technique for producing artificial radioactives.

So American foreign policy had to change.

Had to. *Had to*. It is very difficult to tuck a bugle call back into a bugle. Pandora's Box is a one-way proposition. You can turn pig into sausage, but not sausage into pig. Broken eggs stay broken. "All the King's horses and all the King's men can't put Humpty together again."

I ought to know—I was one of the King's men.

By rights I should not have been. I was not a professional military man when World War II broke out, and when Congress passed the draft law I drew a high number, high enough to keep me out of the army long enough to die of old age.

Not that very many died of old age that generation!

But I was the newly appointed secretary to a freshman congressman; I had been his campaign manager and my former job had left me. By profession, I was a high-school teacher of economics and sociology— school boards don't like teachers of social subjects actually to deal with social problems—and my contract was not renewed. I jumped at the chance to go to Washington.

My congressman was named Manning. Yes, *the* Manning, Colonel Clyde C. Manning, U. S. Army retired—Mr. Commissioner Manning. What you may not know about him is that he was one of the Army's No. 1 experts in chemical warfare before a leaky heart put him on the shelf. I had picked him, with the help of a group of my political associates, to run against the two-bit chiseler who was the incumbent in our district. We needed a strong liberal candidate and Manning was tailor-made for the job. He had served one term in the grand jury, which cut his political eye teeth, and had stayed active in civic matters thereafter.

Being a retired army officer was a political advantage in vote-getting among the more conservative and well-to-do citizens, and his record was O.K. for the other side of the fence. I'm not primarily concerned with vote-getting; what I liked about him was that, though he was liberal, he was tough-minded, which most liberals aren't. Most liberals believe that water runs downhill, but, praise God, it'll never reach the bottom.

Manning was not like that. He could see a logical necessity and act on it, no matter how unpleasant it might be.

We were in Manning's suite in the House Office Building, taking a little blow from that stormy first session of the Seventy-eighth Congress and trying to catch up on a mountain of correspondence, when the War Department called. Manning answered it himself.

I had to overhear, but then I was his secretary. "Yes," he said, "speaking. Very well, put him on. Oh . . . hello, General . . . Fine, thanks. Yourself?" Then there was a long silence. Presently, Manning said, "But I can't do that, General, I've got this job to take

care of . . . . What's that? . . . Yes, who is to do my
committee work and represent my district? . . . I think
so." He glanced at his wrist watch. "I'll be right over."

He put down the phone, turned to me, and said, "Get
your hat, John. We are going over to the War Department."

"So?" I said, complying.

"Yes," he said with a worried look, "the Chief of
Staff thinks I ought to go back to duty." He set off at a
brisk walk, with me hanging back to try to force him
not to strain his bum heart. "It's impossible, of
course." We grabbed a taxi from the stand in front of
the office building and headed for the Department.

But it *was* possible, and Manning agreed to it, after
the Chief of Staff presented his case. Manning had to
be convinced, for there is no way on earth for anyone,
even the President himself, to order a congressman to
leave his post, even though he happens to be a member
of the military service, too.

The Chief of Staff had anticipated the political difficulty and had been forehanded enough to have already dug up an opposition congressman with whom
to pair Manning's vote for the duration of the emergency. This other congressman, the Honorable Joseph
T. Brigham, was a reserve officer who wanted to go to
duty himself—or was willing to; I never found out
which. Being from the opposite political party, his
vote in the House of Representatives could be permanently paired against Manning's and neither party
would lose by the arrangement.

There was talk of leaving me in Washington to handle the political details of Manning's office, but Manning decided against it, judging that his other
secretary could do that, and announced that I must go
along as his adjutant. The Chief of Staff demurred, but
Manning was in a position to insist, and the Chief had
to give in.

A chief of staff can get things done in a hurry if he
wants to. I was sworn in as a temporary officer before

we left the building; before the day was out I was at the bank, signing a note to pay for the sloppy service uniforms the Army had adopted and to buy a dress uniform with a beautiful shiny belt—a dress outfit which, as it turned out, I was never to need.

We drove over into Maryland the next day and Manning took charge of the Federal nuclear research laboratory, known officially by the hush-hush title of War Department Special Defense Project No. 347. I didn't know a lot about physics and nothing about modern atomic physics, aside from the stuff you read in the Sunday supplements. Later, I picked up a smattering, mostly wrong, I suppose, from associating with the heavyweights with whom the laboratory was staffed.

Colonel Manning had taken an Army p.g. course at Massachusetts Tech and had received a master of science degree for a brilliant thesis on the mathematical theories of atomic structure. That was why the Army had to have him for this job. But that had been some years before; atomic theory had turned several cartwheels in the meantime; he admitted to me that he had to bone like the very devil to try to catch up to the point where he could begin to understand what his highbrow charges were talking about in their reports.

I think he overstated the degree of his ignorance; there was certainly no one else in the United States who could have done the job. It required a man who could direct and suggest research in a highly esoteric field, but who saw the problem from the standpoint of urgent military necessity. Left to themselves, the physicists would have reveled in the intellectual luxury of an unlimited research expense account, but, while they undoubtedly would have made major advances in human knowledge, they might never have developed anything of military usefulness, or the military possibilities of a discovery might be missed for years.

It's like this: It takes a smart dog to hunt birds, but it takes a hunter behind him to keep him from wasting time chasing rabbits. And the hunter needs to know nearly as much as the dog.

No derogatory reference to the scientists is intended—by no means! We had all the genius in the field that the United States could produce, men from Chicago, Columbia, Cornell, M. I. T., Cal Tech, Berkeley, every radiation laboratory in the country, as well as a couple of broad-A boys lent to us by the British. And they had every facility that ingenuity could think up and money could build. The five-hundred-ton cyclotron which had originally been intended for the University of California was there, and was already obsolete in the face of the new gadgets these brains had thought up, asked for, and been given. Canada supplied us with all the uranium we asked for—tons of the treacherous stuff—from Great Bear Lake, up near the Yukon, and the fractional-residues technique of separating uranium isotope 235 from the commoner isotope 238 had already been worked out, by the same team from Chicago that had worked up the earlier expensive mass spectograph method.

Someone in the United States government had realized the terrific potentialities of uranium 235 quite early and, as far back as the summer of 1940, had rounded up every atomic research man in the country and had sworn them to silence. Atomic power, if ever developed, was planned to be a government monopoly, at least till the war was over. It might turn out to be the most incredibly powerful explosive ever dreamed of, and it might be the source of equally incredible power. In any case, with Hitler talking about secret weapons and shouting hoarse insults at democracies, the government planned to keep any new discoveries very close to the vest.

Hitler had lost the advantage of a first crack at the secret of uranium through not taking precautions. Dr. Hahn, the first man to break open the uranium atom, was a German. But one of his laboratory assistants had fled Germany to escape a pogrom. She came to this country, and told us about it.

We were searching, there in the laboratory in Maryland, for a way to use U235 in a controlled explosion. We had a vision of a one-ton bomb that would be a whole air raid in itself, a single explosion that would flatten out an entire industrial center. Dr. Ridpath, of Continental Tech, claimed that he could build such a bomb, but that he could not guarantee that it would not explode as soon as it was loaded and as for the force of the explosion—well, he did not believe his own figures; they ran out to too many ciphers.

The problem was, strangely enough, to find an explosive which would be weak enough to blow up only one county at a time, and stable enough to blow up only on request. If we could devise a really practical rocket fuel at the same time, one capable of driving a war rocket at a thousand miles an hour, or more, then we would be in a position to make most anybody say "uncle" to Uncle Sam.

We fiddled around with it all the rest of 1943 and well into 1944. The war in Europe and the troubles in Asia dragged on. After Italy folded up, England was able to release enough ships from her Mediterranean fleet to ease the blockade of the British Isles. With the help of the planes we could now send her regularly and with the additional over-age destroyers we let her have, England hung on somehow, digging in and taking more and more of her essential defense industries underground. Russia shifted her weight from side to side as usual, apparently with the policy of preventing either side from getting a sufficient advantage to bring the war to a successful conclusion. People were beginning to speak of "permanent war."

I was killing time in the administrative office, trying to improve my typing—a lot of Manning's reports had to be typed by me personally—when the orderly on duty stepped in and announced Dr. Karst. I flipped the interoffice communicator. "Dr. Karst is here, chief. Can you see her?"

"Yes," he answered, through his end.

I told the orderly to show her in.

Estelle Karst was quite a remarkable old girl and, I suppose, the first woman ever to hold a commission in the Corps of Engineers. She was an M.D. as well as an Sc.D. and reminded me of the teacher I had had in fourth grade. I guess that was why I always stood up instinctively when she came into the room—I was afraid she might look at me and sniff. It couldn't have been her rank; we didn't bother much with rank.

She was dressed in white coveralls and a shop apron and had simply thrown a hooded cape over herself to come through the snow. I said, "Good morning, ma'am," and led her into Manning's office.

The Colonel greeted her with the urbanity that had made him such a success with women's clubs, seated her, and offered her a cigarette.

"I'm glad to see you, Major," he said. "I've been intending to drop around to your shop."

I knew what he was getting at; Dr. Karst's work had been primarily physiomedical; he wanted her to change the direction of her research to something more productive in a military sense.

"Don't call me 'major,' " she said tartly.

"Sorry, Doctor—"

"I came on business, and must get right back. And I presume you are a busy man, too. Colonel Manning, I need some help."

"That's what we are here for."

"Good. I've run into some snags in my research. I think that one of the men in Dr. Ridpath's department could help me, but Dr. Ridpath doesn't seem disposed to be cooperative."

"So? Well, I hardly like to go over the head of a departmental chief, but tell me about it; perhaps we can arrange it. Whom do you want?"

"I need Dr. Obre."

"The spectroscopist. Hm-m-m. I can understand Dr. Ridpath's reluctance, Dr. Karst, and I'm disposed to agree with him. After all, the high-explosives research is really our main show around here."

She bristled and I thought she was going to make him stay in after school at the very least. "Colonel Manning, do you realize the importance of artificial radioactives to modern medicine?"

"Why, I believe I do. Nevertheless, Doctor, our primary mission is to perfect a weapon which will serve as a safeguard to the whole country in time of war—"

She sniffed and went into action. "Weapons—fiddlesticks! Isn't there a medical corps in the Army? Isn't it more important to know how to heal men than to know how to blow them to bits? Colonel Manning, you're not a fit man to have charge of this project! You're a . . . you're a, a warmonger, that's what you are!"

I felt my ears turning red, but Manning never budged. He could have raised Cain with her, confined her to her quarters, maybe even have court-martialed her, but Manning isn't like that. He told me once that every time a man is court-martialed, it is a sure sign that some senior officer hasn't measured up to his job.

"I am sorry you feel that way, Doctor," he said mildly, "and I agree that my technical knowledge isn't what it might be. And, believe me, I do wish that healing were all we had to worry about. In any case, I have not refused your request. Let's walk over to your laboratory and see what the problem is. Likely there is some arrangement that can be made which will satisfy everybody."

He was already up and getting out his greatcoat. Her set mouth relaxed a trifle and she answered, "Very well. I'm sorry I spoke as I did."

"Not at all," he replied. "These are worrying times. Come along, John."

I trailed after them, stopping in the outer office to get my own coat and to stuff my notebook in a pocket. By the time we had trudged through mushy snow the eighth of a mile to her lab they were talking about gardening!

Manning acknowledged the sentry's challenge with a wave of his hand and we entered the building. He started casually on into the inner lab, but Karst stopped him. "Armor first, Colonel."

We had trouble finding overshoes that would fit over Manning's boots, which he persisted in wearing, despite the new uniform regulations, and he wanted to omit the foot protection, but Karst would not hear of it. She called in a couple of her assistants who made jury-rigged moccasins out of some soft-lead sheeting.

The helmets were different from those used in the explosives lab, being fitted with inhalers. "What's this?" inquired Manning.

"Radioactive dust guard," she said. "It's absolutely essential."

We threaded a lead-lined meander and arrived at the workroom door which she opened by combination. I blinked at the sudden bright illumination and noticed the air was filled with little shiny motes.

"Hm-m-m—it *is* dusty," agreed Manning. "Isn't there some way of controlling that?" His voice sounded muffled from behind the dust mask.

"The last stage has to be exposed to air," explained Karst. "The hood gets most of it. We could control it, but it would mean a quite expensive new installation."

"No trouble about that. We're not on a budget, you know. It must be very annoying to have to work in a mask like this."

"It is," acknowledged Karst. "The kind of gear it would take would enable us to work without body armor, too. That would be a comfort."

I suddenly had a picture of the kind of thing these researchers put up with. I am a fair-sized man, yet I found that armor heavy to carry around. Estelle Karst was a small woman, yet she was willing to work maybe fourteen hours, day after day, in an outfit which was about as comfortable as a diving suit. But she had not complained.

Not all the heroes are in the headlines. These radiation experts not only ran the chance of cancer and nasty radioaction burns, but the men stood a chance of damaging their germ plasm and then having their wives present them with something horrid in the way of offspring—no chin, for example, and long hairy ears. Nevertheless, they went right ahead and never seemed to get irritated unless something held up their work.

Dr. Karst was past the age when she would be likely to be concerned personally about progeny, but the principle applies.

I wandered around, looking at the unlikely apparatus she used to get her results, fascinated as always by my failure to recognize much that reminded me of the physics laboratory I had known when I was an undergraduate, and being careful not to touch anything. Karst started explaining to Manning what she was doing and why, but I knew that it was useless for me to try to follow that technical stuff. If Manning wanted notes, he would dictate them. My attention was caught by a big boxlike contraption in one corner of the room. It had a hopperlike gadget on one side and I could hear a sound from it like the whirring of a fan with a background of running water. It intrigued me.

I moved back to the neighborhood of Dr. Karst and the Colonel and heard her saying, "The problem amounts to this, Colonel: I am getting a much more highly radioactive end product than I want, but there is considerable variation in the half-life of otherwise equivalent samples. That suggests to me that I am using a mixture of isotopes, but I haven't been able to prove it. And frankly, I do not know enough about that end of the field to be sure of sufficient refinement in my methods. I need Dr. Obre's help on that."

I think those were her words, but I may not be doing her justice, not being a physicist. I understood the part about "half-life." All radioactive materials keep right on radiating until they turn into something else, which takes theoretically forever. As a matter of practice their periods, or "lives," are described in terms of how long it takes the original radiation to drop to one-half strength. That time is called a "half-life" and each radioactive isotope of an element has its own specific characteristic half-lifetime.

One of the staff—I forget which one—told me once that any form of matter can be considered as radioactive in some degree; it's a question of intensity and period, or half-life.

"I'll talk to Dr. Ridpath," Manning answered her, "and see what can be arranged. In the meantime you might draw up plans for what you want to reequip your laboratory."

"Thank you, Colonel."

I could see that Manning was about ready to leave, having pacified her; I was still curious about the big box that gave out the odd noises.

"May I ask what that is, Doctor?"

"Oh, that? That's an air conditioner."

"Odd-looking one. I've never seen one like it."

"It's not to condition the air of this room. It's to remove the radioactive dust before the exhaust air goes outdoors. We wash the dust out of the foul air."

"Where does the water go?"

"Down the drain. Out into the bay eventually, I suppose."

I tried to snap my fingers, which was impossible because of the lead mittens. "That accounts for it, Colonel!"

"Accounts for what?"

"Accounts for those accusing notes we've been getting from the Bureau of Fisheries. This poisonous dust is being carried out into Chesapeake Bay and is killing the fish."

Manning turned to Karst. "Do you think that possible, Doctor?"

I could see her brows draw together through the window in her helmet. "I hadn't thought about it," she admitted. "I'd have to do some figuring on the possible concentrations before I could give you a definite answer. But it is possible—yes. However," she added anxiously, "it would be simple enough to divert this drain to a sink hole of some sort."

"Hm-m-m—yes." He did not say anything for some minutes, simply stood there, looking at the box.

Presently he said, "This dust is pretty lethal?"

"Quite lethal, Colonel." There was another long silence.

At last I gathered he had made up his mind about something for he said decisively, "I am going to see to it that you get Obre's assistance, Doctor—"

"Oh, good!"

"—but I want you to help me in return. I am very much interested in this research of yours, but I want it carried on with a little broader scope. I want you to investigate for maxima both in period and intensity as well as for minima. I want you to drop the strictly utilitarian approach and make an exhaustive research along lines which we will work out in greater detail later."

She started to say something but he cut in ahead of her. "A really thorough program of research should prove more helpful in the long run to your original purpose than a more narrow one. And I shall make it my business to expedite every possible facility for such a research. I think we may turn up a number of interesting things."

He left immediately, giving her no time to discuss it. He did not seem to want to talk on the way back and I held my peace. I think he had already gotten a glimmering of the bold and drastic strategy this was to lead

to, but even Manning could not have thought out that
early the inescapable consequences of a few dead
fish—otherwise he would never have ordered the research.

No, I don't really believe that. He would have gone
right ahead, knowing that if he did not do it, someone
else would. He would have accepted the responsibility
while bitterly aware of its weight.

1944 wore along with no great excitement on the
surface. Karst got her new laboratory equipment and
so much additional help that her department rapidly
became the largest on the grounds. The explosives research was suspended after a conference between
Manning and Ridpath, of which I heard only the end,
but the meat of it was that there existed not even a
remote possibility at that time of utilizing U235 as an
explosive. As a source of power, yes, sometime in the
distant future when there had been more opportunity
to deal with the extremely ticklish problem of controlling the nuclear reaction. Even then it seemed likely
that it would not be a source of power in prime movers
such as rocket motors or mobiles, but would be used
in vast power plants at least as large as the Boulder
Dam installation.

After that Ridpath became a sort of co-chairman of
Karst's department and the equipment formerly used
by the explosives department was adapted or replaced
to carry on research on the deadly artificial radioactives. Manning arranged a division of labor and Karst
stuck to her original problem of developing techniques for tailor-making radioactives. I think she was
perfectly happy, sticking with a one-track mind to the
problem at hand. I don't know to this day whether or
not Manning and Ridpath ever saw fit to discuss with
her what they intended to do.

As a matter of fact, I was too busy myself to think
much about it. The general elections were coming up
and I was determined that Manning should have a

constituency to return to, when the emergency was over. He was not much interested, but agreed to let his name be filed as a candidate for re-election. I was trying to work up a campaign by remote control and cursing because I could not be in the field to deal with the thousand and one emergencies as they arose.

I did the next best thing and had a private line installed to permit the campaign chairman to reach me easily. I don't think I violated the Hatch Act, but I guess I stretched it a little. Anyhow, it turned out all right; Manning was elected as were several other members of the citizen-military that year. An attempt was made to smear him by claiming that he was taking two salaries for one job, but we squelched that with a pamphlet entitled "For Shame!" which explained that he got *one* salary for *two* jobs. That's the Federal law in such cases and people are entitled to know it.

It was just before Christmas that Manning first admitted to me how much the implications of the Karst-Obre process were preying on his mind. He called me into his office over some inconsequential matter, then did not let me go. I saw that he wanted to talk.

"How much of the K-O dust do we now have on hand?" he asked suddenly.

"Just short of ten thousand units," I replied. "I can look up the exact figures in half a moment." A unit would take care of a thousand men, at normal dispersion. He knew the figure as well as I did, and I knew he was stalling.

We had shifted almost imperceptibly from research to manufacture, entirely on Manning's initiative and authority. Manning had never made a specific report to the Department about it, unless he had done so orally to the Chief of Staff.

"Never mind," he answered to my suggestion, then added, "Did you see those horses?"

"Yes," I said briefly.

I did not want to talk about it. I like horses. We had requisitioned six broken-down old nags, ready for the bone yard, and had used them experimentally. We knew now what the dust would do. After they had died, any part of their carcasses would register on a photographic plate and tissue from the apices of their lungs and from the bronchia glowed with a light of its own.

Manning stood at the window, staring out at the dreary Maryland winter for a minute or two before replying, "John, I wish that radioactivity had never been discovered. Do you realize what that devilish stuff amounts to?"

"Well," I said, "it's a weapon, about like poison gas—maybe more efficient."

"Rats!" he said, and for a moment I thought he was annoyed with me personally. "That's about like comparing a sixteen-inch gun with a bow and arrow. We've got here the first weapon the world has ever seen against which there is no defense, none whatsoever. It's death itself, C.O.D.

"Have you seen Ridpath's report?" he went on.

I had not. Ridpath had taken to delivering his reports by hand to Manning personally.

"Well," he said, "ever since we started production I've had all the talent we could spare working on the problem of a defense against the dust. Ridpath tells me and I agree with him that there is no means whatsoever to combat the stuff, once it's used."

"How about armor," I asked, "and protective clothing?"

"Sure, sure," he agreed irritatedly, "provided you never take it off to eat, or to drink or for any purpose whatever, until the radioaction has ceased, or you are out of the danger zone. That is all right for laboratory work; I'm talking about war."

I considered the matter. "I still don't see what you are fretting about, Colonel. If the stuff is as good as you say it is, you've done just exactly what you set out to do—develop a weapon which would give the United States protection against aggression."

He swung around. "John, there are times when I think you are downright stupid!"

I said nothing. I knew him and I knew how to discount his moods. The fact that he permitted me to see his feelings is the finest compliment I have ever had.

"Look at it this way," he went on more patiently; "this dust, as a weapon, is not just simply sufficient to safeguard the United States, it amounts to a loaded gun held at the head of every man, woman, and child on the globe!"

"Well," I answered, "what of that? It's our secret, and we've got the upper hand. The United States can put a stop to this war, and any other war. We can declare a *Pax Americana*, and enforce it."

"Hm-m-m—I wish it were that easy. But it won't remain our secret; you can count on that. It doesn't matter how successfully we guard it; all that anyone needs is the hint given by the dust itself and then it is just a matter of time until some other nation develops a technique to produce it. You can't stop brains from working, John; the reinvention of the method is a mathematical certainty, once they know what it is they are looking for. And uranium is a common enough substance, widely distributed over the globe—don't forget that!

"It's like this: Once the secret is out—and it will be out if we ever use the stuff!—the whole world will be comparable to a room full of men, each armed with a loaded .45. They can't get out of the room and each one is dependent on the good will of every other one to stay alive. All offense and no defense. See what I mean?"

I thought about it, but I still didn't guess at the difficulties. It seemed to me that a peace enforced by us was the only way out, with precautions taken to see that we controlled the sources of uranium. I had the usual American subconscious conviction that our

country would never use power in sheer aggression.
Later, I thought about the Mexican War and the Span-
ish-American War and some of the things we did in
Central America, and I was not so sure—

It was a couple of weeks later, shortly after inauguration day, that Manning told me to get the Chief of
Staff's office on the telephone. I heard only the tail end
of the conversation. "No, General, I won't," Manning
was saying. "I won't discuss it with you, or the Secretary, either. This is a matter the Commander in Chief
is going to have to decide in the long run. If he turns it
down, it is imperative that no one else ever knows
about it. That's my considered opinion. . . . What's
that? . . . I took this job under the condition that I was
to have a free hand. You've got to give me a little lee-
way this time. . . . Don't go brass hat on me. I knew
you when you were a plebe. . . . O.K., O.K., sorry. . . .
If the Secretary of War won't listen to reason, you tell
him I'll be in my seat in the House of Representatives
tomorrow, and that I'll get the favor I want from the
majority leader. . . . All right. Good-bye."

Washington rang up again about an hour later. It
was the Secretary of War. This time Manning listened
more than he talked. Toward the end, he said, "All I
want is thirty minutes alone with the President. If
nothing comes of it, no harm has been done. If I convince him, then you will know all about it. . . . No, sir,
I did not mean that you would avoid responsibility. I
intended to be helpful. . . . Fine! Thank you, Mr. Secretary."

The White House rang up later in the day and set a
time.

We drove down to the District the next day through
a nasty cold rain that threatened to turn to sleet. The
usual congestion in Washington was made worse by
the weather; it very nearly caused us to be late in arriving. I could hear Manning swearing under his

breath all the way down Rhode Island Avenue. But we were dropped at the west wing entrance to the White House with two minutes to spare. Manning was ushered into the Oval Office almost at once and I was left cooling my heels and trying to get comfortable in civilian clothes. After so many months of uniform they itched in the wrong places.

The thirty minutes went by.

The President's reception secretary went in, and came out very promptly indeed. He stepped on out into the outer reception room and I heard something that began with, "I'm sorry, Senator, but—" He came back in, made a penciled notation, and passed it out to an usher.

Two more hours went by.

Manning appeared at the door at last and the secretary looked relieved. But he did not come out, saying instead, "Come in, John. The President wants to take a look at you."

I fell over my feet getting up.

Manning said, "Mr. President, this is Captain De-Fries." The President nodded, and I bowed, unable to say anything. He was standing on the hearth rug, his fine head turned toward us, and looking just like his pictures—but it seemed strange for the President of the United States not to be a tall man.

I had never seen him before, though, of course, I knew something of his record the two years he had been in the Senate and while he was Mayor before that.

The President said, "Sit down, DeFries. Care to smoke?" Then to Manning. "You think he can do it?"

"I think he'll have to. It's Hobson's choice."

"And you are sure of him?"

"He was my campaign manager."

"I see."

The President said nothing more for a while and God knows I didn't!—though I was bursting to know what they were talking about. He commenced again with,

"Colonel Manning, I intend to follow the procedure you have suggested, with the changes we discussed. But I will be down tomorrow to see for myself that the dust will do what you say it will. Can you prepare a demonstration?"

"Yes, Mr. President."

"Very well, we will use Captain DeFries unless I think of a better procedure." I thought for a moment that they planned to use me for a guinea pig! But he turned to me and continued, "Captain, I expect to send you to England as my representative."

I gulped. "Yes, Mr. President." And that is every word I had to say in calling on the President of the United States.

After that, Manning had to tell me a lot of things he had on his mind. I am going to try to relate them as carefully as possible, even at the risk of being dull and obvious and of repeating things that are common knowledge.

We had a weapon that could not be stopped. Any type of K-O dust scattered over an area rendered that area uninhabitable for a length of time that depended on the half-life of the radioactivity.

Period. Full stop.

Once an area was dusted there was nothing that could be done about it until the radioactivity had fallen off to the point where it was no longer harmful. The dust could not be cleaned out; it was everywhere. There was no possible way to counteract it—burn it, combine it chemically; the radioactive isotope was still there, still radioactive, still deadly. Once used on a stretch of land, for a predetermined length of time that piece of earth *would not tolerate life*.

It was extremely simple to use. No complicated bomb-sights were needed, no care need be taken to hit "military objectives." Take it aloft in any sort of aircraft, attain a position more or less over the area you wish to sterilize, and drop the stuff. Those on the ground in the contaminated area are dead men, dead in an hour, a day, a week, a month, depending on the degree of the infection—but *dead*.

Manning told me that he had once seriously considered, in the middle of the night, recommending that every single person, including himself, who knew the Karst-Obre technique be put to death, in the interests of all civilization. But he had realized the next day that it had been sheer funk; the technique was certain in time to be rediscovered by someone else.

Furthermore, it would not do to wait, to refrain from using the grisly power, until someone else perfected it and used it. The only possible chance to keep the world from being turned into one huge morgue was for us to use the power first and drastically—get the upper hand and keep it.

We were not at war, legally, yet we had been in the war up to our necks with our weight on the side of democracy since 1940. Manning had proposed to the President that we turn a supply of the dust over to Great Britain, under conditions we specified, and enable them thereby to force a peace. But the terms of the peace would be dictated by the United States—for we were not turning over the secret.

After that, the *Pax Americana*.

The United States was having power thrust on it, willy-nilly. We had to accept it and enforce a worldwide peace, ruthlessly and drastically, or it would be seized by some other nation. There could not be coequals in the possession of this weapon. The factor of time predominated.

I was selected to handle the details in England because Manning insisted, and the President agreed with him, that every person technically acquainted with the Karst-Obre process should remain on the laboratory reservation in what amounted to protective custody—imprisonment. That included Manning himself.

I could go because I did not have the secret—I could
not even have acquired it without years of schooling—
and what I did not know I could not tell, even under,
well, drugs. We were determined to keep the secret as
long as we could to consolidate the *Pax;* we did not
distrust our English cousins, but they were Britishers,
with a first loyalty to the British Empire. No need to
tempt them.

I was picked because I understood the background
if not the science, and because Manning trusted me. I
don't know why the President trusted me, too, but
then my job was not complicated.

We took off from the new field outside Baltimore on
a cold, raw afternoon which matched my own feelings.
I had an all-gone feeling in my stomach, a runny nose,
and, buttoned inside my clothes, papers appointing
me a special agent of the President of the United
States. They were odd papers, papers without precedent; they did not simply give me the usual diplomatic
immunity; they made my person very nearly as sacred
as that of the President himself.

At Nova Scotia we touched ground to refuel, the
F.B.I. men left us, we took off again, and the Canadian
transfighters took their stations around us. All the dust
we were sending was in my plane; if the President's
representative were shot down, the dust would go to
the bottom with him.

No need to tell of the crossing. I was airsick and miserable, in spite of the steadiness of the new six-engined
jobs. I felt like a hangman on the way to an execution,
and wished to God that I were a boy again, with nothing more momentous than a debate contest, or a track
meet, to worry me.

There was some fighting around us as we neared
Scotland, I know, but I could not see it, the cabin being
shuttered. Our pilot-captain ignored it and brought
his ship down on a totally dark field, using a beam, I

suppose, though I did not know nor care. I would have welcomed a crash. Then the lights outside went on and I saw that we had come to rest in an underground hangar.

I stayed in the ship. The Commandant came to see me to his quarters as his guest. I shook my head. "I stay here," I said. "Orders. You are to treat this ship as United States soil, you know."

He seemed miffed, but compromised by having dinner served for both of us in my ship.

There was a really embarrassing situation the next day. I was commanded to appear for a Royal audience. But I had my instructions and I stuck to them. I was sitting on that cargo of dust until the President told me what to do with it. Late in the day I was called on by a member of Parliament—nobody admitted out loud that it was the Prime Minister—and a Mr. Windsor. The M.P. did most of the talking and I answered his questions. My other guest said very little and spoke slowly with some difficulty. But I got a very favorable impression of him. He seemed to be a man who was carrying a load beyond human strength and carrying it heroically.

There followed the longest period in my life. It was actually only a little longer than a week, but every minute of it had that split-second intensity of imminent disaster that comes just before a car crash. The President was using the time to try to avert the need to use the dust. He had two face-to-face television conferences with the new Fuehrer. The President spoke German fluently, which should have helped. He spoke three times to the warring peoples themselves, but it is doubtful if very many on the Continent were able to listen, the police regulations there being what they were.

The Ambassador from the Reich was given a special demonstration of the effect of the dust. He was flown out over a deserted stretch of Western prairie and allowed to see what a single dusting would do to a herd of steers. It should have impressed him and I think that it did—*nobody* could ignore a visual demonstration!—but what report he made to his leader we never knew.

The British Isles were visited repeatedly during the wait by bombing attacks as heavy as any of the war. I was safe enough but I heard about them, and I could see the effect on the morale of the officers with whom I associated. Not that it frightened them—it made them coldly angry. The raids were not directed primarily at dockyards or factories, but were ruthless destruction of anything, particularly villages.

"I don't see what you chaps are waiting for," a flight commander complained to me. "What the Jerries need is a dose of their own *shrecklichkeit*, a lesson in their own Aryan culture."

I shook my head. "We'll have to do it our own way."

He dropped the matter, but I knew how he and his brother officers felt. They had a standing toast, as sacred as the toast to the King: "Remember Coventry!"

Our President had stipulated that the R. A. F. was not to bomb during the period of negotiation, but their bombers were busy nevertheless. The continent was showered, night after night, with bales of leaflets, prepared by our own propaganda agents. The first of these called on the people of the Reich to stop a useless war and promised that the terms of peace would not be vindictive. The second rain of pamphlets showed photographs of that herd of steers. The third was a simple direct warning to get out of cities and to stay out.

As Manning put it, we were calling "Halt!" three times before firing. I do not think that he or the President expected it to work, but we were morally obligated to try.

The Britishers had installed for me a televisor, of the Simonds-Yarley nonintercept type, the sort whereby the receiver must "trigger" the transmitter in order for the transmission to take place at all. It made assurance of privacy in diplomatic rapid communication for the first time in history, and was a real help in the crisis. I had brought along my own technician, one of the F. B. I.'s new corps of specialists, to handle the scrambler and the trigger.

He called to me one afternoon. "Washington signaling."

I climbed tiredly out of the cabin and down to the booth on the hangar floor, wondering if it were another false alarm.

It was the President. His lips were white. "Carry out your basic instructions, Mr. DeFries."

"Yes, Mr. President!"

The details had been worked out in advance and, once I had accepted a receipt and token payment from the Commandant for the dust, my duties were finished. But, at our instance, the British had invited military observers from every independent nation and from the several provisional governments of occupied nations. The United States Ambassador designated me as one at the request of Manning.

Our task group was thirteen bombers. One such bomber could have carried all the dust needed, but it was split up to insure most of it, at least, reaching its destination. I had fetched forty percent more dust than Ridpath calculated would be needed for the mission and my last job was to see to it that every canister actually went on board a plane of the flight. The extremely small weight of dust used was emphasized to each of the military observers.

We took off just at dark, climbed to twenty-five thousand feet, refueled in the air, and climbed again. Our escort was waiting for us, having refueled thirty minutes before us. The flight split into thirteen groups, and cut the thin air for middle Europe. The bombers we rode had been stripped and hiked up to permit the utmost maximum of speed and altitude.

Elsewhere in England, other flights had taken off shortly before us to act as a diversion. Their destinations were every part of Germany; it was the intention to create such confusion in the air above the Reich that our few planes actually engaged in the serious work might well escape attention entirely, flying so high in the stratosphere.

The thirteen dust carriers approached Berlin from different directions, planning to cross Berlin as if following the spokes of a wheel. The night was appreciably clear and we had a low moon to help us. Berlin is not a hard city to locate, since it has the largest square-mile area of any modern city and is located on a broad flat alluvial plain. I could make out the River Spree as we approached it, and the Havel. The city was blacked out, but a city makes a different sort of black from open country. Parachute flares hung over the city in many places, showing that the R. A. F. had been busy before we got there and the A. A. batteries on the ground helped to pick out the city.

There was fighting below us, but not within fifteen thousand feet of our altitude as nearly as I could judge.

The pilot reported to the captain, "On line of bearing!" The chap working the absolute altimeter steadily fed his data into the fuse pots of the canister. The canisters were equipped with a light charge of black powder, sufficient to explode them and scatter the dust at a time after release predetermined by the fuse pot setting. The method used was no more than an efficient expedient. The dust would have been almost as effective had it simply been dumped out in paper bags, although not as well distributed.

The Captain hung over the navigator's board, a slight frown on his thin sallow face. "Ready one!" reported the bomber.

"Release!"

"Ready two!"

The Captain studied his wristwatch. "Release!"

"Ready three!"

"Release!"

When the last of our ten little packages was out of the ship we turned tail and ran for home.

No arrangements had been made for me to get home; nobody had thought about it. But it was the one thing I wanted to do. I did not feel badly; I did not feel much of anything. I felt like a man who has at last screwed up his courage and undergone a serious operation; it's over now, he is still numb from shock but his mind is relaxed. But I wanted to go home.

The British Commandant was quite decent about it; he serviced and manned my ship at once and gave me an escort for the offshore war zone. It was an expensive way to send one man home, but who cared? We had just expended some millions of lives in a desperate attempt to end the war; what was a money expense? He gave the necessary orders absentmindedly.

I took a double dose of nembutal and woke up in Canada. I tried to get some news while the plane was being serviced, but there was not much to be had. The government of the Reich had issued one official news bulletin shortly after the raid, sneering at the much vaunted "secret weapon" of the British and stating that a major air attack had been made on Berlin and several other cities, but that the raiders had been driven off with only minor damage. The current Lord Haw-Haw started one of his sarcastic speeches but was unable to continue it. The announcer said that he had been seized with a heart attack, and substituted some recordings of patriotic music. The station cut off in the middle of the "Horst Wessel" song. After that there was silence.

I managed to promote an Army car and a driver at the Baltimore field which made short work of the Annapolis speedway. We almost overran the turnoff to the laboratory.

Manning was in his office. He looked up as I came in, said, "Hello, John," in a dispirited voice, and dropped his eyes again to the blotter pad. He went back to drawing doodles.

I looked him over and realized for the first time that the chief was an old man. His face was gray and flabby, deep furrows framed his mouth in a triangle. His clothes did not fit.

I went up to him and put a hand on his shoulder. "Don't take it so hard, chief. It's not your fault. We gave them all the warning in the world."

He looked up again. "Estelle Karst suicided this morning."

Anybody could have anticipated it, but nobody did. And somehow I felt harder hit by her death than by the death of all those strangers in Berlin. "How did she do it?" I asked.

"Dust. She went into the canning room, and took off her armor."

I could picture her—head held high, eyes snapping, and that set look on her mouth which she got when people did something she disapproved of. One little old woman whose lifetime work had been turned against her.

"I wish," Manning added slowly, "that I could explain to her why we *had* to do it."

We buried her in a lead-lined coffin, then Manning and I went on to Washington.

While we were there, we saw the motion pictures that had been made of the death of Berlin. You have not seen them; they never were made public, but they were of great use in convincing the other nations of the world that peace was a good idea. I saw them when Congress did, being allowed in because I was Manning's assistant.

They had been made by a pair of R. A. F. pilots, who had dodged the *Luftwaffe* to get them. The first shots showed some of the main streets the morning after the raid. There was not much to see that would show up in telephoto shots, just busy and crowded streets, but if you looked closely you could see that there had been an excessive number of automobile accidents.

The second day showed the attempt to evacuate. The inner squares of the city were practically deserted save for bodies and wrecked cars, but the streets leading out of town were boiling with people, mostly on foot, for the trams were out of service. The pitiful creatures were fleeing, not knowing that death was already lodged inside them. The plane swooped down at one point and the cinematographer had his telephoto lens pointed directly into the face of a young woman for several seconds. She stared back at it with a look too woebegone to forget, then stumbled and fell.

She may have been trampled. I hope so. One of those six horses had looked like that when the stuff was beginning to hit his vitals.

The last sequence showed Berlin and the roads around it a week after the raid. The city was dead; there was not a man, a woman, a child—nor cats, nor dogs, not even a pigeon. Bodies were all around, but they were safe from rats. There were no rats.

The roads around Berlin were quiet now. Scattered carelessly on shoulders and in ditches, and to a lesser extent on the pavement itself, like coal shaken off a train, were the quiet heaps that had been the citizens of the capital of the Reich. There is no use in talking about it.

But, so far as I am concerned, I left what soul I had in that projection room and I have not had one since.

The two pilots who made the pictures eventually died—systemic, cumulative infection, dust in the air over Berlin. With precautions it need not have happened, but the English did not believe, as yet, that our extreme precautions were necessary.

The Reich took about a week to fold up. It might have taken longer if the new Fuehrer had not gone to Berlin the day after the raid to "prove" that the British boasts had been hollow. There is no need to recount the provisional governments that Germany had in the following several months; the only one we are concerned with is the so-called restored monarchy which used a cousin of the old Kaiser as a symbol, the one that sued for peace.

Then the trouble started.

When the Prime Minister announced the terms of the private agreement he had had with our President, he was met with a silence that was broken only by cries of "Shame! Shame! Resign!" I suppose it was inevitable; the Commons reflected the spirit of a people who had been unmercifully punished for four years. They were in a mood to enforce a peace that would have made the Versailles Treaty look like the Beatitudes.

The vote of no confidence left the Prime Minister no choice. Forty-eight hours later the King made a speech from the throne that violated all constitutional precedent, for it had not been written by a Prime Minister. In this greatest crisis in his reign, his voice was clear and unlabored; it sold the idea to England and a national coalition government was formed.

I don't know whether we would have dusted London to enforce our terms or not; Manning thinks we would have done so. I suppose it depended on the character of the President of the United States, and there is no way of knowing about that since we did not have to do it.

The United States, and in particular the President of the United States, was confronted by two inescapable problems. First, we had to consolidate our position at once, use our temporary advantage of an overwhelmingly powerful weapon to insure that such a weapon would not be turned on us. Second, some means had to be worked out to stabilize American foreign policy so that it could handle the tremendous power we had suddenly had thrust upon us.

The second was by far the most difficult and serious. If we were to establish a reasonably permanent peace—say a century or so—through a monopoly on a weapon so powerful that no one dare fight us, it was imperative that the policy under which we acted be more lasting than passing political administrations. But more of that later—

The first problem had to be attended to at once—time was the heart of it. The emergency lay in the very simplicity of the weapon. It required nothing but aircraft to scatter it and the dust itself, which was easily and quickly made by anyone possessing the secret of the Karst-Obre process and having access to a small supply of uranium-bearing ore.

But the Karst-Obre process was simple and might be independently developed at any time. Manning reported to the President that it was Ridpath's opinion, concurred in by Manning, that the staff of any modern radiation laboratory should be able to work out an equivalent technique in six weeks, working from the hint given by the events in Berlin alone, and should then be able to produce enough dust to cause major destruction in another six weeks.

Ninety days—ninety days *provided* they started from scratch and were not already halfway to their goal. Less than ninety days—perhaps no time at all—

By this time Manning was an unofficial member of the Cabinet; "Secretary of Dust," the President called him in one of his rare jovial moods. As for me, well, I attended Cabinet meetings, too. As the only layman who had seen the whole show from beginning to end, the President wanted me there.

I am an ordinary sort of man who, by a concatenation of improbabilities, found himself shoved into the councils of the rulers. But I found that the rulers were ordinary men, too, and frequently as bewildered as I was.

But Manning was no ordinary man. In him ordinary hard sense had been raised to the level of genius. Oh, yes, I know that it is popular to blame everything on him and to call him everything from traitor to mad dog, but I still think he was both wise and benevolent. I don't care how many second-guessing historians disagree with me.

"I propose," said Manning, "that we begin by immobilizing all aircraft throughout the world."

The Secretary of Commerce raised his brows. "Aren't you," he said, "being a little fantastic, Colonel Manning?"

"No, I'm not," answered Manning shortly. "I'm being realistic. The key to this problem is aircraft. Without aircraft the dust is an inefficient weapon. The only way I see to gain time enough to deal with the whole problem is to ground all aircraft and put them out of operation. All aircraft, that is, not actually in the service of the United States Army. After that we can deal with complete world disarmament and permanent methods of control."

"Really now," replied the Secretary, "you are not proposing that commercial airlines be put out of operation. They are an essential part of world economy. It would be an intolerable nuisance."

"Getting killed is an intolerable nuisance, too," Manning answered stubbornly. "I do propose just that. All aircraft. *All*."

The President had been listening without comment to the discussion. He now cut in. "How about aircraft on which some groups depend to stay alive, Colonel, such as the Alaskan lines?"

"If there are such, they must be operated by American Army pilots and crews. No exceptions."

The Secretary of Commerce looked startled. "Am I to infer from that last remark that you intended this prohibition to apply to the *United States* as well as other nations?"

"Naturally."

"But that's impossible. It's unconstitutional. It violates civil rights."

"Killing a man violates his civil rights, too," Manning answered stubbornly.

"You can't do it. Any Federal Court in the country would enjoin you in five minutes."

"It seems to me," said Manning slowly, "that Andy Jackson gave us a good precedent for that one when he told John Marshall to go fly a kite." He looked slowly around the table at faces that ranged from undecided to antagonistic. "The issue is sharp, gentlemen, and we might as well drag it out in the open. We can be dead men, with everything in due order, constitutional, and technically correct; or we can do what has to be done, stay alive, and try to straighten out the legal aspects later." He shut up and waited.

The Secretary of Labor picked it up. "I don't think the Colonel has any corner on realism. I think I see the problem, too, and I admit it is a serious one. The dust must never be used again. Had I known about it soon enough, it would never have been used on Berlin. And I agree that some sort of worldwide control is necessary. But where I differ with the Colonel is in the method. What he proposes is a military dictatorship imposed by force on the whole world. Admit it, Colonel. Isn't that what you are proposing?"

Manning did not dodge it. "That is what I am proposing."

"Thanks. Now we know where we stand. I, for one, do not regard democratic measures and constitutional procedure as of so little importance that I am willing to jettison them any time it becomes convenient. To me, democracy is more than a matter of expediency, it is a faith. Either it works, or I go under with it."

"What do you propose?" asked the President.

"I propose that we treat this as an opportunity to create a worldwide democratic commonwealth! Let us use our present dominant position to issue a call to all nations to send representatives to a conference to form a world constitution."

"League of Nations," I heard someone mutter.

"No!" he answered the side remark. "Not a League of Nations. The old League was helpless because it had no real existence, no power. It was not implemented to enforce its decisions; it was just a debating society, a sham. This would be different *for we would turn over the dust to it!*"

Nobody spoke for some minutes. You could see them turning it over in their minds, doubtful, partially approving, intrigued but dubious.

"I'd like to answer that," said Manning.

"Go ahead," said the President.

"I will. I'm going to have to use some pretty plain language and I hope that Secretary Larner will do me the honor of believing that I speak so from sincerity and deep concern and not from personal pique.

"I think a world democracy would be a very fine thing and I ask that you believe me when I say I would willingly lay down my life to accomplish it. I also think it would be a very fine thing for the lion to lie down with the lamb, but I am reasonably certain that only the lion would get up. If we try to form an actual world democracy, we'll be the lamb in the setup.

"There are a lot of good, kindly people who are internationalists these days. Nine out of ten of them are soft in the head and the tenth is ignorant. If we set up a worldwide democracy, what will the electorate be? Take a look at the facts: Four hundred million Chinese with no more concept of voting and citizen responsibility than a flea; three hundred million Hindus who aren't much better indoctrinated; God knows how many in the Eurasian Union who believe in God knows what; the entire continent of Africa only semicivilized; eighty million Japanese who really believe that they are Heaven-ordained to rule; our Spanish-American friends who might trail along with us and might not, but who don't understand the Bill of Rights the way we think of it; a quarter of a billion people of two dozen different nationalities in Europe, all with revenge and black hatred in their hearts.

"No, it won't wash. It's preposterous to talk about a world democracy for many years to come. If you turn the secret of the dust over to such a body, you will be arming the whole world to commit suicide."

Larner answered at once. "I could resent some of your remarks, but I won't. To put it bluntly, I consider the source. The trouble with you, Colonel Manning, is that you are a professional soldier and have no faith in people. Soldiers may be necessary, but the worst of them are martinets and the best are merely paternalistic." There was quite a lot more of the same.

Manning stood it until his turn came again. "Maybe I am all those things, but you haven't met my argument. *What are you going to do about the hundreds of millions of people who have no experience in, nor love for, democracy?* Now, perhaps, I don't have the same concept of democracy as yourself, but I do know this: Out West there are a couple of hundred thousand people who sent me to Congress; I am *not* going to stand quietly by and let a course be followed which I think will result in their deaths or utter ruin.

"Here is the probable future, as I see it, potential in the smashing of the atom and the development of lethal artificial radioactives. Some power makes a supply of the dust. They'll hit us first to try to knock us out and give them a free hand. New York and Washington overnight, then all of our industrial areas while we are still politically and economically disorganized. But our army would not be in those cities; we would have planes and a supply of dust somewhere where the first dusting wouldn't touch them. Our boys would bravely and righteously proceed to poison their big cities. Back and forth it would go until the organization of each country had broken down so completely that they were no longer able to maintain a sufficiently high level of industrialization to service planes and manufacture dust. That presupposes starvation and plague in the process. You can fill in the details.

"The other nations would get in the game. It would be silly and suicidal, of course, but it doesn't take brains to take a hand in this. All it takes is a very small group, hungry for power, a few airplanes and a supply of dust. *It's a vicious circle that cannot possibly be*

*stopped until the entire planet has dropped to a level of
economy too low to support the techniques necessary to
maintain it.* My best guess is that such a point would
be reached when approximately three-quarters of the
world's population were dead of dust, disease, or hunger, and culture reduced to the peasant-and-village
type.

"Where is your Constitution and your Bill of Rights
if you let that happen?"

I've shortened it down, but that was the gist of it. I
can't hope to record every word of an argument that
went on for days.

The Secretary of the Navy took a crack at him next.
"Aren't you getting a bit hysterical, Colonel? After all,
the world has seen a lot of weapons which were going
to make war an impossibility too horrible to contem-
plate. Poison gas, and tanks, and airplanes—even fire-
arms, if I remember my history."

Manning smiled wryly. "You've made a point, Mr.
Secretary. 'And when the wolf *really* came, the little
boy shouted in vain.' I imagine the Chamber of Commerce in Pompeii presented the same reasonable
argument to any early vulcanologist so timid as to fear
Vesuvius. I'll try to justify my fears. The dust differs
from every earlier weapon in its deadliness and ease of
use, but most importantly in that we have developed
no defense against it. For a number of fairly technical
reasons, I don't think we ever will, at least not this
century."

"Why not?"

"Because there is no way to counteract radioactivity
short of putting a lead shield between yourself and it,
an *airtight* lead shield. People might survive by living
in sealed underground cities, but our characteristic
American culture could not be maintained."

"Colonel Manning," suggested the Secretary of
State, "I think you have overlooked the obvious alternative."

"Have I?"

"Yes—to keep the dust as our own secret, go our own

way, and let the rest of the world look out for itself.
That is the only program that fits our traditions." The
Secretary of State was really a fine old gentleman, and
not stupid, but he was slow to assimilate new ideas.

"Mr. Secretary," said Manning respectfully, "I wish
we could afford to mind our own business. I do wish
we could. But it is the best opinion of all the experts
that we can't maintain control of this secret except by
rigid policing. The Germans were close on our heels in
nuclear research; it was sheer luck that we got there
first. I ask you to imagine Germany a year hence—with
a supply of dust."

The Secretary did not answer, but I saw his lips form
the word Berlin.

They came around. The President had deliberately
let Manning bear the brunt of the argument, conserv-
ing his own stock of goodwill to coax the obdurate. He
decided against putting it up to Congress; the dusters
would have been overhead before each senator had
finished his say. What he intended to do might be unconstitutional, but if he failed to act there might not
be any Constitution shortly. There was precedent—
the Emancipation Proclamation, the Monroe Doctrine, the Louisiana Purchase, suspension of habeas
corpus in the War between the States, the Destroyer
Deal.

On February 22nd the President declared a state of
full emergency internally and sent his Peace Proclamation to the head of every sovereign state. Divested
of its diplomatic surplusage, it said: *The United States
is prepared to defeat any power, or combination of powers, in jig time. Accordingly, we are outlawing war and
are calling on every nation to disarm completely at once.
In other words, "Throw down your guns, boys; we've got
the drop on you!"*

A supplement set forth the procedure: All aircraft
capable of flying the Atlantic were to be delivered in
one week's time to a field, or rather a great stretch of
prairie, just west of Fort Riley, Kansas. For lesser aircraft, a spot near Shanghai and a rendezvous in Wales

were designated. Memoranda would be issued later
with respect to other war equipment. Uranium and its
ores were not mentioned; that would come later.

No excuses. Failure to disarm would be construed
as an act of war against the United States.

There were no cases of apoplexy in the Senate; why
not, I don't know.

There were only three powers to be seriously worried about, England, Japan, and the Eurasian Union.
England had been forewarned, we had pulled her out
of a war she was losing, and she—or rather her men in
power—knew accurately what we could and would
do.

Japan was another matter. They had not seen Berlin
and they did not really believe it. Besides, they had
been telling each other for so many years that they
were unbeatable, they believed it. It does not do to get
too tough with a Japanese too quickly, for they will die
rather than lose face. The negotiations were conducted very quietly indeed, but our fleet was halfway
from Pearl Harbor to Kobe, loaded with enough dust
to sterilize their six biggest cities, before they were
concluded. Do you know what did it? This never hit
the newspapers but it was the wording of the pamphlets we proposed to scatter before dusting.

The Emperor was pleased to declare a New Order of
Peace. The official version, built up for home consumption, made the whole matter one of collaboration
between two great and friendly powers, with Japan
taking the initiative.

The Eurasian Union was a puzzle. After Stalin's unexpected death in 1941, no western nation knew very
much about what went on in there. Our own diplomatic relations had atrophied through failure to replace men called home nearly four years before.
Everybody knew, of course, that the new group in
power called themselves Fifth Internationalists, but
what that meant, aside from ceasing to display the
pictures of Lenin and Stalin, nobody knew.

But they agreed to our terms and offered to cooperate in every way. They pointed out that the Union had never been warlike and had kept out of the recent world struggle. It was fitting that the two remaining great powers should use their greatness to insure a lasting peace.

I was delighted; I had been worried about the E. U.

They commenced delivery of some of their smaller planes to the receiving station near Shanghai at once. The reports on the number and quality of the planes seemed to indicate that they had stayed out of the war through necessity; the planes were mostly of German make and in poor condition, types that Germany had abandoned early in the war.

Manning went west to supervise certain details in connection with immobilizing the big planes, the transoceanic planes, which were to gather near Fort Riley. We planned to spray them with oil, then dust from a low altitude, as in crop dusting, with a low concentration of one-year dust. Then we could turn our backs on them and forget them, while attending to other matters.

But there were hazards. The dust must not be allowed to reach Kansas City, Lincoln, Wichita—any of the nearby cities. The smaller towns roundabout had been temporarily evacuated. Testing stations needed to be set up in all directions in order that accurate tab on the dust might be kept. Manning felt personally responsible to make sure that no bystander was poisoned.

We circled the receiving station before landing at Fort Riley. I could pick out the three landing fields which had hurriedly been graded. Their runways were white in the sun, the twenty-four-hour cement as yet undirtied. Around each of the landing fields were crowded dozens of parking fields, less perfectly graded. Tractors and bulldozers were still at work on some of them. In the easternmost fields, the German and British ships were already in place, jammed wing to body as tightly as planes on the flight deck of a car-

rier—save for a few that were still being towed into
position, the tiny tractors looking from the air like
ants dragging pieces of leaf many times larger than
themselves.

Only three flying fortresses had arrived from the
Eurasian Union. Their representatives had asked for a
short delay in order that a supply of high-test aviation
gasoline might be delivered to them. They claimed a
shortage of fuel necessary to make the long flight over
the Arctic safe. There was no way to check the claim
and the delay was granted while a shipment was
routed from England.

We were about to leave, Manning having satisfied
himself as to safety precautions, when a dispatch
came in announcing that a flight of E. U. bombers
might be expected before the day was out. Manning
wanted to see them arrive; we waited around for four
hours. When it was finally reported that our escort of
fighters had picked them up at the Canadian border,
Manning appeared to have grown fidgety and stated
that he would watch them from the air. We took off,
gained altitude and waited.

There were nine of them in the flight, cruising in column of echelons and looking so huge that our little
fighters were hardly noticeable. They circled the field
and I was admiring the stately dignity of them when
Manning's pilot, Lieutenant Rafferty, exclaimed,
"What the devil! They are preparing to land down-
wind!"

I still did not tumble, but Manning shouted to the
copilot, "Get the field!"

He fiddled with his instruments and announced,
"Got 'em, sir!"

"General alarm! Armor!"

We could not hear the sirens, naturally, but I could
see the white plumes rise from the big steam whistle
on the roof of the Administration Building—three long
blasts, then three short ones. It seemed almost at the
same time that the first cloud broke from the E. U.
planes.

Instead of landing, they passed low over the receiving station, jampacked now with ships from all over the world. Each echelon picked one of three groups centered around the three landing fields and streamers of heavy brown smoke poured from the bellies of the E. U. ships. I saw a tiny black figure jump from a tractor and run toward the nearest building. Then the smoke screen obscured the field.

"Do you still have the field?" demanded Manning.

"Yes, sir."

"Cross connect to the chief safety technician. Hurry!"

The copilot cut in the amplifier so that Manning could talk directly. "Saunders? This is Manning. How about it?"

"Radioactive, chief. Intensity seven point four."

They had paralleled the Karst-Obre research.

Manning cut him off and demanded that the communication office at the field raise the Chief of Staff. There was nerve-stretching delay, for it had to be routed over land wire to Kansas City, and some chief operator had to be convinced that she should commandeer a trunk line that was in commercial use. But we got through at last and Manning made his report. "It stands to reason," I heard him say, "that other flights are approaching the border by this time. New York, of course, and Washington. Probably Detroit and Chicago as well. No way of knowing."

The Chief of Staff cut off abruptly, without comment. I knew that the U.S. air fleets, in a state of alert for weeks past, would have their orders in a few seconds, and would be on their way to hunt out and down the attackers, if possible before they could reach the cities.

I glanced back at the field. The formations were broken up. One of the E. U. bombers was down, crashed, half a mile beyond the station. While I watched, one of our midget dive bombers screamed down on a behemoth E. U. ship and unloaded his eggs. It was a center hit, but the American pilot had cut it too fine, could not pull out, and crashed before his victim.

There is no point in rehashing the newspaper stories of the Four-Days War. The point is that we should have lost it, and we would have, had it not been for an unlikely combination of luck, foresight, and good management. Apparently, the nuclear physicists of the Eurasian Union were almost as far along as Ridpath's crew when the destruction of Berlin gave them the tip they needed. But we had rushed them, forced them to move before they were ready, because of the deadline for disarmament set forth in our Peace Proclamation.

If the President had waited to fight it out with Congress before issuing the proclamation, there would not be any United States.

Manning never got credit for it, but it is evident to me that he anticipated the possibility of something like the Four-Days War and prepared for it in a dozen different devious ways. I don't mean military preparation; the Army and the Navy saw to that. But it was no accident that Congress was adjourned at the time. I had something to do with the vote-swapping and compromising that led up to it, and I know.

But I put it to you—would he have maneuvered to get Congress out of Washington at a time when he feared that Washington might be attacked if he had had dictatorial ambitions?

Of course, it was the President who was back of the ten-day leaves that had been granted to most of the civil-service personnel in Washington and he himself must have made the decision to take a swing through the South at that time, but it must have been Manning who put the idea in his head. It is inconceivable that the President would have left Washington to escape personal danger.

And then, there was the plague scare. I don't know how or when Manning could have started that—it certainly did not go through my notebook—but I simply do not believe that it was accidental that a completely unfounded rumor of bubonic plague caused New York City to be semideserted at the time the E. U. bombers struck.

At that, we lost over eight hundred thousand people in Manhattan alone.

Of course, the government was blamed for the lives that were lost and the papers were merciless in their criticism at the failure to anticipate and force an evacuation of all the major cities.

If Manning anticipated trouble, why did he not ask for evacuation?

Well, as I see it, for this reason:

A big city will not be, never has been, evacuated in response to rational argument. London never was evacuated on any major scale and we failed utterly in our attempt to force the evacuation of Berlin. The people of New York City had considered the danger of air raids since 1940 and were long since hardened to the thought.

But the fear of a nonexistent epidemic of plague caused the most nearly complete evacuation of a major city ever seen.

And don't forget what we did to Vladivostok and Irkutsk and Moscow—those were innocent people, too. War isn't pretty.

I said luck played a part. It was bad navigation that caused one of our ships to dust Ryazan instead of Moscow, but that mistake knocked out the laboratory and plant which produced the only supply of military radioactives in the Eurasian Union. Suppose the mistake had been the other way around—suppose that one of the E. U. ships in attacking Washington, D.C., by mistake had included Ridpath's shop forty-five miles away in Maryland?

Congress reconvened at the temporary capital in St. Louis, and the American Pacification Expedition started the job of pulling the fangs of the Eurasian Union. It was not a military occupation in the usual sense; there were two simple objectives: to search out and dust all aircraft, aircraft plants, and fields, and to locate and dust radiation laboratories, uranium supplies, and lodes of carnotite and pitchblende. No attempt was made to interfere with, or to replace, civil government.

We used a two-year dust, which gave a breathing spell in which to consolidate our position. Liberal rewards were offered to informers, a technique which worked remarkably well not only in the E. U., but in most parts of the world.

The "weasel," an instrument to smell out radiation, based on the electroscope-discharge principle and refined by Ridpath's staff, greatly facilitated the work of locating uranium and uranium ores. A grid of weasels, properly spaced over a suspect area, could locate any important mass of uranium almost as handily as a direction-finder can spot a radio station.

But, notwithstanding the excellent work of General Bulfinch and the Pacification Expedition as a whole, it was the original mistake of dusting Ryazan that made the job possible of accomplishment.

Anyone interested in the details of the pacification work done in 1945–6 should see the "Proceedings of the American Foundation for Social Research" for a paper entitled *A Study of the Execution of the American Peace Policy from February*, 1945. The *de facto* solution of the problem of policing the world against war left the United States with the much greater problem of perfecting a policy that would insure that the deadly power of the dust would never fall into unfit hands.

The problem is as easy to state as the problem of squaring the circle and almost as impossible of accomplishment. Both Manning and the President believed that the United States must of necessity keep the power for the time being, until some permanent institution could be developed fit to retain it. The hazard was this: Foreign policy is lodged jointly in the hands of the President and the Congress. We were fortunate at the time in having a good President and an adequate Congress, but that was no guarantee for the future. We have had unfit Presidents and power-hungry Congresses—oh, yes! Read the history of the Mexican War.

We were about to hand over to future governments of the United States the power to turn the entire globe into an empire, our empire. And it was the sober opinion of the President that our characteristic and beloved democratic culture would not stand up under the temptation. Imperialism degrades both oppressor and oppressed.

The President was determined that our sudden power should be used for the absolute minimum of maintaining peace in the world—the simple purpose of outlawing war and nothing else. It must not be used to protect American investments abroad, to coerce trade agreements, for any purpose but the simple abolition of mass killing.

There is no science of sociology. Perhaps there will be, some day, when a rigorous physics gives a finished science of colloidal chemistry and that leads in turn to a complete knowledge of biology, and from there to a definitive psychology. After that we may begin to know something about sociology and politics. Sometime around the year 5000 A. D., maybe—if the human race does not commit suicide before then.

Until then, there is only horse sense and rule of thumb and observational knowledge of probabilities. Manning and the President played by ear.

The treaties with Great Britain, Germany and the Eurasian Union, whereby we assumed the responsibility for world peace and at the same time guaranteed the contracting nations against our own misuse of power, were rushed through in the period of relief and goodwill that immediately followed the termination of the Four-Days War. We followed the precedents established by the Panama Canal treaties, the Suez Canal agreements, and the Philippine Independence policy.

But the purpose underneath was to commit future governments of the United States to an irrevocable benevolent policy.

The act to implement the treaties by creating the
Commission of World Safety followed soon after, and
Colonel Manning became Mr. Commissioner Manning. Commissioners had a life tenure and the intention was to create a body with the integrity,
permanence and freedom from outside pressure possessed by the Supreme Court of the United States.
Since the treaties contemplated an eventual joint
trust, commissioners need not be American citizens—
and the oath they took was *to preserve the peace of the
world.*

There was trouble getting the clause past the Congress! Every other similar oath had been to the Constitution of the United States.

Nevertheless the Commission was formed. It took
charge of world aircraft, assumed jurisdiction over radioactives, natural and artificial, and commenced the
long slow task of building up the Peace Patrol.

Manning envisioned a corps of world policemen, an
aristocracy which, through selection and indoctrination, could be trusted with unlimited power over the
life of every man, every woman, every child on the face
of the globe. For the power *would* be unlimited; the
precautions necessary to insure the unbeatable
weapon from getting loose in the world again made it
axiomatic that its custodians would wield power that
is safe only in the hands of Deity. There would be no
one to guard those selfsame guardians. Their own
characters and the watch they kept on each other
would be all that stood between the race and disaster.

For the first time in history, supreme political power
was to be exerted with no possibility of checks and
balances from the outside. Manning took up the task
of perfecting it with a dragging subconscious conviction that it was too much for human nature.

The rest of the Commission was appointed slowly,
the names being sent to the Senate after long joint consideration by the President and Manning. The director
of the Red Cross, an obscure little professor of history

from Switzerland, Dr. Igor Rimski who had developed
the Karst-Obre technique independently and whom
the A. P. F. had discovered in prison after the dusting
of Moscow—those three were the only foreigners. The
rest of the list is well known.

Ridpath and his staff were of necessity the original
technical crew of the Commission; United States
Army and Navy pilots its first patrolmen. Not all of the
pilots available were needed; their records were
searched, their habits and associates investigated,
their mental processes and emotional attitudes examined by the best psychological research methods
available—which weren't good enough. Their final
acceptance for the Patrol depended on two personal
interviews, one with Manning, one with the President.

Manning told me that he depended more on the
President's feeling for character than he did on all the
association and reaction tests the psychologists could
think up. "It's like the nose of a bloodhound," he said.
"In his forty years of practical politics he has seen
more phonies than you and I will ever see and each one
was trying to sell him something. He can tell one in
the dark."

The long-distance plan included the schools for the
indoctrination of cadet patrolmen, schools that were
to be open to youths of any race, color, or nationality,
and from which they would go forth to guard the peace
of every country but their own. To that country a man
would never return during his service. They were to be
a deliberately expatriated band of Janizaries, with an
obligation only to the Commission and to the race, and
welded together with a carefully nurtured esprit de
corps.

It stood a chance of working. Had Manning been allowed twenty years without interruption, the original
plan might have worked.

The President's running mate for reelection was the
result of a political compromise. The candidate for

Vice President was a confirmed isolationist who had opposed the Peace Commission from the first, but it was he or a party split in a year when the opposition was strong. The President sneaked back in but with a greatly weakened Congress; only his power of veto twice prevented the repeal of the Peace Act. The Vice President did nothing to help him, although he did not publicly lead the insurrection. Manning revised his plans to complete the essential program by the end of 1952, there being no way to predict the temper of the next administration.

We were both overworked and I was beginning to realize that my health was gone. The cause was not far to seek; a photographic film strapped next to my skin would cloud in twenty minutes. I was suffering from cumulative minimal radioactive poisoning. No well-defined cancer that could be operated on, but a systemic deterioration of function and tissue. There was no help for it, and there was work to be done. I've always attributed it mainly to the week I spent sitting on those canisters before the raid on Berlin.

February 17, 1951. I missed the televue flash about the plane crash that killed the President because I was lying down in my apartment. Manning, by that time, was requiring me to rest every afternoon after lunch, though I was still on duty. I first heard about it from my secretary when I returned to my office, and at once hurried into Manning's office.

There was a curious unreality to that meeting. It seemed to me that we had slipped back to that day when I returned from England, the day that Estelle Karst died. He looked up. "Hello, John," he said.

I put my hand on his shoulder. "Don't take it so hard, chief," was all I could think of to say.

Forty-eight hours later came the message from the newly sworn-in President for Manning to report to him. I took it in to him, an official despatch which I decoded. Manning read it, face impassive.

"Are you going, chief?" I asked.

"Eh? Why, certainly."

I went back into my office, and got my topcoat, gloves, and briefcase.

Manning looked up when I came back in. "Never mind, John," he said. "You're not going." I guess I must have looked stubborn, for he added, "You're not to go because there is work to do here. Wait a minute."

He went to his safe, twiddled the dials, opened it and removed a sealed envelope which he threw on the desk between us. "Here are your orders. Get busy."

He went out as I was opening them. I read them through and got busy. There was little enough time.

The new President received Manning standing and in the company of several of his bodyguards and intimates. Manning recognized the senator who had led the movement to use the Patrol to recover expropriated holdings in South America and Rhodesia, as well as the chairman of the committee on aviation with whom he had had several unsatisfactory conferences in an attempt to work out a *modus operandi* for reinstituting commercial airlines.

"You're prompt, I see," said the President. "Good."

Manning bowed.

"We might as well come straight to the point," the Chief Executive went on. "There are going to be some changes of policy in the administration. I want your resignation."

"I am sorry to have to refuse, sir."

"We'll see about that. In the meantime, Colonel Manning, you are relieved from duty."

"Mr. Commissioner Manning, if you please."

The new President shrugged. "One or the other, as you please. You are relieved, either way."

"I am sorry to disagree again. My appointment is for life."

"That's enough," was the answer. "This is the United States of America. There can be no higher authority. You are under arrest."

I can visualize Manning staring steadily at him for

a long moment, then answering slowly, "You are physically able to arrest me, I will concede, but I advise you to wait a few minutes." He stepped to the window. "Look up into the sky."

Six bombers of the Peace Commission patrolled over the Capitol. "None of those pilots is American born," Manning added slowly. "If you confine me, none of us here in this room will live out the day."

There were incidents thereafter, such as the unfortunate affair at Fort Benning three days later, and the outbreak in the wing of the Patrol based in Lisbon and its resultant wholesale dismissals, but for practical purposes, that was all there was to the *coup d'état*.

Manning was the undisputed military dictator of the world.

Whether or not any man as universally hated as Manning can perfect the Patrol he envisioned, make it self-perpetuating and trustworthy, I don't know, and—because of that week of waiting in a buried English hangar—I won't be here to find out. Manning's heart disease makes the outcome even more uncertain—he may last another twenty years; he may keel over dead tomorrow—and there is no one to take his place. I've set this down partly to occupy the short time I have left and partly to show there is another side to any story, even world dominion.

Not that I would like the outcome, either way. If there is anything to this survival-after-death business, I am going to look up the man who invented the bow and arrow and take him apart with my bare hands. For myself, I can't be happy in a world where any man, or group of men, has the power of death over you and me, our neighbors, every human, every animal, every living thing. I don't like anyone to have that kind of power.

And neither does Manning.

FOREWORD

After World War II I resumed writing with two objectives: first, to explain the meaning of atomic weapons through popular articles; second, to break out from the limitations and low rates of pulp science-fiction magazines into anything and everything: slicks, books, motion pictures, general fiction, specialized fiction not intended for SF magazines, and nonfiction.

My second objective I achieved in every respect, but in my first and much more important objective I fell flat on my face.

Unless you were already adult in August 1945 it is almost impossible for me to convey emotionally to you how people felt about the A-bomb, how many different ways they felt about it, how nearly totally ignorant 99.9% of our citizens were on the subject, including almost all of our military leaders and governmental officials.

And including editors!

(The general public is just as dangerously ignorant as to the significance of nuclear weapons today, 1979, as in 1945—but in different ways. In 1945 we were smugly ignorant; in 1979 we have the Pollyannas, and the Ostriches, and the Jingoists who think we can "win" a nuclear war, and the group—a majority?—who regard World War III as of no importance compared with inflation, gasoline rationing, forced school-busing, or you name it. There is much excuse for the ignorance of 1945; the citizenry had been hit by ideas utterly new and strange. But there is no excuse for the ignorance of 1979. Ignorance today can be charged only to stupidity and laziness—both capital offences.)

I wrote nine articles intended to shed light on the post-Hiroshima age, and I have never worked harder on any writing, researched the background more thoroughly, tried harder to make the (grim and horrid) message entertaining and readable. I offered them to commercial markets, not to make money, but because the only propaganda

*that stands any chance of influencing people is packaged
so attractively that editors will buy it in the belief that the
cash customers will be entertained by it.*

Mine was not packaged that attractively.

I was up against some heavy tonnage:

*General Groves, in charge of the Manhattan District
(code name for A-bomb R&D), testified that it would take
from twenty years to forever for another country to build
an A-bomb. (USSR did it in 4 years.)*

*The Chief of Naval Operations testified that the "only"
way to deliver the bomb to a target across an ocean was
by ship.*

*A very senior Army Air Force general testified that
"blockbuster" bombs were just as effective and cheaper.*

*The chairman of NACA (shortly to become NASA) tes-
tified (Science News Letter 25 May 1946) that intercon-
tinental rockets were impossible.*

*Ad nauseum—the old sailors want wooden ships, the
old soldiers want horse cavalry.*

*But I continued to write these articles until the
U.S.S.R. rejected the United States' proposals for controlling and outlawing atomic weapons through open
skies and mutual on-the-ground inspection, i.e., every
country in the world to surrender enough of its sover-
eignty to the United Nations that mass-weapons war
would become impossible (and lesser war unnecessary).*

*The U.S.S.R. rejected inspection—and I stopped trying
to peddle articles based on tying the Bomb down through
international policing.*

*I wish that I could say that thirty-three years of
"peace" (i.e., no A- or H- or C- or N- or X- bombs dropped)
indicates that we really have nothing to fear from such
weapons, because the human race has sense enough not
to commit suicide. But I am sorry to say that the situation is even more dangerous, even less stable, than it was
in 1946.*

Here are three short articles, each from a different ap-

proach, with which I tried (and failed) to beat the drum for world peace.

Was I really so naif that I thought that I could change the course of history this way? No, not really. But, damn it, I had to try!

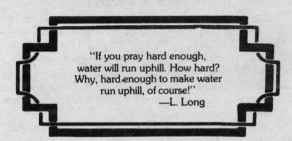

"If you pray hard enough, water will run uphill. How hard? Why, hard enough to make water run uphill, of course!"
—L. Long

THE LAST DAYS OF THE UNITED STATES

"Here lie the bare bones of the United States of America, conceived in freedom, died in bondage. 1776–1986. Death came mercifully, in one stroke, during senility.

"Rest in Peace!"

No expostulations, please. Let us not kid ourselves. The next war can destroy us, utterly, as a nation—and World War III is staring us right in the face. So far, we have done little to avert it and less to prepare for it. Once upon a time the United Nations Organization stood a fair chance of preventing World War III. Now, only a major operation can equip the UNO to cope with the horrid facts of atomics and rocketry—a major operation which would take away the veto power of the Big Five and invest the world organization with the sole and sovereign power to possess atomic weapons.

Are we, as a people, prepared to make the necessary sacrifices to achieve a world authority?

Take a look around you. Many of your friends and neighbors believe that the mere possession of the atomic bomb has rendered us immune to attack. So—the country settles back with a sigh of relief, content to leave foreign affairs to William Randolph Hearst, the Denver Post, and the Chicago Tribune. We turn our backs on world responsibility and are now hell-bent on new washing machines and new cars.

From such an attitude, with dreadful certainty, comes World War III, the Twenty Minute War, the Atomic War, the War of Final Destruction. The "secret" of the atomic bomb cannot be kept, the experts have told us repeatedly, for the "secret" is simply engineering know-how which can be developed by any industrial nation.

From this fact it can be predicted that any industrial nation, even though small and comparatively weak, will in a few years be able to create the means to destroy the United States at will in one all-out surprise attack. What constitutes a strong power in the Atomic Era? Scientific knowledge, engineering skill, and access to the ores of uranium—no more is needed. Under such circumstances the pretensions of the Big Five to veto powers over the affairs of this planet are preposterous. At the moment there is only the Big One, the United States, through its temporary exclusive possession of the Bomb. Tomorrow—five to ten years—the list might include any of the many nations with the two requirements.

Belgium and Canada have the greatest known deposits of uranium. Both are small but both possess science and skill in abundance. Potentially they are more powerful than any of the so-called Big Five, more powerful than the United States or Russia. Will they stand outside indefinitely, hat in hand, while the "Big Five" determine the fate of the human race? The developments of atomic weapons and of rocketry are analogous to the development of the revolver in individual affairs—it has made the little ones and the big ones all the same size. Some fine day some little nation may decide she is tired of having us around, give us one twenty-minute treatment with atomic rocket bombs, and accept our capitulation.

We have reason to fear such an attack. We have been through one Pearl Harbor; we *know* that it can happen to us. Our present conduct breeds fear and distrust in the hearts of men all over the globe. No matter how we think of ourselves, no matter how peaceful and good hearted we think ourselves to be, two facts insure that we will be hated by many. We have the Bomb—it is like a loaded revolver pointed at the heads of all men. Oh, we won't pull the trigger! Nevertheless, do you suppose they love us for it?

Our other unforgivable sin is being rich while they are poor. Never mind our rationalizations—they see our wasteful luxury while much of the globe starves. Hungry men do not reason calmly. We are getting ourselves caught in a situation which should lead us to expect attack from any quarter, from whoever first produces atomic weapons and long-distance rockets.

Knowing these things, the professional gentlemen who are charged with the defense of this country, the generals and the admirals and the members of the military and naval affairs committees of both houses, are cudgelling their brains in a frenzied but honest attempt to persuade the rest of the country to follow this course or that, which, in their several opinions, will safeguard the country in any coming debacle.

But there is a tragic sameness to their proposals. With few exceptions, they favor preparedness for the *last* war. Thusly:

Conscription in peacetime to build up a reserve;
Emphasis on aircraft carriers rather than battleships;
Decentralization of cities;
An armaments race to keep our head start in atomic weapons;
Agreements to "outlaw" atomic weapons;
Consolidation of the Army and the Navy;
Buying enough war planes each year to insure new development;
An active military and foreign affairs intelligence corps;
Moving the aircraft industry inland;

Placing essential war industry underground.

These are the *progressive* proposals. (Some still favor infantry and battleships!) In contrast, General Arnold says to expect war in which *space ships* cruise outside the atmosphere and launch super-high-speed, atomic-armed rockets on cities below. Hap Arnold tells his boys to keep their eyes on Buck Rogers. Somebody is wrong—is it Hap Arnold or his more conservative colleagues?

Compulsory military training—France had that, for both wars. The end was Vichy.

Aircraft carriers *vs.* battleships. Look, pals, the aircraft carrier was the weapon of *this* war, before Hiroshima. Carriers don't look so good against space ships. Let's build galleons instead; they are cheaper, prettier, and just as useful.

Decentralization of large cities—let's table this one for a moment. There is some sense to it, if carried to its logical conclusion. But not with half measures and not for $250,000,000,000, the sum mentioned by Sumner Spaulding, its prime proponent.

Bigger and better atomic weapons for the United States—this has a reasonable and reassuring sound. We've got the plant and the trained men; let's stay ahead in the race. Dr. Robert Wilson says that atomic bombs a hundred or a thousand times as powerful as the Hiroshima bomb are now in prospect. Teddy Roosevelt advised us to "Speak softly but carry a big stick."

It is a tempting doctrine, but the great-hearted Teddy died long before Hiroshima; his day was the day of the charge up San Juan Hill. A hundred obsolete atomic bombs could destroy the United States—if the enemy struck first. Our super bombs would not save us, unless we were willing to strike first, without declaring war. If two men are locked in a basement, one armed with a 50-calibre machine gun, the other with an 18th century ball-and-powder pistol, victory goes to the man who shoots first, not to the one with the better weapon. That is the logic of atomics and now is the time to learn it by heart.

Agreements to "outlaw" atomic weapons? Swell! Remember the Kellogg Pact? It "outlawed" war.

Consolidation of the armed forces: A proposition sensible in itself, but disastrously futile unless we realize that *all* previous military art is obsolete in the atomic age. The best pre-Hiroshima weapons are now no more than the sidearms of the occupying military police. Buck Rogers must be the new chief of staff. Otherwise we will find ourselves with the most expensive luxury in the world—a second-best military establishment.

Purchase of military aircraft in quantities to insure new development—we bought sailing ships-of-the-line in the 1880's. This makes the same sort of pseudo-sense. Airplanes are already obsolete—slow, clumsy, and useless. The V-2 is credited with a speed of 3600 miles per hour. Here is a simple problem in proportion: The Wright Brothers crate at Kittyhawk bears the same relation to the B-29 that the V-2 bears to the rocket ship of the coming war. Complete the equation by visualizing the coming rocket ship. Then stop wasting taxes on airplanes.

An efficient intelligence system—Fine! But no answer in itself. The British intelligence was quite efficient before this war. Mr. Chamberlain's desk was piled high with intelligence reports, reports which showed that Munich need never have happened. This has since been confirmed by high German General Staff officers. But Mr. Chamberlain did not read the reports. *Intelligence reports are useful only to the intelligent.*

Moving the aircraft industry inland—excellent preparation for World War II. Move an industry which we don't need for World War III inland where it will be safe from the weapons of World War II. While we are about it let's put stockades around them to keep the Indians out. In the meantime our potential enemies will have plenty of time to perfect long-range rockets.

Placing key war industry underground—assembly lines underground are all very well, but blast furnaces and many other things simply won't fit. Whatever digging in we do, be sure we do it so secretly that the enemy will never suspect, lest he drop an earthquake-type atomic bomb somewhere near-by and bury all hands. Let us be certain, too, that he does not introduce a small atomic bomb inside the underground works, disguised as a candy vending machine, a lunch pail, or a fire extinguisher. The age of atomics is a field day for saboteurs; underground works could be colossal death traps.

No one wants this new war, no sane men anywhere. Yet we are preparing for it and a majority, by recent Gallup polls, believe it will come. We have seen the diplomats and prime ministers and presidents and foreign affairs committees and state departments manage to get things messed up in the past; from where we sit it looks as if they were hell-bent on messing them up again. We hear the rumble of the not-so-distant drum.

What we want, we little men everywhere, is planetary organization so strong that it can enforce peace, forbid national armaments, atomic or otherwise, and in general police the globe so that a decent man can raise his kids and his dog and smoke his pipe free from worry of sudden death. But we see the same old messing around with half measures.

(If you want to help to try to stop the messing-up process, you might write Congressman Jerry Voorhis, or Senator Fulbright, or Senator Ball, or Beardsley Ruml, or Harold Stassen. Or even the President himself.)

If things go from bad to worse and we have to fight a war, can we prepare to win it? First let us try to grasp what kind of a war it will be. Look at LIFE, Nov. 19, 1945, page 27: *THE 36-HOUR WAR: Arnold Report Hints at the Catastrophe of the Next Great Conflict.* The first picture shows Washington, D.C., being destroyed by an atomic rocket bomb. The text and pictures go on to show 13 U.S. cities being destroyed the same way, enemy airborne troops attempting to occupy, the U.S. striking back with its own rockets from underground emplacements, and eventually winning—at a cost of 13 cities and at least 10,000,000 American lives.

Horrible as the picture is, it is much too optimistic. There is no reason at all to assume that the enemy will attack in too little force, destroying only 13 cities, or to assume that he will attempt to occupy until we have surrendered, or to assume that we will be able to strike back after we are attacked.

It is not safe to assume that the enemy will be either faint-hearted or foolish. If he follows our example with Japan, he will smash us until we surrender, then land. If his saboteurs are worth their blood money, our own rocket emplacements may be blown up by concealed atomic bombs just in advance of the attack.

Atomic rocket warfare has still another drawback— it is curiously anonymous. We might think we knew who had attacked us but be entirely mistaken.

You can think of at least three nations which dislike both us and Russia. What better joke for them than to select a time when suspicion has been whipped up between the two giants to lob just a few atomic rockets from a ship in the North Atlantic, or from a secret emplacement in the frozen north of Greenland—half at us, half at Russia, and with the attack in each case apparently coming from the other, and then sit back while we destroyed each other!

A fine joke! You would die laughing.

Don't think it can't be done, to us and to Russia.

What *can* we do?

The first thing is to get Congress to take a realistic

view of the situation. The most certain thing about LIFE's description of the coming war was the destruction of Washington. Washington is the prime military target on earth today for it is the center of the nervous system of the nation that now has the Bomb. It must be destroyed first and it will be destroyed, if war ever comes. Your congressman has the most dangerous job in the world today. You may live through World War III—*he* can't. Make yours realize this; he may straighten up and fly right.

What we want him to work for is world order and world peace. But we may not get it. The other nations may be fed up with our shilly-shallying and may not go along with us, particularly any who believe they are close to solving the problems of atomic weapons. We may have to go it alone. In such cases, is there anything we can do to preserve ourselves?

Yes, probably—but the price is high.

We can try for another Buck Rogers weapon with which to ward off atomic bomb rockets. It would need to be better than anything we have now or can foresee. To be 100% effective (with atom bombs, anything less is hardly good enough!) it should be something which acts with much greater speed than guns or anti-aircraft rockets. There is a bare possibility that science could cook up some sort of a devastatingly powerful beam of energy, acting with the speed of light, which would be a real anti-aircraft weapon, even against rockets. But the scientists don't promise it.

We would need the best anti-aircraft devices possible, in the meantime. A robot hook-up of target-seeking rockets, radar, and computing machines might give considerable protection, if extensive enough, but there is a lot of research and test and production ahead before any such plan is workable. Furthermore, it could not be air tight and it would be very expensive—and very annoying, for it would end civilian aviation. If we hooked the thing up to ignore civilian planes, we would leave ourselves wide open to a Trojan Horse tactic in which the enemy would use ordinary planes to deliver his atomic bombs.

Such a defense, although much more expensive and much more trouble than all our pre-War military establishment, would be needed. If we are not willing to foot the bill, we can at least save money by not buying flame throwers, tanks, or battleships.

We can prepare to attack. We can be so bristlingly savage that other nations may fear to attack us. If we are not to have a super-state and a world police, then the United States needs the fastest and the most long-range rockets, the most powerful atomic blasts, and every other dirty trick conceived in comic strip or fantastic fiction. We must have space ships and we must have them first. We must land on the Moon and take possession of it in order to forbid its use to other nations as a base against us and in order to have it as a base against any enemy of ours. We must set up, duplicate, and reduplicate rocket installations intended to destroy almost automatically any spot on earth; we must let the world know that we have them and that we are prepared to use them at the drop of a diplomat's silk hat. We must be prepared to tell uncooperative nations that there are men sitting in front of switches, day and night, and that an attack on Washington would cause those switches to be thrown.

And we must guard the secrets of the locations and natures of our weapons in a fashion quite impossible for a normal democracy in peace time. More of that later.

Decentralization we would have to have. Not the picayune $250,000,000,000 job which has been proposed—

("Wait a minute! Why should we disperse our cities if we are going to have that Buck Rogers super-dooper death ray screen?")

We haven't *got* such a screen. Nor is it certain that we will ever have such a screen, no matter how much money we spend. Such a screen is simply the one re-mote possibility which modern physics admits. It may turn out to be impossible to develop it; we simply don't know.

We must disperse thoroughly, so thoroughly that no single concentration of population in the United States is an inviting target. Mr. Sumner Spaulding's timid proposal of a quarter of a trillion dollars was based on the pleasant assumption that Los Angeles was an example of a properly dispersed city for the Atomic Age. This is an incredible piece of optimism which is apparently based on the belief that Hiro-shima is the pattern for all future atomic attacks. Hiroshima was destroyed with *one* bomb. Will the en-emy grace the city of the Angels with only *one* bomb? Why not a dozen?

The Hiroshima bomb was the gentlest, least de-structive atomic bomb ever likely to be loosed. Will the enemy favor us with a love tap such as that?

Within twenty miles of the city hall of Los Angeles lives half the population of the enormous state of Cal-ifornia. An atomic bomb dropped on that City Hall would not only blast the swarming center of the city, it would set fire to the surrounding mountains ("WARNING! No Smoking, In or Out of Cars—$500 fine and six months imprisonment") from Mount Wil-son Observatory to the sea. It would destroy the rail-road terminal half a dozen blocks from the City Hall and play hob with the water system, water fetched clear from the State of Arizona.

If that is dispersion, I'll stay in Manhattan.

Los Angeles is a modern miracle, an enormous city kept alive in a desert by a complex and vulnerable concatenation of technical expedients. The first three colonies established there by the Spaniards starved to death to the last man, woman, and child. If the fragile structure of that city were disrupted by a single atomic bomb, those who survived the blast would in a few short days be reduced to a starving, thirst-crazed mob, ready for murder and cannibalism.

No, if we are to defend ourselves we must not assume that Los Angeles is "dispersed" despite the jokes about her far-flung city line. The Angelenos must be relocated from Oregon to Mexico, in the Mojave Desert, in Imperial Valley, in the great central valley, in the Coast Range, and in the High Sierras.

The same principles apply everywhere. Denver must be scattered out toward Laramie and Boulder, while Colorado Springs must flow around Pike's Peak to Cripple Creek. Kansas City and Des Moines must meet at the Iowa-Missouri line, while Joplin flows up toward Kansas City and on down into the Ozarks. As for Manhattan, that is almost too much to describe— from Boston to Baltimore all the great east coast cities must be abandoned and the population scattered like leaves.

The cities must go. Only villages must remain. If we are to rely on dispersion as a defense in the Atomic Age, then we must spread ourselves out so thin that the enemy cannot possibly destroy us with one bingo barrage, so thin that we will be too expensive and too difficult to destroy.

It would be difficult. It would be incredibly difficult and expensive—Mr. Spaulding's estimate would not cover the cost of new housing alone, but new housing would be the least of our problems. We would have to rebuild more than half of our capital plant—shops, warehouses, factories, railroads, highways, power plants, mills, garages, telephone lines, pipe lines, aqueducts, granaries, universities. We would have to take the United States apart and put it back together again according to a new plan and for a new purpose. The financial cost would be unimportant, because we could not buy it, we would have to *do* it, with our own hands, our own sweat. It would mean a sixty-hour week for everyone, no luxury trades, and a bare minimum standard of living for all for some years. Thereafter the standard of living would be permanently depressed, for the new United States would be organized for defense, not for mass production, nor efficient marketing, nor convenient distribution. We would have to pay for our village culture in terms of lowered consumption. Worse, a large chunk of our lowered productivity must go into producing and supporting the atomic engines of war necessary to strike back against an aggressor—for dispersion alone would not protect us from invasion.

If the above picture is too bleak, let us not prate about dispersion. There are only three real alternatives open to us: One, to form a truly sovereign superstate to police the globe; two, to prepare realistically for World War III in which case dispersion, real and thorough dispersion, is utterly necessary, or, third, to sit here, fat, dumb, and happy, wallowing in our luxuries, until the next Hitler annihilates us!

The other necessary consequences of defense by dispersion are even more chilling than the economic disadvantages. If we go it alone and depend on ourselves to defend ourselves we must be prepared permanently to surrender that democratic freedom of action which we habitually enjoyed in peace time. We must resign ourselves to becoming a socialistic, largely authoritarian police state, with freedom of speech, freedom of occupation, and freedom of movement subordinated to military necessity, as defined by those in charge.

Oh, yes! I dislike the prospect quite as much as you do, but I dislike still more the idea of being atomized, or of being served up as a roast by my starving neighbors. Here is what you can expect:

The front door bell rings. Mr. Joseph Public, solid citizen, goes to answer it. He recognizes a neighbor. "Hi, Jack! What takes you out so late?"

"Got some dope for you, Joe. Relocation orders—I was appointed an emergency deputy, you know."

"Hadn't heard, but glad to hear. Come in and sit down and tell me about it. How do the orders read? We stay, don't we?"

"Can't come in—thanks. I've got twenty-three more stops to make tonight. I'm sorry to say you don't stay. Your caravan will rendezvous at Ninth and Chelsea, facing west, and gets underway at noon tomorrow."

"What!"

"That's how it is. Sorry."

"Why, this is a damned outrage! I put in to stay here—with my home town as second choice."

The deputy shrugged. "So did everybody else. But you weren't even on the list of essential occupations from which the permanent residents were selected. Now, look—I've got to hurry. Here are your orders. Limit yourself to 150 pounds of baggage, each, and take food for three days. You are to go in your own car—you're getting a break—and you will be assigned two more passengers by the convoy captain, two more besides your wife I mean."

Joe Public shoved his hands in his pockets and looked stubborn. "I won't be there."

"Now, Joe, don't take that attitude. I admit it's kinda rough, being in the first detachment, but you've had lots of notice. The newspapers have been full of it. It's been six months since the President's proclamation."

"I won't go. There's some mistake. I saw the councilman last week and he said he thought I would be all right. He—"

"He told everybody that, Joe. This is a *Federal* order."

"I don't give a damn if it's from the Angel Gabriel. I tell you I won't go. I'll get an injunction."

"You can't, Joe. This has been declared a military area and protests have to go to the Provost Marshal. I'd hate to tell you what he does with them. Anyhow, you can't stay here—it's no business of mine to put you out; I just have to tell you—but the salvage crews will be here tomorrow morning to pull out your plumbing."

"They won't get in."

"Maybe not. But the straggler squads will go through all of these houses first."

"I'll shoot!"

"I wouldn't advise it. They're mostly ex-Marines."

Mr. Public was quiet for a long minute. Marines. "Look, Jack," he said slowly, "suppose I do go. I've got to have an exemption on this baggage limitation and I can't carry passengers. My office files alone will fill up the back seat."

"You won't need them. You are assigned as an apprentice carpenter. The barracks you are going to are only temporary."

"*Joseph! Joseph!* Don't stand there with the door open! Who is it?" His wife followed her voice in.

He turned to tell her; the deputy took that as a good time to leave.

At eleven the next morning he pulled out of the driveway, gears clashing. He had the white, drawn look of a man who has been up all night. His wife slept beside him, her hysteria drowned in a triple dose of phenobarbital.

That is dispersion. If you don't believe it, ask any native-born citizen of Japanese blood. Nothing less than force and police organization will drive the peasants off the slopes of Vesuvius. The bones of Pompeii and Herculaneum testify to that. Or, ask yourself— will you go willingly and cheerfully to any spot and any occupation the government assigns to you? If not, unless you are right now working frantically to make World War III impossible, you have not yet adjusted yourself to the horrid facts of the Atomic Age.

For these *are* the facts of the Atomic Age. If we are not to have a World State, then we must accept one of two grim alternatives: A permanent state of total war, even in "peace" time, with every effort turned to offense and defense, or relax to our fate, make our peace with God, and wait for death to come out of the sky. The time in which to form a World State is passing rapidly; it may be gone by the time this is printed. It is worthwhile to note that the publisher of the string of newspapers most bitterly opposed to "foreign entanglements," particularly with Russia, and most insistent on us holding on to the vanishing "secret" of the atomic bomb—this man, this publisher, lives on an enormous, self-sufficient ranch, already dispersed. Not for him is the peremptory knock on the door and the uprooting relocation order. Yet he presumes daily to tell our Congress what must be done with us and for us.

Look at the facts! Go to your public library and read the solemn statements of the men who built the atomic bomb. Do not let yourself be seduced into a false serenity by men who do not understand that the old world is dead. Regularly, in the past, our State Department has bungled us into wars and with equal regularity our military establishment has been unprepared for them. Then the lives and the strength of the common people have bought for them a victory.

Now comes a war which cannot be won after such mistakes.

If we are to die, let us die like men, eyes open, aware of our peril and striving to cope with it—not as fat and fatuous fools, smug in the belief that the military men and the diplomats have the whole thing under control.

"It is later than you think."

HOW TO BE A SURVIVOR

The Art of Staying Alive
in the Atomic Age

Thought about your life insurance lately?

Wait a minute—sit back down! We don't want to sell you any insurance.

Let's put it another way: How's your pioneer blood these days? Reflexes in fine shape? Muscle tone good? Or do you take a taxi to go six blocks?

How are you at catching rabbits? The old recipe goes, "First, catch the rabbit—" Suppose your supper depended on catching a rabbit? Then on building a fire without matches? Then on cooking it? What kind of shape will you be in after the corner delicatessen is atomized?

When a committee of Senators asked Dr. J. Robert Oppenheimer whether or not a single attack on the United States could kill forty million people, he testified, "I am afraid it is true."

This is not an article about making the atom bomb safe for democracy. This is an article about *you*—and how you can avoid being one of the forty million knocked off in the first attack in World War III. How, if worst comes to worst, you can live through the next war, survive the aftermath, and build a new life.

If you have been reading the newspapers you are aware that World War III, if it ever comes, is expected to start with an all-out surprise attack by long-distance atomic bombing on the cities of America. General Marshall's final report included this assumption, General Arnold has warned us against such an attack, General Spaatz has described it and told us that it is almost impossible to ward it off if it ever comes. Innumerable scientists, especially the boys who built the A-bomb, have warned us of it.

From the newspapers you may also have gathered that world affairs are not in the best of shape—the Balkans, India, Palestine, Iran, Argentina, Spain, China, The East Indies, etc., etc.—and the UNO does not seem as yet to have a stranglehold on all of the problems that could lead to another conflict.

Maybe so, maybe not—time will tell. Maybe we will form a real World State strong enough to control the atom bomb. If you are sure there will never be war again, don't let me waste your time. But if you think it possible that another Hitler or Tojo might get hold of the atomic bomb and want to try his luck, then bend an ear and we'll talk about how you and your kids can live through it. We'll start with the grisly assumption that the war will come fast and hard, when it comes, killing forty million or so at once, destroying the major cities, wrecking most of our industry and utterly disorganizing the rest. We will assume a complete breakdown of government and communication which will throw the survivors—that's you, chum!—on their own as completely as ever was Dan'l Boone.

No government—remember that. The United States will cease to be a fact except in the historical sense. You will be on your own, with no one to tell you what to do and no policeman on the corner to turn to for protection. And you will be surrounded with dangerous carnivores, worse than the grizzlies Daniel Boone tackled—the two-legged kind.

Perhaps we had better justify the assumption of complete breakdown in government. It might not happen, but, if the new Hitler has sense enough to write

Mein Kampf, or even to read it as a textbook, he will do his very best to destroy and demoralize us by destroying our government—and his best could be quite efficient. If he wants to achieve political breakdown in his victim, Washington, D.C., will be his prime target, the forty-eight state capitals his secondary targets, and communication centers such as Kansas City his tertiary targets. The results should be roughly comparable to the effect on a man's organization when his head is chopped off.

Therefore, in this bad dream we are having, let us assume no government, no orders from Washington, no fireside chats, no reassurances. You won't be able to write to your congressman, because he, poor devil!, is marked for the kill. You can live through it, he can't. He will be radioactive dust. His profession is so hazardous that there is no need for him to study up on how to snare rabbits.

But *you* should— if you are smart, you can live through it.

Now as to methods—there is just one known way to avoid being killed by an atomic bomb. The formula is very simple:

Don't be there when it goes off!

Survival methods in the atomic age can be divided into two headings, strategical and tactical. The first or strategical aspect is entirely concerned with how not to be where the bomb is; the second, tactical part has to do with how to keep yourself and your family alive if you live through the destruction of the cities and the government.

Strategy first—the simplest way to insure long life for yourself and family is to move to Honduras or some other small and nonindustrialized country, establish yourself there, and quit worrying. It is most unlikely that such places will be subjected to atomic bombardment; if war comes, they will move into the economic and political sphere of the winner, to be sure, but probably without bloodshed, since resistance would be so obviously futile.

However, you probably cannot afford, or feel that you can't afford, any move as drastic as that. (Whether or not you can in truth afford it is a moot point, to be settled by your own notion of the degree of danger. The pre-War refugees from Nazi Germany could not "afford" to flee, either, but events proved the wisdom of doing so. There is an old Chinese adage, "In the course of a long life a wise man will be prepared to abandon his baggage several times." It has never been more true than it is today.)

There are several moves open to you which are less drastic. If you live on a farm or in a small village, several miles—fifty is a good figure—from the nearest large city, rail junction, power dam, auto factory, or other likely military target, strategy largely takes care of itself. If you are blasted, it will probably be an accident, a rocket gone wild, or something equally unforeseeable. If you are not in such a location, you had better make some plans.

Just a moment—a gentleman in the back row has a question. A little louder please. He asks, "Isn't it true that the government is planning to disperse the cities so we will be safe from atomic bombs?"

I don't know—is it? The only figure I have heard mentioned so far is $250,000,000,000. Quite aside from the question of whether or not large scale dispersion can be made effective, there is still the question as to whether or not Congress would appropriate a quarter of a trillion dollars in peacetime for any purpose. That is a political question, beyond the scope of this discussion. We are concerned here with how you, unassisted, with your two hands, your brain, and your ability to plan ahead, can keep yourself alive during and after any possible Next War.

If you have to live in a large city or other target area, your strategical planning has to be a good bit more detailed, alert, and shifty. You need an emergency home, perhaps an abandoned farm picked up cheaply or a cabin built on government land. What it is depends on the part of the country you live in and how much money you can put into it, but it should be chosen with view to the possibilities it offers of eating off the country—fish, game, garden plot—and it should be near enough for you to reach it on one tank of gasoline. If the tank in your car is too small, have a special one built, or keep enough cans of reserve permanently in the trunk of your car. Your car should also be equipped with a survival kit, but that comes under tactics.

Having selected and equipped your emergency base, you must then, if you are to live in a target area, keep your ear to the ground and your eyes open with respect to world affairs. *There will be no time to get out after rockets are launched.* You will have to outguess events. This is a tricky assignment at best and is the principal reason why it is much better to live in the country in the first place, but you stand a fair chance of accomplishing it if you do not insist on being blindly optimistic and can overcome a natural reluctance to make a clean break with your past—business, home, clubs, friends, church—when it becomes evident that the storm clouds are gathering. Despite the tragic debacle at Pearl Harbor, quite a number of people, laymen among them, knew that a war with Japan was coming. If you think you can learn to spot the signs of trouble long enough in advance to jump, you may get away with living on the spot with the X mark.

Let us suppose that you were quick-witted, far sighted, and fast on your feet; you brought yourself and your family safely through the bombing and have them somewhere out in the country, away from the radioactive areas that were targets a short time before. The countryside is swarming with survivors from the edges of the bombed areas, survivors who are hungry, desperate, some of them armed, all of them free of the civilizing restrictions of organized living. Enemy troops, moving in to occupy, may already be present or may be dropping in from the skies any day.

How, on that day, will you feed and protect yourself and your family?

The tactical preparations for survival after the debacle fall mainly into three groups. First is the overhaul of your own bodily assets, which includes everything from joining the YMCA, to get rid of that paunch and increase your wind and endurance, to such things as getting typhoid and cholera shots, having that appendix out, and keeping your teeth in the best shape possible. If you wear glasses, you will need several pairs against the day when there will be no opticians in practice. Second is the acquisition of various materials and tools which you will be unable to make or grow in a sudden, synthetic stone age— items such as a pickax or a burning glass, for example, will be worth considerably more than two college degrees or a diamond bracelet. Third is training in various fundamental pioneer skills, not only how to snare and cook rabbits, but such things as where and when to plant potatoes, how to tell edible fungi from deadly toadstools without trying them on Junior, and how to walk silently.

All these things are necessary, but more important, much more important, is the acquiring of a survival point of view, the spiritual orientation which will enable you to face hardship, danger, cold, and hunger without losing your zest and courage and sense of humor. If you think it is going to be too hard to be worthwhile, if you can't face the prospect of coming back to the ruins of your cabin, burned down by drunken looters, other than with the quiet determination to build another, then don't bother to start. Move to a target area and wait for the end. It does not take any special courage or skill to accept the death that moves like lightning. You won't even have the long walk the steers have to make to get from the stockyard pens to the slaughter-house.

But if your ancestors still move in your bones, you will know that it is worthwhile, just as they did. "The cowards never started and the weaklings died on the way." That was the spirit that crossed the plains, and such was the spirit of every emigrant who left Europe. There is good blood in your veins, *compadre!*

It is not possible to tell exactly what to do to prepare yourself best to survive, even if this were a book instead of a short article, for the details must depend on the nature of the countryside you must rely on, your opportunities for planning and preparing, the numbers, ages and sex of your dependents if any, your present skills, talents, and physical condition, and whether or not you are at present dispersed from target areas or must plan for such dispersal. But the principles under which you can make your plans and the easiest means by which to determine them can be indicated.

Start out by borrowing your son's copy of the *Boy Scout Manual.* It is a practical book of the sort of lore you will need. If you can't borrow it because he is not a member of the Scouts, send him down at once and make him join up. Then make him study. Get him busy on those merit badges—woodcraft, cooking, archery, carpentry. *Somebody* is going to have to make that fire without matches, if that rabbit is ever to be cooked and eaten. See to it that he learns how, from experts. Then make him teach you.

Can you fell a tree? Can you trim a stone? Do you know where to dig a cesspool? Where and how to dig a well? Can you pull a tooth? Can you shoot a rifle accurately and economically? Can you spot tularemia (we are back to that ubiquitous rabbit again!) in cleaning a rabbit? Do you know the rudiments of farming? Given simple tools, could you build a log, or adobe, or rammed-earth, or native-stone cabin from materials at hand and have it be weather-tight, varmint-proof, and reasonably comfortable?

You can't learn all the basic manual trades in your spare time in a limited number of years but you can acquire a jackleg but adequate knowledge of the more important ones, in the time we have left.

But how much time have we?

All we can do is estimate. How long will it be before other nations have the atomic bomb? Nobody knows—one estimate from the men who made it was "two to five years." Dr. Vannevar Bush spoke of "five to fifteen years" while another expert, equally distinguished, mentioned "five or ten years." Major General Leslie Groves, the atom general, thinks it will be a long time.

Let us settle on five years as a reasonable minimum working time. Of course, even if another nation, unfriendly to us, solved the production problems of atomic weapons in that length of time, there still might not be a war for a number of years, nor would there necessarily ever be one. However, since we don't know what world conditions will be like in five years, let's play it safe; let's try to be ready for it by 1950.

Four or five years is none too long to turn a specialized, soft, city dweller into a generalized, hardened pioneer. However, it is likely that you will find that you are enjoying it. It will be an interesting business and there is a deep satisfaction in learning how to do things with your own hands.

First get that *Scout Manual*. Look over that list of merit badges. Try to figure out what skills you are likely to need, what ones you now have, and what ones you need to study up on. The Manual will lead you in time to other books. Ernest Thompson Seton's *Two Little Savages* is full of ideas and suggestions.

Presently you will find that there are handbooks of various trades you have not time to master; books which contain information you could look up in an emergency if you have had the forethought to buy the book and hide it away in your out-of-town base. There are books which show how to build fireplaces, giving the exact dimensions of reflector, throat, ledge, and flue. You may not remember such details; being able to look them up may save you from a winter in a smoke-filled cabin. If there is any greater domestic curse than a smoking fireplace, I can't recall it, unless it be the common cold.

There are little handbooks which show, in colored pictures, the edible mushrooms and their inedible cousins. It is possible to live quite well on practically nothing but fungi, with comparatively little work; they exist in such abundance and variety.

You will need a medical reference book, selected with the advice of a wise and imaginative medical man. Tell him why you want it. Besides that, the best first-aid and nursing instruction you can get will not be too much. Before you are through with this subject you will find yourself selecting drugs, equipment, and supplies to be stored against the darkness, in your base as well as a lesser supply to go into the survival kit you keep in your automobile.

What goes into that survival kit, anyhow? You will have to decide; you won't take any present advice in any case. By the time you get to it you will think, quite correctly, that you are the best judge. But the contents of the survival kits supplied our aviators in this latest war will be very illuminating. The contents varied greatly, depending on climate and nature of mission— from pemmican to quinine, fish hooks to maps.

What to put in your cabin is still more difficult to state definitely. To start with, you might obtain a Sears-Roebuck or Montgomery-Ward catalog and go through it, item by item. Ask yourself "Do I have to have this?," then from the list that produces ask yourself "Could I make this item, or a substitute, in a pinch?"

If shoes wear out, it is possible to make moccasins— although shoes should be hoarded in preference to any

other item of clothing. But you can't—unless you are
Superman—make an ax. You will need an ax.

You will need certain drugs. Better be liberal here.
Salt is difficult to obtain, inland.

It is difficult to reject the idea of hoarding canned
goods. A few hundred dollars worth, carefully selected, could supplement the diet of your family to the
point of luxury for several years. It might save you
from starvation, or the cannibalism that shamed the
Donner Party, during your first winter of the Dark
Ages, and it could certainly alleviate some of the sugar
hunger you are sure to feel under most primitive conditions. But it is a very great risk to have canned goods.
If you have them, you will be one of the hated rich if
anybody finds out about them. We are assuming that
there will be no government to protect you. To have
canned goods—and have it known by anyone outside
your own household—is to invite assassination. If you
do not believe that a man will commit murder for one
can of tomatoes, then you have never been hungry.

If you have canned goods, open them when the win-
dows are shuttered and bury the cans. Resist the
temptation to advertise your wealth by using the
empty tins as receptacles.

Don't forget a can opener—two can openers.

You will have a rifle, high-powered and with telescopic sights, but you won't use it much. Cartridges
are nearly irreplaceable. A deer or a man should be
about the limit of the list of your targets . . . a deer
when you need meat; a man when hiding or running is
not enough.

That brings us to another subject and the most interesting of all. We have not talked much about the
enemy, have we? And yet he was there, from the start.
It was his atom bombs which reduced you to living off
the country and performing your own amputations
and accouchements. If you have laid your plans carefully, you won't see much of him for quite a while; this
is a very, very big country. Where you are hidden out

there never were very many people at any time; the chances of occupation forces combing all of the valleys, canyons, and hills of our back country in less than several years is negligible. It is entirely conceivable that an enemy could conquer or destroy our country, as a state, in twenty minutes, with atom bomb and rocket. Yet, when his occupation forces move in, they will be almost lost in this great continent. He may not find you for years.

There is your chance. It has been proved time and again, by the Fighting French, the recalcitrant Irish, the deathless Poles, yes and by our own Apache and Yaqui Indians, that you cannot conquer a free man; you can only kill him.

After the immediate problems of the belly, comes the Underground!

You'll need your rifle. You will need knives. You will need dynamite and fuses. You will need to know how to turn them into grenades. You must learn how to harry the enemy in the dark, how to turn his conquest into a mockery, too expensive to exploit. Oh, it can be done, it can be done! Once he *occupies*, his temporary advantage of the surprise attack with the atom bomb is over, for once his troops are scattered among you, *he cannot use the atom bomb.*

Then is your day. Then is the time for the neighborhood cell, the mountain hideout, the blow in the night. Yes, and then is the time for the martyr to freedom, the men and women who die painfully, with sealed lips.

Can we then win our freedom back? There is no way of telling. History has some strange quirks. It was a conflict between England and France that gave us our freedom in the first place. A quarrel in enemy high places, a young hopeful feeling his oats and anxious to displace the original dictator, might give us unexpected opportunity, opportunity we could exploit if we were ready.

There are ways to study for that day, too. There are

books, many of them, which you may read to learn how other people have done it. One such book is Tom Wintringham's *New Ways of War*. It is almost a blueprint of what to do to make an invader wish he had stayed at home. It is available in a 25 cent Penguin-Infantry Journal edition. You can study up and become quite deadly, even though 4-F, or fifty.

If you plan for it, you can survive. If you study and plan and are ready to organize when the time comes, you can hope not only to survive but to play a part in winning back lost freedoms. General George Washington once quoted Scripture to describe what we were fighting for then—a time when "everyone shall sit in safety under his own vine and figtree, and none shall make him afraid!"

It is worth planning for.

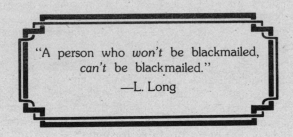

"A person who *won't* be blackmailed, *can't* be blackmailed."
—L. Long

PIE FROM THE SKY

Since we have every reason to expect a sudden rain of death from the sky sometime in the next few years, as a result of a happy combination of the science of atomics and the art of rocketry, it behooves the Pollyanna Philosopher to add up the advantages to be derived from the blasting of your apartment, row house, or suburban cottage.

It ain't all bad, chum. While you are squatting in front of your cave, trying to roast a rabbit with one hand while scratching your lice-infested hide with the other, there will be many cheerful things to think about, the assets of destruction, rather than torturing your mind with thoughts of the good old, easy days of taxis and tabloids and Charlie's Bar Grill.

There are so many, many things in this so-termed civilization of ours which would be mightily improved by a once over lightly of the Hiroshima treatment. There is that dame upstairs, for instance, the one with the square bowling ball. Never again would she take it out for practice right over your bed at three in the morning. Isn't that some consolation?

No more soap operas. No more six minutes of good old Mom facing things bravely, interspersed with eight minutes of insistent, syrupy plugging for commercial junk you don't want and would be better off without. Never again will you have to wait breathlessly for "same time, same station" to find out what beautiful Mamie Jukes, that priceless moron, does about her nameless babe. She will be gone, along with the literary prostitute who brought her into being.

No more alarm clocks. *No more alarm clocks!* No more of the frenzied keeping of schedules, appointments, and deadlines that they imply. You won't have to gulp your coffee to run for the 8:19 commuters' special, nor keep your eye on the clock while you lunch. A few of the handy little plutonium pills dropped from the sky will end the senseless process of running for the bus to go to work to make the money to buy the food to get the strength to run for the bus. You will swap the pressure of minutes for the slow tide of eternity.

But best of all, you will be freed of the plague of the alarm that yanks you from the precious nirvana of sleep and sets you on your weary feet, with every nerve screaming protest. If you are snapped suddenly out of sleep in the Atomic Stone Age, it will be a mountain lion, a wolf, a man, or some other carnivore, not a mechanical monstrosity.

Westbrook Pegler will no longer exhibit to you his latest hate, nor will Lolly Parsons stuff you with her current girlish enthusiasm.(If your pet dislikes among the columnists are not these two, fill in names to suit yourself; none of them will bother you after the fission treatment.)

In fact, all the impact of world-wide troubles will fade away. Divorces, murders, and troubles in China will no longer smite from headline and radio. Your only worries will be your own worries.

No more John L. Lewis.

No more jurisdictional strikes.

No more "Hate-Roosevelt" clubs.

No more "Let's-Hate-Eleanor,-Too" clubs.

No more Petrillo.

No more damn fools who honk right behind your car while the lights are changing. I'll buy this one at a black market price right now.

No more Gerald L. K. Smith. . . . and, conversely, no more people who think that the persecution of their particular minority is the only evil in the entire world worth talking about, or working to correct.

No more phony "days." You won't have to buy a red carnation to show that Mom is alive nor a white one to show that she's not. (It's even money that you will have lost track of her in the debacle and not know whether she is alive or dead.) No more "Boy's Day" in our city governments with pre-adolescent little stinkers handing out fines and puritanical speeches to tired street walkers while the elected judge smiles blandly for the photographers. No more "Eat More Citrus Fruit" or "Eat More Chocolate Candy" or "Read More Comic Books" weeks thought up by the advertising agents of industries.

While we are on the subject of phony buildups, let's give a cheer for the elimination of debutantes with press agents, for the blotting out of "cafe" society, for the consignment to oblivion of the whole notion of the "coming-out" party. The resumption of the coming-out party in the United States, with its attendant, incredibly callous, waste, at the very time that Europe starves, is a scandal to the jay birds. A few atom bombs would be no more than healthy fumigation of this imbecilic evil.

No more toothsome mammals built up by synthetic publicity into movie "stars" before they have played a part in a picture. This is probably a relatively harmless piece of idiocy in our whipped-cream culture, but the end of it, via A-bombs, may stop Sarah Bernhardt from spinning in her grave.

No more over-fed, under-worked, rapacious female tyrants. I won't say "mothers-in-law"; your mother-in-law may be a pretty good Joe. If not, you may have a chance to cut her up for steak.

There is actually nothing to prevent American women from being able, adult, useful citizens, and many of them are. But our society is so rigged that a

worthless female can make a racket of it—but not after
a brisk one-two with uranium! The parasites will
starve when that day comes, from the cheerful idiots
of the Helen Hokinson cartoons to the female dinosaurs who use sacrosanct sex as a club to bullyrag,
blackmail, and dominate every man they can reach.

The parasite males will die out, too. Yes, pal, if you
can manage to zig while the atomic rockets zag you
will find society much changed and in many respects
improved.

There are a lot of other minor advantages you
should get firmly in mind now, lest you fall prey to a
fatal nostalgia after this great, fantastic, incredible,
somewhat glorious and very fragile technological culture crashes about your ears. Subway smell, for example. The guy who coughs on the back of your neck
in the theater. Men who bawl out waitresses. The
woman who crowds in ahead of you at the counter.
The person who asks how much you paid for it. The
preacher with the unctuous voice and the cash register
heart. The millionairess who wills her money to found
a home for orphan guppies. The lunkhead who dials a
wrong number (your number) in the middle of the
night and then is sore at you for not being the party he
wanted. The sportsman who turns his radio up loud so
that he can boo the Dodgers while out in his garden.
The Dodgers. People who don't curb their dogs. People
who spit on sidewalks. People who censor plays and
suppress books. Breach-of-promise suits. People who
stare at wounded veterans.

A blinding flash, a pillar of radioactive dust, and all
this will be gone.

I don't mean to suggest that it will all be fun. Keeping alive after our cities have been smashed and our
government disintegrated will be a grim business at
best, as the survivors in central Europe could tell you.
In spite of the endless list that could be made of the

things we are better off without I do not think it will
be very much fun to scrabble around in the woods for
a bite to eat. For that reason I am thinking of liquidat-
ing, in advance, the next character who says to me,
"Well, what difference does it make if we are atom-
bombed—you gotta die sometime!"

I shall shoot him dead, blow through the barrel, and
say, "You asked for it, chum."

Conceding that we will all die some day, is that a
reason why I should let this grinning ape drag me
along toward disaster just because he will take no
thought of tomorrow?

Since there are so many of him the chances of us, as
a nation, being able to avert disaster are not good. Perhaps some of us could form an association to live
through World War III. Call it the *League for the Pres-
ervation of the Human Race*, or the *Doom's Day Men*, or
something like that. Restrict the membership to sur-
vivor types, sound in tooth and wind, trained in useful
trades or science, reasonably high I.Q.'s and proved
fertility. Then set up two or three colonies remote from
cities and other military targets.

It might work.

Maybe I will start it myself if I can find an angel to
put up the dough for the original promotion. That
should get me in as an *ex-officio* member, I hope. I have
looked over my own qualifications and I don't seem to
measure up to the standards.

My ancestors got into America by a similar dodge.
They got here early, when the immigration restrictions were pretty lax. Maybe I can repeat.

I am sure I shall not resign myself to death simply
because Joe Chucklehead points out that atomization
is quick and easy. Even if that were good I would not
like it. Furthermore, it is not true. Death comes fast at
the center of the blast; around the edges is a big area
of the fatal burn and the slow death, with plenty of
time to reconsider the disadvantages of chucklehead-

ness in the Atomic Age, before your flesh sloughs off and you give up the ghost. No, thank you, I plan to disperse myself to the country.

Of course, if you are so soft that you *like* innerspring mattresses and clean water and regular meals, despite the numerous advantages of blowing us off the map, but are not too soft to try to do something to avoid the coming debacle, there is something you can do about it, other than forming Survival Leagues or cultivating an attitude of philosophical resignation.

If you really want to hang on to the advantages of our slightly wacky pseudo-civilization, there is just one way to do it, according to the scientists who know the most about the new techniques of war—and that is to form a sovereign world authority to prevent the Atomic War.

Run, do not walk, to the nearest Western Union, and telegraph your congressman to get off the dime and get on with the difficult business of forming an honest-to-goodness world union, with no jokers about Big Five vetoes or national armaments . . . to get on with it promptly, while there is still time, before Washington, D.C., is reduced to radioactive dust—and he with it, poor devil!

FOREWORD

While I was failing at World-Saving, I was beginning to achieve my second objective: to spread out, not limit myself to pulp science fiction. *THEY DO IT WITH MIRRORS* was my first attempt in the crime-mystery field, and from it I learned three things: a) whodunnits are fairly easy to write and easy to sell; b) I was no threat to Raymond Chandler or Rex Stout as the genre *didn't* interest me that much; and c) Crime Does Not Pay— Enough (the motto of the Mystery Writers of America).

It may amuse you to know that this story was considered to be (in 1945) too risqué; the magazine editor laundered it before publication. You are seeing the original "dirty" version; try to find in it *anything at all that could bring a blush to the cheek of your maiden aunt.*

In late 1945 this magic mirror existed in a bar at (as I recall) the corner of Hollywood and Gower Gulch; the rest is fiction.

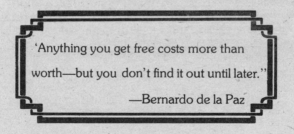

'Anything you get free costs more than

worth—but you don't find it out until later.''

—Bernardo de la Paz

THEY DO IT WITH MIRRORS
An Edison Hill Crime Case

I was there to see beautiful naked women. So was everybody else. It's a common failing.

I climbed on a stool at the end of the bar in Jack Joy's Joint and spoke to Jack himself, who was busy setting up two old-fashioneds. "Make it three," I said. "No, make it four and have one with me. What's the pitch, Jack? I hear you set up a peep show for the suckers."

"Hi, Ed. Nope, it's not a peep show—it's Art."

"What's the difference?"

"If they hold still, it's Art. If they wiggle around, it's illegal. That's the ruling. Here." He handed me a program.

It read:

THE JOY CLUB
PRESENTS
The Magic Mirror

Beautiful Models in a series of Entertaining
and Artistic Pageants

10 p.m.	"Aphrodite"	Estelle
11 p.m.	"Sacrifice to the Sun"	Estelle and Hazel
12 p.m.	"The High Priestess"	Hazel
1 a.m.	"The Altar Victim"	Estelle
2 a.m.	"Invocation to Pan"	Estelle and Hazel

(Guests are requested to refrain stomping, whistling, or otherwise disturbing the artistic serenity of the presentations)

The last was a giggle. Jack's place was strictly a joint. But on the other side of the program I saw a new schedule of prices which informed me that the drink in my hand was going to cost me just twice what I had figured. And the place was jammed. By suckers—including me.

I was about to speak to Jack, in a kindly way, promising to keep my eyes closed during the show and then pay the old price for my drink, when I heard two sharp *beeps!*—a high tension buzzer sound, like radio code— from a spot back of the bar. Jack turned away from me, explaining, "That's the eleven o'clock show." He busied himself underneath the bar.

Being at the end of the bar I could see under the long side somewhat. He had enough electrical gear there to make a happy Christmas for a Boy Scout—switches, a rheostat dingus, a turntable for recordings, and a hand microphone. I leaned over and sized it up. I have a weakness for gadgets, from my old man. He named me Thomas Alva Edison Hill in hopes that I would emulate his idol. I disappointed him—I didn't invent the atom bomb, but I do sometimes try to repair my own typewriter.

Jack flipped a switch and picked up the hand mike. His voice came out of the juke box: "We now present the Magic Mirror." Then the turntable picked up with *Hymn to the Sun* from *Coq d'Or*, and he started turning the rheostat slowly.

The lights went down in the joint and came up slowly in the Magic Mirror. The "Mirror" was actually a sheet of glass about ten feet wide and eight high which shut off a little balcony stage. When the house lights were on bright and the stage was dark, you could not see through the glass at all; it looked like a mirror. As the house lights went out and the stage lights came on, you could see through the glass and a picture slowly built up in the "Mirror."

Jack had a single bright light under the bar which lighted him and the controls and which did not go out

with the house lights. Because of my position at the
end of the bar it hit me square in the eye. I had to block
it with my hand to see the stage.

It was something to see.

Two girls, a blonde and a brunette. A sort of altar or
table, with the blonde sprawled across it, volup'. The
brunette standing at the end of the altar, grabbing the
blonde by the hair with one hand while holding a
fancy dagger upraised with the other. There was a
backdrop in gold and dark blue—a sunburst in a
phony Aztec or Egyptian design, but nobody was looking at it; they were looking at the girls.

The brunette was wearing a high show-girl head
dress, silver sandals, and a G-string in glass jewels.
Nothing more. No sign of a brassiere. The blonde was
naked as an oyster, with her downstage knee drawn up
just enough to get past sufficiently broad-minded cen-
sors.

But I was not looking at the naked blonde; I was
looking at the brunette.

It was not just the two fine upstanding breasts nor
the long graceful legs nor the shape of her hips and
thighs; it was the overall effect. She was so beautiful it
hurt. I heard somebody say, "Great jumping jeepers!"
and was about to shush him when I realized it was me.

Then the lights went down and I remembered to
breathe.

I paid the clip price for my drink without a quiver
and Jack assured me: "They are hostesses between
shows." When they showed up at the stairway leading
down from the balcony he signalled them to come over
and then introduced me.

"Hazel Dorn, Estelle d'Arcy—meet Eddie Hill."

Hazel, the brunette, said, "How do you do?" but the
blonde said,

"Oh, I've met the Ghost before. How's business?
Rattled any chains lately?"

I said, "Good enough," and let it pass. I knew her all

right—but as Audrey Johnson, not as Estelle d'Arcy. She had been a steno at the City Hall when I was doing an autobiography of the Chief of Police. I had not liked her much; she had an instinct for finding a sore point and picking at it.

I am not ashamed of being a ghost writer, nor is it a secret. You will find my name on the title page of *Forty Years a Cop* as well as the name of the Chief—in small print but it is there: "with Edison Hill."

"How did you like the show?" Hazel asked, when I had ordered a round.

"I liked *you*," I said, softly enough to keep it private. "I can't wait for the next show to see more of you."

"You'll see more," she admitted and changed the subject. I gathered an impression that she was proud of her figure and liked to be told she was beautiful but was not entirely calloused about exhibiting it in public.

Estelle leaned across the bar to Jack. "Jackie Boy," she said in sweetly reasonable tones, "you held the lights too long again. It doesn't matter to me in that pose, but you had poor old Hazel trembling like a leaf before you doused the glim."

Jack set a three-minute egg timer, like a little hourglass on the bar. "Three minutes it says—three minutes you did."

"I don't think it was more than three minutes," Hazel objected. "I wasn't tired."

"You were trembling, dear. I saw you. You mustn't tire yourself—it makes lines. Anyhow," she added, "I'll just keep this," and she put the egg timer in her purse. "We'll time it ourselves."

"It was three minutes," Jack insisted.

"Never mind," she answered. "From now on it'll be three minutes, or mamma will have to lock Jackie in the dark closet."

Jack started to answer, thought better of it, then walked away to the other end of the bar. Estelle shrugged, then threw down the rest of her drink and left us. I saw her speak to Jack again, then join some customers at one of the tables.

Hazel looked at her as she walked away. "I'd paddle that chippie's pants," she muttered, "if she wore any."

"A bum beef?"

"Not exactly. Maybe Jack is a friend of yours—"

"Just an acquaintance."

"Well . . . I've had worse bosses—but he is a bit of a jerk. Maybe he doesn't stretch the poses just out of meanness—I've never timed him—but some of those poses are too long for three minutes. Take Estelle's Aphrodite pose—you saw it?"

"No."

"She balances on the ball of one foot, no costume at all, but with one leg raised enough to furnish a fig leaf. Jack's got a blackout switch to cover her if she breaks, but, just the same, it's a strain."

"To cover himself with the cops, you mean."

"Well, yes. Jack wants us to make it just as strong as the vice squad will stand for."

"You ought not to be in a dive like this. You ought to have a movie contract."

She laughed without mirth. "Eddie, did you ever try to get a movie contract? I've tried."

"Just the same—oh, well! But why are you sore at Estelle? What you told me doesn't seem to cover it."

"She— Skip it. She probably means well."

"You mean she shouldn't have dragged you into it?"

"Partly."

"What else?"

"Oh, nothing—look, do you think I need any wrinkle remover?" I examined her quite closely, until she actually blushed a little, then assured her that she did not.

"Thanks," she said. "Estelle evidently thinks so. She's been advising me to take care of myself lately and has been bringing me little presents of beauty preparations. I thank her for them and it appears to be sheer friendliness on her part . . . but it makes me squirm."

I nodded and changed the subject. I did not want to talk about Estelle; I wanted to talk about *her*—and me. I mentioned an agent I knew (my own) who could help her and that got her really interested, if not in me, at least in what I was saying.

Presently she glanced at the clock back of the bar and squealed. "I've got to peel for the customers. 'Bye now!" It was five minutes to twelve. I shifted from the end of the bar to the long side, just opposite Jack's Magic Mirror controls. I did not want that bright light of his interfering with me seeing Hazel.

It was just about twelve straight up when Jack came up from the rear of the joint, elbowed his other barman out of the way, and took his place near the controls. "Just about that time," he said to me. "Has she rung the buzzer?"

"Not a buzz."

"Okay, then." He cleared dirty glasses off the top of the bar while we waited, changed the platter on the turntable, and generally messed around. I kept my eyes on the mirror.

I heard the two *beeps*! sharp and clear. When he did not announce the show at once, I glanced around and saw that, while he had the mike in his hand, he was staring past it at the door, and looking considerably upset.

There were two cops just inside the door, Hannegan and Feinstein, both off the beat. I supposed he was afraid of a raid, which was silly. Pavement pounders don't pull raids. I knew what they were there for, even before Hannegan gave Jack a broad grin and waved him the okay sign—they had just slipped in for a free gander at the flesh under the excuse of watching the public morals.

"We now present the Magic Mirror," said Jack's

voice out of the juke box. Somebody climbed on the stool beside me and slipped a hand under my arm. I looked around. It was Hazel.

"You're not here; you're up there," I said foolishly.

"Huh-uh. Estelle said— I'll tell you after the show."

The lights were coming up in the Mirror and the juke box was cranking out *Valse Triste*. The altar was in this scene, too, and Estelle was sprawled over it much as she had been before. As it got lighter you could see a red stain down her side and the prop dagger. Hazel had told me what each of the acts were; this was the one called "The Altar Victim," scheduled for the one o'clock show.

I was disappointed not to be seeing Hazel, but I had to admit it was good—good theater, of the nasty sort, sadism and sex combined. The red stuff—catsup I guessed—trickling down her bare side and the handle of the prop dagger sticking up as if she had been stabbed through—the customers liked it. It was a natural follow-up to the "Sacrifice to the Sun".

Hazel screamed in my ear.

Her first scream was solo. The next thing I can recall it seemed as if every woman in the place was screaming—soprano, alto, and some tenor, but mostly screeching soprano. Through it came the bull voice of Hannegan. "Keep your seats, folks! Somebody turn on the lights!"

I grabbed Hazel by the shoulders and shook her. "What's the matter? What's up?"

She looked dazed, then pointed at the Mirror. "She's dead . . . she's dead . . . she's dead!" she chanted. She scrambled down from the stool and took out for the back of the house. I started after her. The house lights came on abruptly, leaving the Mirror lights still on.

We finished one, two, three, up the stairway, through a little dressing room, and onto the stage. I almost caught up with Hazel, and Feinstein was close on my heels.

We stood there, jammed in the door, blinking at the flood lights, and not liking what we saw under them. She was dead all right. The dagger, which should have been faked between her arm and her breast with catsup spilled around to maintain the illusion—this prop dagger, this slender steel blade, was three inches closer to her breastbone than it should have been. It had been stabbed straight into her heart.

On the floor at the side of the altar away from the audience, close enough to Estelle to reach it, was the egg timer. As I looked at it the last of the sand ran out.

I caught Hazel as she fell—she was a big armful—and spread her on the couch. "Eddie," said Feinstein, "call the Station for me. Tell Hannegan not to let anyone out. I'm staying here." I called the station but did not have to tell Hannegan anything. He had them all seated again and was jollying them along. Jack was still standing back of the bar, shock on his face, and the bright light at the control board making him look like a death's head.

By twelve-fifteen Spade Jones, Lieutenant Jones of Homicide, showed up and from there on things slipped into a smooth routine. He knew me well, having helped me work up some of the book I did for the Chief, and he grabbed onto me at once for some of the background. By twelve-thirty he was reasonably sure that none of the customers could have done it. "I won't say one of them *didn't* do it, Eddie my boy—anybody could have done it who knew the exact second to slip upstairs, grab the knife, and slide it into her ribs. But the chances are against any of them knowing just when and how to do it."

"Anybody inside or outside," I corrected.

"So?"

"There's a fire exit at the foot of the stairs."

"You think I haven't noticed that?" He turned away and gave Hannegan instructions to let anybody go who could give satisfactory identification with a local address. The others would have to go downtown to have closer ties as material witnesses put on them by the night court. Perhaps some would land in the tank for further investigation, but in any case—clear 'em out!

The photographers were busy upstairs and so were the fingerprint boys. The Assistant Medical Examiner showed up, followed by reporters. A few minutes later, after the house was cleared, Hazel came downstairs and joined me. Neither of us said anything, but I patted her on the back. When they carried down the basket stretcher a little later, with a blanket-wrapped shape in it, I put my arm around her while she buried her eyes in my shoulders.

Spade talked to us one at a time. Jack was not talking. "It ain't smart to talk without a lawyer," was all Spade could get out of him. I thought to myself that it would be better to talk to Spade now than to be sweated and maybe massaged a little under the lights. My testimony would clear him even though it would show that there was a spat between him and Estelle. Spade would not frame a man. He was an honest cop, as cops go. I've known honest cops. Two, I think.

Spade took my story, then he took Hazel's, and called me back. "Eddie my boy," he said, "help me dig into this thing. As I understand it, this girl Hazel should have had the twelve o'clock show."

"That's right."

He studied one of the Joy Club's programs. "Hazel says she went upstairs to undress for the show about eleven-fifty-five."

"Exactly that time."

"Yeah. She was with you, wasn't she? She says she went up and that Estelle followed her in with a song-and-dance that the boss said to swap the two shows around."

"I wouldn't know about that."

"Naturally not. She says she beefed a little but gave in and came on downstairs, where she joined you. Correct?"

"Correct."

"Mmmm . . . By the way, your remark about the fire door might lead to something. Hazel put me onto a boy friend for Estelle. Trumpeter in that rat race across the street. He could have ducked across and stabbed her. Wouldn't take long. Trumpet players can't be pushing wind all the time; they'd lose their lip."

"How would he know when to do it? It was supposed to be Hazel's show."

"Mmmm . . . Well, maybe he did know. Swapping shows sounds like Estelle had made a date, and that sounds like a man. In which case he'd know about it. One of the boys is looking into it. Now about the way these shows worked—do you suppose you could show me how they were staged? Hannegan tried it but all he got was a shock."

"I'll try it," I said, getting up. "It's nothing very fancy. Did you ask Jack about Hazel's statement that Estelle had permission from him to swap the shows?"

"That's the one thing he cracked on. He states flatly that he didn't know that the shows were swapped. He says he expected to see Hazel in the Mirror."

The controls looked complicated but weren't. I showed Jones the rheostat and told him it enabled Jack to turn either set of lights down slowly while the other set went up. I found a bypass switch back of the rheostat which accounted for the present condition— all lights burning brightly, house and stage. There was a blackout switch and there was a switch that cut the hand microphone and the turntable in through the juke box. Near the latter was the buzzer—a small black case with two binding posts—which the girls used to signal Jack. Centered on the under side of the bar was a hundred-and-fifty watt bulb hooked in on its own line separate from the rheostat. Except for the line to this light all the wires from all the equipment disappeared into a steel conduit underneath the bar. It was this light which had dazzled me during the eleven o'clock show. It seemed excessive; a peanut bulb would have been more appropriate. Apparently Jack liked lots of light.

I explained the controls to Spade, then gave him a dry run. First I switched the rheostat back to "House" and threw off the bypass switch, leaving the room brightly lighted and the Magic Mirror dark. "The time is five minutes of twelve. Hazel leaves me to go upstairs. I shift around to the bar stool just opposite where I am now standing. At midnight Jack comes up and asks me if I've heard the buzzer. I say 'No.' He fiddles around a bit, clearing away glasses and the like. Then come two beeps on the buzzer. He picks up the microphone but he doesn't announce the show for a few seconds—he's just noticed Hannegan and Feinstein. Hannegan gives him the high sign and he goes ahead." Then I picked up the mike myself and spoke into it:

"We now present the Magic Mirror!"

I put down the mike and flipped on the turntable switch. The same platter was on and the juke box started playing *Valse Triste.* Hazel looked up at me sharply, from where she had been resting her head on her arms a few tables away. She looked horrified, as if the reconstruction were too much for her stomach.

I turned the rheostat slowly from "House" to "Stage." The room darkened and the stage lit up. "That's all there was to it," I said. "Hazel sat down beside me just as Jack announced the show. As the lights came on she screamed."

Spade scratched his chin. "You say Joy was standing in front of you when the buzzer signal came from upstairs?"

"Positive."

"You gave him a motive—the war he was having with Estelle. But you've given him an alibi too."

"That's right. Either Estelle punched that buzzer herself, then lay down and stabbed herself, or she was murdered and the murderer punched it to cover up, then ducked out while everybody had their eyes on the Mirror. Either way I had Jack Joy in sight."

"It's an alibi all right," he conceded. "Unless you were in cahoots with him," he said hopefully.

"Prove it," I answered, grinning. "Not with him. I think he's a jerk."

"We're all jerks, more or less, Eddie my boy. Let's look around upstairs."

I switched the bypass on, leaving both stage and house lighted, and followed him. I pointed out the buzzer to him, after searching for it myself. A conduit came up through the floor and ended in a junction box on the wall, from which cords ran to the flood lights. The button was on the junction box. I wondered why it was not on the "altar," then saw that the altar was a movable prop. Apparently the girls punched the button, then fell quickly into their poses. Spade tried the button meditatively, then wiped print powder off on his trousers. "I can't hear it," he said.

"Naturally not. This stage is almost a soundproof booth."

He had seen the egg timer but I had not told him until then about seeing the last of the sand run out. He pursed his lips. "You're sure?"

"Call it hallucination. *I* think I saw it. I'll testify to it."

He sat down on the altar, avoiding the blood stain, and said nothing for quite a long time. Finally he said, "Eddie my boy—"

"Yes?"

"You've not only given Jack Joy an alibi, you've damn' near made it impossible for anyone to have done it."

"I know it. Could it have been suicide?"

"Could be. Could be. From the mechanics angle but not from the psychological angle. Would she have started that egg timer for her own suicide? Another thing. Take a look at that blood. Taste it."

"Huh?"

"Don't throw up. Smell it then."

I did, very gingerly. Then I smelled it again. Two smells. Tomato. Blood. Blood and tomato catsup. I thought I could detect differences in appearance as well. "You see, son? If she's going to have blood on her chest she won't bother with catsup. Aside from that and the timer it's a perfect, dramatic, female-style suicide. But it won't wash. It's murder, Eddie."

Feinstein stuck his head in. "Lieutenant—"

"What is it?"

"That musician punk. He had a date with her all right."

"Oh, he did, eh?"

"But he's clear. The band was on the air at midnight, in a number that features him in a trumpet solo."

"Damn! Get out of here."

"That ain't all. I called the Assistant Medical Examiner, like you said. The motive you suggested won't go—she not only wasn't expecting; she hadn't ever been had. *Virgo intacta*," he added in passable high school Latin.

"Feinstein, you'll be wanting to be a sergeant next," Spade answered placidly, "using big words like that. Get out."

"Okay, Lieutenant." I was more than a little surprised at the news. I would have picked Estelle as a case of round heels. Evidently she was a tease in more ways than one.

Spade sat a while longer, then said, "When it's light in here, it's dark out there; when it's light out there, it's dark in here."

"That's right. Ordinarily, that is. Right now we've got both sides lighted with the bypass."

"Ordinarily is what I mean. Light, dark; dark, light. Eddie my boy—"

"Yes?"

"Are you sweet on that Hazel girl?"

"I'm leaning that way," I admitted.

"Then keep an eye on her. The murderer was in here

for just a few seconds—the egg timer and the buzzer prove that. He wasn't any of the few people who knew about the swap in the shows—not since the trumpet-playing boy friend got knocked out of the running. And it was dark. He murdered the wrong party, Eddie my boy. There's another murder coming up.''

"Hazel," I said slowly.

"Yes, Hazel."

Spade Jones shooed us all home, me, Hazel, the two waiters, the other barman, and Jack Joy. I think he was tempted to hold Jack simply because he wouldn't talk but he compromised by telling him that if he stuck his head outside his hotel, he would find a nice police-man ready to take him down to a nice cell. He tipped me a wink and put a finger on his lips as he said good night to me.

But I didn't keep quiet. Hazel let me take her home readily enough. When I saw that she lived alone in a single apartment in a building without a doorman, I decided it called for an all night vigil and some ex-plaining.

She stepped into the kitchenette and mixed me a drink. "One drink and out you go, Ed," she called to me. "You've been very sweet and I want to see you again and thank you, but tonight this girl goes to bed. I'm whipped."

"I'm staying all night," I announced firmly.

She came out with a drink in her hand and looked at me, both annoyed and a little puzzled. "Ed," she said, "aren't you working just a bit too fast? I didn't think you were that clumsy."

"Calm yourself, beautiful," I told her. "It's not nec-essarily a proposition. I'm going to watch over you. Somebody is trying to kill you."

She dropped the drink.

I helped her clean it up and explained the situation. "Somebody stabbed a girl in a dark room," I finished. "That somebody thought it was you. He knows better by now and he will be looking for a chance to finish the job. What you and I have got to figure out is: *Who wants to kill you*?"

She sat down and started to manhandle a handkerchief. "Nobody wants to kill me, Eddie. It was Estelle."

"No, it wasn't."

"But it couldn't have been me. I *know*."

"What do you know?"

"I— Oh, it's impossible. Stay all night if you want to. You can sleep on the couch." She got up and pulled the bed down out of the wall, went in the bath, closed the door, and splashed around for a while. "That bath is too small to dress and undress in," she stated flatly. "Anyhow I sleep raw. If you want to get undressed you won't scare me."

"Thanks," I said. "I'll take my coat and tie and shoes off."

"Suit yourself." Her voice was a little bit smothered as she was already wiggling her dress over her head.

She wore pants, whether Estelle ever did or not—a plain, white knit that looked clean and neat. She did not wear a brassiere and did not need to. The conception I had gotten of her figure in the Magic Mirror was entirely justified. She was simply the most magnificently beautiful thing I had ever seen in my life. In street clothes she was a beautiful, well-built woman; in her skin—wars have started over less.

I was beginning to doubt my ability to stay on the couch. I must have showed it, for she snorted, "Wipe the drool off your chin!" and stepped out of her pants.

" 'Scuse, please," I answered and started unlacing my shoes. She stepped over and switched off the light, then went over to the one big window and raised the shade. It was closed but, with the light out, you could see outside easily. "Stand back from that window," I said. "You're too good a target."

"Huh? Oh, very well." She backed up a few steps but

continued to stare thoughtfully out the window. I stared thoughtfully at her. There was a big neon sign across the street and the colored lights, pouring in the window, covered her from head to foot with a rosy liquid glow. She looked like something out of a dream of fairyland.

Presently I wasn't thinking how she looked; I was thinking about another room, where a girl had lain murdered, with the lights of a night club shining through a pane of glass, shining through like this neon.

My thoughts rearranged themselves rapidly and very painfully. I added them up a second time and still got the same answer. I did not like the answer. I was glad, damn glad, she was bare naked, with no way to conceal a gun, or a knife, or any other sort of deadly weapon. "Hazel," I said softly.

She turned to me. "Yes, Eddie?"

"I've just had a new idea . . . why should anyone want to kill you?"

"You said that before. There isn't any reason."

"I know. You're right; there isn't any. But put it this way—*why should you want to kill Estelle?*"

I thought she was going to faint again, but I didn't care—I wanted to shock her. Her lusciousness meant nothing to me now but a trap that had confused my thoughts. I had not wanted to think her guilty, so I had disregarded the fact that of all the persons involved she was the only one with the necessary opportunity, the knowledge of the swapped shows, and at least some motive. She had made it plain that she detested Estelle. She had covered it up but it was still evident.

But most important of all, the little stage had not been dark! True, it *looked* dark—from the outside. You can't see through glass when all the light comes from one side and you are on that same side—but light passes through the glass just the same. The neon on the street illuminated this room we were in fairly brightly; the brilliant lights of Jack's bar illuminated the little stage even when the stage floodlights were out.

She knew that. She knew it because she had been in there many times, getting ready to pose for the suckers. Therefore she knew that it was not a case of mistaken identity in the dark—there was no dark! And it would have to be nearly pitch black for anyone to mistake Hazel's blue-black mane for Estelle's peroxided mop.

She knew—why hadn't she said so? She was letting me stay all night, not wanting me around but risking her reputation and more, because I had propounded the wrong-girl-in-the-dark theory. She knew it would not hold water; why had she not said so?

"Eddie, have you gone crazy?" Her voice was frightened.

"No—gone sane. I'll tell you how you did it, my beautiful darling. You both were there—you admitted that. Estelle got in her pose, and asked you to punch the buzzer. You did—but first you grabbed the knife and slid it in her ribs. You wiped the handle, looked around, punched the buzzer, and lammed. About ten seconds later you were slipping your arm in mine. Me—your alibi!"

"It *had* to be you," I went on, "for no one else would have had the guts to commit murder with nothing but glass between him and an audience. The stage was lighted—from the outside. You knew that, but it didn't worry you. You were used to parading around naked in front of that glass, certain you could not be seen while the house lights were on! No one else would have dared!"

She looked at me as if she could not believe her ears and her chin began to quiver. Then she squatted down on the floor and burst into tears. Real tears—they dripped. It was my cue to go soft, but I did not. I don't like killing.

I stood over her. "Why did you kill her? *Why did you kill her?*"

"Get out of here."

"Not likely. I'm going to see you fry, my big-busted angel." I headed for the telephone, keeping my eyes on her. I did not dare turn my back, even naked as she was.

She made a break, but it was not for me; it was for the door. How far she thought she could get in the buff I don't know.

I tripped her and fell on her. She was a big armful and ready to bite and claw, but I got a hammer lock on one arm and twisted it. "Be good," I warned her, "or I'll break it."

She lay still and I began to be aware that she was not only an armful but a very female armful. I ignored it. "Let me go, Eddie," she said in a tense whisper, "or I'll scream rape and get the cops in."

"Go right ahead, gorgeous," I told her. "The cops are just what I want, and quick."

"Eddie, Eddie, listen to reason—I didn't kill her, but *I know who did*."

"Huh? Who?"

"I know . . . I do know—but he *couldn't* have. That's why I haven't said anything."

"Tell me."

She didn't answer at once; I twisted her arm. "Tell me!"

"*Oh!* It was Jack."

"Jack? Nonsense—I was watching him."

"I know. But he did it, just the same. I don't know how—but he did it."

I held her down, thinking. She watched my face. "Ed?"

"Huh?"

"If I punched the buzzer, wouldn't my fingerprint be on it?"

"Should be."

"Why don't you find out?"

It stonkered me. I thought I was right but she seemed quite willing to make the test. "Get up," I said. "On your knees and then on your feet. But don't try to get your arm free and don't try any tricks, or, so help me, I'll kick you in the belly."

She was docile enough and I moved us over to the phone, dialled it with one hand and managed to get to Spade Jones through the police exchange. "Spade? This is Eddie—Eddie Hill. Was there a fingerprint on the buzzer button?"

"Now I wondered when you would be getting around to thinking of that. There was."

"Whose?"

"The corpse's."

"Estelle's?"

"The same. And Estelle's on the egg timer. None on the knife—wiped clean. Lots from both girls around the room, and a few odd ones—old, probably."

"Uh . . . yes . . . . well, thanks."

"Not at all. Call me if you get any bright ideas, son."

I hung up the phone and turned to Hazel. I guess I had let go her arm when Spade told me the print was not hers, but I don't remember doing so. She was standing there, rubbing her arm and looking at me in a very odd way. "Well," I said, "you can twist my arm, or kick me anywhere you like. I was wrong. I'm sorry. I'll try to prove it to you."

She started to speak and then started to leak tears again. It finished up with her accepting my apology in the nicest way possible, smearing me with lipstick and tears. I loved it and I felt like a heel.

Presently I wiped her face with my handkerchief and said, "You put on a robe or something and sit on the bed and I'll sit on the couch. We've got to dope this out and I can think better with that lovely chassis of yours covered up."

She trotted obediently and I sat down. "You say

Jack killed her, but you admit you don't know how he could have done it. Then why do you think he did?"

"The music."

"Huh?"

"The music he played for the show was *Valse Triste*. That's Estelle's music, for Estelle's act. My act, the regular twelve o'clock act, calls for *Bolero*. He must have known that Estelle was up there; he used the right music."

"Then you figure he must have been lying when he claimed Estelle never arranged with him to swap the shows. But it's a slim reason to hang a man—he might have gotten that record by accident."

"Could, but not likely. The records were kept in order and were the same ones for the same shows every night. Nobody touched them but him. He would fire a man for touching anything around the control box. However," she went on, "I knew it had to be him before I noticed the music. Only it couldn't be."

"Only it couldn't be. Go ahead."

"He hated her."

"Why?"

"She teased him."

" 'She teased him.' Suppose she did. Lots of people get teased. She teased lots of people. She teased you. She teased me. So what?"

"It's not the same thing," she insisted. "Jack was afraid of the dark."

It was a nasty story. The lunk was afraid of total darkness, really afraid, the way some kids are. Hazel told me he would not go back of the building to get his parked car at night without a flashlight. But that would not have given away his weakness, nor the fact that he was ashamed of it—lots of people use flashlights freely, just to be sure of their footing. But he had fallen for Estelle and apparently made a lot of progress—had actually gotten into bed with her. It never came to anything because she had snapped out the

lights. Estelle had told Hazel about it, gloating over
the fact that she had found out about what she termed
his cowardice "soon enough."

"She needled him after that," Hazel went on.
"Nothing that anyone could tumble to, if they didn't
know. But *he* knew. He was afraid of her, afraid to fire
her for fear she would tell. He hated her—at the same
time he wanted her and was jealous of her. There was
one time in the dressing room. I was there—" He had
come in while they were dressing, or undressing, and
had picked a fight with Estelle over one of the customers. She told him to get out. When he did not do it,
she snapped out the light. "He went out of there like a
jack rabbit, falling over his feet." She stopped. "How
about it, Eddie? Motive enough?"

"Motive enough," I agreed. "You've got me thinking
he did it. Only he couldn't."

" 'Only he couldn't.' That's the trouble."

I told her to get into bed and try to get some sleep—
that I planned to sit right where I was till the pieces
fitted. I was rewarded with another sight of the con-
tours as she chucked the robe, then I helped myself to
a good-night kiss. I don't think she slept; at least she
did not snore.

I started pounding my brain. The fact that the stage
was not dark when it *seemed* dark changed the whole
picture and eliminated, I thought, everyone not familiar with the mechanics of the Mirror. It left only Hazel,
Jack, the other barman, the two waiters—and Estelle
herself. It was physically possible for an Unknown
Stranger to have slipped upstairs, slid the shiv in her,
ducked downstairs, but psychologically—no. I made a
mental note to find out what other models had worked
in the Mirror.

The other barman and the two waiters Spade had
eliminated—all of them had been fully alibied by one
or more customers. *I* had alibied Jack. Estelle—but it
wasn't suicide. And Hazel.

If Estelle's fingerprint meant what it seemed; Hazel

was out—not time enough to commit a murder, arrange a corpse, wipe a handle, and get downstairs to my side before Jack started the show.

But in that case nobody could have done it—except a hypothetical sex maniac who did not mind a spot of butchery in front of a window full of people. Nonsense!

Of course the fingerprint was not conclusive. Hazel *could* have pushed the button with a coin or a bobby pin, without destroying an old print or making a new one. I hated to admit it but she was not clear yet.

Again, if Estelle did not push the button, then it looked still more like an insider; an outsider would not know where to find the button nor have any reason to push it.

For that matter, why should Hazel push it? It had not given her an alibi—it didn't make sense.

Round and round and round till my head ached.

It was a long time later that I went over and tugged at the covers. "Hazel—"

"Yes, Eddie?"

"Who punched the buzzer in the *eleven* o'clock show?"

She considered. "That show is both of us. She did—she always took charge."

"Mmmm. . . . What other girls have worked in the Mirror?"

"Why, none. Estelle and I opened the show."

"Okay. Maybe I've got it. Let's call Spade Jones."

Spade assured me he would be only too happy to get out of a warm bed to play games with me and would I like a job waking the bugler, too? But he agreed to come to the Joy Club, with Joy in tow, and to fetch enough flat feet, fire arms, and muscles to cope.

I was standing back of the bar in the Joy Club, with Hazel seated where she had been when she screamed and a cop from the Homicide Squad in my seat. Jack and Spade were at the end of the bar, where Spade could see.

"We will now show how a man can be two places at

one time," I announced. "I am now Mr. Jack Joy. The time is shortly before midnight. Hazel has just left the dressing room and come downstairs. She stops off for a moment at the little girls room at the foot of the stairs, and thereby misses Jack, who is headed for those same stairs. He goes up and finds Estelle in the dressing room, peeled and ready for her act—probably."

I took a glance at Jack. His face was a taut mask, but he was a long way from breaking. "There was an argument—what about, I don't know, but it might have been over the trumpet boy she had swapped shows to meet. In any case, I am willing to bet that she stopped it by switching out the dressing room light to chase him out."

First blood. He flinched at that—his mask cracked. "He didn't stay out more than a few moments," I went on. "Probably he had a flashlight in his pocket—he's probably got one on him now—and that let him go back into that terrible, dark room, and switch on the light. Estelle was already on the stage, anointing herself with catsup, and almost ready to push the buzzer. She must have been about to do so, for she had started the egg timer. He grabbed the prop dagger and stabbed her, stabbed her dead."

I stopped. No blood from Jack this time. His mask was on firmly. "He arranges her in the pose—ten seconds for that; it was nothing but a sprawl—wipes the handle and ducks out. Ten seconds more to this spot. Or make it twenty. He asks me if the buzzer has sounded and I tell him No. He really had to know, for Estelle might have punched it before he got to her."

"Hearing the answer he wanted, he bustles around a bit like this—" I monkeyed with some glassware and picked up a bar spoon and pointed with it to the stage. "Note that the Mirror is lighted and empty—I've got the bypass on. Imagine it dark, with Estelle on the altar, a knife in her heart." I dropped the spoon down and, while their eyes were still on the Mirror, I brought metal spoon across the two binding posts which carried the two leads to the push button on the stage. The buzzer gave out with a loud *beep*! I broke the connection by lifting the spoon for a split second, and brought it down again for a second *beep*! "And that is how a man can—*Catch him, Spade!*"

Spade was at him before I yelled. The three cops had him helpless in no time. He was not armed; it had been sheer reflex—a break for freedom. But he was not giving up, even now. "You've got nothing on me. No evidence. Anybody could have jimmied those wires anywhere along the line."

"No, Jack," I contradicted. "I checked for that. Those wires run through the same steel conduit as the power wires, all the way from the control box to the stage. It was here or there, Jack. It couldn't be there; it had to be here."

He shut up. "I want to see my lawyer," was his only answer.

"You'll see your lawyer," Spade assured him jovially. "Tomorrow, or the next day. Right now you're going to go downtown and sit under some nice hot lights for a few hours."

"No, Lieutenant!" It was Hazel.

"Eh? And why not, Miss Dorn?"

"Don't put him under lights. Shut him in a dark closet!"

"Eh? Well, I'll be— That's what I call a bright girl!"

It was the mop closet they used. He lasted thirteen minutes, then he started to whimper and then to scream. They let him out and took his confession.

I was almost sorry for him when they led him away. I should not have been—second degree was the most he could get as premeditation was impossible to prove and quite unlikely anyhow. "Not guilty by reason of insanity" was a fair bet. Whatever his guilt, that woman had certainly driven him to it. And imagine the nerve of the man, the pure colossal nerve, that enabled him to go through with lighting up that stage just after he looked up and saw two cops standing inside the door!

I took Hazel home the second time. The bed was still pulled down and she went straight for it, kicking off her shoes as she went. She unzipped the side of her dress and started to pull it over her head, when she stopped. "Eddie!"

"Yes, Beautiful?"

"If I take off my clothes again, are you going to accuse me of another murder?"

I considered this. "That depends," I informed her, "on whether you are really interested in me, or in that agent I was telling you about."

She grinned at me, then scooped up a shoe and threw it. "In you, you lug!" Then she went on shucking off her clothes. After a bit I unlaced my shoes.

FOREWORD

My next attempt to branch out was my first book: *ROCKET SHIP GALILEO*. I attempted book publication earlier than I had intended to because a boys' book was solicited from me by a major publisher. I was unsure of myself—but two highly respected friends, Cleve Cartmill and Fritz Lang, urged me to try it. So I did . . . and the publisher who had asked for it rejected it. A trip to the Moon? Preposterous! He suggested that I submit another book-length MS without that silly space-travel angle.

Instead I sold it to Scribner's and thereby started a sequence: one boys' book each year timed for the Christmas trade. This lasted twelve years and was a very strange relationship, as my editor disliked science fiction, disliked me (a sentiment I learned to reciprocate), and kept me on for the sole reason that my books sold so well that they kept her department out of the red—her words. Eventually she bounced one with the suggestion that I shelve it for a year and then rewrite it.

But by bouncing it she broke the chain of options. Instead of shelving it, I took it across the street. . . and won a Hugo with it.

ROCKET SHIP GALILEO was a fumbling first attempt; I have never been satisfied with it. But it has never been out of print, has appeared in fourteen languages, and has earned a preposterous amount in book royalties alone; I should not kick. Nevertheless I cringe whenever I consider its shortcomings.

My next fiction (here following) was *FREE MEN*. Offhand it appears to be a routine post-Holocaust story, and the details—idioms, place names, etc.—justify that assumption. In fact it is *any* conquered nation in *any* century—

FREE MEN

"That makes three provisional presidents so far,"
the Leader said. "I wonder how many more there
are?" He handed the flimsy sheet back to the runner,
who placed it in his mouth and chewed it up like gum.

The third man shrugged. "No telling. What worries
me—" A mockingbird interrupted. "Doity, doity, doity," he sang. "Terloo, terloo, terloo, purty-purty-
purty-purty."

The clearing was suddenly empty.

"As I was saying," came the voice of the third man
in a whisper in the Leader's ear, "it ain't how many
worries me, but how you tell a de Gaulle from a Laval.
See anything?"

"Convoy. Stopped below us." The Leader peered
through bushes and down the side of a bluff. The high
ground pushed out toward the river here, squeezing
the river road between it and the water. The road
stretched away to the left, where the valley widened
out into farmland, and ran into the outskirts of Barclay ten miles away.

The convoy was directly below them, eight trucks
preceded and followed by halftracks. The following
halftrack was backing, vortex gun cast loose and ready
for trouble. Its commander apparently wanted elbow
room against a possible trap.

At the second truck helmeted figures gathered

around its rear end, which was jacked up. As the Leader watched he saw one wheel removed.

"Trouble?"

"I think not. Just a breakdown. They'll be gone soon." He wondered what was in the trucks. Food, probably. His mouth watered. A few weeks ago an opportunity like this would have meant generous rations for all, but the conquerors had smartened up.

He put useless thoughts away. "It's not that that worries me, Dad," he added, returning to the subject. "We'll be able to tell quislings from loyal Americans. But how do you tell men from boys?"

"Thinking of Joe Benz?"

"Maybe. I'd give a lot to know how far we can trust Joe. But I could have been thinking of young Morrie."

"You can trust him."

"Certainly. At thirteen he doesn't drink—and he wouldn't crack if they burned his feet off. Same with Cathleen. It's not age or sex—but how can you tell? And you've *got* to be able to tell."

There was a flurry below. Guards had slipped down from the trucks and withdrawn from the road when the convoy had stopped, in accordance with an orderly plan for such emergencies. Now two of them returned to the convoy, hustling between them a figure not in uniform.

The mockingbird set up a frenetic whistling.

"It's the messenger," said the Leader. "The dumb fool! Why didn't he lie quiet? Tell Ted we've seen it."

Dad pursed his lips and whistled: "Keewah, keewah, keewah, terloo."

The other "mockingbird" answered, "Terloo," and shut up.

"We'll need a new post office now," said the Leader. "Take care of it, Dad."

"Okay."

"There's no real answer to the problem," the Leader said. "You can limit size of units, so that one person can't give away too many—but take a colony like ours.

It needs to be a dozen or more to work. That means they all have to be dependable, or they all go down together. So each one has a loaded gun at the head of each other one."

Dad grinned, wryly. "Sounds like the United Nations before the Blow Off. Cheer up, Ed. Don't burn your bridges before you cross them."

"I won't. The convoy is ready to roll."

When the convoy had disappeared in the distance, Ed Morgan, the Leader, and his deputy Dad Carter stood up and stretched. The "mockingbird" had announced safety loudly and cheerfully. "Tell Ted to cover us into camp," Morgan ordered.

Dad wheepled and chirruped and received acknowledgement. They started back into the hills. Their route was roundabout and included check points from which they could study their back track and receive reports from Ted. Morgan was not worried about Ted being followed—he was confident that Ted could steal baby 'possums from mama's pouch. But the convoy breakdown might have been a trap—there was no way to tell that all of the soldiers had got back into the trucks. The messenger might have been followed; certainly he had been trapped too easily.

Morgan wondered how much the messenger would spill. He could not spill much about Morgan's own people, for the "post office" rendezvous was all that he knew about them.

The base of Morgan's group was neither better nor worse than average of the several thousand other camps of recalcitrant guerrillas throughout the area that once called itself the United States. The Twenty Minute War had not surprised everyone. The mushrooms which had blossomed over Washington, Detroit, and a score of other places had been shocking but expected—by some.

Morgan had made no grand preparations. He had simply conceived it as a good period in which to stay footloose and not too close to a target area. He had taken squatter's rights in an abandoned mine and had stocked it with tools, food, and other useful items. He had had the simple intention to survive; it was during the weeks after Final Sunday that he discovered that there was no way for a man with foresight to avoid becoming a leader.

Morgan and Dad Carter entered the mine by a new shaft and tunnel which appeared on no map, by a dry rock route which was intended to puzzle even a blood-hound. They crawled through the tunnel, were able to raise their heads when they reached the armory, and stepped out into the common room of the colony, the largest chamber, ten by thirty feet and as high as it was wide.

Their advent surprised no one, else they might not have lived to enter. A microphone concealed in the tunnel had conveyed their shibboleths before them. The room was unoccupied save for a young woman stirring something over a tiny, hooded fire and a girl who sat at a typewriter table mounted in front of a radio. She was wearing earphones and shoved one back and turned to face them as they came in.

"Howdy, Boss!"

"Hi, Margie. What's the good word?" Then to the other, "What's for lunch?"

"Bark soup and a notch in your belt."

"Cathleen, you depress me."

"Well . . . mushrooms fried in rabbit fat, but darn few of them."

"That's better."

"You better tell your boys to be more careful what they bring in. One more rabbit with tularemia and we won't have to worry about what to eat."

"Hard to avoid, Cathy. You must be sure you handle them the way Doc taught you." He turned to the girl. "Jerry in the upper tunnel?"

"Yes."

"Get him down here, will you?"

"Yes, sir." She pulled a sheet out of her typewriter and handed it to him, along with others, then left the room.

Morgan glanced over them. The enemy had abolished soap opera and singing commercials but he could not say that radio had been improved. There was an unnewsy sameness to the propaganda which now came over the air. He checked through while wishing for just one old-fashioned, uncensored newscast.

"Here's an item!" he said suddenly. "Get this, Dad—"

"Read it to me, Ed." Dad's spectacles had been broken on Final Sunday. He could bring down a deer, or a man, at a thousand yards—but he might never read again.

" 'New Center, 28 April—It is with deep regret that Continental Coordinating Authority for World Unification, North American District, announces that the former city of St. Joseph, Missouri, has been subjected to sanitary measures. It is ordered that a memorial plaque setting forth the circumstances be erected on the former site of St. Joseph as soon as radioactivity permits. Despite repeated warnings the former inhabitants of this lamented city encouraged and succored marauding bands of outlaws skulking around the outskirts of their community. It is hoped that the sad fate of St. Joseph will encourage the native authorities of all North American communities to take all necessary steps to suppress treasonable intercourse with the few remaining lawless elements in our continental society.' "

Dad cocked a brow at Morgan. "How many does that make since they took over?"

"Let's see . . . Salinas . . . Colorado Springs . . . uh, six, including St. Joe."

"Son, there weren't more than sixty million Americans left after Final Sunday. If they keep up, we'll be kind of thinned out in a few years."

"I know." Morgan looked troubled. "We've got to work out ways to operate without calling attention to the towns. Too many hostages."

A short, dark man dressed in dirty dungarees entered from a side tunnel, followed by Margie. "You wanted me, boss?"

"Yes, Jerry. I want to get word to McCracken to come in for a meeting. Two hours from now, if he can get here."

"Boss, you're using radio too much. You'll get him shot and us, too."

"I thought that business of bouncing it off the cliff face was foolproof?"

"Well . . . a dodge I can work up, somebody else can figure out. Besides, I've got the chassis unshipped. I was working on it."

"How long to rig it?"

"Oh, half an hour—twenty minutes."

"Do it. This may be the last time we'll use radio, except as utter last resort."

"Okay, boss."

The meeting was in the common room. Morgan called it to order once all were present or accounted for. McCracken arrived just as he had decided to proceed without him. McCracken had a pass for the countryside, being a veterinarian, and held proxy for the colony's underground associates in Barclay.

"The Barclay Free Company, a provisional unit of the United States of America, is now in session." Morgan announced formally. "Does any member have any item to lay before the Company?"

He looked around; there was no response. "How about you?" he challenged Joe Benz. "I heard that you had some things you thought the Company ought to hear."

Benz started to speak, shook his head. "I'll wait."

"Don't wait too long," Morgan said mildly. "Well, I have two points to bring up for discussion—"

"Three," corrected Dr. McCracken. "I'm glad you sent for me." He stepped up to Morgan and handed him a large, much folded piece of paper. Morgan looked it over, refolded it, and put it in his pocket.

"It fits in," he said to McCracken. "What do the folks in town say?"

"They are waiting to hear from you. They'll back you up—so far, anyway."

"All right." Morgan turned back to the group. "First item—we got a message today, passed by hand and about three weeks old, setting up another provisional government. The courier was grabbed right under our noses. Maybe he was a stooge; maybe he was careless—that's neither here nor there at the moment. The message was that the Honorable Albert M. Brockman proclaimed himself provisional President of these United States, under derived authority, and appointed Brigadier General Dewey Fenton commander of armed forces including irregular militia—meaning us—and called on all citizens to unite to throw the Invader out. All formal and proper. So what do we do about it?"

"And who the devil is the Honorable Albert M. Brockman?" asked someone in the rear.

"I've been trying to remember. The message listed government jobs he's held, including some assistant secretary job—I suppose that's the 'derived authority' angle. But I can't place him."

"I recall him," Dr. McCracken said suddenly. "I met him when I was in the Bureau of Animal Husbandry. A career civil servant . . . and a stuffed shirt."

There was a gloomy silence. Ted spoke up. "Then why bother with him?"

The Leader shook his head. "It's not that simple, Ted. We can't assume that he's no good. Napoleon might have been a minor clerk under different circumstances. And the Honorable Mr. Brockman may be a revolutionary genius disguised as a bureaucrat. But that's not the point. We need nationwide unification more than anything. It doesn't matter right now who the titular leader is. The theory of derived authority may be shaky but it may be the only way to get everybody to accept one leadership. Little bands like ours can never win back the country. We've got to have unity—and that's why we can't ignore Brockman."

"The thing that burns me," McCracken said savagely, "is that it need never have happened at all! It could have been prevented."

"No use getting in a sweat about it," Morgan told him. "It's easy to see the government's mistakes now, but just the same I think there was an honest effort to prevent war right up to the last. It takes all nations to keep the peace, but it only takes one to start a war."

"No, no, no—I don't mean that, Captain," McCracken answered. "I don't mean the War could have been prevented. I suppose it could have been—once. But everybody knew that another war could happen, and everybody—*everybody*, I say, knew that if it came, it would start with the blasting of American cities. Every congressman, every senator knew that a war would destroy Washington and leave the country with no government, flopping around like a chicken with its head off. They *knew*—why didn't they *do* something!"

"What could they do? Washington couldn't be protected."

"Do? Why, they could have made plans for their own deaths! They could have slapped through a constitutional amendment calling for an alternate president and alternate congressmen and made it illegal for the alternates to be in target areas—or any scheme to provide for orderly succession in case of disaster. They could have set up secret and protected centers of government to use for storm cellars. They could have planned the same way a father takes out life insurance for his kids. Instead they went stumbling along, fat, dumb, and happy, and let themselves get killed, with no provision to carry out their sworn duties after they were dead. Theory of 'derived authority,' pfui! It's not just disastrous; it's ridiculous! We used to be the greatest country in the world—now look at us!"

"Take it easy, Doc," Morgan suggested. "Hindsight is easier than foresight."

"Hummm! *I* saw it coming. I quit my Washington job and took a country practice, five years ahead of time. Why couldn't a congressman be as bright as I am?"

"Hmmm . . . well—you're right. But we might just as well worry over the Dred Scott Decision. Let's get on with the problem. How about Brockman? Ideas?"

"What do you propose, boss?"

"I'd rather have it come from the floor."

"Oh, quit scraping your foot, boss," urged Ted. "We elected you to lead."

"Okay. I propose to send somebody to backtrack on the message and locate Brockman—smell him out and see what he's got. I'll consult with as many groups as we can reach in this state and across the river, and we'll try to manage unanimous action. I was thinking of sending Dad and Morrie."

Cathleen shook her head. "Even with faked registration cards and travel permits they'd be grabbed for the Reconstruction Battalions. I'll go."

"In a pig's eye," Morgan answered. "You'd be grabbed for something a danged sight worse. It's got to be a man."

"I am afraid Cathleen is right," McCracken commented. "They shipped twelve-year-old boys and old men who could hardly walk for the Detroit project. They don't care how soon the radiation gets them—it's a plan to thin us out."

"Are the cities still that bad?"

"From what I hear, yes. Detroit is still 'hot' and she was one of the first to get it."

"I'm going to go." The voice was high and thin, and rarely heard in conference.

"Now, Mother—" said Dad Carter.

"You keep out of this, Dad. The men and young women would be grabbed, but they won't bother with *me*. All I need is a paper saying I have a permit to rejoin my grandson, or something."

McCracken nodded. "I can supply that."

Morgan paused, then said suddenly, "Mrs. Carter will contact Brockman. It is so ordered. Next order of business," he went on briskly. "You've all seen the news about St. Joe—this is what they posted in Barclay last night." He hauled out and held up the paper McCracken had given him. It was a printed notice, placing the City of Barclay on probation, subject to the ability of "local authorities" to suppress "bands of roving criminals."

There was a stir, but no comment. Most of them had lived in Barclay; all had ties there.

"I guess you're waiting for me," McCracken began. "We held a meeting as soon as this was posted. We weren't all there—it's getting harder to cover up even the smallest gathering—but there was no disagreement. We're behind you but we want you to go a little easy. We suggest that you cut out pulling raids within, oh, say twenty miles of Barclay, and that you stop all killing unless absolutely necessary to avoid capture. It's the killings they get excited about—it was killing of the district director that touched off St. Joe."

Benz sniffed. "So we don't do anything. We just give up—and stay here in the hills and starve."

"Let me finish, Benz. We don't propose to let them scare us out and keep us enslaved forever. But casual raids don't do them any real harm. They're mostly for food for the Underground and for minor retaliations. We've got to conserve our strength and increase it and organize, until we can hit hard enough to make it stick. We won't let you starve. I can do more organizing among the farmers and some animals can be hidden out, unregistered. We can get you meat—some, anyhow. And we'll split our rations with you. They've got us on 1800 calories now, but we can share it. Something can be done through the black market, too. There are ways."

Benz made a contemptuous sound. Morgan looked at him.

"Speak up, Joe. What's on your mind?"

"I will. It's not a plan; it's a disorderly retreat. A year from now we'll be twice as hungry and no further along—and they'll be better dug in and stronger. Where does it get us?"

Morgan shook his head. "You've got it wrong. Even if we hadn't had it forced on us, we would have been moving into this stage anyhow. The Free Companies have got to quit drawing attention to themselves. Once the food problem is solved we've got to build up our strength and weapons. We've got to have organization and weapons—nationwide organization and guns, knives, and hand grenades. We've got to turn this mine into a factory. There are people down in Barclay who can use the stuff we can make here—but we can't risk letting Barclay be blasted in the meantime. Easy does it."

"Ed Morgan, you're kidding yourself and you know it."

"How?"

" 'How?' Look, you sold me the idea of staying on the dodge and joining up—"

"You volunteered."

"Okay, I volunteered. It was all because you were so filled with fire and vinegar about how we would throw the enemy back into the ocean. You talked about France and Poland and how the Filipinos kept on fighting after they were occupied. You sold me a bill of goods. But there was something you didn't tell me—"

"Go on."

"There never was an Underground that freed its own country. All of them had to be pulled out of the soup by an invasion from outside. Nobody is going to pull *us* out."

There was silence after this remark. The statement

had too much truth in it, but it was truth that no member of the Company could afford to think about. Young Morrie broke it. "Captain?"

"Yes, Morrie." Being a fighting man, Morrie was therefore a citizen and a voter.

"How can Joe be so sure he knows what he's talking about? History doesn't repeat. Anyhow, maybe we will get some help. England, maybe—or even the Russians."

Benz snorted. "Listen to the punk! Look, kid, England was smashed like we were, only worse—and Russia, too. Grow up; quit daydreaming."

The boy looked at him doggedly. "You don't know that. We only know what they chose to tell us. And there aren't enough of them to hold down the whole world, everybody, everywhere. We never managed to lick the Yaquis, or the Moros. And they can't lick us *unless we let them.* I've read some history too."

Benz shrugged. "Okay, okay. Now we can all sing 'My Country 'Tis of Thee' and recite the Scout oath. That ought to make Morrie happy—"

"Take it easy, Joe!"

"We have free speech here, don't we? What I want to know is: How long does this go on? I'm getting tired of competing with coyotes for the privilege of eating jackrabbits. You know I've fought with the best of them. I've gone on the raids. Well, haven't I? Haven't I? You can't call *me* yellow."

"You've been on some raids," Morgan conceded.

"All right. I'd go along indefinitely if I could see some sensible plan. That's why I ask, 'How long does this go on?' When do we move? Next spring? Next year?"

Morgan gestured impatiently. "How do I know? It may be next spring; it may be ten years. The Poles waited three hundred years."

"That tears it," Benz said slowly. "I was hoping you could offer some reasonable plan. Wait and arm ourselves—that's a pretty picture! Homemade hand grenades against atom bombs! Why don't you quit kidding yourselves? We're *licked!*" He hitched at his belt. "The rest of you can do as you please—I'm through."

Morgan shrugged. "If a man won't fight, I can't make him. You're assigned noncombatant duties. Turn in your gun. Report to Cathleen."

"You don't get me, Ed. I'm *through.*"

"You don't get *me*, Joe. You don't resign from an Underground."

"There's no risk. I'll leave quietly, and let myself be registered as a straggler. It doesn't mean anything to the rest of you. I'll keep my mouth shut—that goes without saying."

Morgan took a long breath, then answered, "Joe, I've learned by bitter experience not to trust statements set off by 'naturally,' 'of course,' or 'that goes without saying.' "

"Oh, so you don't trust me?"

"As Captain of this Company I can't afford to. Unless you can get the Company to recall me from office, my rulings stand. You're under arrest. Hand over your gun."

Benz glanced around, at blank, unfriendly faces. He reached for his waist, "With your left hand, Joe!"

Instead of complying, Benz drew suddenly, backed away. "Keep clear!" he said shrilly. "I don't want to hurt anybody—but keep clear!"

Morgan was unarmed. There might have been a knife or two in the assembly, but most of them had come directly from the dinner table. It was not their custom to be armed inside the mine.

Young Morrie was armed with a rifle, having come from lookout duty. He did not have room to bring it into play, but Morgan could see that he intended to try. So could Benz.

"Stop it, Morrie!" Morgan assumed obedience and turned instantly to the others. "Let him go. Nobody move. Get going, Joe."

"That's better." Benz backed down the main tunnel, toward the main entrance, weed and drift choked for years. Its unused condition was their principal camouflage, but it could be negotiated.

He backed away into the gloom, still covering them. The tunnel curved; shortly he was concealed by the bend.

Dad Carter went scurrying in the other direction as soon as Benz no longer covered them. He reappeared at once, carrying something. "Heads down!" he shouted, as he passed through them and took out after Benz.

"Dad!" shouted Morgan. But Carter was gone.

Seconds later a concussion tore at their ears and noses.

Morgan picked himself up and brushed at his clothes, saying in annoyed tones, "I never did like explosives in cramped quarters. Cleve—Art. Go check on it. Move!"

"Right, boss!" They were gone.

"The rest of you get ready to carry out withdrawal plan—full plan, with provisions and supplies. Jerry, don't disconnect either the receiver or the line-of-sight till I give the word. Margie will help you. Cathleen, get ready to serve anything that can't be carried. We'll have one big meal. 'The condemned ate hearty.'"

"Just a moment, Captain." McCracken touched his sleeve. "I had better get a message into Barclay."

"Soon as the boys report. You better get back into town."

"I wonder. Benz knows me. I think I'm here to stay."

"Hm . . . well, you know best. How about your family?"

McCracken shrugged. "They can't be worse off than they would be if I'm picked up. I'd like to have them warned and then arrangements made for them to rejoin me if possible."

"We'll do it. You'll have to give me a new contact."

"Planned for. This message will go through and my number-two man will step into my shoes. The name is Hobart—runs a feed store on Pelham Street."

Morgan nodded. "Should have known you had it

worked out. Well, what we don't know—" He was interrupted by Cleve, reporting.

"He got away, Boss."

"Why didn't you go after him?"

"Half the roof came down when Dad chucked the
grenade. Tunnel's choked with rock. Found a place
where I could see but couldn't crawl through. He's not
in the tunnel."

"How about Dad?"

"He's all right. Got clipped on the head with a splinter but not really hurt."

Morgan stopped two of the women hurrying past,
intent on preparations for withdrawal. "Here—Jean,
and you, Mrs. Bowen. Go take care of Dad Carter and
tell Art to get back here fast. Shake a leg!"

When Art reported Morgan said, "You and Cleve go
out and find Benz. Assume that he is heading for Barclay. Stop him and bring him in if you can. Otherwise
kill him. Art is in charge. Get going." He turned to
McCracken. "Now for a message." He fumbled in his
pocket for paper, found the poster notice that Mc-
Cracken had given him, tore off a piece, and started to
write. He showed it to McCracken. "How's that?" he
asked.

The message warned Hobart of Benz and asked him
to try to head him off. It did not tell him that the Barclay Free Company was moving but did designate the
"post office" through which next contact would be expected—the men's rest room of the bus station.

"Better cut out the post office," McCracken advised.
"Hobart knows it and we may contact him half a
dozen other ways. But I'd like to ask him to get my
family out of sight. Just tell him that we are sorry to
hear that Aunt Dinah is dead."

"Is that enough?"

"Yes."

"Okay." Morgan made the changes, then called,
"Margie! Put this in code and tell Jerry to get it out
fast. Tell him it's the strike-out edition. He can knock
down his sets as soon as it's out."

"Okay, boss." Margie had no knowledge of cryptography. Instead she had command of jive talk, adolescent slang, and high school double-talk which would be meaningless to any but another American bobby-soxer. At the other end a fifteen-year-old interpreted her butchered English by methods which impressed her foster parents as being telepathy—but it worked.

The fifteen-year-old could be trusted. Her entire family, save herself, had been in Los Angeles on Final Sunday.

Art and Cleve had no trouble picking up Benz's trail. His tracks were on the tailings spilling down from the main entrance to the mine. The earth and rock had been undisturbed since the last heavy rain; Benz's flight left clear traces.

But trail was cold by more than twenty minutes; they had left the mine by the secret entrance a quarter of a mile from where Benz had made his exit.

Art picked it up where Benz had left the tailings and followed it through brush with the woodsmanship of the Eagle Scout he had been. From the careless signs he left behind Benz was evidently in a hurry and heading by the shortest route for the highway. The two followed him as fast as they could cover ground, discarding caution for speed.

They checked just before entering the highway. "See anything?" asked Cleve.

"No."

"Which way would he go?"

"The Old Man said to head him off from Barclay."

"Yeah, but suppose he headed south instead? He used to work in Wickamton. He might head that way."

"The Boss said to cover Barclay. Let's go."

They had to cache their guns; from here on it would be their wits and their knives. An armed American on a highway would be as conspicuous as a nudist at a garden party.

Their object now was speed; they must catch up with him, or get ahead of him and waylay him.

Nine miles and two and a half hours later—one

hundred and fifty minutes of dog trot, with time lost
lying in the roadside brush when convoys thundered
past—they were in the outskirts of Barclay. Around a
bend, out of sight, was the roadblock of the Invaders'
check station. The point was a bottleneck; Benz must
come this way if he were heading for Barclay.

"Is he ahead or behind us?" asked Cleve, peering out
through bushes.

"Behind, unless he was picked up by a convoy—or
sprouted wings. We'll give him an hour."

A horse-drawn hayrack lumbered up the road. Cleve
studied it. Americans were permitted no power vehicles except under supervision, but this farmer and his
load could go into town with only routine check at the
road block. "Maybe we ought to hide in that and look
for him in town."

"And get a bayonet in your ribs? Don't be silly."

"Okay. Don't blow your top." Cleve continued to
watch the rig. "Hey," he said presently. "Get a load of
that!"

"That" was a figure which dropped from the tail of
the wagon as it started around the bend, rolled to the
ditch on the far side, and slithered out of sight.

"That was Joe!"

"Are you sure?"

"Sure! Here we go."

"How?" Art objected. "Take it easy. Follow me."
They faded back two hundred yards, to where they
could cross the road on hands and knees through a
drainage pipe. Then they worked up the other side to
where Benz had disappeared in weeds.

They found the place where he had been; grass and
weeds were still straightening up. The route he must
have taken was evident—down toward the river bank,
then upstream to the city. There were drops of blood.
"Dad must have missed stopping him by a gnat's
whisker," Cleve commented.

"Bad job he didn't."

"Another thing—he said he was going to give himself up. I don't think he is, or he would have stayed

with the wagon and turned himself in at the check station. He's heading for some hideout. Who does he know in Barclay?"

"I don't know. We'd better get going."

"Wait a minute. If he touches off an alarm, they'll shoot him for us. If he gets by the 'eyes,' we've lost him and we'll have to pick him up inside. Either way, we don't gain anything by blundering ahead. We've got to go in by the chute."

Like all cities the Invader had consolidated, Barclay was girdled by electric-eye circuits. The enemy had trimmed the town to fit, dynamiting and burning where necessary to achieve unbroken sequence of automatic sentries. But the "chute"—an abandoned and forgotten aqueduct—passed under the alarms. Art knew how to use it; he had been in town twice since Final Sunday.

They worked back up the highway, crossed over, and took to the hills. Thirty minutes later they were on the streets of Barclay, reasonably safe as long as they were quick to step off the sidewalk for the occasional Invader.

The first "post office," a clothesline near their exit, told them nothing—the line was bare. They went to the bus station. Cleve studied the notices posted for inhabitants while Art went into the men's rest room. On the wall, defaced by scrawlings of every sort, mostly vulgar, he found what he sought: "Killroy was here." The misspelling of Kilroy was the clue—exactly eighteen inches below it and six to the right was an address: "1745 Spruce—ask for Mabel."

He read it as 2856 Pine—one block beyond Spruce.

Art passed the address to Cleve, then they set out separately, hurrying to beat the curfew but proceeding with caution—at least one of them must get through. They met in the backyard of the translated address. Art knocked on the kitchen door. It was opened a crack by a middle-aged man who did not seem glad to see them. "Well?"

"We're looking for Mabel."

"Nobody here by that name."

"Sorry," said Art. "We must have made a mistake." He shivered. "Chilly out," he remarked. "The nights are getting longer."

"They'll get shorter by and by," the man answered.

"We've got to think so, anyhow," Art countered.

"Come in," the man said. "The patrol may see you." He opened the door and stepped aside. "My name's Hobart. What's your business?"

"We're looking for a man named Benz. He may have sneaked into town this afternoon and found someplace to—"

"Yes, yes," Hobart said impatiently. "He got in about an hour ago and he's holed up with a character named Moyland." As he spoke he removed a half loaf of bread from a cupboard, cut four slices, and added cold sausage, producing two sandwiches. He did not ask if they were hungry; he simply handed them to Art and Cleve.

"Thanks, pal. So he's holed up. Haven't you done anything about it? He has got to be shut up at once or he'll spill his guts."

"We've got a tap in on the telephone line. We had to wait for dark. You can't expect me to sacrifice good boys just to shut his mouth unless it's absolutely necessary."

"Well, it's dark now, and we'll be the boys you mentioned. You can call yours off."

"Okay." Hobart started pulling on shoes.

"No need for you to stick your neck out," Art told him. "Just tell us where this Moyland lives."

"And get your throat cut, too. I'll take you."

"What sort of a guy is this Moyland? Is he safe?"

"You can't prove it by me. He's a black market broker, but that doesn't prove anything. He's not part of the organization but we haven't anything against him."

Hobart took them over his back fence, across a dark side street, through a playground, where they lay for several minutes under bushes because of a false alarm, then through many more backyards, back alleys, and dark byways. The man seemed to have a nose for the enemy; there were no more alarms. At last he brought them through a cellar door into a private home. They went upstairs and through a room where a woman was nursing a baby. She looked up, but otherwise ignored them. They ended up in a dark attic. "Hi, Jim," Hobart called out softly. "What's new?"

The man addressed lay propped on his elbows, peering out into the night through opera glasses held to slots of a ventilating louvre. He rolled over and lowered the glasses, pushing one of a pair of earphones from his head as he did so. "Hello, Chief. Nothing much. Benz is getting drunk, it looks like."

"I'd like to know where Moyland gets it," Hobart said. "Has he telephoned?"

"Would I be doing nothing if he had? A couple of calls came in, but they didn't amount to anything, so I let him talk."

How do you know they didn't amount to anything?"

Jim shrugged, turned back to the louvre. "Moyland just pulled down the shade," he announced.

Art turned to Hobart. "We can't wait. We're going in."

Benz arrived at Moyland's house in bad condition. The wound in his shoulder, caused by Carter's grenade, was bleeding. He had pushed a handkerchief up against it as a compress, but his activity started the blood again; he was shaking for fear his condition would attract attention before he could get under cover.

Moyland answered the door. "Is that you, Zack?" Benz demanded, shrinking back as he spoke.

"Yes. Who is it?"

"It's me—Joe Benz. Let me in, Zack—quick!"

Moyland seemed about to close the door, then suddenly opened it. "Get inside." When the door was bolted, he demanded, "Now—what's your trouble? Why come to me?"

"I had to go someplace, Zack. I had to get off the street. They'd pick me up."

Moyland studied him. "You're not registered. Why not?"

Benz did not answer. Moyland waited, then went on, "You know what I can get for harboring a fugitive. You're in the Underground—aren't you?"

"Oh, no, Zack! I wouldn't do that to you. I'm just a— a straggler. I gotta get registered, Zack."

"That's blood on your coat. How?"

"Uh . . . just an accident. Maybe you could let me have clean rags and some iodine."

Moyland stared at him, his bland face expressionless, then smiled. "You've got no troubles we can't fix. Sit down." He stepped to a cabinet and took out a bottle of bourbon, poured three fingers in a water glass, and handed it to Benz. "Work on that and I'll fix you up."

He returned with some torn toweling and a bottle. "Sit here with your back to the window, and open your shirt. Have another drink. You'll need it before I'm through."

Benz glanced nervously at the window. "Why don't you draw the shade?"

"It would attract attention. Honest people leave their shades up these days. Hold still. This is going to hurt."

Three drinks later Benz was feeling better. Moyland seemed willing to sit and drink with him and to soothe his nerves. "You did well to come in," Moyland told him. "There's no sense hiding like a scared rabbit. It's just butting your head against a stone wall. Stupid."

Benz nodded. "That's what I told them."

"Told who?"

"Hunh? Oh, nobody. Just some guys I was talking to. Tramps."

Moyland poured him another drink. "As a matter of fact you *were* in the Underground."

"Me? Don't be silly, Zack."

"Look, Joe, you don't have to kid me. I'm your friend. Even if you did tell me it wouldn't matter. In the first place, I wouldn't have any proof. In the second place, I'm sympathetic to the Underground—any American is. I just think they're wrong-headed and foolish. Otherwise I'd join 'em myself."

"They're foolish all right! You can say that again."

"So you *were* in it?"

"Huh? You're trying to trap me. I gave my word of honor—"

"Oh, relax!" Moyland said hastily. "Forget it. I didn't hear anything; I can't tell anything. Hear no evil, see no evil—that's me." He changed the subject.

The level of the bottle dropped while Moyland explained current events as he saw them. "It's a shame we had to take such a shellacking to learn our lesson but the fact of the matter is, we were standing in the way of the natural logic of progress. There was a time back in '45 when we could have pulled the same stunt ourselves, only we weren't bright enough to do it. World organization, world government. We stood in the way, so we got smeared. It had to come. A smart man can see that."

Benz was bleary but he did not find this comment easy to take. "Look, Zack—you don't mean you *like* what happened to us?"

"Like it? Of course not. But it was necessary. You don't have to like having a tooth pulled—but it has to be done. Anyhow," he went on, "it's not all bad. The big cities were economically unsound anyway. We should have blown them up ourselves. Slum clearance, you might call it."

Benz banged his empty glass down. "Maybe so—but they made slaves out of us!"

"Take it easy, Joe," Moyland said, filling his glass, "you're talking abstractions. The cop on the corner could push you around whenever he wanted to. Is that freedom? Does it matter whether the cop talks with an Irish accent or some other accent? No, chum, there's a lot of guff talked about freedom. No man is free. There is no such thing as freedom. There are only various privileges. Free speech—we're talking freely now, aren't we? After all, you don't want to get up on a platform and shoot off your face. Free press? When did *you* ever own a newspaper? Don't be a chump. Now that you've shown sense and come in, you are going to find that things aren't so very different. A little more orderly and no more fear of war, that's all. Girls make love just like they used to, the smart guys get along, and the suckers still get the short end of the deal."

Benz nodded. "You're right, Zack. I've been a fool."

"I'm glad you see it. Now take those wild men you were with. What freedom have they got? Freedom to starve, freedom to sleep on the cold ground, freedom to be hunted."

"That was it," Benz agreed. "Did you ever sleep in a mine, Zack? Cold. That ain't half of it. Damp, too."

"I can imagine," Moyland agreed. "The Capehart Lode always was wet."

"It wasn't the Capehart; it was the Harkn—" He caught himself and looked puzzled.

"The Harkness, eh? That's the headquarters?"

"I didn't say that! You're putting words in my mouth! You—"

"Calm yourself, Joe. Forget it." Moyland got up and drew down the shade. "You didn't say anything."

"Of course I didn't." Benz stared at his glass. "Say, Zack, where do I sleep? I don't feel good."

"You'll have a nice place to sleep any minute now."

"Huh? Well, show me. I gotta fold up."

"Any minute. You've got to check in first."

"Huh? Oh, I can't do that tonight, Zack. I'm in no shape."

"I'm afraid you'll have to. See me pull that shade down? They'll be along any moment."

Benz stood up, swaying a little. "You framed me!" he yelled, and lunged at his host.

Moyland sidestepped, put a hand on his shoulder

and pushed him down into the chair. "Sit down, sucker," he said pleasantly. "You don't expect me to get A-bombed just for you and your pals, do you?"

Benz shook his head, then began to sob.

Hobart escorted them out of the house, saying to Art as they left, "If you get back, tell McCracken that Aunt Dinah is resting peacefully."

"Okay."

"Give us two minutes, then go in. Good luck."

Cleve took the outside; Art went in. The back door was locked, but the upper panel was glass. He broke it with the hilt of his knife, reached in and unbolted the door. He was inside when Moyland showed up to investigate the noise.

Art kicked him in the belly, then let him have the point in the neck as he went down. Art stopped just long enough to insure that Moyland would stay dead, then went looking for the room where Benz had been when the shade was drawn.

He found Benz in it. The man blinked his eyes and tried to focus them, as if he found it impossible to believe what he saw. "Art!" he got out at last. "Jeez, boy! Am I glad to see you! Let's get out of here—this place is 'hot.' "

Art advanced, knife out.

Benz looked amazed. "Hey, Art! Art! You're making a mistake. Art. You can't do this—" Art let him have the first one in the soft tissues under the breast bone, then cut his throat to be sure. After that he got out quickly.

Thirty-five minutes later he was emerging from the country end of the chute. His throat was burning from exertion and his left arm was useless—he could not tell whether it was broken or simply wounded.

Cleve lay dead in the alley behind Moyland's house, having done a good job of covering Art's rear.

It took Art all night and part of the next morning to get back near the mine. He had to go through the hills the entire way; the highway was, he judged, too warm at the moment.

He did not expect that the Company would still be there. He was reasonably sure that Morgan would have carried out the evacuation pending certain evidence that Benz's mouth had been shut. He hurried.

But he did not expect what he did find—a helicopter hovering over the neighborhood of the mine.

He stopped to consider the matter. If Morgan had got them out safely, he knew where to rejoin. If they were still inside, he had to figure out some way to help them. The futility of his position depressed him—one man, with a knife and a bad arm, against a helicopter.

Somewhere a bluejay screamed and cursed. Without much hope he chirped his own identification. The bluejay shut up and a mockingbird answered him— Ted.

Art signaled that he would wait where he was. He considered himself well hidden; he expected to have to signal again when Ted got closer, but he underestimated Ted's ability. A hand was laid on his shoulder.

He rolled over, knife out, and hurt his shoulder as he did so. "Ted! Man, do you look good to me!"

"Same here. Did you get him?"

"Benz? Yes, but maybe not in time. Where's the gang?"

"A quarter mile north of back door. We're pinned down. Where's Cleve?"

"Cleve's not coming back. What do you mean 'pinned down'?"

"That damned 'copter can see right down the draw we're in. Dad's got 'em under an overhang and they're safe enough for the moment, but we can't move."

"What do you mean 'Dad's got 'em'?" demanded Art. "Where's the Boss?"

"He ain't in such good shape, Art. Got a machine gun slug in the ribs. We had a dust up. Cathleen's dead."

"The hell you say!"

"That's right. Margie and Maw Carter have got her baby. But that's one reason why we're pinned down—the Boss and the kid, I mean."

A mockingbird's call sounded far away. "There's Dad," Ted announced. "We got to get back."

"Can we?"

"Sure. Just keep behind me. I'll watch out that I don't get too far ahead."

Art followed Ted in, by a circuitous and, at one point, almost perpendicular route. He found the Company huddled under a shelf of rock which had been undercut by a stream, now dry. Against the wall Morgan was on his back, with Dad Carter and Dr. Mc-Cracken squatting beside him. Art went up and made his report.

Morgan nodded, his face gray with pain. His shirt had been cut away; bandaging was wrapped around his ribs, covering a thick pad. "You did well, Art. Too bad about Cleve. Ted, we're getting out of here and you're going first, because you're taking the kid."

"The baby? How—"

"Doc'll dope it so that it won't let out a peep. Then you strap it to your back, papoose fashion."

Ted thought about it. "No, to my front. There's some knee-and-shoulder work on the best way out."

"Okay. It's your job."

"How do *you* get out, boss?"

"Don't be silly."

"Look here, boss, if you think we're going to walk off and leave you, you've got another—"

"Shut up and scram!" The exertion hurt Morgan; he coughed and wiped his mouth.

"Yes, sir." Ted and Art backed away.

"Now, Ed—" said Carter.

"You shut up, too. You still sure you don't want to be Captain?"

"You know better than that, Ed. They took things from me while I was your deppity, but they wouldn't have me for Captain."

"That puts it up to you, Doc."

McCracken looked troubled. "They don't know me that well, Captain."

"They'll take you. People have an instinct for such things."

"Anyhow, if I am Captain, I won't agree to your plan of staying here by yourself. We'll stay till dark and carry you out."

"And get picked up by an infrared spotter, like sitting ducks? That's supposing they let you alone until sundown—that other 'copter will be back with more troops before long."

"I don't think they'd let me walk off on you."

"It's up to you to *make* them. Oh, I appreciate your kindly thoughts, Doc, but you'll think differently as soon as you're Captain. You'll know you have to cut your losses."

McCracken did not answer. Morgan turned his head to Carter. "Gather them around, Dad."

They crowded in, shoulder to shoulder. Morgan looked from one troubled face to another and smiled. "The Barclay Free Company, a provisional unit of the United States of America, is now in session," he announced, his voice suddenly firm. "I'm resigning the captaincy for reasons of physical disability. Any nominations?"

The silence was disturbed only by calls of birds, the sounds of insects.

Morgan caught Carter's eyes. Dad cleared his throat. "I nominate Doc McCracken."

"Any other nominations?" He waited, then continued, "All right, all in favor of Doc make it known by raising your right hand. Okay—opposed the same sign. Dr. McCracken is unanimously elected. It's all yours, Captain. Good luck to you."

McCracken stood up, stooping to avoid the rock overhead. "We're evacuating at once. Mrs. Carter, give the baby about another tablespoon of the syrup, then help Ted. He knows what to do. You'll follow Ted.

Then Jerry. Margie, you are next. I'll assign the others presently. Once out of the canyon, spread out and go it alone. Rendezvous at dusk, same place as under Captain Morgan's withdrawal plan—the cave." He paused. Morgan caught his eye and motioned him over, "That's all until Ted and the baby are ready to leave. Now back away and give Captain Morgan a little air."

When they had withdrawn McCracken leaned over Morgan the better to hear his weak words. "Don't be too sure you've seen the last of me, Captain. I might join up in a few days."

"You might at that. I'm going to leave you bundled up warm and plenty of water within reach. I'll leave you some pills, too—that'll give you some comfort and ease. Only half a pill for you—they're intended for cows." He grinned at his patient.

"Half a pill it is. Why not let Dad handle the evacuation? He'll make you a good deputy—and I'd like to talk with you until you leave."

"Right." He called Carter over, instructed him, and turned back to Morgan.

"After you join up with Powell's outfit," whispered Morgan, "your first job is to get into touch with Brockman. Better get Mrs. Carter started right away, once you've talked it over with Powell."

"I will."

"That's the most important thing we've got to worry about, Doc. We've got to have unity, and one plan, from coast to coast. I look forward to a day when there will be an American assigned, by name, to each and every one of them. Then at a set time—zzzt!" He drew a thumb across his throat.

McCracken nodded. "Could be. It *will* be. How long do you think it will take us?"

"I don't know. I don't think about 'how long'. Two years, five years, ten years—maybe a century. That's not the point. The only question is whether or not there are any guts left in America." He glanced out where the fifth person to leave was awaiting a signal from Carter, who in turn was awaiting a signal from Art, hidden out where he could watch for the helicopter. "Those people will stick."

"I'm sure of that."

Presently Morgan added, "There's one thing this has taught me: You can't enslave a free man. Only person can do that to a man is himself. No, sir—you can't enslave a free man. The most you can do is kill him."

"That's a fact, Ed."

"It is. Got a cigarette, Doc?"

"It won't do you any good, Ed."

"It won't do me any harm, either—now, will it?"

"Well, not much." McCracken unregretfully gave him his last and watched him smoke it.

Later, Morgan said, "Dad's ready for you, Captain. So long."

"So long. Don't forget. Half a pill at a time. Drink all the water you want, but don't take your blankets off, no matter how hot you get."

"Half a pill it is. Good luck."

"I'll have Ted check on you tomorrow."

Morgan shook his head. "That's too soon. Not for a couple of days at least."

McCracken smiled. "I'll decide that, Ed. You just keep yourself wrapped up. Good luck." He withdrew to where Carter waited for him. "You go ahead, Dad. I'll bring up the rear. Signal Art to start."

Carter hesitated. "Tell me straight, Doc. What kind of shape is he in?"

McCracken studied Carter's face, then said in a low voice, "I give him about two hours."

"I'll stay behind with him."

"No, Dad, you'll carry out your orders." Seeing the distress in the old man's eyes, he added, "Don't you worry about Morgan. A free man can take care of himself. Now get moving."

"Yes, sir."

FOREWORD

This story was tailored in length (1500 words) for Colliers as a short-short. I then tried it on the American Legion magazine—and was scolded for suggesting that the treatment given our veterans was ever less than perfect. I then offered it to several SF editors—and was told that it was not a science fiction story. (Gee whiz and Gosh wollickers!—space warps and FTL are science but therapy and psychology are not. I must be in the wrong church.)

But this story does have a major shortcoming, one that usually is fatal. Try to spot it. I will put the answer just after the end.

NO BANDS PLAYING, NO FLAGS FLYING—

"The bravest man I ever saw in my life!" Jones said, being rather shrill about it.

We—Jones and Arkwright and I—were walking toward the parking lot at the close of visiting hours out at the veterans hospital. Wars come and wars go, but the wounded we have always with us—and damned little attention they get between wars. If you bother to look (few do), you can find some broken human remnants dating clear back to World War One in some of our wards.

So our post always sends out a visiting committee every Sunday, every holiday. I'm usually on it, have been for thirty years—if you can't pay a debt, you can at least try to meet the interest. And you do get so that you can stand it.

But Jones was a young fellow making his first visit. Quite upset, he was. Well, surely, I would have despised him if he hadn't been—this crop was fresh in from Southeast Asia. Jones had held it in, then burst out with that remark once we were outside.

"What do you mean by 'bravery'?" I asked him. (Not but what Jones had plenty to back up his opinion—this lad he was talking about was shy both legs and his eyesight, yet he was chin-up and merry.)

"Well, what do *you* mean by 'bravery'? Jones demanded, then added, "sir." Respect for my white hair rather than my opinions, I think; there was an edge in his voice.

"Keep your shirt on, son," I answered. "What that lad back there has I'd call 'fortitude,' the ability to endure adversity without losing your morale. I'm not disparaging it; it may be a higher virtue than bravery—but I define 'bravery' as the capacity to *choose* to face danger when you are frightened by it."

"Why do you say 'choose'?"

"Because nine men out of ten meet the test when it's forced on them. But it takes something extra to face up to danger when it scares the crap out of you and there's an easy way to bug out." I glanced at my watch. "Give me three minutes and I'll tell you about the bravest man I've ever met."

I was a young fellow myself back between War One and War Two and had been in a hospital much like this one Arkwright and Jones and I had visited— picked up a spot on my lung in the Canal Zone and had been sent there for the cure. Mind you, this was years ago when lung therapy was primitive. No antibiotics, no specific drugs. The first thing they would try was a phrenectomy—cut the nerve that controls the diaphragm to immobilize the lung and let it get well. If that didn't work, they used artificial pneumothorax. If that failed, they did a "backdoor job"—chop out some ribs and fit you with a corset.

All these were just expedients to hold a lung still so it could get well. In artificial pneumothorax they shove a hollow needle between your ribs so that the end is between rib wall and lung wall, then pump the space in between full of air; this compresses the lung like a squeezed sponge.

But the air would be absorbed after a while and you had to get pumped up again. Every Friday morning those of us on pneumo would gather in the ward surgeon's office for the needle. It wasn't grim—lungers are funny people; they are almost always cheerful. This was an officers' ward and we treated it like a club. Instead of queuing up outside the surgeon's office we would swarm in, loll in his chair, sit on his desk, smoke his cigarettes, and swap lies while he took care of us. Four of us that morning and I was the first.

Taking the air needle isn't bad—just a slight prick as it goes in and you can even avoid that if you want to bother with skin anesthesia. It's over in a few minutes; you put your bathrobe back on and go back to bed. I hung around after I was through because the second patient, chap named Saunders, was telling a dirty story that was new to me.

He broke off in the middle of it to climb up on the table when I got off. Our number-one ward surgeon was on leave and his assistant was taking care of us— a young chap not long out of school. We all liked him and felt he had the makings of a great surgeon.

Getting pumped up is not dangerous in any reasonable sense of the word. You can break your neck falling off a step ladder, choke to death on a chicken bone. You can slip on a rainy day, knock yourself out, and drown in three inches of rain water. And there is just as unlikely a way to hit the jackpot in taking artificial pneumothorax. If the needle goes a little too far, penetrates the lung, and if an air bubble then happens to be forced into a blood vessel and manages to travel all the way back to the heart without being absorbed, it is possible though extremely unlikely to get a sort of vapor lock in the valves of your heart—air embolism, the doctors call it. Given all these improbable events, you can die.

We never heard the end of Saunders' dirty joke. He konked out on the table.

The young doc did everything possible for him and sent for help while he was doing it. They tried this and that, used all the tricks, but the upshot was that they brought in the meat basket and carted him off to the morgue.

Three of us were still standing there, not saying a word—me, reswallowing my breakfast and thanking my stars that I was through with it, an ex-field-clerk named Josephs who was next up, and Colonel Hostetter who was last in line. The surgeon turned and looked at us. He was sweating and looked bad—may have been the first patient he had ever lost; he was still a kid. Then he turned to Dr. Armand who had come in from the next ward. I don't know whether he was going to ask the older man to finish it for him or whether he was going to put it off for a day, but it was clear from his face that he did not intend to go ahead right then.

Whatever it was, he didn't get a chance to say it. Josephs stood up, threw off his bathrobe and climbed up on the table. He had just lighted a cigarette; he passed it to a hospital orderly and said, "Hold this for me, Jack, while Doctor"—he named our own surgeon—"pumps me up." With that he peels up his pajama coat.

You know the old business about sending a student pilot right back up after his first crack up. That was the shape our young doctor was in—he had to get right back to it and prove to himself that it was just bad luck and not because he was a butcher. But he couldn't send himself back in; Josephs had to do it for him. Josephs could have ruined him professionally that moment, by backing out and giving him time to work up a real case of nerves—but instead Josephs forced his hand, made him do it.

Josephs died on the table.

The needle went in and everything seemed all right, then Josephs gave a little sigh and died. Dr. Armand was on hand this time and took charge, but it did no good. It was like seeing the same horror movie twice. The same four men arrived to move the body over to the morgue—probably the same basket.

Our doctor now looked like a corpse himself. Dr. Armand took over. "You two get back to bed," he said to

Colonel Hostetter and me. "Colonel, come over to my ward this afternoon; I'll take care of your treatment."

But Hostetter shook his head. "No, thank you," he said crisply, "My ward surgeon takes care of my needs." He took off his robe. The young fellow didn't move. The Colonel went up to him and shook his arm. "Come, now Doctor—you'll make us both late for lunch." With that he climbed up on the table and exposed his ribs.

A few moments later he climbed off again, the job done, and our ward surgeon was looking human again, although still covered with sweat.

I stopped to catch my breath. Jones nodded soberly and said, "I see what you mean. To do what Colonel Hostetter did takes a kind of cold courage way beyond the courage needed to fight."

"He doesn't mean anything of the sort," Arkwright objected. "He wasn't talking about Hostetter; he meant the intern. The doctor had to steady down and do a job—not once but twice. Hostetter just had to hold still and let him do it."

I felt tired and old. "Just a moment," I said. "You're both wrong. Remember I defined 'bravery' as requiring that a man had to have a choice . . . and chooses to be brave in spite of his own fear. The ward surgeon had the decisions forced on him, so he is not in the running. Colonel Hostetter was an old man and blooded in battle—and he had Josephs' example to live up to. So he doesn't get first prize."

"But that's silly," Jones protested. "Josephs was brave, sure—but, if it was hard for Josephs to offer himself, it was four times as hard for Hostetter. It would begin to look like a jinx—like a man didn't stand a chance of coming off that table alive."

"Yes, yes!" I agreed. "I know, that's the way *I* felt at the time. But you didn't let me finish. I know for *certain* that it took more bravery to do what Josephs did.

"The autopsy didn't show an air embolism in Josephs, or anything else. Josephs died of fright."

The End

The Answer: I'll bury this in other words to keep your eye from picking it up at once; the shortcoming is that this is a true story. I was there. I have changed names, places, and dates but not the essential facts.

FOREWORD

You may not be old enough to remember the acute housing shortage following World War II (the subject of this story) but if you are over six but not yet old enough for the undertaker, you are aware of the current problem of getting in out of the rain . . . a problem especially acute for the young couple with one baby and for the retired old couple trying to get by on Social "Security" plus savings if any. (I am not suggesting that it is easy for those between youth and old age; the present price of mortgage money constitutes rape with violence; the price tag on an honestly-constructed—if you can find one—two-bedroom house makes me feel faint.)

In 1960 in Moscow Mrs. Heinlein and I had as Intourist courier a sweet child named Ludmilla—23, unmarried, living with her father, mother, brother and sisters. She told us that her ambition in life was for her family not to have to share a bathroom with another family.

The next aesthete who sneers at our American "plumbing culture" in my presence I intend to cut into small pieces and flush him down that W.C. he despises.

Any old pol will recognize the politics in this story as the Real McCoy. Should be. Autobiographical in many details. Which details? Show me a warrant and I'll take the Fifth.

A BATHROOM OF HER OWN

Ever step on a top step that wasn't there?

That's the way I felt when I saw my honorable opponent for the office of city councilman, third district.

Tom Griffith had telephoned at the close of filing, to let me know my opponents. "Alfred McNye," he said, "and Francis X. Nelson."

"McNye we can forget," I mused. "He files just for the advertising. It's a three-way race—me, this Nelson party, and the present encumbrance, Judge Jorgens. Maybe we'll settle it in the primaries." Our fair city has the system laughingly called "non-partisan"; a man can be elected in the primary by getting a clear majority.

"Jorgens didn't file, Jack. The old thief isn't running for re-election."

I let this sink in. "Tom, we might as well tear up those photostats. Do you suppose Tully's boys are conceding our district?"

"The machine *can't* concede the third district, not this year. It must be Nelson."

"I suppose so . . . it can't be McNye. What d'you know about him?"

"Nothing."

"Nor I. Well, we'll look him over tonight." The Civic League had called a "meet-the-candidates" meeting that night. I drove out to the trailer camp where I hang

245

my hat—then a shower, a shave, put on my hurtin' shoes, and back to town. It gave me time to think.

It's not unusual for a machine to replace—temporarily—a man whose record smells too ripe with a citizen of no background to be sniped at. I could visualize Nelson—young, manly looking, probably a lawyer and certainly a veteran. He would be so politically naive that he would stand without hitching, or so ambitious that it would blind him to what he must do to keep the support of the machine. Either way the machine could use him.

I got there just in time to be introduced and take a seat on the platform. I couldn't spot Nelson but I did see Cliff Meyers, standing with some girl. Meyers is a handyman for Boss Tully—Nelson would be around close.

McNye accepted the call of the peepul in a few hundred well-worn words, then the chairman introduced Nelson. "—a veteran of this war and candidate for the same office."

The girl standing with Meyers walked up and took the stage.

They clapped and somebody in the balcony gave a wolf whistle. Instead of getting flustered, she smiled up and said, "Thank you!"

They clapped again, and whistled and stomped. She started talking. I'm not bright—I had trouble learning to wave bye-bye and never did master patty-cake. I expected her to apologize for Nelson's absence and identify herself as his wife or sister or something. She was into her fourth paragraph before I realized that *she* was Nelson.

Francis X. Nelson—*Frances* X. Nelson. I wondered what I had done to deserve this. Female candidates are poison to run against at best; you don't dare use the ordinary rough-and-tumble, while she is free to use anything from a blacksnake whip to mickeys in your coffee.

Add to that ladylike good looks, obvious intelligence, platform poise—and a veteran. I couldn't have lived that wrong. I tried to catch Tom Griffith's eye to share my misery, but he was looking at *her* and the lunk was lapping it up.

Nelson—*Miss* Nelson—was going to town on housing. "You promised him that when he got out of that foxhole nothing would be too good for him. And what did he get? A shack in shanty-town, the sofa in his in-laws' parlor, a garage with no plumbing. If I am elected I shall make it my first concern—"

You couldn't argue against it. Like good roads, good weather, and the American Home, everybody is for veterans' housing.

When the meeting broke up, I snagged Tom and we rounded up the leaders of the Third District Association and adjourned to the home of one of the members. "Look, folks," I told them, "when we caucused and I agreed to run, our purpose was to take a bite out of the machine by kicking out Jorgens. Well, the situation has changed. It's not too late for me to forfeit the filing fee. How about it?"

Mrs. Holmes—Mrs. Bixby Holmes, as fine an old warhorse as ever swung a gavel—looked amazed. "What's gotten into you, Jack? Getting rid of Jorgens is only half of it. We have to put in men we can depend on. For this district, you're it."

I shook my head. "I didn't want to be the candidate; I wanted to manage. We should have had a veteran—"

"There's nothing wrong with your war record," put in Dick Blair.

"Maybe not, but it's useless politically. We needed a veteran." I had shuffled papers in the legal section of the Manhattan project—in civilian clothes. Dick Blair, a paratrooper and Purple Heart, had been my choice. But Dick had begged off, and who is to tell a combat veteran that he has got to make further sacrifice for the dear peepul?

"I abided by the will of the group, because Jorgens

was not a veteran either. Now look at the damn thing—What makes you think I can beat her? She's got political sex-appeal."

"She's got more than political sex-appeal"—this from Tom.

When Dr. Potter spoke we listened; he's the old head in our group. "That's the wrong tack, Jack. It does not matter whether you win."

"I don't believe in lost causes, Doctor."

"I do. And so will you, someday. If Miss Nelson is Tully's choice to succeed Jorgens, then we must oppose her."

"She *is* with the machine, isn't she?" asked Mrs. Holmes.

"Sure she is," Tom told her. "Didn't you see that Cliff Meyers had her in tow? She's a stooge—the Stooge with the Light Brown Hair."

I insisted on a vote; they were all against me. "Okay," I agreed, "if you can take it, I can. This means a tougher campaign. We thought the dirt we had on Jorgens was enough; now we've got to dig."

"Don't fret, Jack," Mrs. Holmes soothed me. "We'll dig. I'll take charge of the precinct work."

"I thought your daughter in Denver was having a baby?"

"So she is. I'll stick."

I ducked out soon after, feeling much better, not because I thought I could win, but because of Mrs. Holmes and Dr. Potter and more like them. The team spirit you get in a campaign is pretty swell; I was feeling it again and recovering my pre-War zip.

Before the War our community was in good shape. We had kicked out the local machine, tightened up civil service, sent a police lieutenant to jail, and had put the bidding for contracts on an honest-to-goodness competitive basis—not by praying on Sunday, either, but by volunteer efforts of private citizens willing to get out and punch doorbells.

Then the War came along and everything came unstuck.

Naturally, the people who can be depended on for the in-and-out-of-season grind of volunteer politics are also the ones who took the War the most seriously. From Pearl Harbor to Hiroshima they had no time for politics. It's a wonder the city hall wasn't stolen during the War—bolted to its foundations, I guess.

On my way home I stopped at a drive-in for a hamburger and some thought. Another car squeezed in close beside me. I glanced up, then blinked my eyes. "Well, I'll be—Miss Nelson! Who let you out alone?"

She jerked her head around, ready to bristle, then turned on the vote-getter. "You startled me. You're Mr. Ross, aren't you?"

"Your future councilman," I agreed. "You startled *me*. How's the politicking? Where's Cliff Meyers? Dump him down a sewer?"

She giggled. "Poor Mr. Meyers! I said goodnight to him at my door, then came over here. I was hungry."

"That's no way to win elections. Why didn't you invite him in and scramble some eggs?"

"Well, I just didn't want—I mean I wanted a chance to think. You won't tell on me?" She gave me the you-great-big-strong-man look.

"I'm the enemy—remember? But I won't. Shall I go away, too?"

"No, don't. Since you are going to be my councilman, I ought to get acquainted. Why are you so sure you will beat me, Mr. Ross?"

"Jack Ross—your friend and mine. Have a cigar. I'm not at all sure I can beat you. With your natural advantages and Tully's gang behind you I should 'a stood in bed."

Her eyes went narrow; the vote-getter smile was gone. "What do you mean?" she said slowly. "I'm an independent candidate."

It was my cue to crawl, but I passed. "You expect

me to swallow that? With Cliff Meyers at your elbow—" The car hop interrupted us; we placed our orders and I resumed. She cut in.

"I *do* want to be alone," she snapped and started to close her window.

I reached out and placed a hand on the glass. "Just a moment. This is politics; you are judged by the company you keep. You show up at your first meeting and Cliff Meyers has you under his wing."

"What's wrong with that? Mr. Meyers is a perfect gentleman."

"And he's good to his mother. He's a man with no visible means of support, who does chores for Boss Tully. I thought what everybody thought, that the boss had sent him to chaperone a green candidate."

"It's not true!"

"No? You're caught in the jam cupboard. What's your story?"

She bit her lip. "I don't have to explain anything to you."

"No. But if you won't, the circumstances speak for themselves." She didn't answer. We sat there, ignoring each other, while we ate. When she switched on the ignition, I said, "I'm going to tail you home."

"It's not necessary, thank you."

"This town is a rough place since the War. A young woman should not be out alone at night. Even Cliff Meyers is better than nobody."

"That's why I let them— Do as you see fit!" I had to skim red lights, but I kept close behind her. I expected her to rush inside and slam the door, but she was waiting by the curb. "Thank you for seeing me home, Mr. Ross."

"Quite all right." I went up on her front porch with her and said goodnight.

"Mr. Ross—I shouldn't care what you think, but I'm not with Boss Tully. I'm independent." I waited. Presently she said, "You don't believe me." The big, beautiful eyes were shiny with tears.

"I didn't say so—but I'm waiting for you to explain."

"But what is there to explain?"

"Plenty." I sat down on the porch swing. "Come here, and tell papa. Why did you decide to run for office?"

"Well . . ." She sat down beside me; I caught a disturbing whiff of perfume. "It started because I couldn't find an apartment. No, it didn't—it was farther back, out in the South Pacific. I could stand the insects and the heat. Even the idiotic way the Army does things didn't fret me much. But we had to queue up to use the wash basins. There was even a time when baths were rationed. I hated it. I used to lie on my cot at night, awake in the heat, and dream about a bathroom of my own. A bathroom of my own! A deep tub of water and time to soak. Shampoos and manicures and big, fluffy towels! I wanted to lock myself in and live there. Then I got out of the Army—"

"Yes?"

She shrugged. "The only apartment I could find carried a bonus bigger than my discharge pay, and I couldn't afford it anyhow."

"What's wrong with your own home?"

"This? This is my aunt's home. Seven in the family and I make eight—one bathroom. I'm lucky to brush my teeth. And I share a three-quarters bed with my eight-year-old cousin."

"I see. But that doesn't tell why you are running for office."

"Yes, it does. Uncle Sam was here one night and I was boiling over about the housing shortage and what I would like to do to Congress. He said I ought to be in politics; I said I'd welcome the chance. He phoned the next day and asked how would I like to run for his seat? I said—"

"Uncle Sam—Sam Jorgens!"

"Yes. He's not my uncle, but I've known him since I was little. I was scared, but he said not to worry, he would help me out and advise me. So I did and that's all there is to it. You see now?"

I saw all right. The political acumen of an Easter bunny—except that the bunny rabbit was likely to lick the socks off me. "Okay," I told her, "but housing isn't the only issue. How about the gas company franchise, for example and the sewage disposal plant? And the tax rate? What airport deal do you favor? Do you think we ought to ease up on zoning and how about the freeways?"

"I'm going after housing. Those issues can wait."

I snorted. "They won't let you wait. While you're riding your hobbyhorse, the boys will steal the public blind—again."

"Hobbyhorse! Mister Smarty-Britches, getting a house is the most important thing in the world to the man who hasn't one. You wouldn't be so smug if you were in that fix."

"Keep your shirt on. Me, I'm sleeping in a leaky trailer. I'm strong for plenty of housing—but how do you propose to get it?"

"How? Don't be silly. I'll back the measures that push it."

"Such as? Do you think the city ought to get into the building business? Or should it be strictly private enterprise? Should we sell bonds and finance new homes? Limit it to veterans, or will you help me, too? Heads of families only, or are you going to cut yourself in on it? How about pre-fabrication? Can we do everything you want to do under a building code that was written in 1911?" I paused for breath. "Well?"

"You're being nasty, Jack."

"I sure am. But that's not half of it. I'll challenge you to debate on everything from dog licenses to patent paving materials. A nice, clean campaign and may the best man win—providing his name is Ross."

"I won't accept."

"You'll wish you had, before we're through. My boys

and girls will be at all your meetings, asking embar-rassing questions."

She looked at me. "Of all the dirty politics!"

"You're a candidate, kid; you're supposed to know the answers."

She looked upset. "I *told* Uncle Sam," she said, half to herself, "that I didn't know enough about such things, but he said—"

"Go on, Frances. What did he say?"

She shook her head. "I've told you too much already."

"I'll tell you. You were not to worry your pretty head, because he would be there to tell you how to vote. That was it, wasn't it?"

"Well, not in so many words. He said—"

"But it amounted to that. And he brought Meyers around and said Meyers would show you the ropes. You didn't want to cause trouble, so you did what Meyers told you to do. Right?"

"You've got the nastiest way of putting things."

"That's not all. You honestly think you are inde-pendent. But you do what Sam Jorgens tells you and Sam Jorgens—your sweet old Uncle Sam—won't change his socks without Boss Tully's permission."

"I don't believe it!"

"Check it. Ask some of the newspaper boys. Sniff around."

"I shall."

"Good. You'll learn about the birds and the bees." I stood up. "I've worn out my welcome. See you at the barricades, comrade."

I was halfway to the street when she called me back. "Jack!"

"Yes, Frances?" I went back up on the porch.

"I'm going to find out what connection, if any, Tully has with Uncle Sam, but, nevertheless and notwith-standing, I'm an independent. If I've been led around by the nose, I won't be for long."

"Good girl!"

"That's not all. I'm going to give you the fight of your life, whip the pants off you, and wipe that know-it-all look off your face!"

"Bravo! That's the spirit, kid. We'll have fun."

"Thanks. Well, goodnight."

"Just a second." I put an arm around her shoulders. She leaned away from me warily. "Tell me, darling: who writes your speeches?"

I got kicked in the shins, then the screen door was between us. "Goodnight, Mr. Ross!"

"One more thing—your middle name, it can't be 'Xavier.' What *does* the X stand for?"

"Xanthippe—want to make something of it?" The door slammed.

I was too busy the following month to worry about Frances Nelson. Ever been a candidate? It is like getting married and having your appendix out, while going over Niagara Falls in a barrel. One or more meetings every evening, breakfast clubs on Saturdays and Sundays, a Kiwanis, Rotary, or Lions, or Chamber of Commerce lunch to hit at noon, an occasional appearance in court, endless correspondence, phone calls, conferences, and, to top it off, as many hours of doorbell pushing as I could force into each day.

It was a grass-roots campaign, the best sort, but strenuous. Mrs. Holmes, by scraping the barrel, rounded up volunteers to cover three-quarters of the precincts; the rest were my problem. I couldn't cover them all, but I could durn well try.

And every day there was the problem of money. Even with a volunteer, unpaid organization, politics costs money—printing, postage, hall rental, telephone bills, and there is gasoline and lunch money for people who can't carry their own expenses. A dollar here and a dollar there and soon you are three thousand bucks in the red.

It is hard to tell how a campaign is going; you tend to kid each other. We made a mid-stream spot check—

phone calls, a reply post-card poll, and a doorbell sampling. And Tom and I and Mrs. Holmes got out and sniffed the air. All one day I bought gasoline here, a cola there, and a pack of cigarettes somewhere else, talking politics as I did so, and never offering my name. By the time I met Tom and Mrs. Holmes at her home I felt that I knew my chances.

We got our estimates together and looked them over. Mine read: "Ross 45%; Nelson 55%; McNye a trace." Tom's was: "fifty-fifty, against us." Mrs. Holmes had written, "A dull campaign, a light vote, and a trend against us." The computed results of the formal polls read; Ross 43%, Nelson 52%, McNye 5%—probable error plus-or-minus 9%.

I looked around. "Shall we cut our losses, or go on gallantly to defeat?"

"We aren't licked yet," Tom pointed out.

"No, but we're going to be. All we offer is the assumption that I'm better qualified than the little girl with the big eyes—a notion in which Joe Public is colossally uninterested. How about it, Mrs. Holmes? Can you make it up in the precincts?"

She faced me. "Jack, to be frank, it's all uphill. I'm working the old faithfuls too hard and I can't seem to stir out any new blood."

"We need excitement," Tom complained. "Let's throw some mud."

"At what?" I asked. "Want to accuse her of passing notes in school, or shall we say she sneaked out after taps when she was a WAC? She's got no record."

"Well, tackle her on housing. You've let her hog the best issue."

I shook my head. "If I knew the answers, I wouldn't be living in a trailer. I won't make phony promises. I've drawn up three bills, one to support the Federal Act, one to revise the building code, and one for a bond election for housing projects—that last one is a hot potato. None of them are much good. This housing shortage will be with us for years."

Tom said, "Jack, you shouldn't run for office. You don't have the fine, free optimism that makes a good public figure."

I grunted. "That's what I told you birds. I'm the manager type. A candidate who manages himself gets a split personality."

Mrs. Holmes knit her brows. "Jack—you know more about housing than she does. Let's hold a rally and debate it."

"Okay with me—I just work here. I once threatened to make her debate everything from streetcars to taxes. How about it, Tom?"

"Anything to make some noise."

I phoned at once. "Is this the Stooge with the Light Brown Hair?"

"That must be Jack Ross. Hello, Nasty. How's the baby-kissing?"

"Sticky. Remember I promised to debate the issues with you? How about 8 p.m. Wednesday the 15th?"

She said, "Hold the line—" I could hear a muffled rumble, then she said, "Jack? You tend to your campaign; I'll tend to mine."

"Better accept, kid. We'll challenge you publicly. Is Miss Nelson afraid to face the issues, quote and unquote."

"Goodbye, Jack."

"Uncle Sam won't let you, will he?" The phone clicked in my ear.

We went ahead anyway. I sold some war bonds and ordered a special edition of the Civic League News, with a Ross-for-Councilman front page, as a throwaway to announce the rally—prizes, entertainment, movies, and a super-colossal, gigantic debate between Ross in this corner and Nelson in that. We piled the bundles of papers in Mrs. Holmes' garage late Sunday night. Mrs. Holmes phoned about seven-thirty the next morning—"Jack," she yipped, "come over right away!"

"On my way. What's wrong?"

"Everything. Wait till you get here." When I did, she led me out to her garage; someone had broken in and had slit open our precious bundles—then had poured dirty motor oil on them.

Tom showed up while we were looking at the mess. "Pixies everywhere," he observed. "I'll call the Commercial Press."

"Don't bother," I said bitterly. "We can't pay for another run." But he went in anyhow. The kids who were to do the distributing started to show up; we paid them and sent them home. Tom came out. "Too late," he announced. "We would have to start from scratch—no time and too expensive."

I nodded and went in the house. I had a call to make myself. "Hello," I snapped, "is this Miss Nelson, the Independent Candidate?"

"This is Frances Nelson. Is this Jack Ross?"

"Yes. You were expecting me to call, I see."

"No, I knew your sweet voice. To what do I owe the honor?"

"I'd like to show you how well your boys have been campaigning."

"Just a moment— I've an appointment at ten; I can spare the time until then. What do you mean; how my boys have been campaigning?"

"You'll find out." I hung up.

I refused to talk until she had seen the sabotage. She stared. "It's a filthy, nasty trick, Jack—but why show it to me?"

"Who else?"

"But— Look, Jack, I don't know who did this, but it has nothing to do with me." She looked around at us. "You've got to believe me!" Suddenly she looked relieved. "I know! It wasn't me, so it must have been McNye."

Tom grunted. I said gently, "Look, darling, McNye is nobody. He's a seventeenth-rater who files to get his name in print. He wouldn't use sabotage because he's not out to win. It *has* to be you—wait!—not you per-

sonally, but the machine. This is what you get into
when you accept the backing of wrong 'uns."

"But you're wrong! You're wrong! I'm not backed
by the machine."

"So? Who runs your campaign? Who pays your
bills?"

She shook her head. "A committee takes care of
those things. My job is to show up at meetings and
speak."

"Where did the committee come from? Did the stork
bring it?"

"Don't be ridiculous. It's the Third District Home-
Owners' League. They endorsed me and set up a campaign committee for me."

I'm no judge of character, but she was telling the
truth, as she saw it. "Ever hear of a dummy organization, kid? Your only connection with this Home-Own-
ers' League is Sam Jorgens . . . isn't it?"

"Why, no—that is— Yes, I suppose so."

"And I told you Jorgens was a tame dog for Boss
Tully."

"Yes, but I checked on that, Jack. Uncle Sam explained the whole thing. Tully used to support him,
but they broke because Uncle Sam wouldn't take the
machine's orders. It's not his fault that the machine
used to back him."

"And you believed him."

"No, I made him prove it. You said to check with the
newspapers—Uncle Sam had me talk with the editor
of the *Herald.*" Tom snorted.

"He means," I told her, "that the *Herald* is part of
the machine. I meant talk to reporters. Most of them
are honest and all of them know the score. But I can't
see how you could be so green. I know you've been
away, but didn't you read the papers before the War?"

It developed that, what with school and the War, she
hadn't been around town much since she was fifteen.
Mrs. Holmes broke in, "Why, she's not eligible, Jack!
She doesn't have the residence requirements."

I shook my head. "As a lawyer, I assure you she does. Those things don't break residence—particularly as she enlisted here. How about making us all some coffee, Mrs. Holmes?"

Mrs. Holmes bristled; I could see that she did not want to fraternize with the enemy, but I took her arm and led her into the house, whispering as I went. "Don't be hard on the kid, Molly. You and I made mistakes while we were learning the ropes. Remember Smythe?"

Smythe was as fine a stuffed shirt as ever took a bribe—we had given him our hearts' blood. Mrs. Holmes looked sheepish and relaxed. We chatted about the heat and presidential possibilities, then Frances said, "I'm conceding nothing, Jack—but I'm going to pay for those papers."

"Skip it," I said. "I'd rather bang Tully's heads together. But see here—you've got an hour yet; I want to show you something."

"Want me along, Jack?" Tom suggested, looking at Frances.

"If you like. Thanks for the coffee, Mrs. Holmes—I'll be back to clean up the mess." We drove to Dr. Potter's office and got the photostats we had on Jorgens out of his safe. We didn't say anything; I just arranged the exhibits in logical order. Frances didn't talk either, but her face got whiter and whiter. At last she said, "Will you take me home now, Mr. Ross?"

We bumped along for the next three weeks, chasing votes all day, licking stamps and stenciling auto-bumper signs late at night and never getting enough sleep. Presently we noticed a curious fact—McNye was coming up. First it was billboards and throwaways, next was publicity—and then we began to get reports from the field of precinct work for McNye.

We couldn't have been more puzzled if the Republican Party had nominated Norman Thomas. We made another spot check. Mrs. Holmes and Dr. Potter and I went over the results. Ross and Nelson, neck and neck—a loss for Nelson; McNye a strong third and coming up fast. "What do you think, Mrs. Holmes?"

"The same you do. Tully has dumped Nelson and bought up McNye."

Potter agreed. "It'll be you and McNye in the run-off. Nelson is coasting on early support from the machine. She'll fizzle."

Tom had come in while we were talking. "I'm not sure," he said. "Tully needs a win in the primary, or, if that fails, a run-off between the girl and McNye. We've got an organization, she hasn't."

"Tully can't count on me running third. In fact, I'll beat out Frances for second place at the very worst."

Tom looked quizzical. "Seen tonight's *Herald*, Jack?"

"No. Have they discovered I'm a secret drinker?"

"Worse than that." He chucked us the paper. "CLAIM ROSS INELIGIBLE COUNCILMANIC RACE" it read; there was a 3-col cut of my trailer, with me in the door. The story pointed out that a city father must have lived two years in the city and six months in his district. The trailer camp was outside the city limits.

Dr. Potter looked worried. "Can they disqualify you, Jack?"

"They won't take it to court," I told him. "I'm legal as baseball. Residence isn't geographical location; it's a matter of intent—your home is where you intend to return when you're away. I'm registered at the flat I had before the War, but I turned it over to my partner when I went to Washington. My junk is still in it, but he's got a wife and twins. Hence the trailer, a temporary exigency of no legal effect."

"Hmmm . . . how about the political effect?"

"That's another matter."

"You betcha it is," agreed Tom. "How about it, Mrs. Holmes?"

She looked worried. "Tom is right. It's tailor-made for a word-of-mouth campaign combined with unfavorable publicity. Why vote for a man who doesn't even live in your district?—that sort of thing."

I nodded. "Well, it's too late to back out, but, let's face it, folks— We've wasted our nickel."

For once they did not argue. Instead Potter said, "What sort of person is Miss Nelson? Could we possibly back her in the finals?"

"She's a good kid," I assured him. "She got taken in and hated to admit it, but she's better than McNye."

"I'll say she is," agreed Tom.

"She's a lady," stated Mrs. Holmes.

"But," I objected, "we can't elect her in the finals. We can't pin anything on McNye and she's too green to stand up to what the machine can do to her in a long campaign. Tully knows what he's doing."

"I'm afraid you're right," Potter agreed.

"Jack," said Tom, "I take it you think we're licked now."

"Ask Mrs. Holmes."

Mrs. Holmes said, "I hate to say so, and I'm not quitting, but it would take a miracle to put Jack on the final ballot."

"Okay," said Tom, "let's quit being boy scouts and have some fun the rest of the campaign. I don't like the way Boss Tully campaigns. We've played fair; what we've gotten in return is shenanigans."

"What do you want to do?"

He explained. Presently I nodded and said, "I'm all for it—and a wrinkle of my own. It'll be fun, and it just might work."

"Well, call her up then!"

I got Frances Nelson on the phone. "Jack Ross, Frances. Haven't seen you around much, sweetheart. How's the campaign?"

She sounded tired. "Oh, that— What campaign, Jack?"

"Did you withdraw? I haven't seen any announcement."

"It wasn't necessary. I had a show-down with

Jorgens and after that my campaign just disappeared. The committee vanished away. Look, Jack, I'd like to see you—to apologize."

"Forget it, I want to see you, too. I'll pick you up."

We laid it on the line. "I'm dropping out of the race, Frances. We want to throw our organizational support to you—provided."

She stared. "But you can't, Jack. I'm going to vote for you."

"Huh? Never mind, you won't get a chance to." I showed her the *Herald* story. "It's a phony, but it licks me anyhow. I should have played up my homeless condition but, like a dope, I let them do it. It's too late now—when a candidate has to explain things he's back on his heels and ready for the knockout. I was a fifty-fifty squeeze at best; this tips the balance."

She was staring at the picture, bug-eyed, knuckles pressed to her mouth. "Jack— Oh, dear! I've gone and done it again."

"Done what?"

"Got you into this mess. I told Sam Jorgens all about our first talk, including how you had to camp out in a trailer. I—"

I brushed it aside. "No matter. They would have stumbled on it anyhow. See here—we're going to take you on. We might even elect you."

"But I don't want the job, Jack. I want you to have it."

"Too late, Frances. But we want to beat that spare tire, McNye. The machine is still using you, to beat me in the primary by splitting the non-machine vote; then they'll settle your hash. I've got a gimmick for that. But first—you call yourself an independent. Well, you aren't now."

"What do you mean? I won't be anything else."

"They gave women the vote! Look, darling, a candidate can be unbossed, but not independent. Independence is an adolescent notion. To merit support you have to commit yourself—and there goes your independence."

"But I— Oh, politics is a rotten business!"

"You make me tired! Politics is just as clean—or as dirty—as the people who practice it. The people who say it's dirty are too lazy to do their part in it." She dropped her face into her hands. I took her by the shoulders, and shook her. "Now you listen to me. I'm going over our program, point by point. If you agree with it and commit yourself, you're our candidate. Right?"

"Yes, Jack." It was just a whisper.

We ran through it. There was no trouble, it was sane and sensible, likely to appeal to anyone with no ax to grind. The points she did not understand we let lay over. She liked especially my housing bills and began to perk up and sound like a candidate.

"Okay," I said finally. "Here's the gimmick. I'll get my name off the ballot so that the race will be over in the primary. It's too late to do it myself, but they've played into my hands. It'll be a court order, for ineligibility through non-residence."

Dr. Potter looked up sharply. "Come again, son? I thought you said your legal position was secure."

I grinned. "It is—if I fight. But I won't. Here's the gag—we bring a citizen's suit through a couple of dummies. The court orders me to show cause. I default. Court has no option but to order my name stricken from the ballot. One, two, three."

Tom cheered. I bowed. "Now Dr. Potter is your new campaign chairman. You go on as before, going where you are sent and speaking your piece. Oh, yes—I'm going to give you some homework on other issues than housing. As for Tom and me—we're the special effects department. Just forget us."

Three days later I was off the ballot. Tom handled it so that it looked like McNye and Tully. Mrs. Holmes had the delicate job of convincing our precinct workers that Frances was our new white hope. Dr. Potter and Dick Blair got Frances endorsed by the Civic League—the League would endorse a giant panda against a Tully man. And Dick Blair worked up a veterans' division.

Leaving Tom and me free for fun and games.

First we got a glamor pic of Frances, one that made her look like Liberty Enlightening the World, with great sorrowful eyes and a noble forehead, and had it blown up for billboards—6-sheets; 24-sheets look like too much dough.

We got a "good" picture of McNye, too—good for us. Like this—you send two photographers to a meeting where your man is to speak. One hits him with a flash bulb; the second does also, right away, before the victim can recover from his reflex. Then you throw the first pic away. We got a picture which showed McNye as pop-eyed, open-mouthed, and idiotic—a Kallikak studying to be a Jukes. It was so good we had to tone it down. Then I went up state and got some printing done, very privately.

We waited until the last few days, then got busy. First we put snipe sheets on our own billboards, right across Frances' beautiful puss so that those eyes looked appealingly at you over the paster. "VOTE FOR McNYE" they read. Two nights later it was quarter cards, this time with his lovely picture: VOTE FOR McNYE—A WOMAN'S PLACE IS IN THE HOME. We stuck them up on private property, too.

Tom and I drove around the next day admiring our handiwork. "It's beautiful," Tom said dreamily. "Jack, do you suppose there is any way we could get the Communist Party to endorse McNye?"

"I don't see how," I admitted, "but if it doesn't cost too much I've still got a couple of war bonds."

He shook his head. "It can't work, but it's a lovely thought."

We saved our double-whammie for the day before election. It was expensive—but wait. We hired some

skid-row characters on Saturday, through connections Tom has, and specified that they must show up
with two-day beards on Monday. We fed each one a
sandwich loaded with garlic, gave him literature and
instructions—ring the doorbell, blow his breath in the
victim's face, and hand her a handbill, saying
abruptly, "Here's how you vote, lady!" The handbill
said, "VOTE FOR McNYE" and had his special picture. It had the rest of Tully's slate too, and some
choice quotes of McNye's best double talk. Around the
edge it said "100% American—100% American."

We pushed the stumblebums through an average of
four precincts apiece, concentrating on the better
neighborhoods.

That night there was an old-fashioned torchlight pa-
rade—Mrs. Holmes' show, and the wind-up of the
proper campaign. It started off with an elephant and
donkey (Heaven knows where she borrowed the elephant!) The elephant carried signs: I'M FOR
FRANCES; the donkey, SO AM I. There was a kid's
band, flambeaux carried by our weary volunteers, and
a platoon of WAC and WAVE veterans marching ahead
of the car that carried Frances. She looked scared and
lovely.

Tom and I watched it, then got to work. No sleep
that night—

More pasters. Windshield size this time, 3"x10",
with glue on the printed side. I suppose half the cars in
town have no garages, housing being what it is. We
covered every block in the district before dawn, Tom
driving and me on the right with a pail of water, a
sponge, and stickers. He would pull alongside a car; I
would slap a sticker on the windshield where it would
stare the driver in the face—and have to be scraped
off. They read: VOTE FOR McNYE—KEEP AMERICA
PURE.

We figured it would help to remind people to vote.

I voted myself when the polls opened, then fell into
bed.

I pulled myself together in time to get to the party at the headquarters—an empty building we had borrowed for the last month of the campaign. I hadn't given a thought to poll watchers or an honest count—that was Mrs. Holmes' baby—but I didn't want to miss the returns.

One election party is like another—the same friendly drunks, the same silent huddle around the radio, the same taut feeling. I helped myself to some beer and potato chips and joined the huddle.

"Anything yet," I asked Mrs. Holmes. "Where's Frances?"

"Not yet. I made her lie down."

"Better get her out here. The candidate has to be seen. When people work for a pat on the back, you've got to give 'em the pat."

But Frances showed up about then, and went through the candidate routine—friendly, gracious, thanking people, etc. I began to think about running her for Congress.

Tom showed up, bleary-eyed, as the first returns came in. All McNye. Frances heard them and her smile slipped. Dr. Potter went over to her and said, "It's not important—the machine's precincts are usually first to report." She plastered her smile back on.

McNye piled up a big lead. Then our efforts began to show—Nelson was pulling up. By 10:30 it was neck and neck. After a while it began to look as if we had elected a councilman.

Around midnight McNye got on the air and conceded.

So I'm a councilman's field secretary now. I sit outside the rail when the council meets; when I scratch my right ear, Councilman Nelson votes "yes"; if I scratch my left ear, she votes "no"—usually.

Marry her? *Me?* Tom married her. They're building a house, one bedroom and *two* bathrooms. When they can get the fixtures, that is.

FOREWORD

When the USSR refused our proposals for controlling the A-bomb, I swore off "World-Saving." No more preaching. No more attempts to explain the mortal peril we were in. No, sir!

A year and a half later, late '47, I backslid. If it could not be done by straightforward exposition, perhaps it could be dramatized as fiction.

Again I fell flat on my face.

Fifteen years later there was a tremendous flap over Soviet medium-range missiles in Cuba. Then they were removed—or so we were told—and the flap died out. Why? Why both ways? For years we have had Soviet submarines on both coasts; are they armed with slingshots? Or powder puffs?

This story is more timely today, over thirty years later, than it was when it was written; the danger is enormously greater.

And again this warning will be ignored. But it won't take much of your time; it's a short-short, a mere 2200 words.

ON THE SLOPES OF VESUVIUS

"Paddy, shake hands with the guy who built the atom bomb," Professor Warner said to the bartender. "He and Einstein rigged it up in their own kitchen one evening."

"With the help of about four hundred other guys," amended the stranger, raising his voice slightly to cut through the rumble of the subway.

"Don't quibble over details. Paddy, this is Doctor Mansfield. Jerry, meet Paddy— Say, Paddy, what *is* your last name?"

"Francis X. Hughes," answered the barkeep as he wiped his hand and stuck it out. "I'm pleased to meet any friend of Professor Warner."

"I'm pleased to meet you, Mr. Hughes."

"Call me Paddy, they all do. You really are one of the scientists who built the atom bomb?"

"I'm afraid so."

"May the Lord forgive you. Are you at N.Y.U., too?"

"No, I'm out at the new Brookhaven Laboratory."

"Oh, yes."

"You've been there?"

Hughes shook his head. "About the only place I go is home to Brooklyn. But I read the papers."

"Paddy's in a well-padded rut," explained Warner. "Paddy, what are you going to do when they blow up New York? It'll break up your routine."

He set their drinks before them and poured himself

a short beer. "If that's all I've got to worry about I guess I'll die of old age and still in my rut, Professor."

Warner's face lost its cheerful expression for a moment; he stared at his drink as if it had suddenly become bitter. "I wish I had your optimism, Paddy, but I haven't. Sooner or later, we're in for it."

"You shouldn't joke about such things, Professor."

"I'm not joking."

"You can't be serious."

"I wish I weren't. Ask him. After all, he built the damned thing."

Hughes raised his brows at Mansfield who replied, "I'm forced to agree with Professor Warner. They will be able to do it—atom-bomb New York I mean. I *know* that; it's not a guess—it's a certainty. Being able to do it, I'm strongly of the opinion that they *will* do it."

"Who do you mean by 'they'?" demanded the bartender. "The Russians?"

"Not necessarily. It might be anybody who first worked up the power to smash us."

"Sure," said Warner. "Everybody wants to kick the fat boy. We're envied and hated. The only reason we haven't been smeared is that no one has had what it takes to do it—up to now, that is!"

"Just a minute, gentlemen—" put in Hughes. "I don't get it. You're talking about somebody—anybody—atom-bombing New York. How can they do it? Didn't we decide to hang on to the secret? Do you think some dirty spy has gotten away with it while we weren't watching?"

Mansfield looked at Warner, then back at Hughes and said gently, "I hate to disturb your peace of mind, Mr. Hughes—Paddy—but there is no secret. Any nation that is willing to go to the trouble and expense can build an atom bomb."

"And that's official," added Warner, "and it's a lead-pipe cinch that, power politics being what it is, a dozen different nations are working on the problem right now."

Hughes had been looking perturbed; his face cleared. "Oh, I see what you mean. In time, they can dig it out for themselves. In that case, gentlemen, let's have a round on the house and drink to their frustration. I can't be worrying about what might happen twenty years from now. We might none of us be spared that long what with taxicabs and the like."

Mansfield's brows shot up. "Why do you say twenty years, Paddy?"

"Eh? Oh, I seem to remember reading it in the papers. That general, wasn't it? The one who was in charge of the atom-bomb business."

Mansfield brushed the general aside. "Poppycock! That estimate is based on entirely unwarranted national conceit. The time will be much shorter."

"How much shorter?" demanded Hughes. Mansfield shrugged.

"What would you do, Paddy," Warner asked curiously, "if you thought some nation—let's say some nation that didn't like us—had already managed to manufacture atom bombs?"

The saloon cat came strolling along the top of the bar. Hughes stopped to feed it a slice of cheese before replying. "I do not have your learning, gentlemen, but Paddy Hughes is no fool. If someone is loose in the world with those devil's contraptions, New York is a doomed city. America is the champion and must be beaten before any new bully boy can hope to win—and New York is one of the spots he would shoot at first. Even Sad Sack—" He jerked a thumb at the cat. "—is bright enough to flee from a burning building."

"Well, what do you think you would do?"

"I don't 'think' what I'd do, I *know* what I'd do; I've done it before. When I was a young man and the Black-and-Tans were breathing down the back o' my neck, I climbed on a ship with never a thought of looking back—and any man who wanted them could have my pigs and welcome to them."

Warner chuckled. "You must have been quite the

lad, Paddy. But I don't believe you would do it—not now. You're firmly rooted in your rut and you like it—like me and six million others in this town. That's why decentralization is a fantasy."

Hughes nodded. "It would be hard." That it would be hard he understood. Like leaving home it would be to quit Schreiber's Bar-Grill after all these years—Schreiber couldn't run it without him; he'd chase all the customers away. It would be hard to leave his friends in the parish, hard to leave his home—what with Molly's grave being just around the corner and all. And if the cities were to be blown up a man would have to go back to farming. He'd promised himself when he hit the new country that he'd never, never, never tackle the heartbreaking load of tilling the soil again. Well, perhaps there would be no landlords when the cities were gone. If a man must farm, at least he might be spared that. Still, it would be hard—and Molly's grave off somewhere in the rubble. "But I'd do it."

"You think you would."

"I wouldn't even go back to Brooklyn to pick up my other shirt. I've my week's pay envelope right here." He patted his vest. "I'd grab my hat and start walking." The bartender turned to Mansfield. "Tell me the truth, Doctor—if it's not twenty years, how long will it be?"

Mansfield took out an envelope and started figuring on the back of it. Warner started to speak, but Hughes cut him off. "Quiet while he's working it out!" he said sharply.

"Don't let him kid you, Paddy," Warner said wryly. "He's been lying awake nights working out this problem ever since Hiroshima."

Mansfield looked up. "That's true. But I keep hoping I'll come out with a different answer. I never do."

"Well, what *is* the answer?" Hughes insisted.

Mansfield hesitated. "Paddy, you understand that there are a lot of factors involved, not all of them too clear. Right? In the first place, it took us about four years. But we were lavish with money and lavish with men, more so maybe than any other nation could be, except possibly Russia. Figured on that alone it might take several times four years for another country to make a bomb. But that's not the whole picture; it's not even the important part. There was a report the War Department put out, the Smyth Report—you've heard of it?—which gives anyone who can read everything but the final answers. With that report, with competent people, uranium ore, and a good deal less money than it cost us, a nation ought to be able to develop a bomb in a good deal less time than it took us."

Hughes shook his head. "I don't expect you to explain, Doctor; I just want to know your answer. How long?"

"I was just explaining that the answer had to be indefinite. I make it not less than two and not more than four years."

The bartender whistled softly. "Two years. Two years to get away and start a new life."

"No, no, no! Mr. Hughes," Mansfield objected, "Not two years from now—two years from the time the first bomb was dropped."

Hughes' face showed a struggle to comprehend. "But, gentlemen," he protested, "it's been *more* than two years since the first bomb was dropped."

"That's right."

"Don't blow your top, Paddy," Warner cautioned him. "The bomb isn't everything. It might be ten years before anybody develops the sort of robot carrier that can go over the north pole or the ocean and seek out a particular city with an atom bomb. In the meantime we don't have too much to fear from an ordinary airplane attack."

Mansfield looked annoyed. "You started this, Dick. Why try to hand out soothing syrup now? With a country as wide open as this one you don't need anything as fancy as guided missiles to pull a Pearl Harbor on it. The bombs would be assembled secretly and set off by remote control. Why, there might be a tramp steamer lying out there in the East River right now—"

Warner let his shoulders slump. "You're right, of course."

Hughes threw down his bar towel. "You're telling me that New York is as likely to be blown up right now as at any other time."

Mansfield nodded. "That's the size of it," he said soberly.

Hughes looked from one to the other. The cat jumped down and commenced rubbing up against his ankle, purring. He pushed it away with his foot. "It's not true! I know it's not true!"

"Why not?"

"Because! If it was true would you be sitting here, drinking quietly? You've been having a bit of fun with me, pulling my leg. Oh, I can't pick the flaw in your argument, but you don't believe it yourselves."

"I wish I didn't believe it," said Mansfield.

"Oh, we believe it, Paddy," Warner told him. "To tell you the truth, I'm planning to get out. I've got letters out to half a dozen cow colleges; I'm just waiting until my contract expires. As for Doc Mansfield, he can't leave. This is where his lab is located."

Hughes considered this, then shook his head. "No, it won't wash. No man in his right mind will hang on to a job when it means sitting on the hot squat, waiting for the Warden to throw the switch. You're pulling my leg."

Mansfield acted as if Hughes had not spoken. "Anyhow," he said to Warner, "the political factors might delay the blow off indefinitely."

Warner shook his head angrily. "Now who's handing out soothing syrup? The political factors speed up the event, not delay it. If a country intends to defeat us someday, it's imperative that she do it as quickly as possible, before we catch wind of her plans and strike first. Or before we work out a real counter weapon—if that's possible."

Mansfield looked tired, as if he had been tired for a long time. "Oh, you're right. I was just whistling to keep my courage up. But we won't develop a counter weapon, not a real one. The only possible defense against atomic explosion is not to be there when it goes off." He turned to the barman. "Let's have another round, Paddy."

"Make mine a Manhattan," added Warner.

"Just a minute. Professor Warner. Doctor Mansfield. You were not fooling with me? Every word you had to say is God's own truth?"

"As you're standing there, Paddy."

"And Doctor Mansfield—Professor Warner, do you trust Doctor Mansfield's figuring?"

"There's no man in the United States better qualified to make such an estimate. That's the truth, Paddy."

"Well, then—" Hughes turned toward where his employer sat nodding over the cash register on the restaurant side of the room and whistled loudly between his teeth. "Schreiber! Come take the bar." He started stripping off his apron.

"Hey!" said Warner, "where you going? I ordered a Manhattan."

"Mix it yourself," said Hughes. "I've quit." He reached for his hat with one hand, his coat with the other, and then he was out the door.

Forty seconds later he was on an uptown express; he got off at 34th Street and three minutes thereafter he was buying a ticket, west. It was ten minutes later that he felt the train start to roll under him, headed out of the city.

But it was less than an hour later when his misgivings set in. Had he been too hasty? Professor Warner was a fine man, to be sure, but given to his little jokes, now and again. Had he been taken in by a carefully contrived hoax? Had Warner said to his friend, we'll have some fun and scare the living daylights out of the old Irishman?

Nor had he made any arrangements for someone to feed Sad Sack. The cat had a weak stomach, he was certain, and no one else gave the matter any attention at all. And Molly's grave—Wednesday was his day to do his gardening there. Of course Father Nelson would see that it was watered, just for kindness' sake, but still—

When the train paused at Princeton Junction he slipped off and sought out a telephone. He had in mind what he meant to say if he was able to reach Professor Warner—a good chance, he thought, for considering the hour the gentlemen probably stayed on for a steak. Professor Warner, he would say, you've had your fun and a fine joke it was as I would be the first to say and to buy a drink on it, but tell me—man to man—was there anything *to* what you and your friend was telling me? That would settle it, he thought.

The call went through promptly and he heard Schreiber's irritated voice. "Hello," he said.

The line went dead. He jiggled the hook. The operator answered, "One moment, please—" then, "This is the Princeton operator. Is this the party with the call to New York?"

"Yes. I—"

"There has been a temporary interruption in service. Will you hang up and try again in a few minutes, please?"

"But I was just talking—"

"Will you hang up and try again in a few minutes, puh*lease*?"

He heard the shouting as he left the booth. As he got outdoors he could see the great, gloriously beautiful, gold and purple mushroom still mounting over where had been the City of New York.

FOREWORD

This story was written twenty-one years before Dr. Neil Armstrong took "one short step for a man, a giant leap for mankind"—but in all important essentials it has not (yet) become dated. True, we do not know that formations such as "morning glories" exist on Luna and we do not know that there are areas where footgear midway between skis and snowshoes would be useful. But the Lunar surface is about equal in area to Africa; a dozen men have explored an area smaller than Capetown for a total of a few days. We will still be exploring Luna and finding new wonders there when the first interstellar explorers return from Proxima Centauri or Tau Ceti.

This story is compatible with the so-called "Future History" stories. It is also part of my continuing post-War-II attempt to leave the SF-pulp field and spread out. I never left the genre pulps entirely, as it turned out to be easy to write a book-length job, then break it into three or four cliff-hangers and sell it as a pulp serial immediately before book publication. I did this with a dozen novels in the '40s and '50s. But I recall only one story (GULF) specifically written for pulp, GULF being for Astounding's unique "prophesied" issue.

Deus volent, I may someday collect my Boy Scout stories as one volume just as I would like to do with the Puddin' stories.

NOTHING EVER HAPPENS ON THE MOON

"I never knew a boy from Earth who wasn't cocky."

Mr. Andrews frowned at his Senior Patrol Leader. "That's childish, Sam. And no answer. I arrive expecting to find the troop ready to hike. Instead I find you and our visitor about to fight. And both of you Eagle Scouts! What started it?"

Sam reluctantly produced a clipping. "This, I guess."

It was from the Colorado Scouting News and read: "Troop 48, Denver—LOCAL SCOUT SEEKS SKY-HIGH HONOR. Bruce Hollifield, Eagle Scout, is moving with his family to South Pole, Venus. Those who know Bruce—and who doesn't—expect him to qualify as Eagle (Venus) in jig time. Bruce will spend three weeks at Luna City, waiting for the Moon-Venus transport. Bruce has been boning up lately on lunar Scouting, and he has already qualified in space suit operation in the vacuum chamber at the Pike's Peak space port. Cornered, Bruce admitted that he hopes to pass the tests for Eagle Scout (Luna) while on the Moon.

"If he does—and we're betting on Bruce!—he's a dead cinch to become the first Triple Eagle in history.

"Go to it, Bruce! Denver is proud of you. Show those Moon Scouts what real Scouting is like."

Mr. Andrews looked up. "Where did this come from?"

"Uh, somebody sent it to Peewee."

"Yes?"

"Well, we all read it and when Bruce came in, the fellows ribbed him. He got sore."

"Why didn't you stop it?"

"Uh . . . well, I was doing it myself."

"Humph! Sam, this item is no sillier than the stuff our own Scribe turns in for publication. Bruce didn't write it, and you yahoos had no business making his life miserable. Send him in. Meantime call the roll."

"Yes, sir. Uh, Mr. Andrews—"

"Yes?"

"What's *your* opinion? Can this kid possibly qualify for lunar Eagle in three weeks?"

"No—and I've told him so. But he's durn well going to have his chance. Which reminds me: you're his instructor."

"Me?" Sam looked stricken.

"You. You've let me down, Sam; this is your chance to correct it. Understand me?"

Sam swallowed. "I guess I do."

"Send Hollifield in."

Sam found the boy from Earth standing alone, pretending to study the bulletin board. Sam touched his arm. "The Skipper wants you."

Bruce whirled around, then stalked away. Sam shrugged and shouted, "Rocket Patrol—fall in!"

Speedy Owens echoed, "Crescent Patrol—fall in!" As muster ended Mr. Andrews came out of his office, followed by Bruce. The Earth Scout seemed considerably chastened.

"Mr. Andrews says I'm to report to you."

"That's right." They eyed each other cautiously. Sam said, "Look, Bruce—let's start from scratch."

"Suits me."

"Fine. Just tag along with me." At a sign from the Scoutmaster Sam shouted, "By twos! Follow me."

Troop One jostled out the door, mounted a crosstown slidewalk and rode to East Air Lock.

Chubby Schneider, troop quartermaster, waited there with two assistants, near a rack of space suits. Duffel was spread around in enormous piles—packaged grub, tanks of water, huge air bottles, frames of heavy wire, a great steel drum, everything needed for pioneers on the airless crust of the Moon.

Sam introduced Bruce to the Quartermaster. "We've got to outfit him, Chubby."

"That new G.E. job might fit him."

Sam got the suit and spread it out. The suit was impregnated glass fabric, aluminum-sprayed to silvery whiteness. It closed from crotch to collar with a zippered gasket. It looked expensive; Bruce noticed a plate on the collar: DONATED BY THE LUNA CITY KIWANIS KLUB.

The helmet was a plastic bowl, silvered except where swept by the eyes of the wearer. There it was transparent, though heavily filtered.

Bruce's uniform was stowed in a locker; Chubby handed him a loose-knit coverall. Sam and Chubby stuffed him into the suit and Chubby produced the instrument belt.

Both edges of the belt zipped to the suit; there were several rows of grippers for the top edge; thus a pleat could be taken. They fastened it with maximum pleat. "How's that?" asked Sam.

"The collar cuts my shoulders."

"It won't under pressure. If we leave slack, your head will pull out of the helmet like a cork." Sam strapped the air, water, radio, and duffel-rack backpack to Bruce's shoulders. "Pressure check, Chubby."

"We'll dress first." While Chubby and Sam dressed, Bruce located his intake and exhaust valves, the spill valve inside his collar, and the water nipple beside it. He took a drink and inspected his belt.

Sam and Bruce donned helmets. Sam switched on Bruce's walkie-talkie, clipped a blood-oxygen indicator to Bruce's ear, and locked his helmet on. "Stand by for pressure," he said, his words echoing in Bruce's helmet. Chubby hooked hose from a wall gauge to Bruce's air intake.

Bruce felt the collar lift. The air in the suit grew stuffy, the helmet fogged. At thirty pounds Chubby cut the intake, and watched the gauge. Mr. Andrews joined them, a Gargantuan helmeted figure, toting a pack six feet high. "Pressure steady, sir," Chubby reported.

Sam hooked up Bruce's air supply. "Open your intake and kick your chin valve before you smother," he ordered. Bruce complied. The stale air rushed out and the helmet cleared. Sam adjusted Bruce's valves. "Watch that needle," he ordered, pointing to the blood-oxygen dial on Bruce's belt. "Keep your mix so that reads steady in the white without using your chin valve."

"I know."

"So I'll say it again. Keep that needle out of the red, or you'll explain it to Saint Peter."

The Scoutmaster asked, "What load are you giving him?"

"Oh," replied Sam, "just enough to steady him—say three hundred pounds, total."

Bruce figured—at one-sixth gravity that meant fifty pounds weight including himself, his suit, and his pack. "I'll carry my full share," he objected.

"We'll decide what's best for you," the Scoutmaster snapped. "Hurry up; the troop is ready." He left.

Sam switched off his radio and touched helmets. "Forget it," he said quietly. "The Old Man is edgy at the start of a hike." They loaded Bruce rapidly—reserve air and water bottles, a carton of grub, short, wide skis and ski poles—then hung him with field gear, first-aid kit, prospector's hammer, two climbing ropes, a pouch of pitons and snap rings, flashlight, knife. The Moon Scouts loaded up; Sam called, "Come on!"

Mr. Andrews handed the lockmaster a list and stepped inside; the three Scouts followed. Bruce felt his suit expand as the air sucked back into the underground city. A light blinked green; Mr. Andrews opened the outer door and Bruce stared across the airless lunar plain.

It dazzled him. The plain was bright under a blazing Sun. The distant needle-sharp hills seemed painted in colors too flat and harsh. He looked at the sky to rest his eyes.

It made him dizzy. He had never seen a whole skyful of stars undimmed by air. The sky was blacker than black, crowded with hard, diamond lights.

"Route march!" the Scoutmaster's voice rang in his helmet. "Heel and toe. Jack Wills out as pathfinder." A boy left the group in long, floating strides, fifteen feet at a bound. He stopped a hundred yards ahead; the troop formed single column fifty yards behind him. The Pathfinder raised his arm, swung it down, and the troop moved out.

Mr. Andrews and a Scout joined Sam and Bruce. "Speedy will help you," he told Sam, "until Bruce gets his legs. Move him along. We can't heel-and-toe and still make our mileage."

"We'll move him."

"Even if we have to carry him," added Speedy.

The Scoutmaster overtook the troop in long leaps. Bruce wanted to follow. It looked easy—like flying. He had not liked the crack about carrying him. But Sam grasped him by his left belt grip while Speedy seized the one on his right. "Here we go," Sam warned. "Feet on the ground and try to swing in with us."

Bruce started off confidently. He felt that three days of low gravity in the corridors of Luna City had given him his "legs"; being taught to walk, like a baby, was just hazing.

Nothing to it—he was light as a bird! True, it was hard to keep heel-and-toe; he wanted to float. He gained speed on a downgrade; suddenly the ground was not there when he reached for it. He threw up his hands.

He hung head down on his belt and could hear his guides laughing. "Wha' happened?" he demanded, as they righted him.

"Keep your feet on the ground."

"I know what you're up against," added Speedy, "I've been to Earth. Your mass and weight don't match and your muscles aren't used to it. You weigh what a baby weighs, Earth-side, but you've got the momentum of a fat man."

Bruce tried again. Some stops and turns showed him what Speedy meant. His pack felt like feathers, but unless he banked his turns, it would throw him, even at a walk. It *did* throw him, several times, before his legs learned.

Presently, Sam asked, "Think you're ready for a slow lope?"

"I guess so."

"Okay—but remember, if you want to turn, you've *got* to slow down first—or you'll roll like a hoop. Okay, Speedy. An eight-miler."

Bruce tried to match their swing. Long, floating strides, like flying. It *was* flying! Up! . . . float . . . brush the ground with your foot and up again. It was better than skating or skiing.

"Wups!" Sam steadied him. "Get your feet out in front."

As they swung past, Mr. Andrews gave orders for a matching lope.

The unreal hills had moved closer; Bruce felt as if he had been flying all his life. "Sam," he said, "do you suppose I can get along by myself?"

"Shouldn't wonder. We let go a couple o' miles back."

"Huh?" It was true; Bruce began to feel like a Moon hand.

Somewhat later a boy's voice called "Heel and toe!"

The troop dropped into a walk. The pathfinder stood
on a rise ahead, holding his skis up. The troop halted
and unlashed skis. Ahead was a wide basin filled with
soft, powdery stuff.

Bruce turned to Sam, and for the first time looked
back to the west. *"Jee . . . miny Crickets!"* he breathed.

Earth hung over the distant roof of Luna City, in half
phase. It was round and green and beautiful, larger
than the harvest Moon and unmeasurably more lovely
in forest greens, desert browns and glare white of
cloud.

Sam glanced at it. "Fifteen o'clock."

Bruce tried to read the time but was stumped by the
fact that the sunrise line ran mostly across ocean. He
questioned Sam. "Huh? See that bright dot on the
dark side? That's Honolulu—figure from there."

Bruce mulled this over while binding his skis, then
stood up and turned around, without tripping.
"Hmmm—" said Sam, "you're used to skis."

"Got my badge."

"Well, this is different. Just shuffle along and try to
keep your feet."

Bruce resolved to stay on his feet if it killed him. He
let a handful of the soft stuff trickle through his glove.
It was light and flaky, hardly packed at all. He wondered what had caused it.

Mr. Andrews sent Speedy out to blaze trail; Sam and
Bruce joined the column. Bruce was hard put to keep
up. The loose soil flew to left and right, settling so
slowly in the weak gravity that it seemed to float in
air—yet a ski pole, swung through such a cloud, cut a
knife-sharp hole without swirling it.

The column swung wide to the left, then back again.
Off to the right was a circular depression perhaps fifty
yards across; Bruce could not see the bottom. He
paused, intending to question Sam; the Scoutmaster's
voice prodded him. "Bruce! Keep moving!"

Much later Speedy's voice called out, "Hard
ground!" Shortly the column reached it and stopped

to remove skis. Bruce switched off his radio and touched his helmet to Sam's.

"What was that back where the Skipper yelled at me?"

"That? That was a morning glory. They're poison!"

"A 'morning glory'?"

"Sort of a sink hole. If you get on the slope, you never get out. Crumbles out from under you and you wind up buried in the bottom. There you stay—until your air gives out. Lot of prospectors die that way. They go out alone and are likely to come back in the dark."

"How do you know what happens if they go out alone?"

"Suppose you saw tracks leading up to one and no tracks going away?"

"Oh!" Bruce felt silly.

The troop swung into a lope; slowly the hills drew closer and loomed high into the sky. Mr. Andrews called a halt. "Camp," he said. "Sam, spot the shelter west of that outcropping. Bruce, watch what Sam does."

The shelter was an airtight tent, framed by a half cylinder of woven heavy wire. The frame came in sections. The Scoutmaster's huge pack was the air bag.

The skeleton was erected over a ground frame, anchored at corners and over which was spread an asbestos pad. The curved roof and wall sections followed. Sam tested joints with a wrench, then ordered the air bag unrolled. The air lock, a steel drum, was locked into the frame and gasketed to the bag. Meanwhile, two Scouts were rigging a Sun shade.

Five boys crawled inside and stood up, arms stretched high. The others passed in all the duffel except skis and poles. Mr. Andrews was last in and closed the air lock. The metal frame blocked radio communication; Sam plugged a phone connection from the lock to his helmet. "Testing," he said.

Bruce could hear the answer, relayed through Sam's radio. "Ready to inflate."

"Okay." The bag surged up, filling the frame. Sam said, "You go on, Bruce. There's nothing left but to adjust the shade."

"I'd better watch."

"Okay." The shade was a flimsy venetian blind, stretched over the shelter. Sam half-opened the slats. "It's cold inside," he commented, "from expanding gas. But it warms up fast." Presently, coached by phone, he closed them a bit. "Go inside," he urged Bruce. "It may be half an hour before I get the temperature steady."

"Maybe I should," admitted Bruce. "I feel dizzy."

Sam studied him. "Too hot?"

"Yeah, I guess so."

"You've held still in the Sun too long. Doesn't give the air a chance to circulate. Here." Sam opened Bruce's supply valve wider; "Go inside."

Gratefully, Bruce complied.

As he backed in, and straightened up, two boys grabbed him. They closed his valves, unlocked his helmet, and peeled off his suit. The suit traveled from hand to hand and was racked. Bruce looked around.

Daylamps were strung from air lock to a curtain at the far end that shut off the sanitary unit. Near this curtain suits and helmets were racked. Scouts were lounging on both sides of the long room. Near the entrance a Scout was on watch at the air conditioner, a blood-oxygen indicator clipped to his ear. Nearby, Mr. Andrews phoned temperature changes to Sam. In the middle of the room Chubby had set up his commissary. He waved. "Hi, Bruce! Siddown—chow in two shakes."

Two Scouts made room for Bruce and he sat. One of them said, "Y'ever been at Yale?" Bruce had not. "That's where I'm going," the Scout confided. "My brother's there now." Bruce began to feel at home.

When Sam came in Chubby served chow, beef stew, steaming and fragrant, packaged rolls, and bricks of peach ice cream. Bruce decided that Moon Scouts had it soft. After supper, the Bugler got out his harmonica and played. Bruce leaned back, feeling pleasantly drowsy.

"Hollifield!" Bruce snapped awake. "Let's try you on first aid."

For thirty minutes Bruce demonstrated air tourniquets and emergency suit patches, artificial respiration for a man in a space suit, what to do for Sun stroke, for anoxia, for fractures. "That'll do," the Scoutmaster concluded. "One thing: What do you do if a man cracks his helmet?"

Bruce was puzzled. "Why," he blurted, "you bury him."

"Check," the Scoutmaster agreed. "So be careful. Okay, sports—six hours of sleep. Sam, set the watch."

Sam assigned six boys, including himself. Bruce asked, "Shouldn't I take a watch?"

Mr. Andrews intervened. "No. And take yourself off, Sam. You'll take Bruce on his two-man hike tomorrow; you'll need your sleep."

"Okay, Skipper." He added to Bruce, "There's nothing to it. I'll show you." The Scout on duty watched several instruments, but, as with suits, the important one was the blood-oxygen reading. Stale air was passed through a calcium oxide bath, which precipitated carbon dioxide as calcium carbonate. The purified air continued through dry sodium hydroxide, removing water vapor.

"The kid on watch makes sure the oxygen replacement is okay," Sam went on. "If anything went wrong, he'd wake us and we'd scramble into suits."

Mr. Andrews shooed them to bed. By the time Bruce had taken his turn at the sanitary unit and found a place to lie down, the harmonica was sobbing: "*Day is done. . . . .Gone the Sun . . .*"

It seemed odd to hear Taps when the Sun was still overhead. They couldn't wait a week for sundown, of course. These colonials kept funny hours ... bed at what amounted to early evening, up at one in the morning. He'd ask Sam. Sam wasn't a bad guy—a little bit know-it-all. Odd to sleep on a bare floor, too—not that it mattered with low gravity. He was still pondering it when his ears were assaulted by *Reveille*, played on the harmonica.

Breakfast was scrambled eggs, cooked on the spot. Camp was struck, and the troop was moving in less than an hour. They headed for Base Camp at a lope.

The way wound through passes, skirted craters. They had covered thirty miles and Bruce was getting hungry when the pathfinder called, "Heel and toe!" They converged on an air lock, set in a hillside.

Base Camp had not the slick finish of Luna City, being rough caverns sealed to airtightness, but each troop had its own well-equipped troop room. Air was renewed by hydroponic garden, like Luna City; there was a Sun power plant and accumulators to last through the long, cold nights.

Bruce hurried through lunch; he was eager to start his two-man hike. They outfitted as before, except that reserve air and water replaced packaged grub. Sam fitted a spring-fed clip of hiking rations into the collar of Bruce's suit.

The Scoutmaster inspected them at the lock. "Where to, Sam?"

"We'll head southeast. I'll blaze it."

"Hmm—rough country. Well, back by midnight, and stay out of caves."

"Yes, sir."

Outside Sam sighed, "Whew! I thought he was going to say not to climb."

"We're going to?"

"Sure. You can, can't you?"

"Got my Alpine badge."

"I'll do the hard part, anyhow. Let's go."

Sam led out of the hills and across a baked plain. He

hit an eight-mile gait, increased it to a twelve-miler. Bruce swung along, enjoying it. "Swell of you to do this, Sam."

"Nuts. If I weren't here, I'd be helping to seal the gymnasium."

"Just the same, I need this hike for my Mooncraft badge."

Sam let several strides pass. "Look, Bruce—you don't really expect to make Lunar Eagle?"

"Why not? I've got my optional badges. There are only four required ones that are terribly different: camping, Mooncraft, pathfinding, and pioneering. I've studied like the dickens and now I'm getting experience."

"I don't doubt you've studied. But the Review Board are tough eggs. You've got to be a real Moon hand to get by."

"They won't pass a Scout from Earth?"

"Put it this way. The badges you need add up to one thing, Mooncraft. The examiners are old Moon hands; you won't get by with book answers. They'll know how long you've been here and they'll *know* you don't know enough."

Bruce thought about it. "It's not fair!"

Sam snorted. "Mooncraft isn't a game; it's the real thing. 'Did you stay alive?' If you make a mistake, you flunk—and they bury you."

Bruce had no answer.

Presently they came to hills; Sam stopped and called Base Camp. "Parsons and Hollifield, Troop One—please take a bearing."

Shortly Base replied, "One one eight. What's your mark?"

"Cairn with a note."

"Roger."

Sam piled up stones, then wrote date, time, and their names on paper torn from a pad in his pouch, and laid it on top. "Now we start up."

The way was rough and unpredictable; this canyon

had never been a watercourse. Several times Sam stretched a line before he would let Bruce follow. At intervals he blazed the rock with his hammer. They came to an impasse, five hundred feet of rock, the first hundred of which was vertical and smooth.

Bruce stared. "We're going up that?"

"Sure. Watch your Uncle Samuel." A pillar thrust up above the vertical pitch. Sam clipped two lines together and began casting the bight up toward it. Twice he missed and the line floated down. At last it went over.

Sam drove a piton into the wall, off to one side, clipped a snap ring to it, and snapped on the line. He had Bruce join him in a straight pull on the free end to test the piton. Bruce then anchored to the snap ring with a rope strap; Sam started to climb.

Thirty feet up, he made fast to the line with his legs and drove another piton; to this he fastened a safety line. Twice more he did this. He reached the pillar and called, "Off belay!"

Bruce unlinked the line; it snaked up the cliff. Presently Sam shouted, "On belay!"

Bruce answered, "Testing," and tried unsuccessfully to jerk down the line Sam had lowered.

"Climb," ordered Sam.

"Climbing." One-sixth gravity, Bruce decided, was a mountaineer's heaven. He paused on the way up only to unsnap the safety line.

Bruce wanted to "leapfrog" up the remaining pitches, but Sam insisted on leading. Bruce was soon glad of it; he found three mighty differences between climbing on Earth and climbing here; the first was low gravity, but the others were disadvantages: balance climbing was awkward in a suit, and chimney climbing, or any involving knees and shoulders, was clumsy and carried danger of tearing the suit.

They came out on raw, wild upland surrounded by pinnacles, bright against black sky. "Where to?" asked Bruce.

Sam studied the stars, then pointed southeast. "The photomaps show open country that way."

"Suits me." They trudged away; the country was too rugged to lope. They had been traveling a long time, it seemed to Bruce, when they came out on a higher place from which Earth could be seen. "What time is it?" he asked.

"Almost seventeen," Sam answered, glancing up.

"We're supposed to be back by midnight."

"Well," admitted Sam, "I expected to reach open country before now."

"We're lost?"

"Certainly not! I've blazed it. But I've never been here before. I doubt if anyone has."

"Suppose we keep on for half an hour, then turn back?"

"Fair enough." They continued for at least that; Sam conceded that it was time to turn.

"Let's try that next rise," urged Bruce.

"Okay." Sam reached the top first. "Hey, Bruce—we made it!"

Bruce joined him. "Golly!" Two thousand feet below stretched a dead lunar plain. Mountains rimmed it except to the south. Five miles away two small craters formed a figure eight.

"I know where we are," Sam announced. "That pair shows up on the photos. We slide down here, circle south about twenty miles, and back to Base. A cinch—how's your air?"

Bruce's bottle showed fair pressure; Sam's was down, he having done more work. They changed both bottles and got ready. Sam drove a piton, snapped on a ring, fastened a line to his belt and passed it through the ring. The end of the line he passed between his legs, around a thigh and across his chest, over his shoulder and to his other hand, forming a rappel seat. He began to "walk" down the cliff, feeding slack as needed.

He reached a shoulder below Bruce. "Off rappel!" he called, and recovered his line by pulling it through the ring.

Bruce rigged a rappel seat and joined him. The pitches became steeper; thereafter Sam sent Bruce down first, while anchoring him above. They came to a last high sheer drop. Bruce peered over. "Looks like here we roost."

"Maybe." Sam bent all four lines together and measured it. Ten feet of line reached the rubble at the base.

Bruce said, "It'll reach, but we have to leave the lines behind us."

Sam scowled. "Glass lines cost money; they're from Earth."

"Beats staying here."

Sam searched the cliff face, then drove a piton. "I'll lower you. When you're halfway, drive two pitons and hang the strap from one. That'll give me a change-over."

"I'm against it," protested Bruce.

"If we lost our lines," Sam argued, "we'll never hear the last of it. Go ahead."

"I still don't like it."

"Who's in charge?"

Bruce shrugged, snapped on the line and started down.

Sam stopped him presently. "Halfway. Pick me a nest."

Bruce walked the face to the right, but found only smooth wall. He worked back and located a crack. "Here's a crack," he reported, "but just one. I shouldn't drive two pitons in one crack."

"Spread 'em apart," Sam directed. "It's good rock."

Reluctantly, Bruce complied. The spikes went in easily but he wished he could hear the firm ring that meant a piton was biting properly. Finished, he hung the strap. "Lower away!"

In a couple of minutes he was down and unsnapped the line. "Off belay!" He hurried down the loose rock at the base. When he reached the edge of it he called, "Sam! This plain is soft stuff."

"Okay," Sam acknowledged. "Stand clear." Bruce

moved along the cliff about fifty feet and stopped to
bind on skis. Then he shuffled out onto the plain, kick-
turned, and looked back. Sam had reached the pitons.
He hung, one foot in the strap, the bight in his elbow,
and recovered his line. He passed his line through the
second piton ring, settled in rappel, and hooked the
strap from piton to piton as an anchor. He started
down.

Halfway down the remaining two hundred feet he
stopped. "What's the matter?" called Bruce.

"It's reached a shackle," said Sam, "and the pesky
thing won't feed through the ring. I'll free it." He
raised himself a foot, then suddenly let what he had
gained slip through the ring above.

To Bruce's amazement Sam leaned out at an impossible angle. He heard Sam cry "Rock!" before he
understood what had happened—the piton had failed.

Sam fell about four feet, then the other piton, connected by the strap, stopped him. He caught himself,
feet spread. But the warning cry had not been point-
less; Bruce saw a rock settling straight for Sam's helmet. Bruce repeated the shout.

Sam looked up, then jumped straight out from the
cliff. The rock passed between him and the wall; Bruce
could not tell if it had struck him. Sam swung in, his
feet caught the cliff—and again he leaned out crazily.
The second piton had let go.

Sam again shouted, "*Rock!*" even as he kicked himself away from the cliff.

Bruce watched him, turning slowly over and over
and gathering momentum. It seemed to take Sam forever to fall.

Then he struck.

Bruce fouled his skis and had to pick himself up. He
forced himself to be careful and glided toward the
spot.

Sam's frantic shove had saved him from crashing
his helmet into rock. He lay buried in the loose debris,
one leg sticking up ridiculously. Bruce felt an hysteri-

cal desire to laugh.

Sam did not stir when Bruce tugged at him. Bruce's skis got in his way; finally he stood astraddle, hauled Sam out. The boy's eyes were closed, his features slack, but the suit still had pressure. "Sam," shouted Bruce, "can you hear me?"

Sam's blood-oxygen reading was dangerously in the red; Bruce opened his intake valve wider—but the reading failed to improve. He wanted to turn Sam face down, but he had no way of straightening Sam's helmeted head, nor would he then be able to watch the blood-oxygen indicator unless he took time to remove the belt. He decided to try artificial respiration with the patient face up. He kicked off skis and belt.

The pressure in the suit got in his way, nor could he fit his hands satisfactorily to Sam's ribs. But he kept at it—swing! and one, and two and up! and one, and two and swing!

The needle began to move. When it was well into the white Bruce paused.

It stayed in the white.

Sam's lips moved but no sound came. Bruce touched helmets. "What is it, Sam?"

Faintly he heard, "Look out! Rock!"

Bruce considered what to do next.

There was little he could do until he got Sam into a pressurized room. The idea, he decided, was to get help—fast!

Send up a smoke signal? Fire a gun three times? Snap out of it, Bruce! You're on the Moon now. He wished that someone would happen along in a desert car.

He would have to try radio. He wasn't hopeful, as they had heard nothing even from the cliff. Still, he must try—

He glanced at Sam's blood-oxygen reading, then climbed the rubble, extended his antenna and tried. "M'aidez!" he called. "Help! Does anybody hear me?" He tried again.

And again.

When he saw Sam move he hurried back. Sam was sitting up and feeling his left knee. Bruce touched helmets. "Sam, are you all right?"

"Huh? This leg won't work right."

"Is it broken?"

"How do I know? Turn on your radio."

"It *is* on. Yours is busted."

"Huh? How'd that happen?"

"When you fell."

"Fell?"

Bruce pointed. "Don't you remember?"

Sam stared at the cliff. "Uh, I don't know. Say, this thing hurts like mischief. Where's the rest of the troop?"

Bruce said slowly, "We're out by ourselves, Sam. Remember?"

Sam frowned. "I guess so. Bruce, we've got to get out of here! Help me get my skis on."

"Do you think you can ski with that knee?"

"I've got to." Bruce lifted him to his feet, then bound a ski to the injured leg while Sam balanced on the other. But when Sam tried shifting his weight he collapsed—and fainted.

Bruce gave him air and noted that the blood-oxygen reading was still okay. He untangled the ski, straightened out Sam's legs, and waited. When Sam's eyes fluttered he touched helmets. "Sam, can you understand me?"

"Yeah. Sure."

"You can't stay on your feet. I'll carry you."

"No."

"What do you mean, 'No'?"

"No good. Rig a toboggan." He closed his eyes.

Bruce laid Sam's skis side by side. Two steel rods were clipped to the tail of each ski; he saw how they were meant to be used. Slide a rod through four ring studs, two on each ski; snap a catch—*so*! Fit the other rods. Remove bindings—the skis made a passable narrow toboggan.

He removed Sam's pack, switched his bottles around in front and told him to hold them. "I'm going to move you. Easy, now!" The space-suited form hung over the edges, but there was no help for it. He found he could thread a rope under the rods and lash his patient down. Sam's pack he tied on top.

He made a hitch by tying a line to the holes in the tips of the skis; there was a long piece left over. He said to Sam, "I'll tie this to my arm. If you want anything, just jerk."

"Okay."

"Here we go." Bruce put on his skis, brought the hitch up to his armpits and ducked his head through, forming a harness. He grasped his ski poles and set out to the south, parallel to the cliff.

The toboggan drag steadied him; he settled down to covering miles. Earth was shut off by the cliff; the Sun gave him no estimate of hour. There was nothing but blackness, stars, the blazing Sun, a burning desert underfoot, and the towering cliff—nothing but silence and the urgency to get back to base.

Something jerked his arm. It scared him before he accounted for it. He went back to the toboggan. "What is it, Sam?"

"I can't stand it. It's too hot." The boy's face was white and sweat-covered.

Bruce gave him a shot of air, then thought about it. There was an emergency shelter in Sam's pack, just a rolled-up awning with a collapsible frame. Fifteen minutes later he was ready to move. One awning support was tied upright to the sole of one of Sam's boots; the other Bruce had bent and wedged under Sam's shoulders. The contraption looked ready to fall apart but it held. "There! Are you okay?"

"I'm fine. Look, Bruce, I think my knee is all right now. Let me try it."

Bruce felt out the knee through the suit. It was twice the size of its mate; he could feel Sam wince. He touched helmets. "You're full of hop, chum. Relax."

Bruce got back into harness.

Hours later, Bruce came across tracks. They swung in from northeast, turned and paralleled the hills. He stopped and told Sam.

"Say, Sam, how can I tell how old they are?"

"You can't. A track fifty years old looks as fresh as a new one."

"No point in following these?"

"No harm in it, provided they go in our direction."

"Roger." Bruce went back to towing. He called hopefully over the radio every few minutes and then listened. The tracks cheered him even though he knew how slim the chance was that they meant anything. The tracks swung out from the hills presently or, rather, the hills swung in, forming a bay. He took the shorter route as his predecessor had.

He should have seen what was coming. He knew that he should keep his eyes ahead, but the need to watch his instruments, the fact that he was leaning into harness, and the circumstance that he was following tracks combined to keep his head down. He had just glanced back at Sam when he felt his skis slipping out from under him.

Automatically he bent his knees and threw his skis into a "snowplow." He might have been able to stop had not the toboggan been scooting along behind. It plowed into him; boy, skis, and toboggan went down, tangled like jackstraws.

He struggled for footing, felt the sand slip under him. He had time to see that he had been caught—in daylight!—by that lunar equivalent of quicksand, a morning glory. Then the sifting dust closed over his helmet.

He felt himself slip, slide, fall, slide again, and come softly to rest.

Bruce tried to get his bearings. Part of his mind was busy with horror, shock, and bitter self blame for having failed Sam; another part seemed able to drive ahead with the business at hand. He did not seem hurt—and he was still breathing. He supposed that he was buried in a morning glory; he suspected that any movement would bury him deeper.

Nevertheless he had to locate Sam. He felt his way up to his neck, pushing the soft flakes aside. The toboggan hitch was still on him. He got both hands on it and heaved. It was frustrating work, like swimming in mud. Gradually he dragged the sled to him—or himself to the sled. Presently he felt his way down the load and located Sam's helmet. "*Sam!* Can you hear me?"

The reply was muffled. "Yeah, Bruce!"

"Are you okay?"

"Okay? Don't be silly! We're in a *morning glory!*"

"Yes, I know. Sam, I'm terribly sorry!"

"Well, don't cry about it. It can't be helped."

"I didn't mean to—"

"Stow it, can't you!" Sam's voice concealed panic with anger. "It doesn't matter. We're goners—don't you realize that?"

"Huh? No, we're not! Sam, I'll get you out—I swear I will."

Sam waited before replying. "Don't kid yourself, Bruce. Nobody ever gets out of a morning glory."

"Don't talk like that. We aren't dead yet."

"No, but we're going to be. I'm trying to get used to the idea." He paused. "Do me a favor, Bruce—get me loose from these confounded skis. I don't want to die tied down."

"Right away!" In total darkness, his hands in gloves, with only memory to guide him, and with the soft, flaky dust everywhere, unlashing the load was nearly impossible. He shifted position, then suddenly noticed something—his left arm was free of the dust.

He shifted and got his helmet free as well. The darkness persisted; he fumbled at his belt, managed to locate his flashlight.

He was lying partly out and mostly in a sloping mass of soft stuff. Close overhead was a rocky roof; many feet below the pile spilled over a floor of rock. Sideways the darkness swallowed up the beam.

He still clutched the toboggan; he hauled at it, trying to drag Sam out. Failing, he burrowed back in. "Hey, Sam! We're in a cave!"

"Huh?"

"Hang on. I'll get you out." Bruce cautiously thrashed around in an attempt to get his entire body outside the dust. It kept caving down on him. Worse, his skis anchored his feet. He kicked one loose, snaked his arm in, and dragged it out. It slid to the base of the pile. He repeated the process, then rolled and scrambled to the floor, still clinging to the hitch.

He set the light on the rock floor, and put the skis aside, then heaved mightily. Sam, toboggan, and load came sliding down, starting a small avalanche. Bruce touched helmets. "Look! We're getting somewhere!"

Sam did not answer. Bruce persisted, "Sam, did you hear me?"

"I heard you. Thanks for pulling me out. Now untie me, will you?"

"Hold the light." Bruce got busy. Shortly he was saying, "There you are. Now I'll stir around and find the way out."

"What makes you think there is a way out?"

"Huh? Don't talk like that. Who ever heard of a cave with no exit?"

Sam answered slowly, "*He* didn't find one."

" 'He'?"

"Look." Sam shined the light past Bruce. On the rock a few feet away was a figure in an old-fashioned space suit.

Bruce took the light and cautiously approached the figure. The man was surely dead; his suit was limp. He lay at ease, hands folded across his middle, as if taking a nap. Bruce pointed the torch at the glass face plate. The face inside was lean and dark, skin clung to the bones; Bruce turned the light away.

He came back shortly to Sam. "He didn't make out

so well," Bruce said soberly. "I found these papers in his pouch. We'll take them with us so we can let his folks know."

"You *are* an incurable optimist, aren't you? Well, all right." Sam took them. There were two letters, an old-style flat photograph of a little girl and a dog, and some other papers. One was a driver's license for the Commonwealth of Massachusetts, dated June 1995 and signed *Abner Green.*

Bruce stared. "1995! Gee Whiz!"

"I wouldn't count on notifying his folks."

Bruce changed the subject. "He had one thing we can use. This." It was a coil of manila rope. "I'll hitch all the lines together, one end to your belt and one to mine. That'll give me five or six hundred feet. If you want me, just pull."

"Okay. Watch your step."

"I'll be careful. You'll be all right?"

"Sure. I've got *him* for company."

"Well . . . . here goes."

One direction seemed as good as another. Bruce kept the line taut to keep from walking in a circle. The rock curved up presently and his flash showed that it curved back on itself, a dead end. He followed the wall to the left, picking his way, as the going was very rough. He found himself in a passage. It seemed to climb, but it narrowed. Three hundred feet and more out by the ropes, it narrowed so much that he was stopped.

Bruce switched off his light and waited for his eyes to adjust. He became aware of a curious sensation. It was panic.

He forced himself not to turn on the light until he was certain that no gleam lay ahead. Then thankfully he stumbled back into the main cavern.

Another series of chambers led steadily downward. He turned back at a black and bottomless hole.

The details varied but the answers did not: At the furthest reach of the lines, or at some impassable ob-

stacle, he would wait in the dark—but no gleam of
light ever showed. He went back to Sam after having
covered, he estimated, about 180°.

Sam had crawled up to the heap of fallen dust. Bruce
hurried to him. "Sam, are you all right?"

"Sure. I just moved to a feather bed. That rock is
terribly cold. What did you find?"

"Well, nothing yet," he admitted. He sat down in the
flaky pile and leaned toward Sam. "I'll start again in
a moment."

"How's your air supply?" asked Sam.

"Uh, I'll have to crack my reserve bottle soon. How's
yours?"

"Mine is throttled to the limit. You're doing all the
work; I can save my reserve bottle for you—I think."

Bruce frowned. He wanted to protest, but the gesture wouldn't make sense. They would have to finish
up all even; naturally he was using much more air
than was Sam.

One thing was sure—time was running out. Finally
he said, "Look, Sam—there's no end of those caves and
passages. I couldn't search them all with all the air in
Luna City."

"I was afraid so."

"But we *know* there's a way out right above us."

"You mean *in*."

"I mean *out*. See here—this morning glory thing is
built like an hour glass; there's an open cone on top,
and this pile of sand down below. The stuff trickled
down through a hole in the roof and piled up until it
choked the hole."

"Where does that get you?"

"Well, if we dug the stuff away we could clear the
hole."

"It would keep sifting down."

"No, it wouldn't, it would reach a point where there
wasn't enough dust close by to sift down any further—
there would still be a hole."

Sam considered it. "Maybe. But when you tried to

climb up it would collapse back on you. That's the bad part about a morning glory, Bruce; you can't get a foothold."

"The dickens I can't! If I can't climb a slope on skis without collapsing it, when I've got my wits about me and am really trying, why, you can have my reserve air bottle."

Sam chuckled. "Don't be hasty. I might hold you to it. Anyhow," he added, "I can't climb it."

"Once I get my feet on the level, I'll pull you out like a cork, even if you're buried. Time's a-wastin'." Bruce got busy.

Using a ski as a shovel he nibbled at the giant pile. Every so often it would collapse down on him. It did not discourage him; Bruce knew that many yards of the stuff would have to fall and be moved back before the hole would show.

Presently he moved Sam over to the freshly moved waste. From there Sam held the light; the work went faster. Bruce began to sweat. After a while he had to switch air bottles; he sucked on his water tube and ate a march ration before getting back to work.

He began to see the hole opening above him. A great pile collapsed on him; he backed out, looked up, then went to Sam. "Turn out the light!"

There was no doubt; a glimmer of light filtered down. Bruce found himself pounding Sam and shouting. He stopped and said, "Sam, old boy, did I ever say what patrol I'm from?"

"No. Why?"

"Badger Patrol. Watch me dig!" He tore into it. Shortly sunlight poured into the hole and reflected dimly around the cavern. Bruce shoveled until he could see a straight rise from the base of the pile clear to the edge of the morning glory high above them. He decided that the opening was wide enough to tackle.

He hitched himself to Sam with the full length of all the glass ropes and then made a bundle of Sam's pack save air and water bottles, tied a bowline on Sam's uninjured foot, using the manila line and secured the bundle to the end of that line. He planned to drag Sam out first, then the equipment. Finished, he bound on skis.

Bruce touched helmets. "This is it, pal. Keep the line clear of the sand."

Sam grabbed his arm. "Wait a minute."

"What's the matter?"

"Bruce—if we don't make it, I just want to say that you're all right."

"Uh . . . oh, forget it. We'll make it." He started up.

A herringbone step suited the convex approach to the hole. As Bruce neared the opening he shifted to side-step to fit the narrow passage and the concave shape of the morning glory above. He inched up, transferring his weight smoothly and gradually, and not remaining in one spot too long. At last his head, then his whole body, were in sunshine; he was starting up the morning glory itself.

He stopped, uncertain what to do. There was a ridge above him, where the flakes had broken loose when he had shoveled away their support. The break was much too steep to climb, obviously unstable. He paused only a moment as he could feel his skis sinking in; he went forward in half side-step, intending to traverse past the unstable formation.

The tow line defeated him. When Bruce moved sideways, the line had to turn a corner at the neck of the hole. It brushed and then cut into the soft stuff. Bruce felt his skis slipping backwards; with cautious haste he started to climb, tried to ride the slipping mass and keep above it. He struggled as the flakes poured over his skis. Then he was fouled, he went down, it engulfed him.

Again he came to rest in soft, feathery, darkness. He lay quiet, nursing his defeat, before trying to get out. He hardly knew which way was up, much less which way was out. He was struggling experimentally when he felt a tug on his belt. Sam was trying to help him.

A few minutes later, with Sam's pull to guide him, Bruce was again on the floor of the cave. The only light came from the torch in Sam's hand; it was enough to show that the pile choking the hole was bigger than ever.

Sam motioned him over. "Too bad, Bruce," was all he said.

Bruce controlled his choking voice to say, "I'll get busy as soon as I catch my breath."

"Where's your left ski?"

"Huh? Oh! Must have pulled off. It'll show up when I start digging."

"Hmmm . . . how much air have you?"

"Uh?" Bruce looked at his belt. "About a third of a bottle."

"I'm breathing my socks. I've got to change."

"Right away!" Bruce started to make the switch; Sam pulled him down again.

"You take the fresh bottle, and give me your bottle."

"But—"

"No 'buts' about it," Sam cut him off. "You have to do all the work; you've *got* to take the full tank."

Silently Bruce obeyed. His mind was busy with arithmetic. The answer always came out the same; he knew with certainty that there was not enough air left to permit him again to perform the Herculean task of moving that mountain of dust.

He began to believe that they would never get out. The knowledge wearied him; he wanted to lie down beside the still form of Abner Green and, like him, not struggle at the end.

However he could not. He knew that, for Sam's sake, he would have to shovel away at that endless sea of sand, until he dropped from lack of oxygen. Listlessly he took off his remaining ski and walked toward his task.

Sam jerked on the rope.

Bruce went back. "What's got into you, kid?" Sam demanded.

"Nothing. Why?"

"It's got you whipped."

"I didn't say so."

"But you think so. I could see it. Now you listen! You convinced me that you could get us out—and, by Jiminy! you're going to! You're just cocky enough to be the first guy to whip a morning glory and you can do it. Get your chin up!"

Bruce hesitated. "Look, Sam, I won't quit on you, but you might as well know the truth: there isn't air enough to do it again."

"Figured that out when I saw the stuff start to crumble."

"You knew? Then if you know any prayers, better say them."

Sam shook his arm. "It's not time to pray; it's time to get busy."

"Okay." Bruce started to straighten up.

"That's not what I meant."

"Huh?"

"There's no point in digging. Once was worth trying; twice is wasting oxygen."

"Well, what do you want me to do?"

"You didn't try *all* the ways out, did you?"

"No." Bruce thought about it. "I'll try again, Sam. But there isn't air enough to try them all."

"You can search longer than you can shovel. But don't search haphazardly; search back toward the hills. Anywhere else will be just another morning glory; we need to come out *at the hills;* away from the sand."

"Uh . . . look, Sam, where *are* the hills? Down here you can't tell north from next week."

"Over that way," Sam pointed.

"Huh? How do you know?"

"You showed me. When you broke through I could tell where the Sun was from the angle of the light."

"But the Sun is overhead."

"Was when we started. Now it's fifteen, twenty degrees to the west. Now listen: these caves must have been big blow holes once, gas pockets. You search off in that direction and find us a blow hole that's not choked with sand."

"I'll do my darndest!"

"How far away were the hills when we got caught?" Bruce tried to remember. "Half a mile, maybe."

"Check. You won't find what we want tied to me with five or six hundred feet of line. Take that pad of paper in my pouch. Blaze your way—and be darn sure you blaze enough!"

"I will!"

"Attaboy! Good luck."

Bruce stood up.

It was the same tedious, depressing business as before. Bruce stretched the line, then set out at the end of it, dropping bits of paper and counting his steps. Several times he was sure that he was under the hills, only to come to an impasse. Twice he skirted the heaps that marked other morning glorys. Each time he retraced his steps he gathered up his blazes, both to save paper and to keep from confusing himself.

Once, he saw a glimmer of light and his heart pounded—but it filtered down from a hole too difficult even for himself and utterly impossible for Sam.

His air got low; he paid no attention, other than to adjust his mix to keep it barely in the white. He went on searching.

A passage led to the left, then down; he began to doubt the wisdom of going further and stopped to check the darkness. At first his eyes saw nothing, then it seemed as if there might be a suggestion of light ahead. Eye fatigue? Possibly. He went another hundred feet and tried again. It was light!

Minutes later he shoved his shoulders up through a twisted hole and gazed out over the burning plain.

"Hi!" Sam greeted him. "I thought you had fallen down a hole."

"Darn near did. Sam, I found it!"

"Knew you would. Let's get going."

"Right. I'll dig out my other ski."

"Nope."

"Why not?"

"Look at your air gauge. We aren't going anywhere on skis."

"Huh? Yeah, I guess not." They abandoned their loads, except for air and water bottles. The dark trek was made piggy-back, where the ceiling permitted. Some places Bruce half dragged his partner. Other places they threaded on hands and knees with Sam pulling his bad leg painfully behind him.

Bruce climbed out first, having slung Sam in a bow-line before he did so. Sam gave little help in getting out; once they were above ground Bruce picked him up and set him against a rock. He then touched helmets. "There, fellow! We made it!"

Sam did not answer.

Bruce peered in; Sam's features were slack, eyes half closed. A check of his belt told why; the blood-oxygen indicator showed red.

Sam's intake valve was already wide open; Bruce moved fast, giving himself a quick shot of air, then transferring his bottle to Sam. He opened it wide.

He could see Sam's pointer crawl up even as his own dropped toward the red. Bruce had air in his suit for three or four minutes if he held still.

He did not hold still. He hooked his intake hose to the manifold of the single bottle now attached to Sam's suit and opened his valve. His own indicator stopped dropping toward the red. They were Siamese twins now, linked by one partly-exhausted bottle of utterly necessary gas. Bruce put an arm around Sam, settled Sam's head on his shoulder, helmet to helmet, and throttled down both valves until each was barely in the white. He gave Sam more margin than himself, then settled down to wait. The rock under them was in shadow, though the Sun still baked the plain. Bruce looked out, searching for anyone or anything, then extended his aerial. *"M'aidez!"* he called. "Help us! We're lost."

He could hear Sam muttering. "May day!" Sam echoed into his dead radio. "May day! We're lost."

Bruce cradled the delirious boy in his arm and repeated again, *"M'aidez!* Get a bearing on us." He paused, then echoed, "May day! May day!"

After a while he readjusted the valves, then went back to repeating endlessly, "May day! Get a bearing on us."

He did not feel it when a hand clasped his shoulder. He was still muttering "May day!" when they dumped him into the air lock of the desert car.

Mr. Andrews visited him in the infirmary at Base Camp. "How are you, Bruce?"

"Me? I'm all right, sir. I wish they'd let me get up."

"My instructions. So I'll know where you are." The Scoutmaster smiled; Bruce blushed.

"How's Sam?" he asked.

"He'll get by. Cold burns and a knee that will bother him a while. That's all."

"Gee, I'm glad."

"The troop is leaving. I'm turning you over to Troop Three, Mr. Harkness. Sam will go back with the grub car."

"Uh, I think I could travel with the Troop, sir."

"Perhaps so, but I want you to stay with Troop Three. You need field experience."

"Uh—" Bruce hesitated, wondering how to say it. "Mr. Andrews?"

"Yes?"

"I might as well go back. I've learned something. You were right. A fellow can't get to be an old Moon hand in three weeks. Uh . . . I guess I was just conceited."

"Is that all?"

"Well—yes, sir."

"Very well, listen to me. I've talked with Sam and with Mr. Harkness. Mr. Harkness will put you through a course of sprouts; Sam and I will take over when you get back. You plan on being ready for the Court of Honor two weeks from Wednesday." The Scoutmaster added, "Well?"

Bruce gulped and found his voice. "Yes, sir!"

PANDORA'S BOX

Once opened, the box could never be closed. But after the myriad swarming Troubles came Hope.

Science fiction is not prophecy. It often reads as if it were prophecy; indeed the practitioners of this odd genre (pun intentional—I won't do it again) of fiction usually strive hard to make their stories sound as if they were true pictures of the future. Prophecies.

Prophesying is what the weatherman does, the race track tipster, the stock market adviser, the fortune-teller who reads palms or gazes into a crystal. Each one is predicting the future—sometimes exactly, sometimes in vague, veiled, or ambiguous language, sometimes simply with a claim of statistical probability, but always with a claim seriously made of disclosing some piece of the future.

This is not at all what a science fiction author does. Science fiction is almost always laid in the future—or at least in a fictional possible-future—and is almost invariably deeply concerned with the shape of that future. But the method is not prediction; it is usually extrapolation and/or speculation. Indeed the author is not required to (and usually does not) regard the fictional "future" he has chosen to write about as being the events most likely to come to pass; his purpose may have nothing to do with the *probability* that these storied events may happen.

"Extrapolation" means much the same in fiction

writing as it does in mathematics: exploring a trend. It means continuing a curve, a path, a trend into the future, by extending its present direction and continuing the *shape* it has displayed in its past performance—i.e., if it is a sine curve in the past, you extrapolate it as a sine curve in the future, not as an hyperbola, nor a Witch of Agnesi, and *most certainly not* as a tangent straight line.

"Speculation" has far more elbowroom than extrapolation; it starts with a "What if?"—and the new factor thrown in by the what-if may be both wildly improbable and so revolutionary in effect as to throw a sine-curve trend (or a yeast-growth trend, or any trend) into something unrecognizably different. What if little green men land on the White House lawn and invite us to join a Galactic union?—or big green men land and enslave us and eat us? What if we solve the problem of immortality? What if New York City really does go dry? And not just the present fiddlin' shortage tackled by fiddlin' quarter-measures—can you imagine a man being lynched for wasting an ice cube? Living, as I do, in a state (Colorado—1965) which has just two sorts of water, too little and too much—we just finished seven years of drought with seven inches of rain in two hours, and one was about as disastrous as the other—I find a horrid fascination in Frank Herbert's *Dune World*, in Charles Einstein's *The Day New York Went Dry*, and in stories about Bible-type floods such as S. Fowler Wright's *Deluge*.

Most science fiction stories use both extrapolation and speculation. Consider "Blowups Happen," elsewhere in this volume. It was written in 1939, updated very slightly for book publication just after World War II by inserting some words such as "Manhattan Project" and "Hiroshima," but not rewritten, and is one of a group of stories published under the pretentious collective title of *The History of the Future* (!) (an editor's title, *not* mine!)—which certainly sounds like prophecy.

I disclaim any intention of prophesying; I wrote that story for the sole purpose of making money to pay off a mortgage and with the single intention of entertaining the reader. As prophecy the story falls flat on its silly face—any tenderfoot Scout can pick it to pieces—but I think it is still entertaining as a *story*, else it would not be here; I have a business reputation to protect and wish to continue making money. Nor am I ashamed of this motivation. Very little of the great literature of our heritage arose solely from a wish to "create art"; most writing, both great and not-so-great, has as its proximate cause a need for money combined with an aversion to, or an inability to perform, hard "honest labor." Fiction writing offers a legal and reasonably honest way out of this dilemma.

A science fiction author may have, and often does have, other motivations *in addition to* pursuit of profit. He may wish to create "art for art's sake," he may want to warn the world against a course he feels to be disastrous (Orwell's *1984*, Huxley's *Brave New World*—but please note that each is intensely entertaining, and that each made stacks of money), he may wish to urge the human race toward a course which he considers desirable (Bellamy's *Looking Backwards*, Wells' *Men Like Gods*), he may wish to instruct, or uplift, or even to dazzle. But the science fiction writer—*any* fiction writer—must keep entertainment consciously in mind as his prime purpose . . . or he may find himself back dragging that old cotton sack.

If he succeeds in this purpose, his story is likely to remain gripping entertainment long years after it has turned out to be false "prophecy." H. G. Wells is perhaps the greatest science fiction author of all time—and his greatest science fiction stories were written around sixty years ago (i.e., about 1895) . . . under the whip. Bedfast with consumption, unable to hold a job, flat broke, paying alimony—he *had* to make money somehow, and writing was the heaviest work he could manage. He was clearly aware (see his autobiography) that to stay alive he must be entertaining. The result was a flood of some of the most brilliant speculative stories about the future ever written. As prophecy they are all hopelessly dated . . . which matters not at all; they are as spellbinding now as they were in the Gay 'Nineties and the Mauve Decade.

Try to lay hands on his *The Sleeper Awakes*. The gadgetry in it is ingenious—and all wrong. The projected future in it is brilliant—and did not happen. All of which does not sully the story; it is a great story of love and sacrifice and blood-chilling adventure set in a matrix of mind-stretching speculation about the nature of Man and his Destiny. I read it first in 1923, and at least a dozen times since . . . and still reread it whenever I get to feeling uncertain about just how one does go about the unlikely process of writing fiction for entertainment of strangers—and again finding myself caught up in the sheer excitement of Wells' story.

"Solution Unsatisfactory" herein is a consciously Wellsian story. No, no, I'm not claiming that it is of H. G. Wells' quality—its quality is for you to judge, not me. But it was written by the method which Wells spelled out for the speculative story: Take one, just one, basic new assumption, then examine all its consequences—but express those consequences in terms of human beings. The assumption I chose was the "Absolute Weapon"; the speculation concerns what changes this forces on mankind. But the "history" the story describes simply did not happen.

However the problems discussed in this story are as fresh today, the issues just as poignant, for the grim reason that we have not reached even an "unsatisfactory" solution to the problem of the Absolute Weapon; we have reached *no* solution.

In the years that have passed since I wrote that story (in 1940) the world situation has grown much worse. Instead of one Absolute Weapon there are now at least five distinct types—an "Absolute Weapon" being defined as one against which there is no effective defense and which kills indiscriminately over a very wide area. The earliest of the five types, the A-bomb, is now known to be possessed by at least five nations; at least twenty-five other nations have the potential to build them in the next few years.

But there is a possible sixth type. Earlier this year (1965–R.A.H.) I attended a seminar at one of the nation's new think-factories. One of the questions discussed was whether or not a "Doomsday Bomb" could be built—a single weapon which would destroy all life of all sorts on this planet; *one* weapon, not an all-out nuclear holocaust involving hundreds of thousands of ICBMs. No, this was to be a world-wrecker of the sort Dr. E. E. Smith used to use in his interstellar sagas back in the days when SF magazines had bug-eyed monsters on the cover and were considered lowbrow, childish, fantastic.

The conclusions reached were: Could the Doomsday Machine be built?—yes, no question about it. What would it cost?—quite cheap.

A seventh type hardly seems necessary.

And that makes the grimness of "Solution Unsatisfactory" seem more like an Oz book in which the most harrowing adventures always turn out happily.

"Searchlight" is almost pure extrapolation, almost no speculation. The gadgets in it are either hardware on the shelf, or hardware which will soon be on the shelf because nothing is involved but straightforward engineering development. "Life-Line" (my first story) is its opposite, a story which is sheer speculation and either impossible or very highly improbable, as the What-If postulate will never be solved—I think. I hope. But the two stories are much alike in that neither depends on when it was written nor when it is read. Both are independent of any particular shape to history; they are timeless.

"Free Men" is another timeless story. As told, it

looks like another "after the blowup" story—but it is
not. Although the place is nominally the United States
and the time (as shown by the gadgetry) is set in the
not-distant future, simply by changing names of persons and places and by inserting other weapons and
other gadgets this story could be any country and any
time in the past or future—or could even be on another
planet and concern a non-human race. But the story
does also apply here-and-now, so I told it that way.

"Pandora's Box" was the original title of an article
researched and written in 1949 for publication in
1950, the end of the half-century. Inscrutable are the
ways of editors: it appeared with the title "Where To?"
and purported to be a nonfiction prophecy concerning
the year 2000 A.D. as seen from 1950. (I agree that a
science fiction writer should avoid marijuana, prophecy, and time payments—but I was tempted by a soft
rustle.)

Our present editor (1965) decided to use this article,
but suggested that it should be updated. Authors who
wish to stay in the business listen most carefully to
editors' suggestions, even when they think an editor
has been out in the sun without a hat; I agreed.

And reread "Where To?" and discovered that our
editor was undeniably correct; it needed updating. At
least.

But at last I decided not to try to conceal my bloopers. Below is reproduced, unchanged, my predictions
of fifteen years back. But here and there through the
article I have inserted signs for footnotes—like this:
(z)— and these will be found at the end of the 1950
article . . . calling attention to bloopers and then
forthrightly excusing myself by rationalizing how
anyone, even Nostradamus, would have made the
same mistake . . . hedging my bets in other cases, or
chucking in brand-new predictions and carefully lay-
ing them farther in the future than I am likely to live
. . . and, in some cases, crowing loudly about successful

predictions. (Addendum 1979: I have interpolated the later comments, and marked each item 1950, or 1965, or 1980.)

So—

WHERE TO?

A bloomin', foolish sparrow
Built his nest in a spout,
And along—

—came a building inspector, looked over the site, and the plans, and okayed them, after requiring the sparrow to buy eleven different licenses totalling 18% of the sparrow's building budget, plus something called special service, and along—

—the bleedin' rains came,
And washed the sparrow out.

Again the foolish sparrow,
Built his nest in the spout,
And again—

—came that building inspector, bawled out the sparrow for failing to get special licenses and permits covering typhoons, sun spots, and ice ages, required him to buy seventeen permits and/or licenses and appear before boards controlling zoning, economic impact, ecological protection, energy conservation, and community esthetics, plus something called "very special service"—and a second mortgage, and along—

—the bleedin' rains came,
And washed the sparrow out. (Around again...and again...and—)

1950 Where To?

Most science fiction consists of big-muscled stories about adventures in space, atomic wars, invasions by extra-terrestrials, and such. All very well—but now we will take time out for a look at ordinary home life half a century hence.

Except for tea leaves and other magical means, the only way to guess at the *future* is by examining the *present* in the light of the *past*. Let's go back half a century and visit your grandmother before we attempt to visit your grandchildren.

1900: Mr. McKinley is President and the airplane has not yet been invented. Let's knock on the door of that house with the gingerbread, the stained glass, and the cupola.

The lady of the house answers. You recognize her—your own grandmother, Mrs. Middleclass. She is almost as plump as you remember her, for she "put on some good, healthy flesh" after she married.

She welcomes you and offers coffee cake, fresh from her modern kitchen (running water from a hand pump; the best coal range Pittsburgh ever produced). Everything about her house is modern—hand-painted china, souvenirs from the Columbian Exposition, beaded portières, shining baseburner stoves, gas lights, a telephone on the wall.

There is no bathroom, but she and Mr. Middleclass

are thinking of putting one in. Mr. Middleclass's
mother calls this nonsense, but your grandmother
keeps up with the times. She is an advocate of clothing
reform, wears only one petticoat, bathes twice a week,
and her corsets are guaranteed rust proof. She has
been known to defend female suffrage—but not in the
presence of Mr. Middleclass.

Nevertheless, you find difficulty in talking with her.
Let's jump back to the present and try again.

The automatic elevator takes us to the ninth floor,
and we pick out a door by its number, that being the
only way to distinguish it.

"Don't bother to ring," you say? What? It's *your*
door and you know exactly what lies beyond it—

Very well, let's move a half century into the future
and try another middle class home.

It's a suburban home not two hundred miles from
the city. You pick out your destination from the air
while the cab is landing you—a cluster of hemispheres
that makes you think of the houses Dorothy found in
Oz.

You set the cab to return to its hangar and go into
the entrance hall. You neither knock nor ring. The
screen has warned them before you touched down on
the landing flat and the autobutler's transparency is
shining with: PLEASE RECORD A MESSAGE.

Before you can address the microphone a voice calls
out, "Oh, it's you! Come in, come in." There is a short
wait, as your hostess is not at the door. The autobutler
flashed your face to the patio—where she was reading
and sunning herself—and has relayed her voice back
to you.

She pauses at the door, looks at you through one-
way glass, and frowns slightly; she knows your old-
fashioned disapproval of casual nakedness. Her kindness causes her to disobey the family psychiatrist; she
grabs a robe and covers herself before signaling the
door to open.

The psychiatrist was right; you have thus been

classed with strangers, tradespeople, and others who
are not family intimates. But you must swallow your
annoyance; you cannot object to her wearing clothes
when you have sniffed at her for not doing so.

There is no reason why she should wear clothes at
home. The house is clean—not somewhat clean, but
clean—and comfortable. The floor is warm to bare
feet; there are no unpleasant drafts, no cold walls. All
dust is precipitated from the air entering this house.
All textures, of floor, of couch, of chair, are comfortable to bare skin. Sterilizing ultra-violet light floods
each room whenever it is unoccupied, and, several
times a day, a "whirlwind" blows house-created dust
from all surfaces and whisks it out. These auto services
are unobstrusive because automatic cut-off switches
prevent them from occurring whenever a mass in a
room is radiating at blood temperature.

Such a house can become untidy, but not dirty. Five
minutes of straightening, a few swipes at children's
fingermarks, and her day's housekeeping is done. Of-
tener than sheets were changed in Mr. McKinley's day,
this housewife rolls out a fresh layer of sheeting on
each sitting surface and stuffs the discard down the
oubliette. This is easy; there is a year's supply on a roll
concealed in each chair or couch. The tissue sticks by
pressure until pulled loose and does not obscure the
pattern and color.

You go into the family room, sit down, and remark
on the lovely day. "Isn't it?" she answers. "Come sun-
bathe with me."

The sunny patio gives excuse for bare skin by anyone's standards; thankfully she throws off the robe
and stretches out on a couch. You hesitate a moment.
After all, she is your own grandchild, so why not? You
undress quickly, since you left your outer wrap and
shoes at the door (only barbarians wear street shoes in
a house) and what remains is easily discarded. Your
grandparents had to get used to a mid-century beach.
It was no easier for them.

On the other hand, their bodies were wrinkled and old, whereas yours is not. The triumphs of endocrinology, of cosmetics, of plastic surgery, of figure control in every way are such that a woman need not change markedly from maturity until old age. A woman can keep her body as firm and slender as she wishes—and most of them so wish. This has produced a paradox: the United States has the highest percentage of old people in all its two and a quarter centuries, yet it seems to have a larger proportion of handsome young women than ever before.

(Don't whistle, son! That's your grandmother—)

This garden is half sunbathing patio, complete with shrubs and flowers, lawn and couches, and half swimming pool. The day, though sunny, is quite cold—but not in the garden, and the pool is not chilly. The garden appears to be outdoors, but is not; it is covered by a bubble of transparent plastic, blown and cured on the spot. You are inside the bubble; the sun is outside; you cannot see the plastic.

She invites you to lunch; you protest. "Nonsense!" she answers, "I like to cook." Into the house she goes. You think of following, but it is deliciously warm in the March sunshine and you are feeling relaxed to be away from the city. You locate a switch on the side of the couch, set it for gentle massage, and let the couch knead your troubles away. The couch notes your heart rate and breathing; as they slow, so does it. As you fall asleep it stops.

Meanwhile your hostess has been "slaving away over a hot stove." To be precise, she has allowed a menu selector to pick out an 800-calory, 4-ration-point luncheon. It is a random-choice gadget, somewhat like a slot machine, which has in it the running inventory of her larder and which will keep hunting until it turns up a balanced meal. Some housewives claim that it takes the art out of cookery, but our hostess is one of many who have accepted it thankfully as an endless source of new menus. Its choice is limited today as it has been three months since she has done grocery shopping. She rejects several menus; the selector continues patiently to turn up combinations until she finally accepts one based around fish disguised as lamb chops.

Your hostess takes the selected items from shelves or the freezer. All are prepared; some are pre-cooked. Those still to be cooked she puts into her—well, her "processing equipment," though she calls it a "stove." Part of it traces its ancestry to diathermy equipment; another feature is derived from metal enameling processes. She sets up cycles, punches buttons, and must wait two or three minutes for the meal to cook. She spends the time checking her ration accounts.

Despite her complicated kitchen, she doesn't eat as well as her great grandmother did—too many people and too few acres.

Never mind; the tray she carries out to the patio is well laden and beautiful. You are both willing to nap again when it is empty. You wake to find that she has burned the dishes and is recovering from her "exertion" in her refresher. Feeling hot and sweaty from your nap you decide to use it when she comes out. There is a wide choice offered by the 'fresher, but you limit yourself to a warm shower growing gradually cooler, followed by warm air drying, a short massage, spraying with scent, and dusting with powder. Such a simple routine is an insult to a talented machine.

Your host arrives home as you come out; he has taken a holiday from his engineering job and has had the two boys down at the beach. He kisses his wife, shouts, "Hi, Duchess!" at you, and turns to the video, setting it to hunt and sample the newscasts it has stored that day. His wife sends the boys in to 'fresh themselves then says, "Have a nice day, dear?"

He answers, "The traffic was terrible. Had to make the last hundred miles on automatic. Anything on the phone for me?"

"Weren't you on relay?"

"Didn't set it. Didn't want to be bothered." He steps to the house phone, plays back his calls, finds nothing he cares to bother with—but the machine goes ahead and prints one message; he pulls it out and tears it off.

"What is it?" his wife asks.

"Telestat from Luna City—from Aunt Jane."

"What does she say?"

"Nothing much. According to her, the Moon is a great place and she wants us to come visit her."

"Not likely!" his wife answers. "Imagine being shut up in an air-conditioned cave."

"When you are Aunt Jane's age, my honey lamb, and as frail as she is, with a bad heart thrown in, you'll go to the Moon and like it. Low gravity is not to be sneezed at—Auntie will probably live to be a hundred and twenty, heart trouble and all."

"Would *you* go to the Moon?" she asks.

"If I needed to and could afford it." He turns to you. "Right?"

You consider your answer. Life still looks good to you—and stairways are beginning to be difficult. Low gravity is attractive even though it means living out your days at the Geriatrics Foundation on the Moon. "It might be fun to visit," you answer. "One wouldn't have to stay."

Hospitals for old people on the Moon? Let's not be silly—

Or is it silly? Might it not be a logical and necessary outcome of our world today?

Space travel we will have, not fifty years from now, but much sooner. It's breathing down our necks. As for geriatrics on the Moon, for most of us no price is too high and no amount of trouble is too great to extend the years of our lives. It is possible that low gravity (one sixth, on the Moon) may not lengthen lives; nevertheless it *may*—we don't know yet—and it will most certainly add greatly to comfort on reaching that inevitable age when the burden of dragging around one's body is almost too much, or when we would otherwise resort to an oxygen tent to lessen the work of a worn-out heart.

By the rules of prophecy, such a prediction is *probable*, rather than impossible.

But the items and gadgets suggested above are examples of *timid* prophecy.

What are the rules of prophecy, if any?

Look at the graph shown here. The solid curve is what has been going on this past century. It represents many things—use of power, speed of transport, numbers of scientific and technical workers, advances in communication, average miles traveled per person per year, advances in mathematics, the rising curve of knowledge. Call it the curve of human achievement.

What is the correct way to project this curve into the future? Despite everything, there is a stubborn "common sense" tendency to project it along dotted line

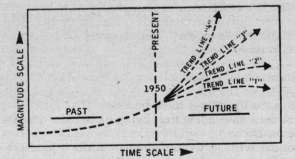

number one—like the patent office official of a hundred years back who quit his job "because everything had already been invented." Even those who don't expect a slowing up at once tend to expect us to reach a point of diminishing returns (dotted line number two).

Very daring minds are willing to predict that we will continue our present rate of progress (dotted line number three—a tangent).

But the proper way to project the curve is dotted line number four—for there is no reason, mathematical, scientific, or historical, to expect that curve to flatten out, or to reach a point of diminishing returns, or simply to go on as a tangent. The correct projection, by all facts known today, is for the curve to go on up indefinitely with *increasing* steepness.

The timid little predictions earlier in this article actually belong to curve one, or, at most, to curve two. You can count on the changes in the next fifty years at least *eight times* as great as the changes of the past fifty years.

The Age of Science *has not yet opened.*

AXIOM: A "nine-days' wonder" is taken as a matter of course on the tenth day.

AXIOM: A "common sense" prediction is sure to err on the side of timidity.

AXIOM: The more extravagant a prediction sounds the more likely it is to come true.

So let's have a few free-swinging predictions about the future.

Some will be wrong——but cautious predictions are *sure* to be wrong.

1. **1950** Interplanetary travel is waiting at your front door—C.O.D. It's yours when you pay for it.

1965 And now we are paying for it and the cost is high. But, for reasons understandable only to bureaucrats, we have almost halted development of a nuclear-powered spacecraft when success was in sight. Never mind; if we don't another country will. By the end of this century space travel will be cheap.

1980 And now the Apollo-Saturn Man-on-the-Moon program has come and gone, and all we have now in the U.S.A. as a new man-in-space program is the Space Shuttle—underfinanced and two years behind schedule. See my article SPINOFF on page 500 of this book, especially the last two pages.

Is space travel dead? *No, because the United States is not the only nation on this planet.* Today both Japan and Germany seem to be good bets—countries aware that endless wealth is out there for the taking. USSR seems to be concentrating on the military aspects rather than on space travel, and the People's Republic of China does not as yet appear to have the means to spare—but don't count out either nation; the potential is there, in both cases.

And don't count out the United States! Today most of our citizens regard the space program as a boondoggle (totally unaware that it is one of the very few Federal programs that paid for themselves, manyfold). But we are talking about twenty years from now, 2000 A.D. Let's see it in perspective. Exactly thirty years ago George Pal and Irving Pichel and I—and ca. 200 others—were making the motion picture DESTINATION MOON. I remember sharply that most of the people working on that film started out thinking that it was a silly fantasy, an impossibility. I had my nose rubbed in it again and again, especially if the speaker was unaware that I had written it. (Correction: written the first version of it. By the time it was filmed, even the banker's wife was writing dialog.)

As for the general public— A trip to the *Moon*? Nonsense!

That was thirty years ago, late 1949.

Nineteen years and ten months later Apollo 11 landed on the Moon.

Look again at the curves on page 322. With respect

to space travel (and industry, power, and colonization) we have dropped to that feeble curve #1—but we
could shift back to curve #4 overnight *if our President
and/or Congress* got it through their heads that not one
but *all* of our crisis problems can be solved by exploiting space. Employment, inflation, pollution, population, energy, running out of nonrenewable resources—
there is pie in the sky for the U.S.A. *and for the entire
planet including the impoverished "Third World."*

I won't try to prove it here. See THE THIRD INDUS-
TRIAL REVOLUTION by G. Harry Stine, 1979, Ace
Books, 51 Madison Avenue, New York, NY 10010,
and see A STEP FARTHER OUT by Dr. Jerry Pournelle, also Ace Books 1979—and accept my assurance
that I have known both authors well for twenty-odd
years, know that each has years of experience in aerospace, and that each has both the formal education
and the continuing study—and the horse sense!—to be
true experts in this matter.

From almost total disbelief about space travel
(99.9% +) to a landing on the Moon in twenty years . . .
from President Kennedy's announcement of intention to that Lunar landing in only *seven* years . . . and
still twenty years to go until the year 2000—we can
still shift to curve #4 (and get rich) almost overnight.
By 2000 A.D. we could have O'Neill colonies, self-sup-
porting and exporting power to Earth, at both La-
grange-4 and Lagrange-5, transfer stations in orbit
about Earth and around Luna, a permanent base on
Luna equipped with an electric catapult—and a geriatrics retirement home.

However, I am not commissioned to predict what
we *could* do but to predict (guess) what is *most likely* to
happen by 2000 A.D.

Our national loss of nerve, our escalating anti-intel-
lectualism, our almost total disinterest in anything
that does not *directly* and *immediately* profit us, the
shambles of public education throughout most of our
nation (especially in New York and California) cause

me to predict that *our space program will continue to dwindle*. It would not surprise me (but would distress me mightily!) to see the Space Shuttle canceled.

In the meantime some other nation or group will start exploiting space—industry, power, perhaps Lagrange-point colonies—and suddenly we will wake up to the fact that we have been left at the post. That happened to us in '57; we came up from behind and passed the competition. Possibly we will do it again. Possibly—

But I am making no cash bets.

2. **1950** Contraception and control of disease is revising relations between the sexes to an extent that will change our entire social and economic structure.

1965 This trend is so much more evident now than it was fifteen years ago that I am tempted to call it a fulfilled prophecy. Vast changes in sex relations are evident all around us—with the oldsters calling it "moral decay" and the youngsters ignoring them and taking it for granted. Surface signs: books such as *Sex and the Single Girl* are smash hits; the formerly-taboo four-letter words are now seen both in novels and popular magazines; the neologism "swinger" has come into the language; courts are conceding that nudity and semi-nudity are now parts of the cultural *mores*. But the end is not yet; this revolution will go much farther and is now barely started.

The most difficult speculation for a science fiction writer to undertake is to imagine correctly the *secondary* implications of a new factor. Many people correctly anticipated the coming of the horseless carriage; some were bold enough to predict that everyone would use them and the horse would virtually disappear. But I know of no writer, fiction or nonfiction, who saw ahead of time the vast change in the courting and mating habits of Americans which would result primarily from the automobile—a change which the diaphragm and the oral contraceptive merely confirmed. So far as I know, no one even dreamed of the change in sex habits the automobile would set off.

There is some new gadget in existence today which will prove to be equally revolutionary in some other way equally unexpected. You and I both know of this gadget, by name and by function—but we don't know which one it is nor what its unexpected effect will be. This is why science fiction is *not* prophecy—and why fictional speculation can be so much fun both to read and to write.

1980 (No, I still don't know what that revolutionary gadget is—unless it is the computer chip.) The sexual revolution: it continues apace—FemLib, GayLib, single women with progeny and never a lifted eyebrow, staid old universities and colleges that permit unmarried couples to room together on campus, group marriages, "open" marriages, miles and miles of "liberated" beaches. Most of this can be covered by one sentence: What used to be concealed is now done openly. But sexual attitudes are in flux; the new ones not yet cultural *mores*.

But I think I see a trend, one that might jell by 2000 A.D. The racial biological function of "family" is the protection of children and pregnant women. To accomplish that, family organization must be rewarding to men as well . . . and I do *not* mean copulation. There is a cynical old adage covering that: "Why keep a cow when milk is so cheap?" A marriage must offer its members emotional, spiritual, and physical comforts superior to those to be found in living alone if that prime function is to be accomplished.

(Stipulated: there are individuals, both sexes, who prefer to live alone. This is racially self-correcting.)

The American core family (father, mother, two or three children) has ceased to be emotionally satisfying—if it ever was. It is a creation of our times: mobility, birth control, easy divorce. Early in this century the core family was mother, father, four to eight children . . . and was itself a unit in an extended family of grandparents, aunts, uncles, and cousins living near enough (if not in the same house) to be mutually supportive. If a child was ill, Aunt Cora came over to help while Aunt Abby took the other kids into her home. See Mauve Decade fiction.

With increased mobility and fewer children this undefined extended-family pattern disappeared almost without its disappearance being noticed. To the extent to which it was noticed there was often glee at being free of the nuisance of in-laws and kinfolk. It took considerably longer to realize that the advantages had also disappeared.

We will not get a return of the extended family of the sort that characterized the 19th century and the early 20th . . . but the current flux of swingers' clubs, group marriages, spouse swapping, etc., is, in my opinion, fumbling and almost unconscious attempts to regain the pleasure, emotional comfort, and mutual security once found in the extended family of two or more generations back.

Prediction: by 2000 A.D. or soon thereafter extended families of several sorts will be more common than core families. The common characteristic of the various types will be increased security for children under legally enforceable contracts.

3. **1950** The most important military fact of this century is that there is no way to repel an attack from outer space.

1965 I flatly stand by this one. True, we are now working on Nike-Zeus and Nike-X and related systems and plan to spend billions on such systems—and we know that others are doing the same thing. True, it is possible to hit an object in orbit or trajectory. Nevertheless this prediction is as safe as predicting tomorrow's sunrise. Anti-aircraft fire never stopped air attacks; it simply made them expensive. The disadvantage in being at the bottom of a deep "gravity well" is very great; gravity gauge will be as crucial in the coming years as wind gauge was in the days when sailing ships controlled empires. The nation that controls the Moon will control the Earth—but no one seems willing these days to speak that nasty fact out loud.

1980 I have just heard a convincing report that the USSR has developed lasers far better than ours that can blind our eyes-in-the-sky satellites and, presumably, destroy our ICBMs in flight. Stipulate that this rumor is true: It does not change my 1950 assertion one iota. Missiles tossed from the Moon to the Earth need not be H-bombs or any sort of bomb—or even missile-shaped. All they need be is massive . . . because they arrive at approximately *seven miles per second.* A laser capable of blinding a satellite and of disabling an ICBM to the point where it can't explode would need to be orders of magnitude more powerful in order to volatilize a house-size chunk of Luna. For further details see my THE MOON IS A HARSH MISTRESS.

4. **1950** It is utterly impossible that the United States will start a "preventive war." We will fight when attacked, either directly or in a territory we have guaranteed to defend.

1965 Since 1950 we have done so in several theaters and are doing so in Viet Nam as this is written. "Preventive" or "pre-emptive" war seems as unlikely as ever, no matter who is in the White House. Here is a new prediction: World War III (as a major, all-out war) will not take place at least until 1980 and could easily hold off until 2000. This is a very happy prediction compared with the situation in 1950, as those years of grace may turn up basic factors which (I hope!) may postpone disaster still longer. We were *much* closer to ultimate disaster around 1955 than we are today—much closer indeed than we were at the time of the Cuban Confrontation in 1962. But the public never knew it. All in all, things look pretty good for survival, for the time being—and that is as good a break as our ancestors ever had. It was far more dangerous to live in London in 1664–5 than it is to live in a city threatened by H-bombs today.

1980 I am forced to revise the 1950 prediction to this extent: It is no longer certain that we will fight to repel attack on territory we have guaranteed to defend; our behavior both with respect to Viet Nam and to Taiwan is a clear warning to our NATO allies. The question is not whether we should ever have been in Viet Nam or whether we should ever have allied ourselves to the Nationalist Chinese. I do not know of *any* professional military man who favored ever getting into combat on the continent of Asia; such war for us is a logistic and strategic disaster.

But to break a commitment to an ally *once it has been made* is to destroy our credibility.

5. **1950** In fifteen years the housing shortage will be solved by a "breakthrough" into new technology which will make every house now standing as obsolete as privies.

1965 Here I fell flat on my face. There has been no breakthrough in housing, nor is any now in prospect— instead the ancient, wasteful methods of building are now being confirmed by public subsidies. The degree of our backwardness in the field is hard to grasp; we have never seen a modern house. Think what an automobile would be if each one were custom-built from materials fetched to your home—what would it look like, what would it do, and how much would it cost. But don't set the cost lower than $100,000 or the speed higher than 10 m/h, if you want to be realistic about the centuries of difference between the housing industry and the automotive industry.

I underestimated (through wishful thinking) the power of human stupidity—a fault fatal to prophecy.

1980 I'm still flat on my face with my nose rubbed in the mud; the situation is worse than ever. See A BATHROOM OF HER OWN on page 244. And that figure of

$100,000 just above was with gold at $35 per troy ounce—so change it to one million dollars—or call it 2700 troy ounces of gold. Or forget it. The point is that it would be very nearly impossible to build even a clunker automobile at any price if we built them the way we build houses.

We have the technology to build cheap, beautiful, efficient, flexible (modular method) houses, extremely comfortable and with the durability of a Rolls Royce. But I cannot guess when (if ever) the powers that be (local bureaucrats, unions, building materials suppliers, county and state officials) will permit us poor serfs to have modern housing.

6. **1950** We'll all be getting a little hungry by and by.
1965 No new comment.
1980 Not necessarily. In 1950 I was too pessimistic concerning population. Now I suspect that the controlling parameter is oil. In modern agriculture oil is the prime factor—as power for farm machinery (obviously) but also for insecticides and for fertilizers. Since our oil policies in Washington are about as boneheaded—counterproductive—as they can be, I have no way to guess how much food we can raise in 2000 A.D. But no one in the United States should be hungry in 2000 A.D.—unless we are conquered and occupied.

7. **1950** The cult of the phony in art will disappear. So-called "modern art" will be discussed only by psychiatrists.
1965 No new comment.
1980 One may hope. But art reflects culture and the world is even nuttier now than it was in 1950; these are the Crazy Years. But, while "fine" art continues to look like the work of retarded monkeys, commercial art grows steadily better.

8. **1950** Freud will be classed as a pre-scientific, intuitive pioneer and psychoanalysis will be replaced by

a growing, changing "operational psychology" based on measurement and prediction.

1965 No new comment.

1980 This prediction is beginning to come true. Freud is no longer taken seriously by informed people. More and more professional psychologists are skilled in appropriate mathematics; most of the younger ones understand inductive methodology and the nature of scientific confirmation and are trying hard to put rigor into their extremely difficult, still inchoate subject. For some of the current progress see Dr. Pournelle's book, cited on page 325.

By 2000 A.D. we will know a great deal about how the brain functions . . . whereas in 1900 what little we knew was wrong.

I do *not* predict that the basic mystery of psychology—how mass arranged in certain complex patterns becomes aware of itself—will be solved by 2000 A.D. I hope so but do not expect it.

9. **1950** Cancer, the common cold, and tooth decay will all be conquered; the revolutionary new problem in medical research will be to accomplish "regeneration," i.e., to enable a man to grow a new leg, rather than fit him with an artificial limb.

1965 In the meantime spectacular progress has been made in organ transplants—and the problem of regeneration is related to this one. Biochemistry and genetics have made a spectacular breakthrough in "cracking the genetic code." It is a tiny crack, however, with a long way to go before we will have the human chromosomes charted and still longer before we will be able to "tailor" human beings by gene manipulation. The possibility is there—but not by year 2000. This is probably just as well. If we aren't bright enough to build decent houses, are we bright enough to play God with the architecture of human beings?

1980 I see no reason to change this prediction if you will let me elaborate (weasel) a little. "The common cold" is a portmanteau expression for upper respiratory infections which appear to be caused by a very large number of different viruses. Viruses are pesky things. It is possible to immunize against them, e.g., vaccination against smallpox, a virus disease. But there are almost no chemotherapies, medicines, against viruses. That is why "the common cold" is treated much the same way today as in 1900, i.e., support the patient with bed rest, liquids, aspirin to make him more comfortable, keep him warm. This was standard in 1900 and it is still standard in 1980.

It is probable that your body makes antibodies against the virus of any cold you catch. But this gives you no protection against that virus's hundreds of close relatives found in any airport, theater, supermarket, or gust of dust off the street. In the meantime, while his kinfolk take turns making you miserable, virus #1 has mutated and you have no antibodies against the mutation.

Good news: Oncology (cancer), immunology, hematology, and "the common cold" turn out to be strongly interrelated subjects; research in all these is moving fast—and a real breakthrough in any one might mean a breakthrough in all.

10. **1950** By the end of this century mankind will have explored this solar system, and the first ship intended to reach the nearest star will be a building.

1965 Our editor suggested that I had been too optimistic on this one—but I still stand by it. It is still thirty-five years to the end of the century. For perspective; look back thirty-five years to 1930—the American Rocket Society had not yet been founded. Another curve, similar to the one herewith in shape but derived entirely from speed of transportation, extrapolates to show faster-than-light travel by year 2000. I guess I'm chicken, for I am not predicting FTL ships by then, if ever. But the prediction still stands without hedging.

1980 My money is still on the table at twenty years

and counting. Senator Proxmire can't live forever. In
the last 10½ years men have been to the Moon several
times; much of the Solar system has been most thoroughly explored within the limits of "black box" technology and more will be visited before this year is out.

Ah, but not explored by *men*—and the distances are
so great. Surely they are . . . by free-fall orbits, which
is all that we have been using. But there are numerous
proposals (and not all ours!) for constant-boost ships,
proposals that require R&D on present art only—no
breakthroughs.

Reach for your pocket calculator and figure how
long it would take to make a trip to Mars and back if
your ship could boost at one-tenth gee. We will omit
some trivia by making it from parking orbit to parking
orbit, use straight-line trajectories, and ignore the
Sun's field—we'll be going uphill to Mars, downhill to
Earth; what we lose on the roundabouts we win on the
shys.

These casual assumptions would cause Dan Alderson, ballistician at Jet Propulsion Laboratory, to faint.
But after he comes out of his faint he would agree that
our answers would be of correct close order of magnitude—and all I'm trying to prove is that even a slight
constant boost makes an enormous difference in tour-
ing the Solar System. (Late in the 21st century we'll
offer the Economy Tour: Ten Planets in Ten Days.)

There are an unlimited number of distances between rather wide parameters for an Earth-Mars-
Earth trip but we will select one that is nearly minimum (it's cheating to wait in orbit at Mars for about a
year in order take the shortest trip each way . . . and
unthinkable to wait years for the closest approach).
We'll do this Space Patrol style: There's Mars, here we
are at L-5; let's scoot over, swing around Mars, and
come straight home. Just for drill.

Conditions: Earth-surface gravity (one "gee") is an
acceleration of 32.2 feet per second squared, or 980.7
centimeters per second squared. Mars is in or near op-

position (Mars is rising as Sun is setting). We will assume that the round trip is 120,000,000 miles. If we were willing to wait for closest approach we could trim that to less than 70,000,000 miles . . . but we might have to wait as long as 17 years. So we'll take a common or garden variety opposition—one every 26 months—for which the distance to Mars is about 50- to 60,000,000 miles and never over 64 million.

(With Mars in conjunction on the far side of the Sun, we could take the scenic route of over 500 million miles—how much over depends on how easily you sunburn. I suggest a minimum of 700 million miles.)

You now have all necessary data to figure the time it takes to travel Earth-Mars-Earth in a constant-boost ship—*any* constant-boost ship—when Mars is at opposition. (If you insist on the scenic route, you can't treat the trajectory approximations as straight lines and you can't treat space as flat but a bit uphill. You'll need Alderson or his equal and a *big* computer, not a pocket calculator; the equations are very hairy and sometimes shoot back.)

But us two space cadets are doing this by eyeballing it, using Tennessee windage, an aerospace almanac, a Mickey Mouse watch, and an SR-50 Pop discarded years ago.

We need just one equation: Velocity equals acceleration times elapsed time: $v = at$

This tells us that our average speed is $\frac{1}{2}at$—and from that we know that the distance achieved is the average speed times the elapsed time: $d = \frac{1}{2}at^2$

If you don't believe me, check any physics text, encyclopedia, or nineteen other sorts of reference books—and I did that derivation without cracking a book but now I'm going to stop and find out whether I've goofed—I've had years of practice in goofing. (Later—seems okay.)

Just two things to remember: 1) This is a 4-piecee trip—boost to midpoint, flip over and boost to brake; then do the same thing coming home. Treat all four legs as being equal or 30,000,000 miles, so figure one of them and multiply by four (Dan, stop frowning; this is an *approximation* . . . done with a Mickey Mouse watch.)

2) You must keep your units straight. If you start with centimeters, you are stuck with centimeters; if you start with feet, you are stuck with feet. So we have ¼ of the trip equals 5280 x 30,000,000 = 1.584 x 10^{11} feet, or 4.827 x 10^{12} centimeters.

One last bit: Since it is elapsed time we are after, we will rearrange that equation (d = ½at²) so that you can get the answer in one operation on your trusty-but-outdated pocket calculator . . . or even on a slide rule, as those four-significant-figures data are mere swank; I've used so many approximations and ignored so many minor variables that I'll be happy to get answers correct to two significant figures.

$$\frac{d}{\frac{1}{2}a} = t^2 \quad \text{This gives us: } t = \sqrt{d/\tfrac{1}{2}a}$$

d is 30,000,000 miles expressed in feet, or 158,400,000,000. Set that into your pocket calculator. Divide it by one half of one tenth of gee, or 1.61. Push the square root button. Multiply by 4. You now have the elapsed time of the round trip expressed in seconds so divide by 3600 and you have it in hours, and divide that by 24 and you have it in days.

At this point you are supposed to be astonished and to start looking for the mistake. While you are looking, I'm going to slide out to the refrigerator.

There is no mistake. Work it again, this time in metric. Find a reference book and check the equation. You will find the answer elsewhere in this book but don't look for it yet; we'll try some other trips you may take by 2000 A.D. if you speak Japanese or German—or even English if Proxmire and his ilk fail of reelection.

Same trip, worked the same way, but at only one

percent of gee. At that boost I would weigh less than my shoes weigh here in my study.

Hmmph! Looks as if one answer or the other must be wrong.

Bear with me. This time we'll work it at a full gee, the acceleration you experience lying in bed, asleep. (See Einstein's 1905 paper.)

(Preposterous. All three answers must be wrong.)

Please stick with me a little longer. Let's run all three problems for a round trip to Pluto—in 2006 A.D., give or take a year. Why 2006? Because today Pluto has ducked inside the orbit of Neptune and won't reach perihelion until 1989—and I want it to be a bit farther away; I've got a rabbit stashed in the hat.

Pluto ducks outside again in 2003 and by 2006 it will be (give or take a few million miles) 31.6 A.U. from the Sun, figuring an A.U. at 92,900,000 miles or 14,950,000,000,000 centimeters as we'll work this both ways, MKS and English units. (All right, all right—1.495×10^{13} centimeters; it gets dull here at this typewriter.)

Now work it all three ways, a round trip of 63.2 A.U. at a constant boost of one gravity, one tenth gravity, and one hundredth of a gee—and we'll dedicate this to Clyde Tombaugh, the only living man to discover a new planet—through months of tedious and painstaking examination of many thousands of films.

Some think that Pluto was once a satellite and its small size makes this possible. But it is *not* a satellite today. It is both far too big and hundreds of millions of miles out of position to be an asteroid. It can't be a comet. So it's a planet—or something so exotic as to be still more of a prize.

Its size made it hard to find and thus still more of an achievment. But Tombaugh continued the search for seventeen weary years and many millions more films. If there is an Earth-size planet out there, it is at least three times as distant as Pluto, and a gas giant would have to be six times as far. Negative data win no prizes but they are the bedrock of science.

Until James W. Christy on 22 June 1978 discovered Pluto's satellite, Charon, it was possible for us romantics to entertain the happy thought that Pluto was loaded with valuable heavy metals; the best estimate of its density made this plausible. But the mass of a planet with a satellite can be calculated quite easily and accurately, and from that, its density.

The new figure was much too low, only half again as heavy as water. Methane snow? Perhaps.

So once again a lovely theory is demolished by an awkward fact.

Nevertheless Pluto remains a most mysterious and most intriguing heavenly body. A planet the size and mass of Mars might not be too much use to us out there . . . but think of it as a fuel dump. Many stories and many nonfictional projections speak of using the gas giants and/or the rings of Saturn as sources of fuel. But if Pluto is methane ice or water ice or frozen hydrogen or all three, as a source of fuel— conventional, or fusion, or even reaction mass—Pluto has one supremely important advantage over the gas giants: Pluto is *not* at the bottom of a horridly deep gravity well.

Finished calculating? Good. Please turn to page 368 and see why I wanted our trip to Pluto to be a distance of 31.6 A.U.—plus other goodies, perhaps.

11. **1950** Your personal telephone will be small enough to carry in your handbag. Your house telephone will record messages, answer simple inquiries, and transmit vision.

1965 No new comment.

1980 This prediction is trivial and timid. Most of it has already come true and the telephone system will hand you the rest on a custom basis if you'll pay for it. In the year 2000, with modern telephones tied into home computers (as common then as flush toilets are today) you'll be able to have 3-dimensional holovision along with stereo speech. Arthur C. Clarke says that this will do away with most personal contact in business. I agree with all of Mr. Clarke's arguments and disagree with his conclusion; with us monkey folk there is no substitute for personal contact; we enjoy it and it fills a spiritual need.

Besides that, the business conference is often an excuse to loaf on the boss's time and the business convention often supplies some of the benefits of the Roman Saturnalia.

Nevertheless I look forward to holovideostereophones *without* giving up personal contacts.

12. **1950** Intelligent life will be found on Mars.

1965 Predicting intelligent life on Mars looks pretty silly after those dismal photographs. But I shan't withdraw it until Mars has been *thoroughly* explored. As yet we really have no idea—and no data—as to just how ubiquitous and varied life may be in this galaxy; it is conceivable that life as we *don't* know it can evolve on *any* sort of a planet . . . and nothing in our present knowledge of chemistry rules this out. All the talk has been about life-as-we-know-it—which means terrestrial conditions.

But if you feel that this shows in me a childish reluctance to give up thoats and zitidars and beautiful Martian princesses until forced to, I won't argue with you—I'll just wait.

1980 The photographs made by the Martian landers of 1976 and their orbiting companions make the prediction of intelligent Martian life look even sillier. But the new pictures and the new data make Mars even more mysterious. I'm a diehard because I suspect that life is ubiquitous—call that a religious opinion if you wish. But remember two things: Almost all discussion has been about Life-as-we-know-it . . . but what about Life-as-we-*don't*-know-it? If there were Martians around the time that those amazing gullies and canyons were formed, perhaps they went underground as their atmosphere thinned. At present, despite wonderful pictures, our data are very sparse; those two fixed landers are analogous to two such landing here: one on Canadian tundra, the other in Antarctica—hardly sufficient to solve the question: Is there intelligent life on Sol III?

(Is there intelligent life in Washington, D.C.?)

Whistling in the dark—I think I goofed on this one. But if in fact Mars is uninhabited, shortly there will be a land rush that will make the Oklahoma land stampede look gentle. Since $E = mc^2$ came into our lives, *all* real estate is potentially valuable; it can be terraformed to suit humans. There has been so much fiction and serious, able nonfiction published on how to terraform Mars that I shan't add to it, save to note one thing:

Power is no problem. Sunshine at that distance has dropped off to about .43% of the maximum here—but Mars gets *all* of it and gets it all day long save for infrequent dust storms . . . whereas the *most* that Philadelphia (and like places) ever gets is .35%—and overcast days are common. Mars won't need solar power from orbit; it will be easier to do it on the ground.

But don't be surprised if the Japanese charge you a very high fee for stamping their visa into your passport plus requiring deposit of a prepaid return ticket or, if you ask for immigrant's visa, charge you a much, much higher fee plus proof of a needed colonial skill.

For there *is* intelligent life in Tokyo.

13. **1950** A thousand miles an hour at a cent a mile will be commonplace; short hauls will be made in evacuated subways at extreme speed.

1965 I must hedge number thirteen; the "cent" I meant was scaled by the 1950 dollar. But our currency has been going through a long steady inflation, and no nation in history has ever gone as far as we have along this route without reaching the explosive phase of inflation. Ten-dollar hamburgers? Brother, we are headed for the hundred-dollar hamburger—for the barter-only hamburger.

But this is only an inconvenience rather than a disaster as long as there is plenty of hamburger.

1980 I must scale that "cent" again. In 1950 gold was $35/troy ounce; this morning the London fix was $374/troy ounce. Just last week my wife and I flew San Francisco to Baltimore and return. We took neither the luxury class nor any of the special discounted fares; we simply flew what we could get.

Applying the inflation factor—35/374—our tickets cost a hair less than one cent a mile in *1950* dollars. From here on I had better give prices in troy ounces of gold, or in Swiss francs; not even the Man in the White House knows where this inflation is going. About those subways: possible, even probable, by 2000 A.D. But I see little chance that they will be financed until the dollar is stablized—a most painful process our government hates to tackle.

14. **1950** A major objective of applied physics will be to control gravity.

1965 This prediction stands. But today physics is in a tremendous state of flux with new data piling up faster than it can be digested; it is anybody's guess as to where we are headed, but the wilder you guess, the more likely you are to hit it lucky. With "elementary particles" of nuclear physics now totaling about half the number we used to use to list the "immutable" chemical elements, a spectator needs a program just to keep track of the players. At the other end of the scale, "quasars"—quasi-stellar bodies—have come along; radio astronomy is now bigger than telescopic astronomy used to be; and we have redrawn our picture of the universe several times, each time enlarging it and making it more complex—I haven't seen this week's theory yet, which is well, as it would be out of date before this gets into print. Plasma physics was barely started in 1950; the same for solid-state physics. This is the Golden Age of physics—and it's an anarchy.

1980 I stick by the basic prediction. There is so much work going on both by mathematical physicists and experimental physicists as to the nature of gravity that it seems inevitable that twenty years from now applied physicists will be trying to control it. But note that I said "trying"—succeeding may take a long time. If and when they do succeed, a spinoff is likely to be a spaceship that is in no way a rocket ship—and the Galaxy is ours! (Unless we meet that smarter, meaner, tougher race that kills us or enslaves us or eats us—or all three.)

Particle physics: the situation is even more confusing than in 1965. Physicists now speak of more than 200 kinds of hadrons, "elementary" heavy particles. To reduce this confusion a mathematical construct called the "quark" was invented. Like Jell-O quarks come in many colors and flavors . . . plus spin, charm, truth, and beauty (or top and bottom in place of truth and beauty—or perhaps "truth" doesn't belong in the list, and no jokes, please, as the physicists aren't joking and neither am I). Put quarks together in their many attributes and you can account for (maybe) all those 200-odd hadrons (and have a system paralleling the leptons or light particles as a bonus).

All very nice . . . except that no one has ever been able to pin down even one quark. Quarks, if they exist, come packaged in clumps as hadrons—not at random but by rules to account for each of that mob of hadrons.

Now comes Kenneth A. Johnson, Ph.D. (Harvard '55), Professor of Physics at the Massachusetts Institute of Technology (which certainly places him in the worldwide top group of physicists) with an article (*Scientific American*, July 1979, p. 112, "The Bag Model of Quark Confinement"), an article which appears to state that quarks will never be pinned down because they are in sort of an eternal purdah, never to be seen even as bubble tracks.

Somehow it reminds me of the dilemma when the snark is a boojum.

I'm not poking fun at Dr. Johnson; he is very learned and trying hard to explain his difficult subject to the unlearned such as I.

But, in the meantime I suggest reading *The Hunting of the Snark* while waiting patiently for 2000 A.D. We have a plethora of data; perhaps in twenty more years the picture will be simplified. Perhaps—

15. **1950** We will not achieve a "World State" in the predictable future. Nevertheless, Communism will vanish from this planet.

1965 I stand flatly behind prediction number fifteen.

1980 I still stand flatly behind the first sentence of that two-part prediction above. The second part I could weasel out of by pointing out that on this planet *no* state that calls itself Marxist or Socialist or Communist has ever established a system approximating that called for by the works of Karl Marx and Friedrich Engels. And never will; Marx's utopia does not fit human beings. The state will not "wither away."

But I shan't weasel as I am utterly dismayed by the political events of the past 15-20 years. At least two thirds of the globe now calls itself Marxist. Another large number of countries are military dictatorships. Another large group (including the United States) are constitutional democratic republics but so heavily tinged with socialism ("welfare state") that all of them are tottering on the brink of bankruptcy and collapse.

So far as I can see today the only thing that could cause the soi-disant Marxist countries to collapse in as little time as twenty years would be for the United States to be conquered and occupied by the USSR— and twenty years ago I thought that this was a strong possibility. (I'm more optimistic now, under the present three-cornered standoff.)

If we were to be conquered and occupied, the Communist world might collapse rather quickly. We have been propping them up whenever they were in real trouble (frequently!) for about half a century.

16. **1950** Increasing mobility will disenfranchise a majority of the population. About 1990 a constitutional amendment will do away with state lines while retaining the semblance.

1965 No further comment.

1980 I goofed. I will be much surprised if either half of this double prediction comes to pass by 2000—at least in the form described and for the reasons I had in mind. The franchise now extends to any warm body over eighteen years of age and that franchise can be transferred to another state in less time than it takes the citizen to find housing in his/her new state.

Thus no constitutional amendment is needed. But the state lines are fading year by year anyhow as power continues to move from the states to the Federal government and especially into the hands of non-elected bureaucrats.

17. **1950** All aircraft will be controlled by a giant radar net run on a continent-wide basis by a multiple electronic "brain."

1965 No further comment.

1980 This prediction still stands—although it may be my wishful thinking. Such a system was designed over thirty years ago; Congress wouldn't buy it. It would be more expensive today . . . and is far more urgently needed. Anyone who has ever been in the tower of a busy field or has ever ridden in the "office" of a commercial plane during a takeoff or landing at a busy field knows what I mean. All our fields are overloaded but anyone who goes in or out of San Diego or of O'Hare-Chicago or—but why go on? Our airplanes are pretty durn wonderful . . . but our method of handling air traffic at fields is comparable to Manhattan without traffic lights.

I shall continue to fly regularly for two reasons: 1) Mrs. Heinlein and I hope to go out in a common disaster. 2) Consider the alternatives: AMTRAK (ugh!), buses (two ughs!), and driving oneself. The latter is fine for short distances (OPEC and Washington permitting) but, while in my younger days I drove across this continent so many times that I've lost count, today I am no longer physically up to such a trip even with a chauffeur.

But that totally-automated traffic control system *ought* to be built. Expensive, yes—but what price do we place on a hundred dead passengers, a flight crew, and a modern airliner? In the present state of the art in computers and in radar neither the pilot nor the controller should be in the loop at landing or take off; they should simply be alert, ready to override, because even the most perfect machinery is subject to Murphy's Law. But all routine (99.9%+)takeoffs and landings should be made by computer.

If this pushes small private planes onto separate and smaller fields, so be it. Bicycles do not belong on freeways. I hate to say that, as there is nothing more fun than a light sports plane.

(Nothing that is not alive, I mean. Vive la difference!)

(On air traffic control I speak with a modicum of authority. I returned to the aircraft industry for a short time in 1948 to research this subject, then wrote an article aimed at the slicks: THE BILLION-DOLLAR EYE. I missed; it is still unpublished.)

18. **1950** Fish and yeast will become our principal sources of proteins. Beef will be a luxury; lamb and mutton will disappear.

1965 I'll hedge number eighteen a little. Hunger is not now a problem in the USA and need not be in the year 2000—but hunger *is* a world problem and would at once become an acute problem for us if we were conquered . . . a distinct possibility by 2000. Between our present status and that of subjugation lies a whole spectrum of political and economic possible shapes to the future under which we would share the worldwide hunger to a greater or lesser extent. And the problem grows. We can expect to have to feed around half a billion Americans circa year 2000—our present huge surpluses would then represent acute shortages even if we never shipped a ton of wheat to India.

1980 It would now appear that the USA population in 2000 A.D. will be about 270,000,000 instead of 500,000,000. I have been collecting clippings on demography for forty years; all that the projections have in common is that all of them are wrong. Even that figure of 270,000,000 may be too high; today the only reason our population continues to increase is that we oldsters are living longer; our current birthrate is not sufficient even to replace the parent generation.

19. **1950** Mankind will *not* destroy itself, nor will "Civilization" be destroyed.

1965 I stand by prediction number nineteen.

1980 I still stand by prediction number nineteen. There will be wars and we will be in some of them— and some may involve atomic weapons. But there will *not* be that all-destroying nuclear holocaust that forms the background of so many SF stories. There are three reasons for this: The United States, the Soviet Union, and the People's Republic of China.

Why? Because the three strongest countries in the world (while mutually detesting each the other two) have nothing to gain and everything to lose in an all-out swapping of H-bombs. Because Kremlin bosses are not idiots and neither are those in Beijing (Peiping)(Peking).

If another country—say Israel, India, or the South African Republic—gets desperate and tosses an A- or H-bomb, that country is likely to receive three phone calls simultaneously, one from each of the Big Three: "You have exactly three minutes to back down. Then we destroy you."

After World War II I never expected that our safety would ever depend on a massive split in Communist International—but that is exactly what has happened.

1950 Here are things we *won't* get soon, if ever:
Travel through time.
Travel faster than the speed of light.
"Radio" transmission of matter.
Manlike robots with manlike reactions.
Laboratory creation of life.
Real understanding of what "thought" is and how it is related to matter.
Scientific proof of personal survival after death.
Nor a permanent end to war. (I don't like that prediction any better than you do.)

1950 Prediction of gadgets is a parlor trick anyone can learn; but only a fool would attempt to predict details of future history (except as fiction, so labeled); there are too many unknowns and no techniques for integrating them even if they were known.

Even to make predictions about overall trends in technology is now most difficult. In fields where before World War II there was one man working in public, there are now ten, or a hundred, working in secret. There may be six men in the country who have a clear picture of what is going on in science today. *There may not be even one.*

This is in itself a trend. Many leading scientists consider it a factor as disabling to us as the nonsense of Lysenkoism is to Russian technology. Nevertheless there are clear-cut trends which are certain to make this coming era enormously more productive and interesting than the frantic one we have just passed through. Among them are:

Cybernetics: The study of communication and control of mechanisms and organisms. This includes the wonderful field of mechanical and electronic "brains"—but is not limited to it. (These "brains" are a factor in themselves that will speed up technical progress the way a war does.)

Semantics: A field which seems concerned only with definitions of words. It is not; it is a frontal attack on epistemology—that is to say, *how* we know *what* we know, a subject formerly belonging to long-haired philosophers.

New tools of mathematics and logic, such as calculus of statement, Boolean logic, morphological analysis, generalized symbology, newly invented mathematics of every sort—there is not space even to name these enormous fields, but they offer us hope in every field—medicine, social relations, biology, economics, anything.

Biochemistry: Research into the nature of protoplasm, into enzyme chemistry, viruses, etc., give hope not only that we may conquer disease, but that we may someday understand the mechanisms of life itself. Through this, and with the aid of cybernetic machines and radioactive isotopes, we may eventually acquire a rigor of chemistry. Chemistry is not a discipline today; it is a jungle. We know that chemical behavior depends on the number of orbital electrons in an atom and that physical and chemical properties follow the pattern called the Periodic Table. We don't know much else, save by cut-and-try, despite the great size and importance of the chemical industry. When chemistry becomes a discipline, mathematical chemists will design new materials, predict their properties, and tell engineers how to make them—without ever entering a laboratory. We've got a *long* way to go on that one!

Nucleonics: We have yet to find out what makes the atom tick. Atomic power?—yes, we'll have it, in convenient packages—when we understand the nucleus. The field of radioisotopes alone is larger than was the entire known body of science in 1900. Before we are through with these problems, we may find out how the universe is shaped and *why*. Not to mention enormous unknown vistas best represented by ?????

Some physicists are now using two time scales, the T-scale, and the *tau*-scale. Three billion years on one scale can equal an incredibly split second on the other scale—and yet both apply to you and your kitchen stove. Of such anarchy is our present state in physics.

For such reasons we must insist that *the Age of Science has not yet opened*.

(Still 1950) The greatest crisis facing us is not Russia, not the Atom bomb, not corruption in government, not encroaching hunger, not the morals of young. It is a crisis in the *organization* and *accessibility* of human knowledge. We own an enormous "encyclopedia"—which isn't even arranged alphabetically. Our "file cards" are spilled on the floor, nor were they ever in order. The answers we want may be buried somewhere in the heap, but it might take a lifetime to locate two already known facts, place them side by side and derive a third fact, the one we urgently need.

Call it the Crisis of the Librarian.

We need a new "specialist" who is not a specialist, but a synthesist. We need a new science to be the perfect secretary to all other sciences.

But we are not likely to get either one in a hurry and we have a powerful lot of grief before us in the meantime.

Fortunetellers can always be sure of repeat customers by predicting what the customer wants to hear . . . it matters not whether the prediction comes true. Contrariwise, the weatherman is often blamed for bad weather.

Brace yourself.

In 1900 the cloud on the horizon was no bigger than a man's hand—but what lay ahead was the Panic of 1907, World War I, the panic following it, the Depression, Fascism, World War II, the Atom Bomb, and Red Russia.

Today the clouds obscure the sky, and the wind that overturns the world is sighing in the distance.

The period immediately ahead will be the roughest, cruelest one in the long, hard history of mankind. It will probably include the worst World War of them all. It might even end with a war with Mars, God save the Mark! Even if we are spared that fantastic possibility, it is certain that there will be no security anywhere, save that which you dig out of your own inner spirit.

But what of that picture we drew of domestic luxury and tranquility for Mrs. Middleclass, style 2000 A.D.?

She lived through it. She survived.

Our prospects need not dismay you, not if you or your kin were at Bloody Nose Ridge, at Gettysburg—or trudged across the Plains. You and I are here because we carry the genes of uncountable ancestors who fought—and won—against death in all its forms. We're tough. We'll survive. Most of us.

We've lasted through the preliminary bouts; the main event is coming up.

But it's not for sissies.

The last thing to come fluttering out of Pandora's Box was Hope—without which men die.

The gathering wind will not destroy everything, nor will the Age of Science change everything. Long after the first star ship leaves for parts unknown, there will still be outhouses in upstate New York, there will still be steers in Texas, and—no doubt—the English will still stop for tea.

Afterthoughts, fifteen years later—(1965)

I see no reason to change any of the negative predictions which follow the numbered affirmative ones. They are all conceivably possible; they are all wildly unlikely by year 2000. Some of them are debatable if the terms are defined to suit the affirmative side—definitions of "life" and "manlike," for example. Let it stand that I am not talking about an amino acid in one case, or a machine that plays chess in the other.

Today the forerunners of synthesists are already at work in many places. Their titles may be anything; their degrees may be in anything—or they may have no degrees. Today they are called "operations researchers," or sometimes "systems development engineers," or other interim tags. But they are all interdisciplinary people, generalists, not specialists— the new Renaissance Man. The very explosion of data which forced most scholars to specialize very narrowly created the necessity which evoked this new non-specialist. So far, this "unspecialty" is in its infancy; its methodology is inchoate, the results are sometimes trivial, and no one knows how to train to become such a man. But the results are often spectacularly brilliant, too—this new man may yet save all of us.

I'm an optimist. I have great confidence in Homo sapiens.

We have rough times ahead—but when didn't we? Things have always been "tough all over." H-bombs, Communism, race riots, water shortage—all nasty problems. But not basic problems, merely current ones.

We have three basic and continuing problems: The problem of population explosion; the problem of data explosion; and the problem of government.

Population problems have a horrid way of solving themselves when they are not solved rationally; the Four Horsemen of the Apocalypse are always saddled up and ready to ride. The data explosion is now being solved, mostly by cybernetics and electronics men rather than by librarians—and if the solutions are less than perfect, at least they are better than what

Grandpa had to work with. The problem of government has not been solved either by the "Western Democracies" or the "Peoples' Democracies," as of now. (Anyone who thinks the people of the United States have solved the problem of government is using too short a time scale.) The peoples of the world are now engaged in a long, long struggle with no end in sight, testing whether one concept works better than another; in that conflict millions have already died and it is possible that hundreds of millions will die in it before year 2000. But not all.

I hold both opinions and preferences as to the outcome. But my personal preference for a maximum of looseness is irrelevant; what we are experiencing is an evolutionary process in which personal preference matters, at most, only statistically. Biologists, ecologists in particular, are working around to the idea that natural selection and survival of the fittest is a notion that applies more to groups and how they are structured than it does to individuals. The present problem will solve itself in the cold terms of evolutionary survival, and in the course of it both sides will make changes in group structure. The system that survives might be called "Communism" or it might be called "Democracy" (the latter is my guess)—but one thing we can be certain of: it will not resemble very closely what either Marx or Jefferson had in mind. Or it might be called by some equally inappropriate neologism; political tags are rarely logical.

For Man is rarely logical. But I have great confidence in Man, based on his past record. He is mean, ornery, cantankerous, illogical, emotional—and amazingly hard to kill. Religious leaders have faith in the spiritual redemption of Man; humanist leaders subscribe to a belief in the perfectibility of Man through his own efforts; but I am not discussing either of these two viewpoints. My confidence in our species lies in its past history and is founded quite as much on Man's so-called vices as on his so-called virtues. When the chips are down, quarrelsomeness and selfishness can be as useful to the survival of the human race as is altruism, and pig-headedness can be a trait superior to sweet reasonableness. If this were not true, these "vices" would have died out through the early deaths of their hosts, at least a half million years back.

I have a deep and abiding confidence in Man as he is, imperfect and often unlovable—plus still greater confidence in his potential. No matter how tough things are, Man copes. He comes up with adequate answers from illogical reasons. But the answers work.

Last to come out of Pandora's Box was a gleaming, beautiful thing—eternal Hope.

(**1980**—I see no point in saying more. R.A.H.)

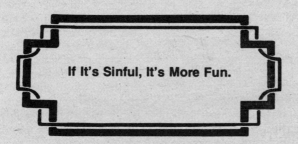

If It's Sinful, It's More Fun.

FOREWORD

The editor who disliked science fiction (and me) but liked my sales grumbled to me, on my delivering my annual boys' novel, that she did wish that someone would write girls' stories. I answered, "Very well, I'll write a story for girls. When do you want it?"

She was simultaneously astonished, offended, and amused at the ridiculous and arrogant notion that a mere man could write stories for girls. So that's how Puddin' was born: I started writing first-person-female-adolescent stories—but not for that old harridan.

Since this is not the first of the Puddin' stories, let me introduce her: her name is Maureen, her nickname derives from her weight problem. She is eternally an undergraduate on a small campus in Somewhere, U.S.A., where her father teaches anthropology, smokes his pipe, and reads—whereas her mother is a Renaissance Man who does everything. Maureen has an unbearable younger brother (all younger brothers are unbearable; I should know, I was one).

I grew so fond of Maureen that I helped her to get rid of that excess weight, changed her name to "Podkayne," and moved her to Mars (along with her unbearable kid brother). And now and again she turns up under other names in other science fiction stories.

Nevertheless Maureen still attends classes on this campus in Never-Neverland. I had intended to do a full book of Puddin' short stories under the title MEN ARE EXASPERATING. I have enough stories for a fat volume but as yet I have not written all of them down. One in particular (MOTHER AND THE ANIMAL KINGDOM) keeps niggling at me to write it—a character in it, a little gray donkey named Mr. Jenkins, keeps looking at me with mournful eyes. I can write that one anytime I get a full day absolutely free of other pressures—say about 1997.

Three others are almost as ready to write, and I would have enough for a book.

And yet . . . and yet—Is Puddin' totally obsolete? This

*campus never has riots. The girls are not "on the Pill."
(Or if they are, the subject is not mentioned.) There is no
drug problem. In short, I have described college life of a
bygone day.*

*But don't misunderstand me. My teens were the Torrid
Twenties and exactly the same things went on then as
now . . . but were kept under cover. When I was a freshman in college, the nearest connection for marijuana
was a drugstore a hundred yards off campus; for H or C
it was necessary to walk another block. But bootleg liquor (taxfree) would be delivered on or off campus at any
hour.*

*Did I avail myself of any of these amenities? None of
your business, Buster!*

*As for sex, each generation thinks it invented sex; each
generation is totally mistaken. Anything along that line
today was commonplace both in Pompeii and in Victo-
rian England; the differences lie only in the degree of cov-
erup—if any.*

*I may never publish the book MEN ARE EXASPER-
ATING; I'm not sure it has a market and, at my age, there
are more stories that I want to write (and are certain of
publication) than I can possibly write before the black
camel kneels at my door.*

I hope you like Puddin'.

CLIFF AND THE CALORIES

According to Daddy, I'll eat anything standing still or even moving slowly. But Mother said nonsense, I simply have a high metabolic rate.

Daddy answered, "You haven't had it checked, so how do you know? Puddin', stand sideways and let me look at you."

Junior said, "She hasn't got a 'sideways,'" and let loose a perfectly horrible laugh that is supposed to sound like Woody Woodpecker and does, only worse. Of what use is the male of the species between the ages of two and sixteen? Later on, they are bearable, even indispensable—at least I would find it difficult to dispense with Cliff, although Junior may never be an asset.

That's how I went on a diet.

It started with Cliff—most things do. I am going to marry Cliff, only I haven't told him yet. I have never had any cause to doubt the sincerity of Cliff's devotion, but I have sometimes wondered what it was he found most attractive about me: my character, disposition, and true worth, or my so-to-speak physical attributes.

The bathroom scales were beginning to make me think it was the former. Perhaps that should have made me happy, but I have yet to find the girl who would swap a twenty-one-inch waist and a good silhouette for sterling merit. Not that I could hope to be a raving beauty, but a few wolf whistles never did any harm and are good for the morale.   .

I had just had a chance to test Cliff's point of view. A girl showed up at school who was exactly my size; we compared measurements. The point is, on Clarice it looked good—cursive and bountiful but good. Maureen, I told myself, here is a chance to get an honest opinion out of Cliff.

I saw to it that he got a good look at her at tennis practice. As we left I said craftily, "That new girl, Clarice—she has a lovely figure."

Cliff looked over his shoulder and replied. "Oh, sure—from her ankles down."

I had my answer and I didn't like it. Cliff didn't care for my type of figure; divorced from my personality it did not appeal to him. I should have felt a warm glow, knowing it for true love. I didn't; I felt terrible.

It was when I refused a second helping of potatoes that evening that the subject of my metabolism came up.

I went to the library next day and looked into this matter of diet. I hadn't known there were so many books about it. Finally I found one that made sense: *Eat and Grow Slender*. That struck me as an excellent idea.

I took it home to study. I got a few crackers and some cheese and ate them absent-mindedly while I thumbed through the book. There was a plan for losing ten pounds in ten days; the menus looked pretty skimpy. There was another for losing ten pounds in a month. That's for me, I said; no need to be fanatic.

There was a chapter about calories. They make it so simple: one ice-cream cone, one hundred and fifty calories; three dates, eighty-four calories.

My eye lit on "soda crackers"; I knew they wouldn't count much and they didn't—only twenty-one calories apiece. Then I looked up "cheese."

Arithmetic stirred in my brain and I had a chilly feeling. I went into Daddy's study and used his postal

scale to weigh the cheese that had not already become
Maureen.

I did the arithmetic three times. Including two little
bits of fudge I had eaten six hundred and seventy calories, *more than half of a day's allowance as given in the
reducing diet*! And I had only meant to stay the pangs
until dinnertime.

Maureen, I said, this time you've got to be a fanatic;
it's the ten-day die-trying diet for you.

I planned to keep my affairs to myself, selecting the
diet from what was placed before me, but such a
course is impossible in a family that combines the
worst aspects of a Senate investigation with the less
brutal methods of a third degree. I got away with passing up the cream-of-tomato soup by being a little bit
late, but when I refused the gravy, there was nothing
to do but show them the book.

Mother said a growing girl needed her food. I
pointed out that I had quit growing vertically and it
was time I quit horizontally. Junior opened his mouth
and I stuffed a roll into it. That gave Daddy a chance
to say, "Let's put it up to Doc Andrews. If he gives her
the green light, she can starve herself gaunt. She's a
free agent."

So Daddy and I went to Doctor Andrews' office next
day. Daddy had an appointment anyhow—he has terrible colds every spring. Doctor Andrews sent Daddy
across the hall to Doctor Grieb who specializes in al-
lergies and things, then he saw me.

I've known Doctor Andrews since my first squawk,
so I told him everything, even about Cliff, and showed
him the book. He thumbed through it, then he weighed
me and listened to my heart and took my blood pressure. "Go ahead," he told me, "but make it the thirty-
day diet. I don't want you fainting in the classroom."

I guess I had counted on him to save me from my
will power. "How about exercise?" I said hopefully.
"I'm pretty active. Won't I need to eat more to offset
it?"

He roared. "Honey child," he said, "do you know how far you would have to hike to burn up one chocolate malt? *Eight miles!* It will help, but not much."

"How long do I keep this up?"—I asked faintly.

"Until you reach the weight you want—or until your character plays out."

I marched out with my jaw set. If a girl doesn't have a figure or character either, what has she got left?

Mother was home when we got there. Daddy picked her up and kissed her and said, "Now you've got two of us on diets!"

"Two?" said Mother.

"Look." Daddy peeled off his shirt. His arms were covered with little red pin pricks, some redder than others, arranged in neat rows. "I'm allergic," he announced proudly. "Those aren't real colds. I'm allergic to practically everything. That one"— he pointed to a red welt— "is bananas. That one is corn. That one is cow's milk protein. And there is pollen in honey. Wait." He hauled out a list: "Rhubarb, tapioca, asparagus, lima beans, coconut, mustard, cow's milk, apricot, beets, carrots, lamb, cottonseed oil, lettuce, oysters, chocolate—here, you read it; it's your problem."

"It's a good thing that I went to the campus today and signed up for an evening class in domestic dietetics. From now on this family is going to be fed scientifically," Mother said.

That should have been the worst of it, but it wasn't. Junior announced that he was training for hockey and he had to have a training-table diet—which to him meant beef, dripping with blood, whole-wheat toast, and practically nothing else. Last season he had discovered that, even with lead weights in his pockets, he didn't have what it took for a body check. Next season he planned to be something between Paul Bunyan and Gorgeous George. Hence the diet.

By now, Mother was on a diet, too, a scientific one, based on what she had learned during the two weeks she had actually attended classes. Mother pored over charts and we each had separate trays like a hospital, the time I broke my ankle playing second base for the West Side Junior Dodgers. Mother says a girl with my figure should not be a tomboy, but I said that a tomboy should not have my figure. Anyhow, I am no longer a tomboy since Cliff came into my life.

Somehow, Mother found things that weren't on Daddy's verboten list—stewed yak and pickled palm fronds and curried octopus and such. I asked if Daddy had been checked for those too? He said, "Tend to your knitting, Puddin'," and helped himself to more venison pasty. I tried not to watch.

Mother's own diet was as esoteric, but less attractive. She tried to tempt Junior and me with her seaweed soup or cracked wheat or raw rhubarb, but we stuck to our own diets. Eating is fun, but only if it's food.

Breakfast was easiest; Daddy breakfasted later than I did—he had no lectures earlier than ten o'clock that semester.

I would lie abed while our budding athlete wolfed down his Breakfast of Champions, then slide out at the last minute, slurp my glass of tomato juice (twenty-eight calories), and be halfway to school before I woke up. By then it would be too late to be tempted.

I carried my pitiful little lunch. Cliff started packing his lunch, too, and we picnicked together. He never noticed what I ate or how much.

I didn't want Cliff to notice, not yet. I planned to make him faint with the way I would look in my new formal at graduation prom.

It did not work out. Cliff took two final exams early and left for California for the summer and I spent the night of the prom in my room, nibbling celery (four calories per stalk) and thinking about life.

We got ready for our summer trip immediately thereafter. Daddy voted for New Orleans.

Mother shook her head. "Impossibly hot. Besides, I don't want you tempted by those Creole restaurants."

"Just what I had in mind," Daddy answered. "Finest gourmet restaurants in the country. You can't keep us on diets while traveling; it isn't practical. Antoine's, here I come!"

"No," said Mother.

"Yes," said Daddy.

So we went to California. I was ready to throw my weight (which was still too much) in with Daddy, when California was mentioned. I hadn't expected to see Cliff until fall. I put thoughts of *bouillabaisse* and Shrimp Norfolk out of mind; Cliff won, but it was nearer than I like to think.

The trip was hardly a case of merrie-merrie-be. Junior sulked because he wasn't allowed to take along his lifting weights, and Mother was loaded with charts and reference books and menus. Each time we stopped she would enter into long negotiations, involving a personal interview with the chef, while we got hungrier, and hungrier.

We were coming to Kingman, Arizona, when Mother announced that she didn't think we could find a restaurant to take care of our needs. "Why not?" demanded Daddy. "The people there must eat."

Mother shuffled her lists and suggested that we go on through to Las Vegas. Daddy said that if he had known this trip was going to be another Donner party, he would have studied up on how to cook human flesh.

While they discussed it we slid through Kingman and turned north toward Boulder Dam. Mother looked worriedly at the rugged hills and said, "Perhaps you had better turn back, Charles. It will be hours before we reach Las Vegas and there isn't a thing on the map."

Daddy gripped the wheel and looked grim. Daddy will not backtrack for less than a landslide, as Mother should have known.

I was beyond caring. I expected to leave my bones whitening by the road with a notice: *She tried and she died.*

We had dropped out of those hills and into the bleakest desert imaginable when Mother said, "You'll have to turn back, Charles. Look at your gasoline gauge."

Daddy set his jaw and speeded up. "Charles!" said Mother.

"Quiet!" Daddy answered. "I see a gas station ahead."

The sign read Santa Claus, Arizona. I blinked at it, thinking I was at last seeing a mirage. There was a gas station, all right, but that wasn't all.

You know what most desert gas stations look like— put together out of odds and ends. Here was a beautiful fairytale cottage with wavy candy stripes in the shingles. It had a broad brick chimney—*and Santa Claus was about to climb down the chimney!*

Maureen, I said, you've overdone this starvation business; now you are out of your head.

Between the station and the cottage were two incredible little dolls' houses. One was marked *Cinderella's House* and Mistress Mary Quite Contrary was making the garden grow. The other one needed no sign; the Three Little Pigs, and Big Bad Wolf was stuck in its chimney.

"Kid stuff!" says Junior, and added, "Hey, Pop, do we eat here? Huh?"

"We just gas up," answered Daddy. "Find a pebble to chew on. Your mother has declared a hunger strike."

Mother did not answer and headed toward the cottage. We went inside, a bell bonged, and a sweet contralto voice boomed, "Come in! Dinner is ready!"

The inside was twice as big as the outside and was the prettiest dining room imaginable, fresh, new, and clean. Heavenly odors drifted out of the kitchen. The owner of the voice came out and smiled at us.

We knew who she was because her kitchen apron

had "Mrs. Santa Claus" embroidered across it. She made me feel slender, but for her it was perfectly right. Can you imagine Mrs. Santa Claus being *skinny*?

"How many are there?" she asked.

"Four," said Mother, "but—" Mrs. Santa Claus disappeared into the kitchen.

Mother sat down at a table and picked up a menu. I did likewise and started to drool—here is why:

Minted Fruit Cup Rouge
Pot-au-feu à la Creole
Chicken Velvet Soup
Roast Veal with Fine Herbs
Ham Soufflé
Yankee Pot Roast
Lamb Hawaii
Potatoes Lyonnaise
Riced Potatoes
Sweet Potatoes Maryland
Glazed Onions
Asparagus Tips with Green Peas
Chicory Salad with
Roquefort Dressing
Artichoke Hearts with Avocado
Beets in Aspic
Cheese Straws
Miniature Cinnamon Rolls
Hot Biscuits
Sherry Almond Ice Cream
Rum Pie
Pêches Flambées Royales
Peppermint Cloud Cake
Devil's Food Cake
Angel Berry Pie
Coffee   Tea   Milk

(Our water is trucked fifteen miles; please help us save it.)

Thank you. Mrs. Santa Claus

It made me dizzy, so I looked out the window. We were still spang in the middle of the grimmest desert in the world.

I started counting the calories in that subversive document. I got up to three thousand and lost track, because fruit cups were placed in front of us. I barely tasted mine—and my stomach jumped and started nibbling at my windpipe.

Daddy came in, said, "Well!" and sat down, too. Junior followed.

Mother said, "Charles, there is hardly anything here you can touch. I think I had better—" She headed for the kitchen.

Daddy had started reading the menu. He said, "Wait, Martha! Sit down." Mother sat.

Presently he said, "Do I have plenty of clean handkerchiefs?"

Mother said, "Yes, of course. Why—"

"Good. I feel an attack coming on. I'll start with the *pot-au-feu* and—"

Mother said, "Charles!"

"Peace, woman! The human race has survived upwards of five million years eating anything that could be chewed and swallowed." Mrs. Santa Claus came back in and Daddy ordered lavishly, every word stabbing my heart. "Now," he finished, "if you will have that carried in by eight Nubian slaves—"

"We'll use a jeep," Mrs. Santa Claus promised and turned to Mother.

Mother was about to say something about chopped grass and vitamin soup but Daddy cut in with, "That was for both of us. The kids will order for themselves." Mother swallowed and said nothing.

Junior never bothers with menus. "I'll have a double cannibal sandwich," he announced.

Mrs. Santa Claus flinched. "What," she asked ominously, "is a cannibal sandwich?"

Junior explained. Mrs. Santa Claus looked at him as

if she hoped he would crawl back into the woodwork. At last she said, "Mrs. Santa Claus always gives people what they want. But you'll have to eat it in the kitchen; other people will be coming in for dinner."

"Oke," agreed Junior.

"Now what would you like, honey?" she said to me.

"I'd like everything," I answered miserably, "but I'm on a reducing diet."

She clucked sympathetically. "Anything special you mustn't eat?"

"Nothing in particular—just food. I mustn't eat food."

She said, "You will have a hard time choosing a low-caloric meal here. I've never been able to work up interest in such cooking. I'll serve you the same as your parents; you can eat what you wish and as little as you wish."

"All right," I said weakly.

Honestly, I tried. I counted up to ten between bites, then I found I was counting faster so as to finish each course before the next one arrived.

Presently I knew I was a ruined woman and I didn't care. I was surrounded by a warm fog of calories. Once my conscience peeked over the edge of my plate and I promised to make up for it tomorrow. It went back to sleep.

Junior came out of the kitchen with his face covered by a wedge of pinkstriped cake. "Is that a cannibal sandwich?" I asked.

"Huh?" he answered. "You should see what she's got out there. She ought to run a training table."

A long time later Daddy said, "Let's hit the road. I hate to."

Mrs. Santa Claus said, "Stay here if you like. We can accommodate you."

So we stayed and it was lovely.

I woke up resolved to skip even my twenty-eight calories of tomato juice, but I hadn't reckoned with Mrs. Santa Claus. There were no menus; tiny cups of coffee appeared as you sat down, then other things, deceptively, one at a time. Like this: grapefruit, milk, oatmeal and cream, sausage and eggs and toast and butter and jam, bananas and cream—then when you were sure that they had played themselves out, in came the fluffiest waffle in the world, more butter and strawberry jam and syrup, and then more coffee.

I ate all of it, my personality split hopelessly between despair and ecstasy. We rolled out of there feeling wonderful. "Breakfast," said Daddy, "should be compulsory, like education. I hypothesize that correlation could be found between the modern tendency to skimp breakfast and the increase in juvenile delinquency."

I said nothing. Men are my weakness; food my ruin—but I didn't care.

We lunched at Barstow, only I stayed in the car and tried to nap.

Cliff met us at our hotel and we excused ourselves because Cliff wanted to drive me out to see the university. When we reached the parking lot he said, "What has happened? You look as if you had lost your last friend—and you are positively emaciated."

"Oh, Cliff!" I said, and blubbered on his shoulder.

Presently he wiped my nose and started the car. As we drove I told him about it. He didn't say anything, but after a bit he made a left turn. "Is this the way to the campus?" I asked.

"Never you mind."

"Cliff, are you disgusted with me?"

Instead of answering me, he pulled up near a big public building and led me inside; it turned out to be the art museum. Still refusing to talk, he steered me into an exhibition of old masters. Cliff pointed at one of them. "That," he said, "is my notion of a beautiful woman."

I looked. It was *The Judgment of Paris* by Rubens. "And that—and that—" added Cliff. Every picture he pointed to was by Rubens, and I'll swear his models had never heard of dieting.

"What this country needs," said Cliff, "is more plump girls—and more guys like me who appreciate them."

I didn't say anything until we got outside; I was too busy rearranging my ideas. Something worried me, so I reminded him of the time I had asked his opinion of Clarice, the girl who is just my size and measurements. He managed to remember. "Oh, yes! Very beautiful girl, a knockout!"

"But, Cliff, you said—"

He grabbed my shoulders. "Listen, featherbrain, think I've got rocks in my head? Would I say anything that might make you jealous?"

"But I'm never jealous!"

"So *you* say! Now where shall we eat? Romanoff's? The Beachcomber? I'm loaded with dough."

Warm waves of happiness flowed over me. "Cliff?"

"Yeah, honey?"

"I've heard of a sundae called Moron's Delight. They take a great big glass and start with two bananas and six kinds of ice cream and—"

"That's passé. Have you ever had a Mount Everest?"

"Huh?"

"They start with a big platter and build up the peak with twenty-one flavors of ice cream, using four bananas, butterscotch syrup, and nuts to bind it. Then they cover it with chocolate syrup, sprinkle malted-milk powder and more nuts for rock, pour marshmallow syrup and whipped cream down from the top for snow, stick parsley around the lower slopes for trees, and set a little plastic skier on one of the snow banks. You get to keep him as a souvenir of the experience."

"Oh, my!" I said.

"Only one to a customer and I don't have to pay if you finish it."

I squared my shoulders. "Lead me to it!"

"I'm betting on you, Puddin'."

Cliff is such a wonderful man.

AFTERWORD

*Santa Claus, Arizona, is still there; just drive from
Kingman toward Boulder Dam on 93; you'll find it. But
Mrs. Santa Claus (Mrs. Douglas) is no longer there, and
her gourmet restaurant is now a fast-food joint. If she is
alive, she is at least in her eighties. I don't want to find
out. In her own field she was an artist equal to Rem-
brandt, Michelangelo, and Shakespeare. I prefer to think
of her in that perfect place where all perfect things go,
sitting in her kitchen surrounded by her gnomes, preparing her hearty ambrosia for Mark Twain and Homer and
Praxiteles and others of her equals.*

THE ANSWERS
(to Problems on Pages 334–338)

N.B.: All trips are Earth parking orbit to Earth parking orbit without stopping at the target planet (Mars
or Pluto). I assume that Hot Pilot Tom Corbett will
handle his gravity-well maneuvers at Mars and at
Pluto so as not to waste mass-energy—but that's his
problem. Now about that assumption of "flat space"
only slightly uphill: The Sun has a fantastically deep
gravity well; its "surface" gravity is 28 times as great
as ours and its escape speed is 55+ times as great—but
at the distance of Earth's orbit that grasp has atten-
uated to about one thousandth of a gee, and at Pluto at
31.6 A.U. it has dropped off to a gnat's whisker, one
millionth of gee.

(No wonder it takes 2½ centuries to swing around
the Sun. By the way, some astronomers seem positively gleeful that *today* Pluto is not the planet farthest
from the Sun. The facts: Pluto spends nine-tenths of its
time outside Neptune's orbit, and it averages being
875,000,000 miles farther out than Neptune—and at
maximum is nearly 2 billion miles beyond Neptune's
orbit (1.79×10^9 miles)—friends, that's more than the

distance from here to Uranus, nearly four times as far as from here to Jupiter. When Pluto is out there—1865 or 2114 A.D.—it takes light 6 hours and 50 minutes to reach it. Pluto—the Winnuh and still Champeen! Sour grapes is just as common among astronomers as it is in school yards.)

ROUNDTRIP BOOST COMPARISON OF ELAPSED TIME		
Earth-Mars-Earth		Earth-Pluto-Earth
	@1 gee	
4.59 days	vs.	**4.59** weeks
	@$^1/_{10}$ gee	
14.5 days	vs.	**14.5** weeks
	@$^1/_{100}$ gee	
45.9 days	vs.	**45.9** weeks
	@$^1/_{1000}$ gee	
145 days	vs.	**145** weeks

—and the rabbit is out of the hat. You will have noticed that the elapsed-time figures are exactly the same in both columns, but in days for Mars, weeks for Pluto—i.e., with constant-boost ships of any sort Pluto is *only 7 times* as far away for these conditions as is Mars *even though in miles Pluto is about 50 times as far away*.

If you placed Pluto at its aphelion (stay alive another century and a quarter—quite possible), at one gee the Pluto round trip would take 5.72 weeks, at $^1/_{10}$ gee 18.1 weeks, at $^1/_{100}$ gee 57.2 weeks—and at $^1/_{1000}$ gee 181 weeks, or 3 yrs & 25 wks.

I have added on the two illustrations at $^1/_{1000}$ of one gravity boost because today (late 1979 as I write) we do not as yet know how to build constant-boost ships for long trips at 1 gee, $^1/_{10}$ gee, or even $^1/_{100}$ gee; Newton's Third Law of Motion (from which may be derived all the laws of rocketry) has us (temporarily) stumped. But only temporarily. There is $E = mc^2$, too, and there are several possible ways of "living off the country" like a foraging army for necessary reaction mass. Be patient; this is all very new. Most of you who read this will live to see constant-boost ships of $1/10$ gee or better—and will be able to afford vacations in space—soon, soon! I probably won't live to see it, but *you* will. (No complaints, Sergeant—I was born in the horse & buggy age; I have lived to see men walk on the Moon and to see live pictures from the soil of Mars. I've had my share!)

But if you are willing to settle today for a constant-boost on the close order of magnitude of $1/1000$ gee, we can start the project later this afternoon, as there are several known ways of building constant-boost jobs with that tiny acceleration—even light-sail ships.

I prefer to talk about light-sail ships (or, rather, ships that sail in the "Solar wind") because those last illustrations I added ($1/1000$ gee) show that we have the entire Solar System available to us *right now*; it is not necessary to wait for the year 2000 and new breakthroughs.

Ten weeks to Mars . . . a round trip to Pluto at 31.6 A.U. in 2 years and 9 months . . . or a round trip to Pluto's aphelion, the most remote spot we know of in the Solar System (other than the winter home of the comets).

Ten weeks—it took the Pilgrims in the *Mayflower* nine weeks and three days to cross the Atlantic.

Two years and nine months—that was a normal commercial voyage for a China clipper sailing out of Boston in the last century . . . and the canny Yankee merchants got rich on it.

Three years and twenty-five weeks is excessive for the China trade in the 19th century . . . but no one will ever take that long trip to Pluto *because Pluto does not reach aphelion until 2113* and by *then* we'll have ships that can get out there (constant boost with turnover near midpoint) *in three weeks*.

Please note that England, Holland, Spain, and Portugal all created worldwide empires with ships that took as long to get anywhere and back as would a $1/1000$-gee spaceship. On the high seas or in space it is not distance that counts but *time*. The magnificent accomplishments of our astronauts up to now were made in free fall and are therefore analogous to floating down the Mississippi on a raft. But even the tiniest constant boost turns sailing the Solar System into a money-making commercial venture.

Now return to page 338.

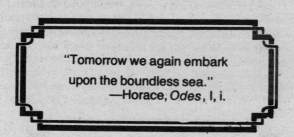

"Tomorrow we again embark
upon the boundless sea."
—Horace, *Odes*, I, i.

FOREWORD

One of the very few advantages of growing old is that one can reach an age at which he can do as he damn well pleases within the limits of his purse.

A younger writer, still striving, has to put up with a lot of nonsense—interviews, radio appearances, TV dates, public speaking here and there, writing he does not want to do—and all of this almost invariably unpaid.

In 1952 I was not a young writer (45) but I was certainly still striving. Here is an unpaid job I did for a librarians' bulletin because librarians can make you or break you. But today, thank Allah, if I don't want to do it, I simply say, "No." If I get an argument, I change that to: "Hell, No!"

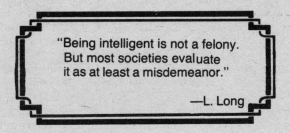

"Being intelligent is not a felony.
But most societies evaluate
it as at least a misdemeanor."

—L. Long

RAY GUNS AND ROCKET SHIPS

"When I make a word do a lot of work like that," said Humpty Dumpty, "I always pay it extra."

"Science Fiction" is a portmanteau term, and many and varied are the things that have been stuffed into it. Just as the term "historical fiction" includes in its broad scope *Quo Vadis*, nickel thrillers about the James Boys or Buffalo Bill, and *Forever Amber*, so does the tag "science fiction" apply both to Alley Oop and to Aldous Huxley's *After Many a Summer Dies the Swan*. It would be more nearly correctly descriptive to call the whole field "speculative fiction" and to limit the name "science fiction" to a sub-class—in which case some of the other sub-classes would be: undisguised fantasy (Thorne Smith, the Oz books), pseudoscientific fantasy (C. S. Lewis's fine novel *Out of the Silent Planet*, Buck Rogers, Bradbury's delightful Martian stories), sociological speculation (More's *Utopia*, Michael Arlen's *Man's Mortality*, H. G. Wells' *World Set Free*, Plato's *Republic*), adventure stories with exotic and non-existent locales (Flash Gordon, Burroughs' Martian stories, the *Odyssey*, *Tom Sawyer Abroad*). Many other classes will occur to you, since the term "speculative fiction" may be defined negatively as being fiction about things that have not happened.

One can see that the name "science fiction" is too Procrustean a bed, too tight a corset, to fit the whole field comfortably. Nevertheless, since language is how we talk, not how we might talk, it seems likely that the term "science fiction" will continue to be applied to the whole field; we are stuck with it, as the American aborigines are stuck with the preposterous name "Indian."

But what, under rational definition, is *science* fiction? There is an easy touchstone: science fiction is speculative fiction in which the author takes as his first postulate the real world as we know it, including all established facts and natural laws. The result can be extremely fantastic in content, but it is not fantasy; it is legitimate—and often very tightly reasoned—speculation about the possibilities of the real world. This category excludes rocket ships that make U-turns, serpent men of Neptune that lust after human maidens, and stories by authors who flunked their Boy Scout merit badge tests in descriptive astronomy.

But the category includes such mindstretchers as Olaf Stapledon's *Last and First Men*, William Sloane's *To Walk the Night*, Dr. Asimov's *The Stars, Like Dust*, even though these stories are stranger than most outright fantasies.

But how is one to distinguish between legitimate science fiction and ridiculous junk? Place of original publication is no guide; some of the best have appeared in half-cent-a-word pulp magazines, with bug-eyed monsters on their covers; some of the silliest have appeared in high-pay slicks or in the "prestige" quality group.

"The Pretzel Men of Pthark"—that one we can skip over; the contents are probably like the title. Almost as easy to spot is the Graustark school of space opera. This is the one in which the dashing Nordic hero comes to the aid of the rightful Martian princess and kicks out the villainous usurper through superscience and sheer grit. It is not being written very often these days, although it still achieves book publication occasionally, sometimes with old and respectable trade book houses. But it does not take a Ph.D. in physics to recognize it for what it is.

But do not be too quick to apply as a test to science fiction what are merely the conventions of better known fields of literature. I once heard a librarian say that she could not stand the unpronounceable names given by science-fiction writers to extraterrestrials. Have a heart, friend! These strings of consonants are honest attempts to give unearthly names to unearthly creatures. As Shaw pointed out, the customs of our tribe are not laws of nature. You would not expect a Martian to be named "Smith." (Say—how about a story about a Martian named "Smith?" Ought to make a good short. Hmmmm—)

But are there reliable criteria by which science fiction can be judged by one who is not well acquainted with the field? In my opinion, there are. Simply the criteria which apply to all fields of fiction, no more, no less.

First of all, an item of science fiction should be a story, i.e., its entertainment value should be as high as that which you expect from other types of stories. It should be entertaining to almost anyone, whether he habitually reads the stuff or not. Second, the degree of literacy should be as high as that expected in other fields. I will not labor this point, since we are simply applying an old rule to a new field, but there is no more excuse here than elsewhere for split infinitives, dangling participles, and similar untidiness, or for obscurity and doubletalk.

The same may be said for plotting, characterization, motivation, and the rest. If a science-fiction writer can't *write*, let him go back to being a fry cook or whatever he was doing before he gave up honest work.

I want to make separate mention of the author's evaluations. Granted that not all stories need be morally edifying, nevertheless I would demand of science-fiction writers as much exercise of moral sense as I would of other writers. I have in mind one immensely popular series which does not hold my own interest very well because the protagonist seems to be guided only by expediency. Neither the writer nor his puppet seems to be aware of good and evil. For my taste this is a defect in any story, nor is the defect mitigated by the wonderful and gaudy trappings of science fiction. In

my opinion, such abstractions as honor, loyalty, fortitude, self-sacrifice, bravery, honesty, and integrity
will be as important in the far reaches of the Galaxy as
they are in Iowa or Korea. I believe that you are entitled to apply your own evaluating standards to science
fiction quite as rigorously as you apply them in other
fiction.

The criteria outlined above take care of every aspect
of science fiction but one—the *science* part. But even
here no new criterion is needed. Suppose you were
called on to purchase or to refuse to purchase a novel
about a Mexican boy growing up on a Mexican cattle
ranch; suppose that you knew no Spanish, had never
been to Mexico and were unacquainted with its history and customs, and were unsure of the competence
of the author. What would you do?

I suspect that you would farm out the decision to
someone who was competent to judge the authenticity
of the work. It might be a high school Spanish teacher,
it might be a friend or neighbor who was well acquainted with our neighboring culture, it might be the
local Mexican consul. If the expert told you that the
background material of the book was nonsense, you
would not give the book shelf room.

The same procedure applies to science fiction. No
one can be expected to be expert in everything. If you
do not happen to know what makes a rocket go when
there is no air to push against, you need not necessarily read Willy Ley's *Rockets, Missiles, and Space
Travel*—although it is a fine book, a "must" for every
library, desirable for any home. You may instead consult anyone of your acquaintance who *does* know
about rocket ships—say an Air Force or Artillery officer, a physics teacher, or almost any fourteen-year-old
boy, especially boys who are active in high school science clubs. If the novel being judged concerns cybernetics, nuclear physics, genetics, chemistry, relativity,
it is necessary only to enlist the appropriate helper.

You would do the same, would you not, with a novel
based on the life of Simón Bolívar?

Of course, there is the alternate, equivalent method of testing the authenticity of any book by checking on the author. If the Simón Bolívar novel was written by a distinguished scholar of South American history, you need concern yourself only with the literary merit of the book. If a book about space travel is written by a world-famous astronomer (as in the case of the one who writes under the pen name of "Philip Latham"), you can put your mind at rest about the correctness of the science therein. In many cases science-fiction writers have more than adequate professional background in the sciences they use as background material and their publishers are careful to let you know this through catalog and dustjacket blurb. I happen to be personally aware of and can vouch for the scientific training of Sprague de Camp, George O. Smith, "John Taine," John W. Campbell, Jr., "Philip Latham," Will Jenkins, Jack Williamson, Isaac Asimov, Arthur C. Clarke, E. E. Smith, Philip Wylie, Olaf Stapledon, H. G. Wells, Damon Knight, Harry Stine, and "J. J. Coupling." This listing refers to qualifications in science only and is necessarily incomplete, nor do I mean to slight the many fine writers without formal scientific training who are well read in science and most careful in their research.

But some means of checking on a writer of alleged science fiction is desirable. Most writers of historical fiction appear to go to quite a lot of trouble to get the facts of their historical scenes correct, but some people seem to feel that all that is necessary to write science fiction is an unashamed imagination and a sprinkling of words like "ray gun," "rocket tube," "mutant," and "space warp." In some cases the offense is as blatant as it would be in the case of an author of alleged historical fiction who founded a book on the premise that Simón Bolívar was a Chinese monk! It follows that, in order to spot these literary fakers it is necessary to know that Bolívar was not a Chinese monk—know something of the sciences yourself or enlist competent advisers.

AFTERWORD

Writers talking about writing are about as bad as parents boasting about their children. I have not done much of it; the few times that I have been guilty, I did not instigate the project, and in almost all cases (all, I think) my arm was twisted.

I promise to avoid it in the future.

The item above, however, I consider worthy of publication (even though my arm was twisted) because there really are many librarians who earnestly wish to buy good science fiction . . . but don't know how to do it. In this short article I tried very hard to define clearly and simply how to avoid the perils of Sturgeon's Law in buying science fiction.

Part way through you will notice the origin of the last name of the STRANGER IN A STRANGE LAND.

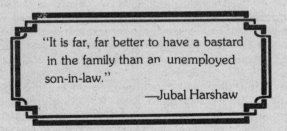

"It is far, far better to have a bastard in the family than an unemployed son-in-law."

—Jubal Harshaw

FOREWORD

*Superficially this looks like the same sort of article as
PANDORA'S BOX; it is not, it is fiction—written by request to celebrate the 50th anniversary of* Amazing
Stories. *In PANDORA'S BOX I was trying hard to
extrapolate rationally to most probable answers 50 years
in the future (and in November 1979 I gave myself a score
of 66%—anybody want to buy a used crystal ball with a
crack in it?).*

*But in this short-short I wrote as if I were alive in 2001
and writing a retrospective of the 20th century. Of course
everyone knows what happened in 2001; they found a big
black monolith on Luna—but in 1956 I didn't know that.
So I wrote as far out as I thought I could get away with
(to be entertaining) while trying to make the items sound
plausible and possible if not likely.*

Figures in parentheses refer to notes at the end.

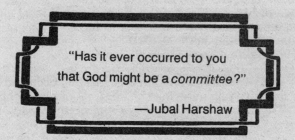

"Has it ever occurred to you
that God might be a *committee*?"

—Jubal Harshaw

THE THIRD MILLENNIUM OPENS

Now, at the beginning of the year 2001, it is time to see where we have been and guess at where we are going. A thousand years ago Otto III ruled the Holy Roman Empire, William the Conqueror was not yet born, and the Discovery of America was almost five hundred years in the future. The condition of mankind had not changed in most important respects since the dawn of history. Aside from language and local custom a peasant of 1000 B.C. would have been right at home in a village of 1001 A.D.

He would not be so today!

The major changes took place in the last two centuries, but the most significant change of all occurred in the last fifty years, during the lifetimes of many of us. In 1950 six out of ten persons could neither read nor write; today an illiterate person is a freak.(1)

More people have learned to read and write in the past fifty years than in all the thousands of years preceding 1950.

This one change is more worldshaking than the establishment this last year of the laboratory outpost on Pluto. We think of this century just closed as the one in which mankind conquered space; it would be more appropriate to think of it as the century in which the human race finally learned to read and write.

(Let's give the Devil his due; the contagious insanities of the past century—communism, xenophobia, aggressive nationalism, the explosions of the formerly colonial peoples—have done more to spread literacy than the efforts of all the do-gooders in history. The Three R's suddenly became indispensable weapons in mankind's bloodiest struggles—learn to read, or die. Out of bad has come good; a man who can read and write is nine-tenths free even in chains.)

But something else has happened as important as the ABC's. The big-muscled accomplishments of the past fifty years—like sea-farming, the fantastic multiplication of horsepower, and spaceships, pantographic factories, the Sahara Sea, reflexive automation, tapping the Sun—overshadow the most radical advance, i.e., the first fumbling steps in founding a science of the human mind.

Fifty years ago hypnotism was a parlor trick, clairvoyance was superstition, telepathy was almost unknown, and parapsychology was on a par with phrenology and not as respectable as the most popular nonsense called astrology.

Do we have a "science of the mind" today? Far from it. But we do have—

A Certainty of Survival after Death, proved with scientific rigor more complete than that which we apply to heat engines. It is hard to believe that it was only in 1952 that Morey Bernstein, using hypnotic regression, established the personal survival of Bridget Murphy—and thereby turned the western world to a research that Asia and Africa had always taken for granted.(2)

Telepathy and Clairvoyance for Military Purposes. The obvious effect was the changing of war from a "closed" game to an "open" game in the mathematical sense, with the consequence that assassination is now more important than mass weapons. It may well be that no fusion bomb or plague weapon will ever again be used—it would take a foolhardy dictator even to consider such when he knows that his thoughts are being monitored . . . and that assassination is so much harder to stop than a rocket bomb. He is bound to remember that Tchaka the Ruthless was killed by one of his own bodyguard.

But the less obvious effect has been to take "secrecy" wraps off scientific research. It is hard to recall that there was once a time when scientific facts could not be freely published, just as it is hard to believe that our grandfathers used to wear things called "swimming suits"—secrecy in science and swimming with clothes on are almost equally preposterous to the modern mind. Yet clothing never hampered a swimmer as much as "classification" hampered science. Most happily, controlled telepathy made secrecy first futile, then obsolete.(3)

But possibly the most important discovery we have made about ourselves is that *Man is a Wild Animal*. He cannot be tamed and remain Man; his genius is bound up in the very qualities which make him wild. With this self-knowledge, bleak, stern, and proud, goes the last hope of permanent peace on Earth; it makes world government unlikely and certainly unstable. Despite the fact that we are (as always) in a condition of marginal starvation, this fact makes all measures of population control futile—other than the ancient, grisly Four Horsemen, and even they are not effective; we finished World War III with a hundred million more people than when we started.

Not even the H-bomb could change our inner nature. We have learned most bloodily that the H-bomb does nothing that the stone axe did not do—and neither weapon could tame us. Man can be chained but he cannot be domesticated, and eventually he always breaks his chains.

Nor can we be "improved" by genetic breeding; it is not in our nature to accept it. Someday we may be conquered by superbeings from elsewhere, then bred according to their notions—and become dogs, rather than wolves. (I'm betting that we will put up a fight!)

But, left to our own resources, improvements in our breed must come the hard way, through survival . . . and we will still remain wild animals.(4)

But we have barely begun to study ourselves. Now that mankind has finally learned to read and write what can we expect him to accomplish?

We have no idea today of how self-awareness is linked to protoplasm. Now that we know that the ego survives the body we should make progress on this mystery.

Personal survival necessitates *Cosmic Purpose* as a "least hypothesis" for the universe. Scientists are tending to take teleology away from theologians and philosophers and give it a shaking. But concrete results this century seem unlikely. As of now, we still don't know why we are here or what we are supposed to do—but for the first time in history it is scientifically probable that the final answers are not null answers. It will be interesting indeed if one of the religious faiths turns out to be correct to nine decimals.

Since ESP talents seem to be independent of space-time it is theoretically possible that we may achieve a mental form of time travel. This is allowable under the mathematics being developed to describe mind phenomena. If so, we may eventually establish history, and even prophecy, as exact sciences.

On the physical side we can be certain that the speed-of-light barrier will be cracked this century. This makes it statistically likely that we will soon encounter races equal or superior to ourselves. This should be the most significant happening to mankind since the discovery of fire. It may degrade or destroy us, it may improve us; it cannot leave us unchanged.

On the mundane side we can expect a population of five billion by the middle of this century. Emigration to other planets will not affect the total here.

Scientific facts will continue to be discovered much faster than they can be classified and cross-referenced, but we cannot expect any accompanying increase in human intelligence. No doubt the few remaining illiterates will continue to be employed in the subscription departments of periodicals; the same bigmouths who now complain about rocket service to Luna (but who can't thread a needle themselves) will in 2050 be complaining about service to the stars (and they still won't be able to thread a needle).

Unquestionably the Twentieth Century will be referred to as the "Good Old Days," we will continue to view with alarm the antics of the younger generation, and we probably will still be after a cure for the common cold.

Notes:1980

1. He's still a freak but he's all too common. There is a special circle in Hell for the "Educators" who decided that the Three R's really weren't all that important. Concerning our public schools today: Never have so many been paid so much for so little. I thank whatever gods there be that I went to school so many years ago that I had no choice but to be tightly disciplined in classes in which the teachers did not hesitate to fail and to punish.

My first-grade class had 63 kids in it, one teacher, no assistant. Before the end of the second semester all 63 could read.

2. Many people seem to feel that the "Bridey Murphy" case has been invalidated. Maybe so, maybe not—the investigative reporter who went to Ireland had no special qualifications and the "disproof" came from TIME magazine. TIME magazine probably publishes many facts . . . but since its founding in the early 1920's I have been on the spot eight or nine times when something that wound up as a news story in TIME happened. Not once—not once—did the TIME magazine story match what I saw and heard.

I have the "Bridey Murphy" recording and Bernstein's book about it. I am not an expert witness . . . but I found the recording highly interesting. To me it sounded like what it purported to be: regression under hypnosis to memory of a former existence. Some years later I learned from an ethical hypnotherapist (i.e., he accepted patients only by referrals from M.D.'s, his own doctorate being in psychology) that regression to what seemed to be former lives was a commonplace among patients of hypnotherapists— they discussed it among themselves but never published because they were bound by much the same rule as physicians and priests taking confession.

I have no data to offer of my own. I decided many years back that I was too busy with this life to fret about what happens afterwards. Long before 2001 I will know . . . or I will know nothing whatever because my universe has ceased to exist.

3. Anyone today who simply brushes off ESP phenomena as being ridiculous is either pigheaded or ignorant. But I do not expect controlled telepathy by 2001; that is sheer fiction, intended to permit me to get in that bit about Tchaka, et al.

4. I lifted this "Man is a wild animal" thesis bodily from Charles Galton Darwin (grandson of the author of THE ORIGIN OF SPECIES) in his book THE NEXT MILLION YEARS, Doubleday, 1953. I am simply giving credit; I shan't elaborate here. But THE NEXT MILLION YEARS is a follow-on to THE ORIGIN OF THE SPECIES and is, in my opinion, one of most important works of this century. It has not been a popular book—but I seem to recall that his grandfather's seminal work wasn't too popular, either.

FOREWORD

This polemic was first published on Saturday 12 April 1958. Thereafter it was printed many other places and reprints of it were widely circulated inside and outside the science fiction community, inside and outside this country.

It brought down on me the strongest and most emotional adverse criticism I have ever experienced—not to my surprise.

After more than twenty years my "misdeed" seems to have been largely forgotten, or perhaps forgiven. But I do not ask to be forgiven and I do not want it to be forgotten. So I now republish it in permanent form. I have not consulted my editor or my publisher; each is free to denounce my opinions here expressed—but is not free to refuse this item while accepting the rest of this book.

A few specific details below are outdated by new technology—e.g., earthquakes can now be distinguished with certainty (we hope) from nuclear explosions, while other aspects of detection and inspection grow more complex. Technical details change; basic principles do not.

"Supreme excellence in war is to subdue the enemy without fighting."

—Sun Tzu, ca. 350 B.C.

The Soviet Union is highly skilled at this—and so are the Chinese leaders. During the last twenty-odd years we have been outmaneuvered endlessly. Today it's the Backfire bomber (a B-1 with a Russian accent); tomorrow it is an international (U.N.) treaty to socialize all aspects of space and thereby kill such enterprise as the L-5 Society, Sabre, Otrag (already killed), Robert Truax's Do-It-Yourself projects. The treaty will permit a KGB agent ("A rose by any other name—") to inspect in detail anything of ours, private or public, on the ground or in the sky, if it is **in any way** connected with space—or the KGB man claims to suspect that it might be.

(But if you think that gives us a free ticket into every

building, every room, at the Byakonur space complex,
you don't know how the USSR does business.)

The President has already announced that he will sign
it. 10 to 1 he will, 7 to 2 the Senate will pass it—and 100
to 1 we will regret it.

This declaration is more timely than ever; I am proud
to reprint it—and deeply sorry that it was ever needed.

Any rational person may well disagree with me on details of this broadside. But on the moral principles expressed here, a free man says: "Give me liberty, or give
me death!" No quibbling, no stopping to "think it over."
He means it.

Fools and poltroons do not.

WHO ARE THE HEIRS OF PATRICK HENRY? STAND UP AND BE COUNTED!

"Is life so dear, or peace so sweet, as to be purchased at the price of chains and slavery? Forbid it, Almighty God! I know not what course others may take, but as for me, give me liberty, or give me death!!"
—Patrick Henry

Last Saturday in this city appeared a full-page ad intended to scare us into demanding that the President stop our testing of nuclear weapons. This manifesto was a curious mixture of truth, half-truth, distortion, exaggeration, untruth, and Communist-line goals concealed in idealistic-sounding nonsense.

The instigators were seventy-odd local people and sixty-odd national names styling themselves "The National Committee for a Sane Nuclear Policy." It may well be that none of the persons whose names are used as the "National" committee are Communists and we have no reason to suppose that any of the local people are Communists—possibly all of them are loyal and merely misguided. But this manifesto is the rankest sort of Communist propaganda.

A tree is known by its fruit. The purpose of their manifesto is to entice or frighten you into signing a letter to President Eisenhower, one which demands that he take three actions. The first demand is the old, old Communist-line gimmick that nuclear weapons and their vehicles should be "considered apart" in disarmament talks. It has had a slight restyling for the post-Sputnik era and now reads: "That nuclear test explosions, missiles, and outer-space satellites be considered apart from other disarmament problems."

This proposal sounds reasonable but is booby-trapped with outright surrender of the free world to the Communist dictators. Mr. Truman knew it, Mr. Eisenhower knows it; both have refused it repeatedly. The gimmick is this: if nuclear weapons and their vehicles are outlawed while conventional weapons (tanks and planes and bayonets and rifles) are not, then—but you figure it out. 170,000,000 of us against 900,000,000 of them. Who wins?

Even if you count our allies (on the assumption that every last one of them will stick by us no matter how bone-headed our behavior), the ratio is still two-to-one against us when it comes to slugging it out with infantry divisions, Yalu River style.

Oh yes! Khrushchev would like very much to have nuclear weapons "considered apart" from infantry divisions. And he is delighted when soft-headed Americans agree with him.

"The Mice Voted to Bell the Cat." —Aesop

Their second proposal has been part of the Communist line for twelve long years. It reads: "That all nuclear test explosions be stopped immediately and that the U.N. then proceed with the mechanics necessary for monitoring this cessation." This is the straight Communist gospel direct from the Kremlin. This was and is today their phony counter-proposal to the Baruch Proposals of 1946—banning first, policing the ban if, when, and maybe . . . and subject to the veto of the U.S.S.R. It would leave us at the "mercy" of the butchers of Budapest, our lives staked on the "honor" of men to whom honesty is a bourgeois weakness, our freedom resting on the promises of a gangster government that has broken every promise it ever made.

The Committee's manifesto claims: "—the problems in monitoring such tests are relatively uncomplicated." This is either an outright lie or ignorant wishful thinking; the problems are so complicated that nothing short of on-the-spot inspection will work—an underground test cannot be told from an earthquake shock by any known method of monitoring.

Before you trust your lives and freedom to the promises of the Kremlin, remember Budapest—

—remember Poland in 1945
—remember Prague
—remember Estonia, Latvia, Lithuania
—remember Korea
—remember brave little Finland .
—and keep your powder dry!

The third proposal is largely pious window-dressing but it has the same sort of booby-trap buried in it. It reads: "That missiles and outer-space satellites be brought under United Nations-monitored control, and that there be a pooling of world science for space exploration under the United Nations." The harmless part could be done if the U.S.S.R. were willing; the booby-trap is the word "missiles."

We Americans live in a goldfish bowl; we could not conceal rocket tests even if we tried. But in the vast spaces of Russia, Siberia, and China missiles of every sort—even the long-range ICBMs—can be tested in secret, manufactured and stockpiled and installed ready to go, despite all "monitoring." Anything less than on-the-spot inspection of the entire vast spaces of the Communist axis would leave us at the mercy of the bland promises of the Butchers of Budapest.

The last paragraph of this letter that they want you to send to the President is not a proposal; it is simply another attempt to strike terror into the hearts of free men by reminding us of the horrors of nuclear war.

" 'Will you walk into my parlor?' said the Spider to the Fly."

It is no accident that this manifesto follows the Communist line, no coincidence that it "happens" to appear all over the United States the very week that Khrushchev has announced smugly that the U.S.S.R. has ended their tests—and demands that we give up our coming, long-scheduled, and publicly announced tests of a weapon with minimum fall-out.

This follows the pattern of a much-used and highly-refined Communist tactic: plan ahead to soften up the free world on some major point, package the propaganda to appeal to Americans with warm hearts and soft heads, time the release carefully, then let the suckers carry the ball while the known Communists stay under cover.

They used this method to gut our army after the Japanese surrender with the slogan of "Bring the Boys Home." They used it to make us feel guilty about the A-bomb—while their spies were stealing it. They dreamed up the pious theme of "Don't Play Politics with Hunger"—then used our charity to play their politics. They used it to put over the infamous "Oxford Oath" and the phony "Peace Strikes" of the thirties. They have used this tactic many times to soften up the free world and will use it whenever they can find dupes.

They are using it now. Today both sides, Freedom and Red Tyranny, are armed with nuclear weapons . . . and the Communists are again using our own people to try to shame or scare us into throwing our weapons away.

These proposals are not a road to world peace, they are abject surrender to tyranny. If we fall for them, then in weeks or months or a few years at most, Old Glory will be hauled down for the last time and the whole planet will be ruled by the Butchers of Budapest.

For more than a hundred years, ever since the original Communist Manifesto, it has been the unswerving aim of the Communist Party to take over all of this planet. The only thing blocking their conquest is the fact that the tragically-shrunken free world still possesses nuclear weapons. They can destroy us . . . but they know that we can destroy them.

So they want us to throw away the equalizer.

If we do, we can expect the same "mercy" that Budapest received. They will say to us: "Surrender—or be destroyed!"

"God grants liberty only to those who love it and are always ready to guard and defend it."

—Daniel Webster

We the undersigned are not a committee but simply two free citizens of these United States. We love life and we want peace . . . but not "peace at any price"— not the price of liberty!

Poltroons and pacifists will think otherwise.

Those who signed that manifesto have made their choice; consciously or unconsciously they prefer enslavement to death. Such is their right and we do not argue with them—we speak to you who are still free in your souls.

In a free country, political action can start anywhere. We read that insane manifesto of the so-called "Committee for a 'Sane' Nuclear Policy" and we despised it. So we are answering it ourselves—by our own free choice and spending only our own money.

We say to the commissars: "You will never enslave us. The worst you can do is kill us. But we are resolved to die free!"

"They that can give up essential liberty to obtain a little temporary safety deserve neither liberty nor safety."

—Benjamin Franklin

No scare talk of leukemia, mutation, or atomic holocaust will sway us. Is "fall-out" dangerous? Of course it is! The risk to life and posterity has been willfully distorted by these Communist-line propagandists— but if it were a hundred times as great we still would choose it to the dead certainty of Communist enslavement. If atomic war comes, will it kill off the entire human race? Possibly—almost certainly so if the Masters of the Kremlin choose to use cobalt bombs on us. Their command of science in these matters seems equal to ours, they appear to be some years ahead of us in the art of rocketry; they almost certainly have the power to destroy the human race.

If it comes to atomic war, the best we can hope for is tens of millions of American dead—perhaps more than half our population wiped out in the first few minutes.

Colorado Springs is at least a secondary target; all of us here may be killed.

These are the risks. The alternative is surrender. We accept the risks.

"The liberties of our country, the freedom of our civil Constitution, are worth defending at all hazards."

—Samuel Adams

We have no easy solution to offer. The risks cannot be avoided other than by surrender; they can be reduced only by making the free world so strong that the evil pragmatists of Communism cannot afford to murder us. The price to us will be year after weary year of higher taxes, harder work, grim devotion . . . and perhaps, despite all this—death. But we shall die free!

To this we pledge our lives, our fortunes, and our sacred honor.

We the undersigned believe that almost all Americans agree with us. Whoever you are, wherever you are, you sons of Patrick Henry—let us know your name! Sign the letter herewith and mail it to us—we will see that it gets to Congressman Chenoweth, to both our Senators, and to the President.

	Robert and Virginia Heinlein
1958 address—	1776 Mesa Avenue
	Colorado Springs, Colorado
1980 address—	Spectrum Literary Agency
	225 West 34th Street
	New York, New York 10122

"WHAT CAN I DO?"

This much has been done by two people acting alone. Let's call ourselves "The Patrick Henry League" and prove to our government that the Spirit of '76 is still alive. We are two, you and your spouse make four, your neighbor and his wife make six—we can snowball this until it sweeps the country.

We can advertise in other counties, in other states.

If you who are reading this are not in Colorado Springs, stand up, speak up, and start your own chapter of "The Patrick Henry League" now. You are a free citizen, you need no permission, nor any charter from us. Run an ad—quote or copy this one if you like. Dig down in the sock to pay for it, or pass the hat, or both—but sound the call in your own home town, mail copies of your ad out of town, and get some more letters started toward Washington.

And let us hear from you!

Let us all stand up and shout aloud again and forever:

"Give Me Liberty or Give Me Death!"

President Eisenhower,
The White House
Washington, D.C.

Dear Mr. President:

We know that you are being pressured to stop our nuclear weapons tests, turn our missile and space program over to the U.N., and in other ways to weaken our defenses.

We urge you to stand steadfast.

We want America made supremely strong and we are resolved to accept all burdens necessary to that end. We ask for total effort—nuclear testing, research, and development, highest priorities for rocketry, sterner education, anything that is needed. We are ready to pay higher taxes, forego luxuries, work harder.

To this we pledge our lives, our fortunes, and our sacred honor.

Respectfully yours,

. . . .
(names)

. . . .
(address)

AFTERWORD

When the soi-disant "SANE" committee published its page ad in Colorado Springs (and many other cities) on 5 April 1958, I was working on THE HERETIC (later to be published as STRANGER IN A STRANGE LAND). I stopped at once and for several weeks Mrs. Heinlein and I did nothing but work on this "Patrick Henry" drive. We published our ad in three newspapers, encouraged its publication elsewhere, mailed thousands of reprints, spoke before countless meetings, collected and mailed to the White House thousands of copies of the letter above— always by registered mail—no acknowledgement of any sort was ever received, not even in response to "Return Receipt Requested."

Then the rug was jerked out from under us; by executive order Mr. Eisenhower canceled all testing without requiring mutual inspection. (The outcome of that is now history; when it suited him, Khrushchev resumed testing with no warning and with the dirtiest bombs ever set off in the atmosphere.)

I was stunned by the President's action. I should not have been as I knew that he was a political general long before he entered politics—stupid, all front, and dependent on his staff. But that gets me the stupid hat, too; I had learned years earlier that many politicians (not all!) will do anything to get elected . . . and Adlai Stevenson had him panting.

Presently I resumed writing—not STRANGER but STARSHIP TROOPERS.

The "Patrick Henry" ad shocked 'em; STARSHIP TROOPERS outraged 'em. I still can't see how that book got a Hugo. It continues to get lots of nasty "fan" mail and not much favorable fan mail . . . but it sells and sells and sells and sells, in eleven languages. It doesn't slow down—four new contracts just this year. And yet I almost never hear of it save when someone wants to chew me out over it. I don't understand it.

The criticisms are usually based on a failure to under-

396

stand simple indicative English sentences, couched in simple words—especially when the critics are professors of English, as they often are. (A shining counter example, a professor who can read and understand English, is one at Colorado College—a professor of history.*)*

We have also some professors of English who write science fiction but I do not know of one who formally reviewed or criticized STARSHIP TROOPERS. However, I have gathered a strong impression over the years that professors of English who write and sell science fiction average being much more grammatical and much more literate than their colleagues who do not (cannot?) write saleable fiction.

Their failures to understand English are usually these:

1. "Veteran" does not mean in English dictionaries or in this novel solely a person who has served in military forces. I concede that in commonest usage today it means a war veteran . . . but no one hesitates to speak of a veteran fireman or veteran school teacher. In STARSHIP TROOPERS it is stated flatly and more than once that nineteen out of twenty veterans are not military veterans. Instead, 95% of voters are what we call today "former members of federal civil service."

Addendum: The volunteer is not given a choice. He/she can't win a franchise by volunteering for what we call civil service. He volunteers . . . then for two years plus-or-minus he goes where he is sent and does what he is told to do. If he is young, male, and healthy, he may wind up as cannon fodder. But there are long chances against it.

2. He/she can resign at any time other than during combat—i.e., 100% of the time for 19 out of 20; 99%+ of the time for those in the military branches of federal service.

3. There is no conscription. (I am opposed to conscription for any reason at any time, war or peace, and have said so repeatedly in fiction, in nonfiction, from platforms, and in angry sessions in think tanks. I was sworn in first in 1923, and have not been off the hook since that time. My principal pride in my family is that I know of not one in over two centuries who was drafted; they all volunteered. But the draft is involuntary servitude, immoral, and unconstitutional no matter what the Supreme Court says.)

4. Criticism: "The government in STARSHIP TROOPERS is militaristic." "Militaristic" is the adjective for the noun "militarism," a word of several definitions but not one of them can be correctly applied to the government described in this novel. No military or civil servant can vote or hold office until after he is discharged and is again a civilian. The military tend to be despised by most civilians and this is made explicit. A career military man is most unlikely ever to vote or hold office; he is more likely to be dead—and if he does live through it, he'll vote for the first time at 40 or older.

"That book glorifies the military!" Now we are getting somewhere. It does indeed. Specifically the P.B.I., the Poor Bloody Infantry, the mudfoot who places his frail body between his loved home and the war's desolation— but is rarely appreciated. "It's Tommy this and Tommy that and chuck him out, the brute!—but it's 'thin red line of heroes when the guns begin to shoot.' "

My own service usually doesn't have too bad a time of it. Save for very special situations such as the rivers in Nam, a Navy man can get killed but he is unlikely to be wounded . . . and if he is killed, it is with hot food in his belly, clean clothes on his body, a recent hot bath, and sack time in a comfortable bunk not more than 24 hours earlier. The Air Force leads a comparable life. But think of Korea, of Guadalcanal, of Belleau Wood, of Viet Nam. The H-bomb did not abolish the infantryman; it made him essential . . . and he has the toughest job of all and should be honored.

Glorify the military? Would I have picked it for my profession and stayed on the rolls the past 56 years were I not proud of it?

I think I know what offends most of my critics the most about STARSHIP TROOPERS: It is the dismaying idea that a voice in governing the state should be earned instead of being handed to anyone who is 18 years old and has a body temperature near 37°C.

But there ain't no such thing as a free lunch.

Democracies usually collapse not too long after the plebs discover that they can vote themselves bread and circuses . . . for a while. Either read history or watch the daily papers; it is now happening here. Let's stipulate for discussion that some stabilizing qualification is needed (in addition to the body being warm) for a voter to vote responsibly with proper consideration for the future of his children and grandchildren—and yours. The Founding Fathers never intended to extend the franchise to everyone; their debates and the early laws show it. A man had to be a stable figure in the community through owning land or employing others or engaged in a journeyman trade or something.

But few pay any attention to the Founding Fathers today—those ignorant, uneducated men—they didn't even have television (have you looked at Monticello lately?)—so let's try some other "poll taxes" to insure a responsible electorate:

a) Mark Twain's "The Curious Republic of Gondor"—if you have not read it, do so.

b) A state where anyone can buy for cash (or lay-away installment plan) one or more franchises, and this is the government's sole source of income other than services sold competitively and non-monopolistically. This would produce a new type of government with several rabbits tucked away in the hat. Rich people would take over the government? Would they, now? Is a wealthy man going to impoverish himself for the privilege of casting a couple of hundred votes? Buying an election today, under the warm-body (and tombstone) system is much cheaper than buying a controlling number of franchises would be. The arithmetic on this one becomes unsolv-

able . . . but I suspect that paying a stiff price (call it 20,000 Swiss francs) for a franchise would be even less popular than serving two years.

c) A state that required a bare minimum of intelligence and education—e.g., step into the polling booth and find that the computer has generated a new quadratic equation just for you. Solve it, the computer unlocks the voting machine, you vote. But get a wrong answer and the voting machine fails to unlock, a loud bell sounds, a red light goes on over that booth—and you slink out, face red, you having just proved yourself too stupid and/or ignorant to take part in the decisions of the grownups. Better luck next election! No lower age limit in this system—smart 12-yr-old girls vote every election while some of their mothers—and fathers—decline to be humiliated twice.

There are endless variations on this one. Here are two: Improving the Breed—No red light, no bell . . . but the booth opens automatically—empty. Revenue—You don't risk your life, just some gelt. It costs you a ¼ oz troy of gold in local currency to enter the booth. Solve your quadratic and vote, and you get your money back. Flunk—and the state keeps it. With this one I guarantee that no one would vote who was not interested and would be most unlikely to vote if unsure of his ability to get that hundred bucks back.

I concede that I set the standards on both I.Q. and schooling too low in calling only for the solution of a quadratic since (if the programming limits the machine to integer roots) a person who deals with figures at all can solve that one with both hands behind him (her) and her-his eyes closed. But I just recently discovered that a person can graduate from high school in Santa Cruz with a straight-A record, be about to enter the University of California on a scholarship . . . but be totally unable to do simple arithmetic. Let's not make things too difficult at the transition.

d) I don't insist on any particular method of achieving a responsible electorate; I just think that we need to *tighten up the present warm-body criterion before it destroys us. How about this? For almost a century and a half women were not allowed to vote. For the past sixty years they have voted . . . but we have not seen the enormous improvement in government that the suffragettes promised us.*

Perhaps we did not go far enough. Perhaps men are still corrupting government . . . so let's try the next century and a half with males disenfranchised. (Fair is fair. My mother was past forty before she was permitted to vote.) But let's not stop there; at present men outnumber women in elective offices, on the bench, and in the legal profession by a proportion that is scandalous.

Make males ineligible to hold elective office, or to serve in the judiciary, elective or appointed, and also reserve the profession of law for women.

Impossible? That was exactly the situation the year I was born, but male instead of female, even in the few states that had female suffrage before the XIXth Amendment, with so few exceptions as to be unnoticed. As for rooting male lawyers out of their cozy niches, this would give us a pool of unskilled manual laborers—and laborers are very hard to hire these days; I've been trying to hire one at any wages he wants for the past three months, with no success.

The really good ones could stay on as law clerks to our present female lawyers, who will be overworked for a while. But not for long. Can you imagine female judges (with no male judges to reverse them) permitting attorneys to take six weeks to pick a jury? Or allowing a trial to ramble along for months?

Women are more practical than men. Biology forces it on them.

Speaking of that, let's go whole hog. Until a female bears a child her socio-economic function is male no matter how orthodox her sexual preference. But a woman who is mother to a child knows she has a stake in the future. So let's limit the franchise and eligibility for office and the practice of law to mothers.

The phasing over should be made gentle. Let males serve out their terms but not succeed themselves. Male lawyers might be given as long as four years to retire or find other jobs while not admitting any more males into law schools. I don't have a candidate for President but the events of the last fifty years prove that anybody can sit in the Oval Office; it's just that some are more impressive in appearance than others.

Brethren and Sistern, have you ever stopped to think that there has not been one rational decision out of the Oval Office for fifty years?

An all-female government could not possibly be worse than what we have been enduring. Let's try it!

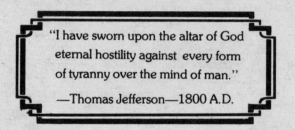

"I have sworn upon the altar of God eternal hostility against every form of tyranny over the mind of man."

—Thomas Jefferson—1800 A.D.

FOREWORD

After I got STARSHIP TROOPERS out of the way, I indulged in some stone masonry (my favorite recreation and reconditioning after writing when I was younger), installed a fountain in our lower irrigation pool and landscaped it—then got back to work on THE HERETIC aka STRANGER IN A STRANGE LAND, and finally finished it more than ten years after I had plotted it. I had been in no hurry to finish it, as that story could not be published commercially until the public mores changed. I could see them changing and it turned out that I had timed it right.

Many people have said that it is clear that STRANGER was written in two parts; the division point showed. But no two people have ever picked the same putative division point . . . and this is the first time I have ever admitted that it was not written in two chunks but in four.

No one ever will spot the actual starts and stops because STRANGER is one of the very few stories in which I plotted every detail before writing it, and then stuck precisely to that plot. What readers pick as places where I "must have" broken the writing are in fact division points planned for dramatic reasons.

Then I had to cut the damned thing; sticking to that complex and ponderous plot resulted in a MS more than twice as long as it should have been, either commercially or dramatically. Cutting it took more working time than writing it.

In the meantime my wife signed up for University of Colorado Extension classes in Russian. She has always believed that anything worth doing at all is worth overdoing; for two solid years she lived and breathed Russian. She never missed a class, was always thoroughly prepared, hired a private conversation tutor to supplement her classroom work, bought every brand of Russian language instruction records available then, kept them stacked on the record changer and played them all day *long while she did other things—our home had a speaker in every room, and a large speaker for the garden.*

(This did not bother my work; since I knew no Russian then, it was random noise to me.)

Two years of this and she could read Russian, write Russian, speak Russian, understand Russian—and think in Russian.

Then we went to the USSR.

Other countries, too, of course—Poland and Czechoslovakia won my undying sympathy, as well as the captive Baltic states. I should include the Turkestan countries, too, but they don't seem quite as oppressed— much farther from Moskva and off the beaten track. All in all we traveled about 10,000 miles inside USSR and saw about twenty cities. Ginny's hard work paid off; we saw and heard far, far more than we could have learned had we been dependent on a politically-cleared guide— we often ducked out without our guide. I picked up some pidgin Russian but never learned to speak it—I could give directions, ask directions, order a meal, pay a bill— and swear in Russian (essential!).

The article below I wrote in Hotel Torni, Helsinki, immediately after "escaping" (that's how it felt) from the Soviet Union. The lighter article following "PRAVDA" I wrote a couple of weeks later in Stockholm. By then my nerves had relaxed in the free air of Scandinavia and I could see humor in things that had not seemed at all funny at the time.

"PRAVDA" Means "TRUTH"

"Pravda" means "truth."

That's what it says, right here in my English-Russian dictionary: Pravda—Truth. Surely one may depend on the dictionary.

In Al Smith's bleak, skeptical words: "Let's take a look at the record."

On May Day, 1960, a United States U-2 reconnaissance plane made some type of unplanned landing in the Soviet Union. This much is both "truth" and "pravda." Beyond this bare fact, "truth" and "pravda" diverge widely.

TRUTH: On May 1 this U-2 plane grounded near Sverdlovsk in the heartland of the Soviet Union about 1,500 miles from the border it crossed. The plane was wrecked but the pilot was not killed. Much of the equipment in the plane, such as radio gear, was undamaged. The pilot's survival and the condition of the wreckage, plus the undamaged equipment, suggest a forced landing in rough country, such as would result from engine failure.

The U-2 is extremely fast and it cruises at very high altitude, 60–70,000 feet. The kinetic energy stored in a moving object varies as the square of its velocity ($E = \frac{1}{2}MV^2$). A staggering amount of kinetic energy is stored in a U-2. If such a plane is hit by anti-aircraft rocket fire what happens in the next split second would make a head-on collision between two hot-rodders seem like a mother's loving pat. The anti-aircraft damage merely triggers the disaster; the major violence comes from the plane's great speed—it explodes! Suddenly the sky is filled with junk.

The chance of the pilot's surviving is small. He may escape if the plane's ejection capsule is not damaged when the plane is hit. But there is only the tiniest chance that radios and other relatively fragile pieces of equipment would reach the ground undamaged. Nevertheless, such items were "recovered" from the "shot-down" U-2. A crate of eggs, uncracked, would be equally convincing.

We may never know the exact truth of what happened to that U-2. Only Soviet officials talked to unlucky pilot Powers before his trial.

But the nervous nellies among us should stop beating their breasts over the shame of it all. Photo reconnaissance is not the same thing as a bombing run. An overflight by an unarmed plane is not in the same league with what Khrushchev did to Budapest. What we are dealing with here is the security of the United States and—very possibly—the survival, and certainly the freedom, of the entire human race.

Espionage is not illegal under International Law. Neither is it immoral. The penalty for getting caught at it is very high. It usually means the spy's neck. It is not illegal under U.S. laws for us to attempt to spy on the U.S.S.R., nor is it illegal under Soviet law for them to attempt to spy on us. Nor, in either case, is it an act of war. Throughout history every country has striven to learn the military secrets of any potential enemy, and to protect its own. Spying is wise and necessary insurance against utter military disaster.

That we have been conducting photo reconnaissance over the Soviet Union so successfully and for four vital years is the most encouraging news in the past decade. Among other things it means we have accurate maps by which to strike back. The Soviet Union does not have to send spy planes over us to obtain sim-

ilar information. Excellent large-scale maps with our
military installations and industrial complexes clearly
marked may be obtained free from Standard Oil or
Conoco. Still better maps may be ordered by the Soviet Embassy from our Coast and Geodetic Survey at
very low prices. Soviet agents move freely among us
and many of them enjoy the immunity and complete
freedom of travel afforded by U.N. passports. If a Red
spy wants aerial color photographs at low altitude of
our Air Defense installation just south of Kansas
City—in America's heartland—until recently he could
hire a pilot and a plane at the Kansas City airport for
about $25 an hour and snap pictures to his heart's con-
tent without taking any of the risks of being hanged or
shot down that Francis Powers took for us. If Mr. Eisenhower had failed to obtain by any possible means
the military intelligence that the U.S.S.R. gets so easily and cheaply about us, he would have been derelict
in his duty.

So, if you hear anyone whining about how "shameful" the U-2 flights were, take his lollipop away and
spank him with it.

PRAVDA: It took the fat boy with the bad manners
five days to decide just what sort of "pravda" to feed
his people. The situation must have been acutely embarrassing for him, much more so than it was to us,
because for four years he had been totally unable to
stop the flights, despite his boasts and missile bran-
dishing, despite the fact that every flight was certainly
observed in Soviet radar screens.

K. could keep quiet, in which case there was little
chance that the Free World news services would ever
learn about it, and no chance that the Russian people
would ever find out. Our Central Intelligence Agency
would know that a reconnaissance plane was missing,
but it would not have advertised a top secret.

K. could refurbish the incident, give it a new paint
job and peddle it as propaganda.

Or K. could tell the simple truth. This alternative is

mentioned simply to keep the record technically complete, as the simple truth is a tactic not contemplated under Marxism-Leninism doctrines. Here we have the essential distinction between truth and pravda.

Truth, to the West, consists of all the facts without distortion.

Pravda is that which serves the World Communist Revolution. Pravda can be a mixture of fact and falsehood, or a flat-footed, brassbound, outright lie. In rare cases and by sheer coincidence, pravda may happen to match the facts. I do not actually know of such a case but it seems statistically likely that such matching must have taken place a few times in the past 43 years.

This comparison is not mere cynicism. I appeal to the authority of V. I. Lenin himself, in his tactics of revolution. By the doctrines of dialectical materialism, simple truth as we know it is abolished as a concept. It can have no existence of its own separate from the needs and purposes of the Communist Party and the World Revolution. Our ingrained habit of believing that the other fellow must be telling the truth at least most of the time is perhaps our greatest weakness in dealing with the Kremlin.

Apparently K. and his cohorts encountered much trouble in deciding just what the pravda should be about the U-2. They spent almost a week making up their minds. I was in Moscow at the time and there was no indication of any sort that anything unusual had happened on May 1. Russians continued to treat us American visitors with their customary almost saccharine politeness and the daily paper (I hesitate to call it a newspaper) known as *Pravda* hinted not of U-2's. This situation continued for several days thereafter. I was not dependent on an Intourist guide-interpreter in reaching this impression as my wife reads, writes, understands and fluently speaks Russian. She's not of Russian descent. She learned it at a University of Colorado Extension night school, plus a private tutor and a lot of hard work.

After May Day, we went on out to Alma Ata in Kazakhstan, north of India and a very short distance from the Red China border, about 2,000 miles beyond Moscow. Be-Kind-To-Americans Week continued. Three Americans, the only travelers in that remote part of Asia, received the undivided attention of the Alma Ata Director of Intourist, two school teachers (pulled off their teaching jobs to act as guides), two chauffeurs, and most of the attention of the hotel staff. We had but to express a wish and it was granted.

As of Thursday morning, May 5, the pravda was still that nothing had happened.

Thursday afternoon the climate abruptly changed. K's cohorts had at last decided on a pravda; to wit: an American military plane had attempted to cross the border of the Soviet Union. Soviet rocket fire had shot it down from an altitude of 60,000 feet as soon as it had crossed the border. The Soviet peoples were very much distressed that America would even attempt such an act of bald aggression. The Soviet peoples wanted peace. Such aggression would not be tolerated. Any other such planes would not only be shot down but the bases from which the attacks were made would be destroyed. Such was K's new pravda at the end of a five-hour speech.

The only connection between pravda and fact lay in the existence of an American plane down on Soviet soil. The locale of the incident shifted 1,500 miles. The plane is "shot down" at an extremely high altitude (if true then those exhibits in Gorky Park were as phony as K's promises of safety to Nagy and Pal Maleter). No mention at all is made of four long years of humiliating defeat. Pravda suppresses the truth and turns the incident into a triumph of Soviet arms. The Soviet newspapers and radio stations, all state-owned, spout the same line. All during this period the Voice of America was jammed. K. made certain his serfs heard nothing but the pravda.

We learned it by being ordered—not requested—to report to the Alma Ata office of the Director of Intourist. There we were given a long, very stern, but fatherly, lecture on the aggressive misbehavior of our government, a lecture that included a careful recital of the U-2 pravda.

Once I understood, I did something no American should ever do in the Soviet Union. I lost my temper completely. I out-shouted the director on the subject of American grievances against the Soviet Union. My red-headed wife most ably supported me by scorching him about Soviet slave labor camps, naming each one by name, pointing out their location to him on the big map of the Soviet Union which hung back of his desk, and telling him how many people had died in them— including Americans.

We stomped out of his office, went to our room and gave way to the shakes. I had lost my temper and with it my judgment and thereby endangered not merely myself but my wife. I had forgotten that I was not protected by our Bill of Rights, that I was not free to bawl out a public official with impunity—that I was more than 2,000 miles from any possible help.

Communism has no concern for the individual. The Soviets have liquidated some 20 to 30 millions of their own in "building socialism." They kept after Trotsky until they got him. They murdered a schoolmate of mine between stations on a train in Western Europe and dumped his body. Terror and death are as fixed a part of their tactics as is distortion of the truth. Their present gang boss is the "liberator" of Budapest, the "pacifier" of the Ukraine—a comic butcher personally responsible for the deaths of millions of innocent people.

All this I knew. I knew, too, that our own policies had softened beyond recognition since the day when Teddy Roosevelt demanded the return of an American citizen alive—or the man who grabbed him, dead— and made his threat stick. In these present sorry days no American citizen abroad can count on protection from our State Department. We have even voluntarily surrendered our own soldier's Constitutional rights, drafted and sent willy-nilly to foreign lands. We still permit the Red Chinese to hold prisoner hundreds of our boys captured nearly ten years ago in Korea. We do nothing about it. I did have the cold comfort of knowing that I had behaved as a free man, an American. I cherished the thought. But I could not honestly pat myself on the back. My anger had been a reflex, not courage. Pride would not be much to chew on if it had got my wife and myself into a Soviet slave labor camp.

I began to listen for that knock on the door, the one you read about in *Darkness at Noon*, the knock that means your next address may be Vorkuta or Karaganda. The address doesn't matter. You are never, never going to receive mail.

My fears were not groundless. I'd read Philip Wylie's *The Innocent Ambassadors* and I knew what had happened to his brother. I vividly recalled Kravchenko's *I Chose Freedom*.

The knock never came because the political climate engendered by the new pravda was "more-in-sorrow-than-in-anger." The next morning, May 6, we were again ordered to report to the Director's office. We had decided to brazen it out. We refused to go. Presently, we were allowed to catch a plane for Tashkent.

Pravda lasted 12 days, until K. shattered the Summit and revealed a new pravda.

We arrived in Leningrad just as the news reached there that the Summit had failed and that President Eisenhower had cancelled his proposed trip to the USSR and that Khrushchev was returning to Moscow via East Berlin.

The climate suddenly turned very chilly.

A month earlier, in Moscow, we had been picked up by two Russians the very first time we went out on the street. One was a technical translator; the other, a lady, was a museum curator. They were very friendly and stayed with us almost three hours, asking questions about the U.S. and inviting questions about the Soviet Union. This happened to us daily thereafter; we were always making casual acquaintance with Soviet citizens, on the street, in parks, in restaurants, during intermissions at the theatre, everywhere. They were always curious about America, very friendly and extremely polite. This attitude on the part of individual Soviet citizens toward individual Americans continued throughout the first pravda, ending May 6. It lessened slightly during the "more-in-sorrow" second pravda.

K's Paris news conference set up a new pravda. From the time we reached Leningrad until we left for Helsinki, Finland, not one Soviet citizen other than Intourist employees—who had to deal with us professionally—spoke to us under any circumstances. Not one.

In dealing with Intourist it is always difficult to tell whether one's frustrations arise from horrendous red tape or from intentional obstructionism. In Leningrad it at once became clear that Intourist now just did not want to give service. Even the porter who took up our bags made trouble.

Our first afternoon we were scheduled to visit the Hermitage, one of the world's great art museums. The tour had been set with Intourist for that particular afternoon before we left the States.

At the appointed time our guide (you have to have one) had not arranged for a car. After awhile it whisked up and the guide said, "Now we will visit the stadium."

We said that we wanted to visit the Hermitage, as scheduled. The guide told us that the Hermitage was closed. We asked to be taken to another museum (Leningrad has many). We explained that we were not interested in seeing another stadium.

We visited the stadium.

That is all Intourist permitted us to see that afternoon.

When we got back to the hotel we found someone in our room, as always in Leningrad. Since maid service in Intourist hotels varies from non-existent to very ubiquitous we did not at once conclude that we were being intentionally inconvenienced. But one afternoon we found six men in our room, busy tearing out all the pipes and the question of intent became academic. A hotel room with its plumbing torn up and its floor littered with pipes and bits of wood and plaster is only slightly better than no hotel room at all.

We went to the ballet once in Leningrad. Intermissions are very long in Soviet theatres, about half an hour, and on earlier occasions these had been our most fruitful opportunity for meeting Russians.

Not now, not after K's Paris pravda. No one spoke to us. No Russian would even meet our eyes as we strolled past. The only personal attention we received that evening at the ballet was an unmistakably intentional elbow jab in the ribs from a Russian major in uniform. Be-Kind-To-Americans Week had adjourned, sine die.

How can the attitudes of 200 million people be switched on and off like a light bulb? How can one set of facts be made to produce three widely differing pravdas? By complete control of all communications from the cradle to the grave.

Almost all Soviet women work. Their babies are placed in kindergartens at an average age of 57 days, so we were told, and what we saw supported the allegation. We visited several kindergartens, on collective farms and in factories. By the posted schedules, these babies spend 13½ hours each day in kindergarten— they are with their mothers for perhaps an hour before bedtime.

At the Forty-Years-Of-October Collective Farm outside Alma Ata some of the older children in one of the kindergartens put on a little show for us. One little girl recited a poem. A little boy gave a prose recitation. The entire group sang. The children were clean and neat, healthy and happy. Our guide translated nothing so, superficially, it was the sort of beguiling performance one sees any day in any American kindergarten.

However, my wife understands Russian:

The poem recounted the life of Lenin.

The prose recitation concerned the Seven-Year Plan.

The group singing was about how "we must protect our Revolution."

These tots were no older than six.

That is how it is done. Starting at the cradle, never let them hear anything but the official version. Thus "pravda" becomes "truth" to the Russian children.

What does this sort of training mean to a person when he is old enough, presumably, to think for himself? We were waiting in the Kiev airport, May 14. The weather was foul, planes were late and some 30 foreigners were in the Intourist waiting room. One of them asked where we were going and my wife answered that we were flying to Vilno.

Vilno? Where is that? My wife answered that it was the capital of Lithuania, one of the formerly independent Baltic republics which the USSR took over 20 years ago—a simple historic truth, as indisputable as the fact of the Invasion of Normandy or the bombing of Pearl Harbor.

But the truth is not pravda.

A young Intourist guide present understood English, and she immediately interrupted my wife, flatly contradicted her and asserted that Lithuania had *always* been part of the Soviet Union.

The only result was noise and anger. There was no possibility of changing this young woman's belief. She was telling the pravda the way she had been taught it in school and that was that. She had probably been about three when this international rape occurred. She had no personal memory of the period. She had never been to Vilno, although it is less than 400 miles from Kiev. (Soviet people do not travel much. With few exceptions the roads are terrible and the railroads are scarce. Russians are required to use internal passports, secure internal visas for each city they visit and travel by Intourist, just like a foreigner. Thus, traveling for pleasure, other than to designated vacation spots on the Black Sea, is almost unheard of.)

In disputing the official pravda we were simply malicious liars and she made it clear that she so considered us.

About noon on Sunday, May 15, we were walking downhill through the park surrounding the castle that dominates Vilno. We encountered a group of six or eight Red Army cadets. Foreigners are a great curiosity in Vilno. Almost no tourists go there. So they stopped and we chatted, myself through our guide and my wife directly, in Russian.

Shortly one of the cadets asked us what we thought of their new manned rocket. We answered that we had had no news lately—what was it and when did it happen? He told us, with the other cadets listening and agreeing, that the rocket had gone up that very day, and at that very moment a Russian astronaut was in orbit around the earth—and what did we think of that?

I congratulated them on this wondrous achievement but, privately, felt a dull sickness. The Soviet Union had beaten us to the punch again. But later that day our guide looked us up and carefully corrected the story: The cadet had been mistaken, the rocket was not manned.

That evening we tried to purchase *Pravda*. No copies were available in Vilno. Later we heard from other Americans that *Pravda* was not available in other cities in the USSR that evening—this part is hearsay, of course. We tried also to listen to the Voice of America. It was jammed. We listened to some Soviet stations but heard no mention of the rocket.

This is the rocket the Soviets tried to recover and

later admitted that they had had some trouble with the retrojets; they had fired while the rocket was in the wrong attitude.

So what is the answer? Did that rocket contain only a dummy, as the pravda now claims? Or is there a dead Russian revolving in space?—an Orwellian "unperson," once it was realized that he could not be recovered.

I am sure of this: At noon on May 15 a group of Red Army cadets were unanimously positive that the rocket was manned. That pravda did not change until later that afternoon.

Concerning unpersons—

Rasputin is a fairly well known name in America. I was unable to find anyone in Russia who would admit to having heard of him. He's an unperson.

John Paul Jones is known to every school child in America. After the American Revolution Catherine the Great called him to Russia where he served as an Admiral and helped found the Russian Navy, negligible up to that time. I tried many, many times to find a picture of him in Russian historical museums and I asked dozens of educated Russians about him—with no results. In Russian history John Paul Jones has become an unperson.

Trotsky and Kerensky are not unpersons yet. Too many persons are still alive who recall their leading roles in recent Russian history. But they will someday be unpersons, even though Dr. Kerensky is living today in California. In the USSR it is always tacitly assumed that the Communists overthrew the Tsar. This leaves no room for Dr. Kerensky. If pinned down, a Soviet guide may admit that there was such a person as Kerensky, then change the subject. The same applies to Trotsky; his role, for good or bad, is being erased from the records. We saw literally thousands of pictures of Lenin, including several hundred group pictures which supposedly portrayed all the Communist VIP's at the time of the Revolution. Not one of these pictures shows Trotsky even though many of them were alleged to be news photos taken at the time when Lenin and Trotsky were still partners and buddies.

This is how unpersons are made. This is how pravda is created.

The theme of the May Day celebration this year was "Miru Mir": "Peace to the World." A sweet sentiment. But it isn't safe to assume that the dictionary definition of peace has any connection with the official Communist meaning, since even yesterday's pravda may be reversed tomorrow.

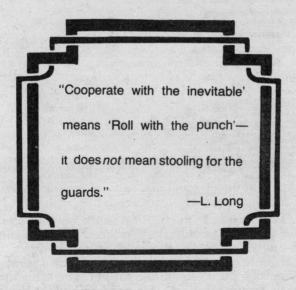

"Cooperate with the inevitable' means 'Roll with the punch'— it does *not* mean stooling for the guards."

—L. Long

FOREWORD

"Don't Go To Russia If You Expect Tidy Toilets" *is the heading on an article by H. Marlin Landwehr (Newspaper Enterprise Association) in the Santa Cruz SENTINEL, Sunday, December 2, 1979. "Russian toilets," writes Mr. Landwehr, "are uniformly filthy, with no toilet seats, coarse (if any) toilet paper, and extremely low pressure."*

From this and from many recent (1979) personal reports I know that my 1960 article INSIDE INTOURIST is still timely despite minor changes. Intourist still has three classes of travel: Bad—Worse—Horrible. These are now called: "Deluxe Suite, Deluxe, and First Class"— i.e., "First Class" is in fact third class—an Orwellian pravda.

Dirty toilets and bad food explain themselves; relative prices are harder to make clear, as the 1960 prices I cite as being outrageously high seem like bargain prices in 1979. So I must adjust for inflation, not too easy when dealing with four sorts of currency: 1) the 1960 dollar fully convertible to gold in the world market at $35 = 1 troy ounce of fine gold; 2) the 1979 floating dollar having today, 3 December 1979, a price per troy ounce of fine gold on the world market of $432 and some odd cents; 3) the 1960 western-tourist ruble, a currency not traded (= "blocked") in the world market, not convertible, not spendable outside its own country, and having its official rate set by decree and in direct consequence a very different black market (= free market) rate; and 4) the 3-Dec-79 western-tourist ruble, a blocked currency not equivalent to the 1960 western-tourist ruble.

To define the relationships between a fully-convertible gold currency, a floating currency, and two different blocked currencies is a task that causes headaches. The arithmetic is simple, the semantic problem is not, and it is further complicated by both conscious and subconscious personal attitudes. You may not "believe in" a gold standard, for example (and I readily concede the

*truth of the old saw that one cannot eat gold), but it does
not matter what I believe or you believe, our floating dollar is now worth in gold whatever the rest of the world
tells us it is worth, i.e., the price at which they will buy
dollars or sell gold. The only yardstick I can apply to all
four currencies is the troy ounce of fine gold (= 480
grains in both troy and apothecary, or 31.1035 grams in
metric).*

*Since the ruble is not traded in the gold market, I must
equate rubles first in dollars, then translate into gold.
(This fiscal discussion is not my idea; our editor complained—correctly—that a much shorter discussion was
unclear.) In 1960 the Kremlin-decreed rate was 4 rubles
= $1.00 USA. Today Monday 3 December 1979 the
Kremlin-decreed rate to U.S. tourists is 1 ruble = $1.52
USA.*

Now to work—

In 1960 $1.00 USA equalled
*1/35 tr. oz. Au. = 13.715 grains = 0.888671+ grams gold,
and one ruble equalled $0.25, or
1/140 tr. oz. Au. = 3.429 grains = 0.222167+ grams gold.*

While on Dec. 3, 1979, $1.00 USA equalled
*1/432 tr. oz. Au. = 1.1111... grains = 0.071998+ grams gold
and one ruble equalled $1.52 USA, or
0.003518+ tr. oz. Au. = 1.7 grains = 0.109438+ grams gold.*

*—which doesn't tell us much, especially as the dollar
floats and changes every day, and the ratio between the
dollar and the U.S.-tourist ruble is by decree and subject
to change without notice. In the following article I show
all prices three ways: 1) 1960 prices; 2) 3-Dec-79 equivalent by world free-market conversion; and 3) 3-Dec-79
equivalent by Kremlin-decreed dollar/ruble ratio.*

*The conversion factor for the world free market is 432/
35 = 12.343; the Kremlin-decreed conversion factor is
152¢/25¢ = 6.08. You are free to believe either one or
neither.*

But the above still doesn't tell you very much as the

*floating dollar changes daily and the ruble/dollar ratio
changes whenever the Kremlin changes it . . . and you
will not be reading this on December 3, 1979. But all is
not lost; you can obtain and apply the conversion factors
for the day you read this in the same fashion in which I
did it:*

*For the world free-market conversion factor first get
that day's gold fix from newspaper or radio, then divide
by 35. For the Kremlin factor telephone a Soviet consul-
ate or Intourist New York, get the current price of a ruble
in dollars and cents, divide by 25¢. Then reach for your
pocket calculator.*

*It would have been simpler to state that travel in USSR
in 1960 was extremely, outrageously expensive—a
planned swindle.*

The Early Worm Deserves the Bird

INSIDE INTOURIST

How to Break Even (or Almost) in the Soviet Union

To enjoy a thing requires that it be approached in the proper mood. A woman who has been promised a luxury suite at Miami Beach won't cheer at the thought of roughing it in the north woods, especially if her husband pulls this switch after the vacation has started.

But, with proper pre-conditioning, it is possible to enjoy anything—some people are addicted to parachute jumping. To experience the Soviet Union without first getting in the mood for it is too much like parachute jumping when the chute fails to open. The proper mood for the Soviet Union is that of the man who hit himself on the head with a hammer because it felt so good when he stopped.

This article assumes that you have already, for good and sufficient reasons, decided to visit the USSR, one good and sufficient reason being a wish to see for yourself this Communist paradise that Khrushchev has promised our grandchildren. But to set out for Russia in the holiday spirit in which you head for the Riviera, Las Vegas, or Rio is like going to a funeral for the ride.

You can avoid the worst shocks to your nervous system by knowing in advance that you are not going to get what you have paid for; then you can soothe the residual nerve jangling with your favorite pacifier. I used small quantities of vodka—"small" by Russian standards, as Russians also use it to insulate themselves from the slings and arrows of outrageous fortune but they dose to unconsciousness. Drunks, passed out in public places, are more truly symbolic of the USSR than is the Hammer & Sickle.

My wife found methyl meprobamate (Equanil, Miltown) more useful. For you it might be yoga, or silent prayer, but, whatever it is, don't neglect it. Travel in the Soviet Union is not like travel anywhere else in the world. My wife and I have visited more than sixty countries on six continents, by freight ship, helicopter, dog sled, safari, jet plane, mule back, canal boat, etc.; as "seasoned travelers" these are our credentials. To visit the USSR we prepared by extensive reading and my wife learned the Russian language. Nevertheless, again and again we ran into surprises, difficulties, and maddening frustrations.

You can travel all through the Soviet Union without knowing a word of Russian—which will suit Khrushchev just fine because you will thereby be a prisoner of "Intourist," the state-owned travel bureau, seeing only what they want you to see, hearing only what they want you to hear.

But the Russian language is difficult; it took my wife two years of hard work to master it. The alphabet is weirdly strange, the pronunciation is hard for us, and the language is heavily inflected—a proper noun, such as "Smith" or "Khrushchev," has eighteen different forms.

Obviously most tourists can't take two years off to master Russian. What then? Depend entirely on Intourist guides?

No, no, no! Better to save your money and stay home. With no Russian at all you'll be as helpless as a bed patient. Instead you should prepare by learning a smattering of Russian. Forget about grammar; grammatical Russian is found only in formal literary compositions. Khrushchev has never learned to speak

Russian well and Mikoyan speaks it with an accent thick enough to slice—so why should you worry?

First learn the alphabet, capitals and lower case, printed and written. This alone is half the battle. You can now find the men's room (or the ladies' room). The men's room is marked with "M" (for "muzhcheen," but think of "M" for "men") and the ladies' room is marked with a letter which looks like two capital K's, back to back: Ж You are now past the greatest crisis confronting a traveler: finding the plumbing.

You now know many of the most useful Russian words just from knowing the alphabet. Hungry? Watch for a sign reading: "РЕСТОРАН." Sound it in your head as "restauran"—and it is!—the same word as in English save that the final "t" has been dropped.

There are hundreds of words which turn out to be the same as the English, or near enough. If you know French or German, your immediate vocabulary is further enriched, as, despite their boasts, Russian culture is very backward and most of their vocabulary for anything more complex than weeding a turnip patch has been borrowed from French, English, or German by converting the foreign word phonetically.

But don't stop with the alphabet; get a set of phonograph records for teaching Russian. Play them while following the lessons in the book—and play them without the book while bathing, shaving, cooking, gardening, etc. A few hours of this will pay off to the point where you will no longer be dependent on an Intourist guide; it will triple what you get out of a trip behind the Iron Curtain. For a few dollars in records and a little work you change it from a losing game into one in which your investment will be well repaid in education if not in pleasure.

But to get fun out of it, too, you must understand the Intourist game, play it, and win. Winning consists in outwitting the system so that you get more than they intend you to get; it does *not* mean fair value in the fashion (for example) that a traveler invariably gets

his money's worth in any Scandinavian country. It is
not possible to get fair value in the USSR; the game is
rigged against the American tourist. But there are
ways to minimize the expense and maximize the return while having quite a lot of fun.

All travel in the USSR is controlled at every point
by Intourist; you must buy from it all travel, all automobile and guide service, all hotel rooms, all meals—
or if you buy a meal not from Intourist you simply
waste a meal already paid for.

You buy from Intourist at four rubles to the dollar—
and you are licked from scratch as the value of the ruble is closer to forty to the dollar (which is the rate the
Soviet government gives to favored visitors such as
Asians they are trying to woo into the Communist
camp).

You can cut costs by ordering cheap accommoda-
tions. Three grades are offered: Luxe, Tourist A, and
Tourist B. A single man might risk Tourist B if he did
not mind public toilets and baths of uncertain clean-
liness, plus sharing sleeping space, dormitory style; a
couple might risk Tourist A, which is supposed to be
(but is not) equal to first-class travel elsewhere. But I
cannot honestly urge anything short of "Luxe" class
because even the best in Russia is often shockingly bad
by our standards—bathrooms without baths, even hotels with no baths, tubs with no hot water, plumbing
that is "quaint" or worse, poor cooking, dirty utensils,
maddening waits. The lodging for Luxe class is often
a huge and fantastically furnished suite, but a first-
class double room & bath in any other country is more
comfortable.

Luxe class costs $30 per day per person (3 Dec 79—
Kremlin   rate $182.40—World   free-market   rate
$370.29) and includes lodging, meal coupons, and
three hours of guide and automobile service per person (thus six hours for a couple)—if you get it. It does
not include *any* train, plane, or bus fares. Add these in,
plus round trip aircoach fares from New York, and a

month in the Soviet Union will cost an American couple at least $4500 (3 Dec 79—Kremlin rate $27,360.00—World rate $55,543.50), plus spending money and extras.

You will get at least twice as much for your money in any other part of Europe, but the real problem always is to get what you have paid for and Intourist has contracted to furnish you.

Start by realizing that Intourist is not really a travel service in the sense in which Thos. Cook or American Express is. It is a bureau of the Communist government and its function is to get those Yankee dollars in advance, channel you through a fixed route, then spill you out at the far end almost as ignorant of their country as when you started. P. T. Barnum's famous sign *"This Way to the Egress"* anticipated the basic Intourist principle: Get the sucker's money first, then get rid of him with the least trouble to the management.

So treat it as a game and don't fret when you lose. Try to get a good night's sleep—the bed may be awful but it will be quiet because there is almost no traffic—and try again the next day.

For example: the guide is not there to guide you, the guide is there to make sure that you see the stadium—so try not to see a stadium anywhere in the Soviet Union. Surely they have stadiums; any people so devoted to "Togetherness" have stadiums—how else could they display ten thousand people all doing physical jerks at once? (A "Spartakiad") But remember that your fixed cost is about $20 just to look at a stadium (with no football game thrown in) and that, in diverting you to the stadium, Intourist has kept you from seeing something of real interest, a factory, a slum area, or a school.

Stadiums haven't changed much since the Romans built the Colosseum; if you have seen Yankee Stadium, Soldiers' Field, or the Rose Bowl—or even the football stands of Podunk High—you've seen enough empty stadiums to last a lifetime. So refuse!

But the guide has orders that you *must* see the stadium; no other theory will account for the persistence with which all Intourist guides *insist* that you see the local stadium. If you manage to get in and out of the Soviet Union without visiting a stadium, award yourself the Order of Hero of Soviet Travel, First Class.

(We saw a lot of them—nobody had warned us.)

Each Intourist hotel has a place called the "Service Bureau." "Service" in this usage is an example of Communist semantics comparable to "co-existence," "peace-loving," "democratic," etc. Here most of your battles with Intourist will take place. Second only to the passed-out drunk, the most typical sight in the Soviet Union is an American tourist seated in a service bureau, his expression getting tighter as the weary, expensive minutes trickle away.

Intourist rarely uses the blunt refusal on this unhappy creature; instead the standard tactics are please-sit-down-and-wait-for-just-a-moment (which usually turns out to be at least an hour), I'm-sorry-but-the-Director-is-out (and won't return as long as *you* keep hanging around), come-back-later (when the desk will be closed), and go-to-that-desk-at-the-far-end-of-the-room (where, after more delay and much consultation, you will be sent back to the desk from which you started).

When facing this, to get part of what you have paid for (and anything over 70% is a triumph, with 50% par for the course) you must stick to pre-planned defensive tactics and never, never, never lose your temper, or you will wind up a fit candidate for wet packs and sedation.

Their first weapon is politeness. You *must* resist this soporific politeness or you will not get anything.

First-Stage Defense: Be just as polite as they are—but utterly stubborn. Above all, *don't sit down when invited to.* If you do, this retires you from the game for an indefinite penalty period. Hold your ground, standing firmly against the desk and taking up as much space as possible—lean on it with hands spread wide to double your combat frontage. Say firmly and politely: "No, thank you, I'll wait right here"—then monopolize that desk and clerk, making it impossible for business to be transacted until Intourist has honored your contract on the point you have raised.

Keep talking. It does not matter what you say nor whether the clerk understands English—*keep talking!* Your purpose is to take that unit of Intourist out of the game until your request has been met, not with promises but with immediate action—whereas *their* purpose is to get *you* out of the game by persuading you to sit down away from the desk.

So hold your ground and be softly, politely stubborn. Usually someone with authority will arrive in a few minutes and satisfy your request.

Defense in Depth: Be prepared to simulate anger at any instant. It is much better to *pretend* to lose your temper *before* things have grown so unbearable that you actually do blow your top; it saves wear and tear on your ulcers and enables you to conduct your tactics more efficiently.

(And I must say a word on behalf of Intourist employees. About three quarters of them are young women, girls really. They are nice people, polite, harassed, overworked, and underpaid. They are prisoners of a system which automatically frustrates the traveler, and they are more imprisoned by it than you are, for you will escape (we hope) on the date set forth on your exit visa. They can't. These poor kids did not invent the silly red tape and mountains of useless paperwork and those in the lower ranks have no authority to vary from it. So don't be too harsh and try not to lose your temper in fact.)

But be prepared to simulate anger whenever the log jam does not break under the pianissimo tactics of the first-stage defense. When you refuse to sit down and wait, the clerk will sometimes turn away and ignore you.

It is then time to throw a fit.

You must (1) hold your blocking position, (2) make lots of noise, and (3) show that you are bitterly and righteously angry and cannot possibly be shut up short of complete satisfaction.

Keep shouting. It helps to cuss a bit and one all-purpose word will do: "*Bor*jemoi!" This is a phonetic approximation of two words meaning "My God!"—which is merely an expression of disgust in this atheistic society. Another good phrase is "Yah Haw*chew*!" which is the abrupt way of saying "I want it!" (The polite idiom is "Mnyeh *Khaw*chettsuh.")

You can shout, "I want to see the Director!"—or, in Russian, "Yah *Khaw*chew veedyets Direktora!" She may possibly answer, "The Director's office (or desk) is over there," but she is more likely to give you what you want rather than let you complain to the boss.

But if she does, *don't move*. Hold your ground, keep on being unreasonable, and let the boss come to you. If you let them chivvy you into his office, away from spectators, and you yourself sitting down and being polite, you've lost that round. The Director will be polite, apologetic, and regretful about "shortages"—but firmly unhelpful. The place to win is in public.

For most of us it is not easy to be intentionally rude. I think one should never be impolite unnecessarily—but we can do much to uphold our national dignity and to improve our relations with the Soviet Union by never keeping quiet when we are cheated, by answering the great stubbornness of Russians by being twice as stubborn, and by being intentionally and loudly rude whenever Intourist refuses to keep its contract despite polite protest. Intourist is an integral part of a government with a forty-three year record (now 63 years—R.A.H.) of not honoring its most solemn commitments; one must assume that its blatant cheating is planned from the top and that every employee of

Intourist is schooled in his role, right down to the sweet little girl who insists that you must see the stadium.

You may prefer to think that this horrendous swindle is merely an unintentional by-product of a fantastic, all embracing, and incredibly inefficient bureaucracy bogged down in its own red tape to the point where it can't give service. Either way, a contract with Intourist works exactly like that long list of broken treaties. You start by making a contract with the Soviet government; you are required to pay in advance and in full. Then you attempt to collect what you have paid for—and discover that a Communist contract is worth what it usually is. "Room with bath" turns out to be without, "jet planes" become prop planes, guide and auto service is less than half the time you have paid for, dining rooms are locked at meal hours, and your extremely expensive time is wasted sitting, sitting, sitting in "service" bureaus.

Unless you raise hell about it, right at the time. No use complaining later, you won't get your money back.

If neither polite stubbornness nor noisy rudeness will work, use the insult direct. Shake your finger in the face of the most senior official present, simulate extreme rage, and shout, "Nyeh Kuhl-*toor*nee!" ("Uncultured!") Hit that middle syllable and roll the r's.

Subordinates will turn a sickly green and pretend to be elsewhere. The official will come close to apoplexy—but will probably make an extreme effort to satisfy your demand in order to shut you up. This is the worst insult you can hand a Russian, one that hits him in cracks of his armor. *Use it only as a last resort.*

I do not think you will be in personal danger as the officials you will meet will probably not be high enough in the hierarchy to punish you for insulting them. But if anything goes wrong and you wind up in Siberia, *please understand that you use it at your own risk.*

If "nyeh kuhltoornee" does not work, I have nothing

more to suggest but a hot bath and a sedative.

But the above campaign usually wins in the first or second stage and rarely fails in the third as it is based on Russian temperament and Communist social organization. Even the most arrogant Soviet citizen suffers from an inferiority complex when faced with free citizens of the western world, especially Americans. The questions they ask most frequently are: How much money do you make? How big is your house? Do you own an automobile? Each one is a dead give-away.

So if you make it clear that Intourist service is contemptible by free-world standards, a Russian may want to take a poke at you but he is much more likely to attempt to restore face by meeting those standards. The rest of the picture has to do with socialist "equality," another example of Communist semantics, because in the egalitarian paradise there is *no* equality, nowhere anything like the easy-going equality between an American taxi driver and his fare. In the USSR you are either on top or underneath—never even.

An American does not fit. Some Soviet citizens react by subordinating themselves to the tourist; grandmothers sweeping the streets will scurry out of your way, taxi drivers will rush to open doors, porters and waitresses and such are servile in a fashion we are not used to. But an employee of Intourist is in an indeterminate position vis-à-vis a tourist. Dominant? Or subordinate? It must be one or the other. Often there is a quick test of wills, then an immediate assumption of one role or the other depending on how the tourist responds. For example, we were met in Kiev by a guide who gave his name as "Sasha." I asked his surname; he told me quite arrogantly that there was no need for me to know it.

We had been in the USSR several weeks and I had had my fill of arrogance; I told him bluntly that I was not interested in his name, that I had asked out of politeness as practiced in all *civilized* countries—but that if good manners were not customary in his country, forget it!

An American or other free man might have given me a rough answer or icy silence; he did neither, he groveled. When he left us at the hotel he thanked us effusively for having been so kind as to talk with him. His manner was cringingly servile.

I don't like servility any more than the next American—but if there is going to be any groveling done it won't be by me. Nor, I hope, by you. In dealing with Intourist people you will often run into situations where one of you must knuckle under—and many are much tougher cases than this man. It will be a clash of will and all too often polite stubbornness won't be enough to get them to honor your contract—then you need to model your behavior after the worst temper tantrums you have seen Khrushchev pull on television; this they understand. In the USSR only a boss ever behaves that way; therefore you *must* be entitled to Red Carpet service. The Intourist functionary *knows* you are just an American tourist, to be frustrated and cheated, but his conditioned reflex bypasses his brain; a lifetime of conditioning tells him to kowtow to any member of the master class . . . which you *must* be, even though his brain tells him you are not.

It usually works. In a bully-boy society often nothing but bullying will work.

The "Coupon Game": When you arrive you will be handed a lot of documents in exchange for your tour voucher; one will be a book of meal tickets, four coupons for each day. For Luxe class their values are twelve rubles for a breakfast coupon, twenty for a lunch, three for tea, thirty for dinner. If you and your spouse have contracted to spend a month in the USSR, your meal tickets have cost you one thousand dollars (3 Dec 79—Kremlin rate $6,080.00—World free-market $12,343.00) (28½ oz. of gold). The gouging starts here, because Diamond Jim Brady and his twin could

not eat a thousand dollars of Intourist food in a month.
Intourist eateries range from passable to very bad. Hotel Berlin in Moscow is perhaps the best but even it
would have trouble making the Duncan Hines list.
There are three or four good restaurants in the Soviet
Union but their prices are *very* high and they won't
accept coupons.

You can minimize your losses in ways that Intourist
does not tell you. You can combine coupons as you
wish—a "lunch" and a "breakfast" to pay for dinner,
for example. The possible combinations in rubles are
3, 6, 9, 12, 15, 18, 20, 21, 23, 24, 26, 27, 29, 30, 32, 33,
35, 36, 38, and all higher numbers—but the hitch is
that too many of them take more than one "tea" coupon. So figure out the best way to work each combination and write it on the back of your coupon book;
this will help you to decide whether to overpay for
food already horribly overpriced, or to pay the difference in cash. Skill in the coupon game can save you
many, many dollars.

There is nothing fair in the coupon system but it
isn't meant to be; it is the prime fashion in which the
Soviet government squeezes more dollars out of
American tourists than they want or need to spend.

There are other ways to reduce your losses. You can
swap coupons for liquor, candy, canned caviar, cigarettes, and bottled water. Tap water in Moscow and
Leningrad is said to be safe but elsewhere it is wise to
buy mineral water—get enough bottles at a time to
come out even in coupons. Their cigarettes are corro-
sive but a brand called "Trud" is smokable. Candy is
extremely expensive but a welcome change in a tedious diet (I lost twelve pounds); caviar is cheap and is
the best buy to use up leftover coupons on your last
day. Don't expect to find whiskey nor any imported
liquor, but local "kawnyahk" and "chahm*pahn*-
skoyeh" are good. The vodka like ours is *"vawt*-kah
stel*leech*nayuh"—the other sorts are very highly
spiced. Their wines are good.

My favorite relief from a hard day with Intourist was a Bloody Mary—"Staw grahm vawt-kee, p'jalst, ee taw*maht*nee sawk." This is "nyeh kuhltoornee" as the proper way to drink vodka is with beer (*pee*vaw), or with black bread, sweet butter, and caviar.

In Moscow and Leningrad very few Russian waiters speak English and almost none elsewhere, but you will usually be handed a huge four-language menu on which you can pick out what you want in English and point to it in Russian. But only the few items with prices written in are offered and maybe half of those will be available—when the waiter says "Nyeh-taw" he means it's all gone. Allow at least two hours for dinner; I've never heard of any way to speed up the service. But, once you are served, the waiter may try to rush you out, claiming that the table is reserved ten minutes hence for a delegation or such. He may simply want to sell food to someone else—he gets a commission. Ignore him—you've waited a long time, paid a high price in advance, and are entitled to eat in peace.

Pick a table as far from the orchestra as possible. Some orchestras are good but most are very loud and sound like a fully automated boiler factory.

Tipping is never necessary but waiters, chambermaids, and porters are paid very little. Tips can be coupons or cash.

The dining room is often locked—for a political delegation from Asia or Africa, for a traveling theatrical troupe, or anything. Any service may be chopped off without warning in any Intourist hotel. Complain . . . but be prepared to fall back on the buffet (pronounced "*boof*-yet"). There are usually three or four on the upper floors of large hotels, open from seven a.m. to eleven at night and serving omelets, snacks, beer, wine, juice, coffee, tea, cakes, etc. The guides and clerks in Intourist often do not know about them because *they have never been upstairs*, so watch for the sign (БУФЕТ) or wander the corridors saying inquiringly to maids and floor clerks: "*Boof*-yet?"

Buffets are cozy, friendly, little places run by cheerful, helpful, dreadfully overworked women. They
won't know English and the menu will be in Russian—
here a memorandum in English & Russian of your favorite foods is most useful. But even the buffet doesn't
serve breakfast before seven and Russian transportation often leaves at such an hour that you must leave
the hotel before then. Russian hotels have room service but not at such hours. If you have your *own* thermos bottle, room service can fetch you hot coffee and
a cold breakfast the night before. (They've heard of
thermos bottles—the word is the same—but the hotel
won't have one.)

Keep iron rations in your room and carry food and
drink on long flights and train trips. Both trains and
planes often stop for meals but you can't count on it
and usually can't find out in advance.

Minor Ways to Improve Your Score: Go for walks
without your guide; you will usually be picked up by
someone who knows English—but you will *never* be
picked up while a guide is with you. This is your
chance to get acquainted and to get answers which are
not the official answers. Don't talk politics—but these
venturesome souls may ask you political questions
and you can learn almost as much by the questions
they ask as by raising such issues yourself.

Your guide may not be a hardshell Communist; he,
or she, may open up once he thinks he can trust you. If
so, be careful not to mention anything even faintly political when others are in earshot, *especially the driver*.
The driver may be a political chaperone who knows
English but pretends not to. More than one guide has
told me this and *all* guides talk more freely when no
one can overhear.

In this country children are brought to Moscow and
decorated for having informed on their parents. *Never
forget this.*

When you are shown a party headquarters, a palace
of culture, a stadium, an auditorium, or such, ask

when it was built. We discovered that, in the areas not occupied by Nazis, many of the biggest and fanciest were built right at the time Americans were dying to keep the Murmansk lend-lease route open.

There is new brick construction all over the Soviet Union. We asked repeatedly to be shown a brick yard, were never quite refused, but the request was never granted. We have since heard a rumor that this is prison labor and that is why a tourist can't see something as unsecret as a brick yard. So try it yourself— you may merely prove to yourself that Intourist exists to keep tourists from seeing what they want to see, rather than vice versa.

Offer your passport to casual acquaintances; they will usually offer theirs in return—*internal* passports. Intourist people have been coached to deny that such a thing exists but everybody in the USSR carries one and the owner must get a visa to go from one Russian city to another. It is a brown book with "ПАСПОРТ" (passport) on the cover. Try it when your guide is not around.

The USSR is the only country in which we were never able to get into a private home. Other tourists report the same but one couple from Los Angeles almost cracked this; they said to their guide, "*Why* can't we see the inside of one of those apartment houses? Are you people *ashamed* of them?" The next day they were shown through a not-yet-occupied one.

This could be varied endlessly, as it works on that Russian basic, their inferiority complex. The key word is "ashamed"—simply asking "Why?" gets you nowhere. I think it could be used to get into farms, schools, courts, factories, anything not a military secret. It tops my list of things I wish I had thought of first.

In meeting anyone, including guides, try to use "democracies" as an antonym for "Communist countries" as soon as possible—drag it in by the heels, i.e., "I think all of us from the democracies earnestly hope for peace with the Communist countries," etc. The much abused word "democratic" means "Communist" in Russia and it always introduces a propaganda pitch. If you deny him his definition by preempting the word, you leave him with his mouth hanging open, unable to proceed.

We got tripped on this several times before we caught on.

The official list of things you must not photograph is short but the unofficial list is long and ranges from old, broken-down buildings to old, broken-down women sweeping the streets. You can photograph such by having them appear "accidentally" in a background but if you are suspected of this, they have a silent counter to it. At some later time you will find that your film has been exposed to light, then respooled. You could keep all your film with you at all times and hope to get it across the border . . . but such behavior might cause you to be arrested on suspicion of espionage, as one American tourist was this summer. At best, sneaking a picture of one passed-out drunk risks losing *all* your pictures—too high a price even if you aren't accused of being a spy.

The most-used plane, the Ilyushin-14, flies very low; you can see a lot and compare it with elsewhere. Are railroads single or double track? How much traffic on the roads? On the rivers? How about factory smokestacks and other signs of industry? How busy are the airfields? Or a dozen other things. I think you will conclude that no Russian claim should be accepted as true until fully verified. A "great industrial center" often turns out to be a jerkwater town.

But don't make written notes about such things! *Don't!!!*

Will your mail be opened? You must assume so. Will your rooms be bugged? It seems impossible to monitor every room of every Intourist hotel—but if the police get interested in *you* it takes just three minutes in these days of miniaturization to bug a room. I do know, from several incidents, that Soviet citizens *believe* that all hotel rooms are bugged.

I wish that a million of us would visit the USSR; the dollars the Kremlin would reap would be more than offset by the profit to us in having so many free men see with their own eyes what Communism is.

But go there with your eyes open—Intourist is as fully an agency of the Kremlin as is Gromyko or Mikoyan. Its functions are (1) to get your money in advance, (2) to deliver as little as possible by downgrading accomodations, by forced overcharges on food, and by clipping you on auto and guide service, (3) to waste your time so that you will see as little as possible, and (4) to see that what little time you have left is spent only on those things the Kremlin does not mind your seeing—"new construction" (from the outside), parks of "rest & culture" (filled with loudspeakers blaring propaganda), ballets, museums, stadiums, and the outsides of public buildings.

The first point you must accept; the game is crooked but it is the only game in town. Points two and three you can struggle against—I hope the tactics suggested in here will help. Point four is the toughest. After trimming you down to about three hours a day of useful time, Intourist can and will use up what is left in "stadium sightseeing" unless you fight it constantly. Even then, Intourist is adept in parrying with: "It's closed today—too bad you're not staying another day," and "That must be arranged in advance through the Ministry of Culture, etc." and "You should have requested that in Moscow."

The essence of Intourist tactics is: "Jam yesterday and jam tomorrow, but never jam today." The way to answer it is: "No! I will *not* look at the stadium, I do *not* want to see another subway station, I will *not* visit a museum to see another five hundred pictures of Lenin. I want to see thus-and-so and I want to see it *now*. Stop the car, get on the phone, and arrange it— or tell the Director that, as far as I am concerned, you're fired! I am keeping the car and the driver and will go on without you— I've got hours more of car service due me today and I *won't* be cheated out of it."

You will find whether your guide is truly a guide . . . or a guard placed with you to make sure you see only the facade of this regime. Whether or not you see "thus-and-so" you are sure to learn a surprising amount about how a police state is run . . . and thereby get your full money's worth in education.

After twenty years it would seem logical for me to return to the USSR to see what improvements, if any, they have made in handling tourism. I could plead age and health but I shan't—one trip to USSR is educational; twice is masochism.

If you have been to the USSR recently and if you know enough Russian that you could and did slip the leash occasionally and poke around and get acquainted without permission of Intourist, please write to me and tell me about it—what you saw with your own eyes, what you touched, what you counted, how you were treated. I am not interested in second-hand reports, not even from other Americans you trust, and I most emphatically am not interested in anything your guides told you.

If you know no Russian and took one of the standard Intourist trips—around the Black Sea, or the Leningrad-Moskva-Sochi trip—don't waste your time writing. I hope you had fun.

If you took the long railway trip, Vladivostok to Leningrad or Moskva—or vice versa—do please write to me. If you knew no Russian at first, I'm betting high odds that you spoke fluent (if ungrammatical) Russian long before you completed the trip. You will know many things I don't know as I have never been across Siberia. Alma Ata, KSSR, north of the Himalayas and just short of Sinkiang, is as far as I got.

Concerning believing what you see and ignoring reports: *In thirty-odd years of habitual travel, Mrs. Heinlein and I have not been simply sightseeing; we have been studying other people's ways. Sometimes trivia—e.g., in Peru they make far better apple pie than Mom ever baked (treason!), Chile has us beat all hollow when it comes to ice-cream sodas, and the Finnish ice-cream cone is a work of art that makes what we call an ice-cream cone look sad.*

But usually we are dead serious. Lately I've been making a global survey of blood services—but that is another

*story. Two things we have done consistently throughout
the world: 1) See the slums; 2) evaluate the diet.*

*The fancy hotels and the museums and the parks are
much the same the world over—but the slums are honest
criteria even though a traveller can't assign a numerical
value. The street people of Bombay and of Calcutta tell
far more about India than does the glorious Taj Mahal.*

*Two other questions give direct, numerical compari-
sons: Q: How many long tonnes of protein (meat, fish,
cheese) does this country consume in one year? (Then,
privately, divide by the population.) Q: How many minutes must a journeyman carpenter work to earn enough
to buy one kilogram of the local standard bread?*

*The first question tells the quality of the average diet;
the second tells you how rich (or poor) that country averages. If you have also managed to see the slums, you
have some idea of the range of wealth. You can't tell by
looking at the extremely wealthy; all over the world they
are careful to dress like upper middle class, no higher.
But slums are honest and the most extreme wealth range
is to be found in India.*

*The range of personal wealth in Russia, in 1960, was
high, possibly greater than the range in the U.S.A. But
the range showed in "perks," not in money—privately-
assigned automobiles and chauffeurs, summer houses,
assigned living quarters. The Latvian Secretary (a Russian, not a Lett) of the Writers Union had as his offices a
marble palace, extremely ornate inside and outside and
loaded with sculpture and paintings (built—I was told—
by the late Tsar for his favorite mistress. True? I don't
know but I've never been in a more lavish palace and I
have been in many). After meeting his colleagues—and
living through a Russian drinking duel better left undes-
cribed—we were taken by him out to the Baltic and
shown his dacha . . . thereby showing us that he had a
private car, a chauffeur, and a summer home, as well as
offices literally fit for a king. No mention of money, no
need to—I was convinced that he was not going home to
a meal of black bread, potatoes, and boiled cabbage.*

Yet he was merely writer boss in Latvia, a small captive country—not *General Secretary of the Writers Union in Moskva.* I was in the Writers Union general headquarters in Moskva, a large office building; I did not meet the General Secretary. I assume that he lived at least as well as his stooge in Latvia.

How many levels are there between this minor boss in Riga and the members of the Praesidium? How well does Khrushchev—excuse me; Brezhnev—live? I shan't guess.

In the USSR it was not politic (risky) to ask the two key questions that I always asked in other countries, and seeing slums was forbidden. Twice we saw slums by accident, were hurried on past—primitive log cabins just outside Moskva, 1st century mud huts in Alma Ata that were concealed by screening but from one elevation we could see over the screening . . . until we were seen and cautioned not to stop there and not to take pictures.

Since we couldn't ask our standard comparison questions, Mrs. Heinlein devised some "innocent" ones, and I concentrated on certain signs; both of us were sizing up population. At that time the USSR claimed a population of 225,000,000 and claimed a population for Moskva of 5,000,000+. (Today, twenty years later, they claim almost 300,000,000 and over 7,000,000.)

For many days we prowled Moskva—by car, by taxi when we did not want Intourist with us, by subway, by bus, and on foot. In the meantime Mrs. Heinlein, in her fluent Russian, got acquainted with many people—Intourist guides, drivers, people who picked us up on the streets, chambermaids, anyone. The Russians are delightful people, always happy to talk with visitors, in English if they know it (and many do), in Russian if they do not.

Let me add that, if it suited her, Ginny could charm pictures off a wall.

She was able to ask personal questions (but ones people anywhere usually are pleased to answer) by freely answering questions about us and showing warm interest *in that person—not faked; she is a warm person.*

But, buried in chitchat, she always learned these things:

How old are you?

Are you married?

How many children do you have?

How many brothers and sisters do you have? What ages?

How many nieces and nephews do you have?

Put baldly, that sounds as offensive as a quiz by a Kinsey reporter. But it was not put baldly—e.g., "Oh, how lucky you are! Gospodin Heinlein and I didn't even meet until the Great Patriotic War . . . and we have no children although we wanted them. But we have lots of nieces and nephews." Etc., etc. She often told more than she got but she accumulated, painlessly, the data she wanted, often without asking questions.

One day we were seated on a park bench, back of the Kremlin and facing the Moskva river, with no one near us— a good spot to talk; a directional mike would have to be clear across the river as long as we kept our backs to the Kremlin.

I said, "How big does that guide book say this city is?"

"Over five million."

"Hmmph! Look at that river. Look at the traffic on it." (One lonely scow—) "Remember the Rhine?" We had taken a steamer up the Rhine three years earlier; the traffic was so dense the river had traffic lights on it, just like the Panama Canal. "Ginny, this dump isn't anything like five million. More the size of Copenhagen, if that. Pittsburgh. New Orleans. San Francisco, possibly." (These are all cities I know well, on foot and by every form of transportation. In 1960 all of them were in the 600,000–800,000 range.) "Yet they are trying to tell us that this dump is bigger than Philadelphia, bigger than Los Angeles, bigger than Chicago. Nonsense."

(I have lived in all three cities. A big city feels big, be it Yokohama or New York.) "Three quarters of a million, not five million."

443

"*I know*," *she agreed.*

"*Huh?*"

(I think I must mention that Mrs. Heinlein is a close student of Russian history, history of the Russian Revolution, history of the Third International or ComIntern, and so skilled in Marxist dialectical materialism that she can argue theory with a Russian party member and get him so mixed up that he's biting his own tail.)

She answered, "They claim to have finished the War with about two hundred million and Moscow at four million. Now they are claiming twenty-five million more in the Union, and over a million increase in Moscow." She thought a bit. "It's a lie. Unless they are breeding like flies everywhere outside Moscow, they have lost population since the War—not gained. I haven't found even one family with more than three children. The average is less than two. And they marry late. Robert, they aren't even replacing themselves."

She looked at that empty river. "Not quite as big as Copenhagen is my guess."

We stopped in many other cities—Alma Ata, Tashkent, Samarkand, Minsk, Vilno, Kiev, Riga, Leningrad, etc.—and she continued her gentle questioning but never found reason to change her opinion. Even out in the Muslim countries of Turkestan the birthrate was low, or the answers seemed to show it. She did not write down her figures (Well, I don't think she did; I warned her not to) but she has a memory that is effectively perfect as long as necessary . . . then she can wash out useless details, which I can't do.)

How was it possible for the Russians to claim that Moscow was seven times as big as it actually was? How could I be right and the whole world wrong? The World Almanac gave the same figures the Russians did, all news services seemed to accept Russian population figures—how could a Big Lie that big not be noticed—and denounced?

About a year later I had a chance to discuss it with an old shipmate, an admiral now retired but then holding a major command. I asked him how many people there were in Moscow.

He answered, "I don't know. Why don't you look it up?" (When a high brass answers, "I don't know," he may mean, "Don't be nosy and let's change the subject." But I persisted.)

"Make a guess. You must have some idea."

"Okay." He closed his eyes and kept quiet for several minutes. "Seven hundred and fifty thousand, not over that."

(Jackpot!)

I said, "Mister Ought Ought Seven, have you made a special study of Russia? Or shouldn't I ask?"

"Not at all. [His command] gives me all the trouble I need without worrying about Russia. I simply worked it as a logistics problem, War College style. But I had to stop and visualize the map first. Roads, rivers, railroads, size of marshalling yards, and so forth. You know." (I did, vaguely. But I wasn't a War College graduate. He is.) "That city just doesn't have the transportation facilities to be any bigger than that. Get much over three quarters of a million and they'd starve. Until they double their tracks and increase their yards they can't risk a bigger population. You don't do that over night. They can pick up some slack with the river—but it doesn't go where they need it most."

And there it stands. Either all three of us are crazy despite the fact that all three of us got the same answer to a numerical question using three entirely different but logical methods . . . or for many, many years the Kremlin lie factory has peddled their biggest and fanciest "Pravda" without ever being questioned.

Look—both the Pentagon and the State Department know exactly how big Moscow is, and the Kremlin knows that they know. We were high-flying 'em with the U-2 for four years; you can bet Moscow was carefully photographed many times. Our present Eye-in-the-Sky satellites are so sharp-eyed that they can come close to reading the license plate on your car; our top officials *know precisely what the logistics situation is for Moscow—and every economist knows that one of the parameters that controls strictly the upper limit to the size of a city is how many tons of food it can ship in, week in and week out, never failing. Most big cities are only a day or two away from hunger, only a week or so away from beginning starvation and panic.*

Moscow isn't even a seaport; she's a riverport and not a good one. Most food must come overland by train or lorry.

Maybe she's built enough more facilities since 1960 . . . but in 1960 she just didn't have what it takes. Since I can't believe the 5,000,000+ figure for 1960, I don't believe the 7,000,000+ figure for this year.

I have one very wild theory. Our State Department may see no advantage in calling them liars on this point. Through several administrations we have been extremely careful not to hurt their feelings. I think this is a mistake . . . but I am neither president nor secretary of state; my opinion is not important and may be wrong.

(" 'But the Emperor is not wearing any clothes,' said the child.")

The three biggest lies in the USA today:
1) The check is in the mail.
2) I gave at the office.
3) (Big, cheery smile) "Hello! I'm from Washington. I'm here to help you!"

—Anon.

FOREWORD

In April 1962 I received a letter from the advertising agents of Hoffman Electronics: They had a wonderful idea—SF stories about electronics, written by well-known SF writers, just long enough to fill one column of Scientific American *or* Technology Review *or such*, with the other two thirds of the page an ad for Hoffman Electronics tied into the gimmick of the story. For this they offered a gee-whiz word rate—compared with SF magazines.

A well-wrought short story is twice as hard to write as a novel; a short-short is at least eight times as hard—but one that *short* . . . there are much easier ways of making a living. I dropped them a postcard saying, "Thanks·but I'm busy on a novel." (True—*GLORY ROAD*)

They upped the ante. This time I answered, "Thanks and I feel flattered—but I don't know anything about electronics." (Almost true.)

They wrote back offering expert advice from Hoffman's engineers on the gimmick—and a word rate six times as high as The Saturday Evening Post *had paid me.*

I had finished *GLORY ROAD;* I sat down and drafted this one—then sweated endlessly to get it under 1200 words as required by contract. Whereas I had written *GLORY ROAD* in 23 days and enjoyed every minute of it. This is why lazy writers prefer novels.

SEARCHLIGHT

"Will she hear you?"

"If she's on this face of the Moon. If she was able to get out of the ship. If her suit radio wasn't damaged. If she has it turned on. If she is alive. Since the ship is silent and no radar beacon has been spotted, it is unlikely that she or the pilot lived through it."

"She's got to be found! Stand by, Space Station. Tycho Base, acknowledge."

Reply lagged about three seconds, Washington to Moon and back. "Lunar Base, Commanding General."

"General, put every man on the Moon out searching for Betsy!"

Speed-of-light lag made the answer sound grudging. "Sir, do you know how big the Moon is?"

"No matter! Betsy Barnes is there somewhere—so every man is to search until she is found. If she's dead, your precious pilot would be better off dead, too!"

"Sir, the Moon is almost fifteen million square miles. If I used every man I have, each would have over a thousand square miles to search. I gave Betsy my best pilot. I won't listen to threats against him when he can't answer back. Not from anyone, sir! I'm sick of being told what to do by people who don't know Lunar conditions. My advice—my official advice, sir—is to let Meridian Station try. Maybe they can work a miracle."

The answer rapped back, "Very well, General! I'll

speak to you later. Meridian Station! Report your plans."

Elizabeth Barnes, "Blind Betsy," child genius of the piano, had been making a USO tour of the Moon. She "wowed 'em" at Tycho Base, then lifted by jeep rocket for Farside Hardbase, to entertain our lonely missile-men behind the Moon. She should have been there in an hour. Her pilot was a safety pilot; such ships shut-tled unpiloted between Tycho and Farside daily.

After lift-off her ship departed from its program-ming, was lost by Tycho's radars. It was . . . some-where.

Not in space, else it would be radioing for help and its radar beacon would be seen by other ships, space stations, surface bases. It had crashed—or made emer-gency landing—somewhere on the vastness of Luna.

"Meridian Space Station, Director speaking—" Lag was unnoticeable; radio bounce between Washington and the station only 22,300 miles up was only a quarter second. "We've patched Earthside stations to blanket the Moon with our call. Another broadcast blankets the far side from Station Newton at the three-body stable position. Ships from Tycho are orbiting the Moon's rim—that band around the edge which is in radio shadow from us and from the Newton. If we hear—"

"Yes, yes! How about radar search?"

"Sir, a rocket on the surface looks to radar like a million other features the same size. Our one chance is to get them to answer . . . if they can. Ultrahigh-reso-lution radar might spot them in months—but suits worn in those little rockets carry only six hours' air. We are praying they will hear and answer."

"When they answer, you'll slap a radio direction finder on them. Eh?"

"No, sir."

"In God's name, why *not*?"

"Sir, a direction finder is useless for this job. It would tell us only that the signal came from the Moon—which doesn't help."

"Doctor, you're saying that you might *hear* Betsy— and not know where she is?"

"We're as blind as she is. We hope that she will be able to lead us to her . . . if she hears us."

"How?"

"With a laser. An intense, very tight beam of light. She'll hear it—"

"*Hear* a beam of light?"

"Yes, sir. We are jury-rigging to scan like radar— that won't show anything. But we are modulating it to give a carrier wave in radio frequency, then modulating that into audio frequency—and controlling that by a piano. If she hears us, we'll tell her to listen while we scan the Moon and run the scale on the piano—"

"All this while a little girl is *dying*?"

"Mister President—*shut up!*"

"*Who was THAT?*"

"I'm Betsy's father. They've patched me from Omaha. *Please*, Mr. President, keep quiet and let them work. I want my daughter back."

The President answered tightly, "Yes, Mr. Barnes. Go ahead, Director. Order anything you need."

In Station Meridian the Director wiped his face. "Getting anything?"

"No. Boss, can't something be done about that Rio Station? It's sitting right on the frequency!"

"We'll drop a brick on them. Or a bomb. Joe, tell the President."

"I heard, Director. They'll be silenced!"

"*Sh!* Quiet! Betsy—do you hear me?" The operator looked intent, made an adjustment.

From a speaker came a girl's light, sweet voice: "—to hear somebody! Gee, I'm glad! Better come quick—the Major is hurt."

The Director jumped to the microphone. "Yes, Betsy, we'll hurry. You've got to help us. Do you know where you are?"

"Somewhere on the Moon, I guess. We bumped hard and I was going to kid him about it when the ship fell over. I got unstrapped and found Major Peters and he isn't moving. Not dead—I don't think so; his suit puffs out like mine and I hear something when I push my helmet against him. I just now managed to get the door open." She added, "This can't be Farside; it's supposed to be night there. I'm in sunshine, I'm sure. This suit is pretty hot."

"Betsy, you must stay outside. You've got to be where you can see us."

She chuckled. "That's a good one. I see with my ears."

"Yes. You'll see us, with your ears. Listen, Betsy. We're going to scan the Moon with a beam of light. You'll hear it as a piano note. We've got the Moon split into the eighty-eight piano notes. When you hear one, yell, 'Now!' Then tell us what note you heard. Can you do that?"

"Of course," she said confidently, "if the piano is in tune."

"It is. All right, we're starting—"

"Now!"

"What note, Betsy?"

"E flat the first octave above middle C."

"This note, Betsy?"

"That's what I said."

The Director called out, "Where's that on the grid? In Mare Nubium? Tell the General!" He said to the microphone, "We're finding you, Betsy honey! Now we scan just that part you're on. We change setup. Want to talk to your Daddy meanwhile?"

"Gosh! Could I?"

"Yes indeed!"

Twenty minutes later the Director cut in and heard:

"—of course not, Daddy. Oh, a teensy bit scared when the ship fell. But people take care of me, always have."

"Betsy?"

"Yes, sir?"

"Be ready to tell us again."

"Now!" She added, "That's a bullfrog G, three octaves down."

"This note?"

"That's right."

"Get that on the grid and tell the General to get his ships up! That cuts it to a square ten miles on a side! Now, Betsy—we know *almost* where you are. We are going to focus still closer. Want to go inside and cool off?"

"I'm not too hot. Just sweaty."

Forty minutes later the General's voice rang out: "They've spotted the ship! *They see her waving!*"

AFTERWORD

In 1931 I was serving in *LEXINGTON (CV-2)*. In March the Fleet held a war game off the coast of Peru and Ecuador; for this exercise I was assigned as radio compass officer. My principal duty was to keep in touch with the plane guards, amphibians (OL8-A), guarding squadrons we had in the air—i.e., the squadrons were carrier-based land planes; if one was forced to ditch, an amphibian was to land on the water and rescue the pilot.

No radar in those days and primitive radio—the pilots of the plane guards were the only ones I could talk to via the radio compass. The fighters had dot-dash gear; the radio compass did not. To get a feeling for the limitations of those days, only 28 years after the Wright brothers' first flight, see my *"The Man Who Was Too Lazy to Fail"* in Time Enough For Love, *Putnam/Berkley/NEL*.

A radio compass depends on the directional qualities of a loop antenna. To talk you rotate the antenna for maximum signal; turn it 90° and you get a minimum signal that marks the direction of the other radio—or 180° from it but you are assumed to know whether your beacon is ahead or behind you—and you do in almost every case where it matters, such as going up a channel in a fog. That minimum will tell you direction within a degree or two if the other radio is close enough, loud enough.

If it's too far away, the signal can fade to zero before you reach the bearing you need to read, and stay zero until well past it. No use turning it back 90° to try to locate it by the maximum signal; that curve is much too flat.

Late afternoon the second day of the exercise we were in trouble; the other squadrons were landing but VF-2 squadron was lost—all too easy with one-man fighter planes before the days of radar. The captain of the squadron, a lieutenant commander, held one opinion; the pilot of the amphib held another—but his opinion did not count; he was a j.g. and not part of the squadron. The *juniors in the squadron hardly had opinions; they were young, green, and depending on their skipper—and probably had fouled up their dead reckoning early in the flight.*

The squadron captain vectored for rendezvous with the carrier, by his reckoning. No carrier. Just lots and lots of ocean. (I was in the air once, off Hawaii, when this happened. It's a lonely feeling.)

No sign of the U.S. Fleet. No SARATOGA (CV-3), no battleships, no cruisers. Not even a destroyer scouting a flank. Just water.

At this point I found myself in exactly the situation described in SEARCHLIGHT; I could talk to the plane guard pilot quite easily—but swing the loop 90° and zero signal was spread through such a wide arc that it meant nothing . . . and, worse, the foulup in navigation was such that there was no rational choice between the two lobes 180° apart.

And I had a personal interest not as strong as that of Betsy Barnes' father but strong. First, it was my duty and my responsibility to give that squadron a homing vector—and I couldn't do it; the equipment wasn't up to it. Had I kept track of vectors on that squadron all day— But that was impossible; Not only had I had four squadrons in the air all day and only one loop but also (and damning) there was war-game radio silence until the squadron commander in trouble was forced to break it.

But, second, the pilot of the plane guard was my closest friend in that ship—from my home town, at the Academy with me, shipmates before then in USS UTAH, shore-leave drinking companion, only other officer in the ship who believed in rocketry and space flight and read "those crazy magazines." My number-one pal—

And I was forced to tell him: "Bud, you're either somewhere northeast of us, give or take twenty or thirty degrees, or somewhere southwest, same wide range of error, and signal strength shows that you must be at least fifty miles over the horizon, probably more; I've got no way to scale the reception."

Bud chuckled. "That's a lot of ocean."

"How much gas do you have?"

"Maybe forty minutes. Most of the fighters don't have as much. Hold the phone; the skipper's calling me."

So I tried again for a minimum—no luck—swung back. "Lex loop to Victor Fox Two guard."

"Gotcha, boy. Skipper says we all ditch before the sun goes down. First I land, then they ditch as close to me as possible. I'll have hitchhikers clinging to the float all night long—be lucky if they don't swamp me."

"What sea?"

"Beaufort three, crowding four."

"Cripes. No white water here at all. Just long swells."

"She'll take it, she's tough. But I'm glad not to have to dead-stick a galloping goose. Gotta sign off; skipper wants me, it's time. Been nice knowing you."

So at last I knew—too late—which lobe they were in, as it was already dark with the suddenness of the tropics where I was, whereas the sun was still to set where they were. That eliminated perhaps five hundred square miles. But it placed them still farther away . . . which added at least a thousand square miles.

Suddenly out of the darkness endless searchlights shot straight up; the Fleet C-in-C had canceled war-condition darken-ship rather than let Victor Fox Two ditch—which was pretty nice of him because all those battleship admirals were veterans of World War One, not one of them had wings, and (with no exceptions worth noting) they hated airplanes, did not believe that planes were good for anything but scouting (if that), and despised pilots, especially those who had not attended the Academy (i.e., most of them).

I was still listening on Bud's frequency and heard some most prayerful profanity. At once Bud had a bearing on the battle line; our navigator had our bearing and distance to the battle line; my talker to the bridge gave me the course and distance VF-2 needed to home on, and I passed it to Bud. End of crisis—

—but not quite the end of tension. The squadron just barely had enough gas to get home, and more than half of those pilots had never checked out on night carrier landings . . . with no margin of fuel to let the landing officer wave a man off for poor approach if there was any possible chance that his tail hook could catch a wire. I am happy to report that every pilot got down safely although one did sort of bend his prop around the crash barrier.

Bud did almost have to make a dead-stick landing with a galloping goose. As he was the only one who could land on water if necessary, he had to come in last . . . and his engine coughed and died just as his tail hook caught the wire.

In one of Jack Williamson's stories a character goes back in time and makes a very slight change in order to effect a major change in later history.

Bud is Albert Buddy Scoles, then a lieutenant (junior grade), now a retired rear admiral, and is the officer who in 1942 gathered me, Isaac Asimov, and L. Sprague de Camp into his R&D labs at Mustin Field, Philadelphia, later solicited help from all technically trained SF writers and, still later, just after World War Two, set up the Navy's first guided missile range at Point Mugu.

I do not assume that history would have changed appreciably had VF-2 been forced to ditch.

But let's assume a change in Buddy Scoles' career just sufficient that he would not have been in charge of those labs on 7 December 1941. It would not have to be his death—although he was in far greater danger than his cheerful attitude admitted. An amphibian of that era did not necessarily make a safe landing on the high seas, and the galloping goose was an awkward beast at best—hard to see out of it in landing. Assume a minor injury in landing, or several days' exposure to tropical sun—that's a big ocean; they would not necessarily have been picked up the next day or even that week.

Assume any one change that would have affected the pattern of Buddy Scoles' career enough to place him elsewhere than at Mustin Field December 1941:

Now let's take it in small, not in terms of history:

I would not have been at Mustin Field. I can't venture to guess where I would have been; the Navy Bureau of Medicine was being stuffy over my past medical history. I would not have met my wife; therefore I would have died at least ten years ago . . . and I would not be writing this book. (All high probabilities. Among the low probabilities is winning the Irish Sweepstakes and moving to Monaco.)

Sprague de Camp would not have been at Mustin Field. He was already headed for a Naval commission but at my suggestion Scoles grabbed him. Perhaps he would have died gloriously in battle . . . or he might have sat out the war in a swivel chair in the Navy Department.

But now I reach the important one. I practically kidnapped Isaac Asimov from Columbia University, where he was a graduate student bucking for his doctorate.

You can write endless scenarios from there. The Manhattan District is recruiting exceptionally bright graduate students in chemistry and physics; Isaac is grabbed and the A-bomb is thereby finished a year sooner. Or he stays on at Columbia, finishes his doctorate, and his draft board never does pick him up because he is already signed as an assistant professor at N.Y.U. the day he is invested. Etc., etc.

Here comes the rabbit— The first two books of the Foundation series (Foundation, Bridle and Saddle, The Big and the Little, The Wedge, Dead Hand, The Mule) *were written while Isaac was a chemist in the labs at Mustin Field.*

What would the Good Doctor have written during those years had I not fiddled with his karma? Exactly the same stories? Very similar stories? Entirely different stories? (Any scenario is plausible except one in which Dr. Asimov does no writing at all.)

All I feel sure of is that there is an extremely high prob-

ability that an almost-too-late decision by a battle-ship admiral in 1931 not only saved the lives of some fighter pilots whose names I do not know ... but also almost certainly changed the lives of Admiral Scoles, myself, L. Sprague de Camp, Dr. Asimov and, by direct concatenation, the lives of wives, sweethearts, and offspring—and quite a major chunk of modern science fiction. (Had Scoles not called me back to Philadelphia I think I would have wound up in a Southern California aircraft factory, and possibly stayed with it instead of going back to writing ... and helped build Apollo-Saturn. Maybe.)

If you think SEARCHLIGHT derives from an incident off Ecuador, you may be right. Possibly I dredged it out of my subconscious and did not spot it until later.

On 5 April 1973 I delivered the James Forrestal Memorial Lecture to the Brigade of Midshipmen at my alma mater the United States Naval Academy. As the first half of the lecture, at the request of the midshipmen, I discussed freelance writing. This is the second half:

On This Site
The Afternoon of June 5th, 1834
Nothing of Any Importance Happened

THE PRAGMATICS OF PATRIOTISM

In this complex world, science, the scientific method, and the consequences of the scientific method are central to everything the human race is doing and to wherever we are going. If we blow ourselves up we will do it by misapplication of science; if we manage to keep from blowing ourselves up, it will be through intelligent application of science. Science fiction is the only form of fiction which takes into account this central force in our lives and futures. Other sorts of fiction, if they notice science at all, simply deplore it—an attitude very chichi in the anti-intellectual atmosphere of today. But we will never get out of the mess we are in by wringing our hands.

Let me make one flat-footed prediction of the science-fiction type. Like all scenarios this one has assumptions—variables treated as constants. The primary assumption is that World War Three will hold off long enough—ten, twenty, thirty years—for this prediction to work out . . . plus a secondary assumption that the human race will not find some other way to blunder into ultimate disaster.

Prediction: In the immediate future—by that I mean in the course of the naval careers of the class of '73—there will be nuclear-powered, constant-boost spaceships—ships capable of going to Mars and back in a couple of weeks—and these ships will be armed with Buck-Rogersish death rays. Despite all treaties now existing or still to be signed concerning the peaceful use of space, these spaceships will be used in warfare. Space navies will change beyond recognition our present methods of warfare and will control the political shape of the world for the foreseeable future. Furthermore—and still more important—these new spaceships will open the Solar System to colonization and will eventually open the rest of this Galaxy.

I did *not* say that the United States will have these ships. The present sorry state of our country does not permit me to make such a prediction. In the words of one of our most distinguished graduates in his *The Influence of Sea Power on History*: "Popular governments are not generally favorable to military expenditures, however necessary—"

Every military officer has had his nose rubbed in the wry truth of Admiral Mahan's observation. I first found myself dismayed by it some forty years ago when I learned that I was expected to maintain the ship's battery of USS ROPER in a state of combat readiness on an allowance of less than a dollar a day—with World War Two staring down our throats.

The United States is capable of developing such spaceships. But the mood today does not favor it. So I am unable to predict that *we* will be the nation to spend the necessary R&D money to build such ships.

(Addressed to a plebe midshipman:)

Mister, how long is it to graduation?

Sixty-two days? Let's make it closer than that. I have . . . 7.59, just short of eight bells. Assuming graduation for ten in the morning that gives . . . 5,320,860 seconds to graduation . . . and I have less than 960 seconds in which to say what I want to say.

(To the Brigade at large:)

Why are you here?

(To a second plebe:)

Mister, why are *you* here?

Never mind, son; that's a rhetorical question. You are here to become a naval officer. That's why this Academy was founded. That is why all of you are here: to become naval officers. If that is *not* why *you* are here, you've made a bad mistake. But I speak to the overwhelming majority who understood the oath they took on becoming midshipmen and look forward to the day when they will renew that oath as commissioned officers.

But why would anyone want to become a naval officer?

In the present dismal state of our culture there is little prestige attached to serving your country; recent public opinion polls place military service far down the list.

It can't be the pay. No one gets rich on Navy pay. Even a 4-star admiral is paid much less than top executives in other lines. As for lower ranks the typical naval officer finds himself throughout his career just catching up from the unexpected expenses connected with the last change of duty when another change of duty causes a new financial crisis. Then, when he is about fifty, he is passed over and retires . . . but he can't really retire because he has two kids in college and one still to go. So he has to find a job . . . and discovers that jobs for men his age are scarce and usually don't pay well.

Working conditions? You'll spend half your life away from your family. Your working hours? "Six days shalt thou work and do all thou art able; the seventh the same, and pound on the cable." A forty-hour week is standard for civilians—but not for naval officers. You'll work that forty-hour week but that's just a starter. You'll stand a night watch as well, and duty weekends. Then with every increase in grade your hours get longer—until at last you get a ship of your own and no longer stand watches. Instead you are on duty twenty-four hours a day . . . and you'll sign your night order book with: "In case of doubt, do not hesitate to call me."

I don't know the average week's work for a naval officer but it is closer to sixty than to forty. I'm speaking of peacetime, of course. Under war conditions it is whatever hours are necessary—and sleep you grab when you can.

Why would anyone elect a career which is unappreciated, overworked, and underpaid? It can't be just to wear a pretty uniform. There has to be a better reason.

As one drives through the bushveldt of East Africa it is easy to spot herds of baboons grazing on the ground. But not by looking at the ground. Instead you look up and spot the lookout, an adult male posted on a limb of a tree where he has a clear view all around him— which is why you can spot him; he has to be where he can see a leopard in time to give the alarm. On the ground a leopard can catch a baboon . . . but if a baboon is warned in time to reach the trees, he can outclimb a leopard.

The lookout is a young male assigned to that duty and there he will stay, until the bull of the herd sends up another male to relieve him.

Keep your eye on that baboon; we'll be back to him.

Today, in the United States, it is popular among self-styled "intellectuals" to sneer at patriotism. They seem to think that it is axiomatic that any civilized man is a pacifist, and they treat the military profession with contempt. "Warmongers"—"Imperialists"— "Hired killers in uniform"—you have all heard such sneers and you will hear them again. One of their favorite quotations is: "Patriotism is the last refuge of a scoundrel."

What they never mention is that the man who made that sneering wisecrack was a fat, gluttonous slob who was pursued all his life by a pathological fear of death.

I propose to prove that that baboon on watch is morally superior to that fat poltroon who made that wise-crack.

Patriotism is the most practical of all human characteristics.

But in the present decadent atmosphere patriots are often too shy to talk about it—as if it were something shameful or an irrational weakness.

But patriotism is *not* sentimental nonsense. Nor something dreamed up by demagogues. Patriotism is as necessary a part of man's evolutionary equipment as are his eyes, as useful to the race as eyes are to the individual.

A man who is *not* patriotic is an evolutionary dead end. This is not sentiment but the hardest sort of logic.

To prove that patriotism is a necessity we must go back to fundamentals. Take any breed of animal—for example, tyrannosaurus rex. What is the most basic thing about him? The answer is that tyrannosaurus rex is dead, gone, extinct.

Now take homo sapiens. The first fact about him is that he is not extinct, he is alive.

Which brings us to the second fundamental question: Will homo sapiens stay alive? Will he survive?

We can answer part of that at once: Individually h. sapiens will *not* survive. It is unlikely that anyone here tonight will be alive eighty years from now; it approaches mathematical certainty that we will all be dead a hundred years from now as even the youngest plebe here would be 118 years old then—if still alive.

Some men do live that long but the percentage is so microscopic as not to matter. Recent advances in biology suggest that human life may be extended to a century and a quarter, even a century and a half—but this will create more problems than it solves. When a man reaches my age or thereabouts, the last great service he can perform is to die and get out of the way of younger people.

Very well, as individuals we all die. This brings us

to the second half of the question: Does homo sapiens *as a breed* have to die? The answer is: No, it is *not* unavoidable.

We have two situations, mutually exclusive: Mankind surviving, and mankind extinct. With respect to morality, the second situation is a null class. An extinct breed has *no* behavior, moral or otherwise.

Since survival is the sine qua non, I now define "moral behavior" as "behavior that tends toward survival." I won't argue with philosophers or theologians who choose to use the word "moral" to mean something else, but I do not think anyone can define "behavior that tends toward extinction" as being "moral" without stretching the word "moral" all out of shape.

We are now ready to observe the hierarchy of moral behavior from its lowest level to its highest.

The simplest form of moral behavior occurs when a man or other animal fights for his own survival. Do not belittle such behavior as being merely selfish. Of course it is selfish . . . but selfishness is the bedrock on which all moral behavior starts and it can be immoral only when it conflicts with a higher moral imperative. An animal so poor in spirit that he won't even fight on his own behalf is already an evolutionary dead end; the best he can do for his breed is to crawl off and die, and not pass on his defective genes.

The next higher level is to work, fight, and sometimes die for your own immediate family. This is the level at which six pounds of mother cat can be so fierce that she'll drive off a police dog. It is the level at which a father takes a moonlighting job to keep his kids in college—and the level at which a mother or father dives into a flood to save a drowning child . . . and it is still moral behavior even when it fails.

The next higher level is to work, fight, and sometimes die for a group larger than the unit family—an extended family, a herd, a tribe—and take another look at that baboon on watch; he's at that moral level. I don't think baboon language is complex enough to permit them to discuss such abstract notions as "morality" or "duty" or "loyalty"—but it is evident that baboons *do* operate morally and *do* exhibit the traits of duty and loyalty; we see them in action. Call it "instinct" if you like—but remember that assigning a name to a phenomenon does not explain it.

But that baboon behavior can be explained in evolutionary terms. Evolution is a process that never stops. Baboons who fail to exhibit moral behavior do not survive; they wind up as meat for leopards. Every baboon generation has to pass this examination in moral behavior; those who bilge it don't have progeny. Perhaps the old bull of the tribe gives lessons . . . but the leopard decides who graduates—and there is no appeal from his decision. We don't have to understand the details to observe the outcome: Baboons behave morally—for baboons.

The next level in moral behavior higher than that exhibited by the baboon is that in which duty and loyalty are shown toward a group of your own kind too large for an individual to know all of them. We have a name for that. It is called "patriotism."

Behaving on a still higher moral level were the astronauts who went to the Moon, for their actions tend toward the survival of the entire race of mankind. The door they opened leads to the hope that h. sapiens will survive indefinitely long, even longer than this solid planet on which we stand tonight. As a direct result of what they did, it is now possible that the human race will *never* die.

Many short-sighted fools think that going to the Moon was just a stunt. But the astronauts knew the meaning of what they were doing, as is shown by Neil Armstrong's first words in stepping down onto the soil of Luna: "One small step for a man, one giant leap for mankind."

Let us note proudly that eleven of the Astronaut Corps are graduates of this our school.

And let me add that James Forrestal was the *first*

high-ranking Federal official to come out flatly for space travel.

I must pause to brush off those parlor pacifists I mentioned earlier . . . for they contend that *their* actions are on this highest moral level. They want to put a stop to war; they say so. Their purpose is to save the human race from killing itself off; they say that too. Anyone who disagrees with them must be a bloodthirsty scoundrel—and they'll tell you that to your face.

I won't waste time trying to judge their motives; my criticism is of their mental processes: Their heads aren't screwed on tight. They live in a world of fantasy.

Let me stipulate that, if the human race managed its affairs sensibly, we could do without war.

Yes—and if pigs had wings, they could fly.

I don't know what planet those pious pacifists are talking about but it can't be the third one out from the Sun. Anyone who has seen the Far East—or Africa—or the Middle East—knows or certainly should know that there is *no* chance of abolishing war in the foreseeable future. In the past few years I have been around the world three times, traveled in most of the communist countries, visited many of the so-called emerging countries, plus many trips to Europe and to South America; I saw nothing that cheered me as to the prospects for peace. The seeds of war are everywhere; the conflicts of interest are real and deep, and will not be abolished by pious platitudes.

The best we can hope for is a precarious balance of power among the nations capable of waging total war—while endless lesser wars break out here and there.

I won't belabor this. Our campuses are loaded with custard-headed pacifists but the yard of the Naval Academy is one place where I will not encounter them. We are in agreement that the United States still needs a navy, that the Republic will always have need for heroes—else you would not be here tonight and in uniform.

Patriotism— Moral behavior at the national level. Non sibi sed Patria. Nathan Hale's last words: "I regret that I have but one life to give for my country." Torpedo Squadron Eight making its suicidal attack. Four chaplains standing fast while the water rises around them. Thomas Jefferson saying, "The Tree of Liberty must be refreshed from time to time with the blood of patriots—" A submarine skipper giving the order "Take her *down*!" while he himself is still topside. Jonas Ingram standing on the steps of Bancroft Hall and shouting, "The Navy has no place for good losers! The Navy needs tough sons of bitches who can go out there and *win*!"

Patriotism— An abstract word used to describe a type of behavior as harshly practical as good brakes and good tires. It means that you place the welfare of your nation ahead of your own even if it costs you your life.

Men who go down to the sea in ships have long had another way of expressing the same moral behavior tagged by the abstract expression "patriotism." Spelled out in simple Anglo-Saxon words "Patriotism" reads "Women and children first!"

And that is the moral result of realizing a self-evident biological fact: Men are expendable; women and children are not. A tribe or a nation can lose a high percentage of its men and still pick up the pieces and go on . . . as long as the women and children are saved. But if you fail to save the women and children, you've had it, you're done, you're *through*! You join tyrannosaurus rex, one more breed that bilged its final test.

I must amplify that. I know that women can fight and often have. I have known many a tough old grandmother I would rather have at my side in a tight spot than any number of pseudo-males who disdain military service. My wife put in three years and a butt active duty in World War Two, plus ten years reserve, and I am proud—very proud!—of her naval service. I am proud of every one of our women in uniform; they are a shining example to us men.

Nevertheless, as a mathematical proposition in the facts of biology, children, and women of child-bearing age, are the ultimate treasure that we must save. Every human culture is based on "Women and children first"—and any attempt to do it any other way leads quickly to extinction.

Possibly extinction is the way we are headed. Great nations have died in the past; it can happen to us.

Nor am I certain how good our chances are. To me it seems self-evident that any nation that loses its patriotic fervor is on the skids. Without that indispensable survival factor the end is only a matter of time. I don't know how deeply the rot has penetrated—but it seems to me that there has been a change for the worse in the last fifty years. Possibly I am misled by the offensive behavior of a noisy but unimportant minority. But it does seem to me that patriotism has lost its grip on a large percentage of our people.

I hope I am wrong . . . because if my fears are well grounded, I would not bet two cents on this nation's chance of lasting even to the end of this century.

But there is no way to force patriotism on anyone. Passing a law will not create it, nor can we buy it by appropriating so many billions of dollars.

You gentlemen of the Brigade are most fortunate. You are going to a school where this basic moral virtue is daily reinforced by precept and example. It is not enough to know what Charlie Noble does for a living, or what makes the wildcat wild, or which BatDiv failed to splice the main brace and why—nor to learn matrix algebra and navigation and ballistics and aerodynamics and nuclear engineering. These things are merely the working tools of your profession and could be learned elsewhere; they do not require "four years together by the Bay where Severn joins the tide."

What you do have here is a tradition of service. Your most important classroom is Memorial Hall. Your most important lesson is the way you feel inside when you walk up those steps and see that shot-torn flag framed in the arch of the door: "Don't Give Up the Ship."

If you feel nothing, you don't belong here. But if it gives you goose flesh just to see that old battle flag, then you are going to find that feeling increasing every time you return here over the years . . . until it reaches a crescendo the day you return and read the list of your own honored dead—classmates, shipmates, friends—read them with grief and pride while you try to keep your tears silent.

The time has come for me to stop. I said that "Patriotism" is a way of saying "Women and children first." And that no one can force a man to feel this way. Instead he must embrace it freely. I want to tell about one such man. He wore no uniform and no one knows his name, or where he came from; all we know is what he did.

In my home town sixty years ago when I was a child, my mother and father used to take me and my brothers and sisters out to Swope Park on Sunday afternoons. It was a wonderful place for kids, with picnic grounds and lakes and a zoo. But a railroad line cut straight through it.

One Sunday afternoon a young married couple were crossing these tracks. She apparently did not watch her step, for she managed to catch her foot in the frog of a switch to a siding and could not pull it free. Her husband stopped to help her.

But try as they might they could not get her foot loose. While they were working at it, a tramp showed up, walking the ties. He joined the husband in trying to pull the young woman's foot loose. No luck—

Out of sight around the curve a train whistled. Perhaps there would have been time to run and flag it down, perhaps not. In any case both men went right ahead trying to pull her free . . . and the train hit them.

The wife was killed, the husband was mortally injured and died later, the tramp was killed—and testimony showed that neither man made the slightest effort to save himself.

The husband's behavior was heroic . . . but what we expect of a husband toward his wife: his right, and his proud privilege, to die for his woman. But what of this nameless stranger? Up to the very last second he could have jumped clear. He did not. He was still trying to save this woman he had never seen before in his life, right up to the very instant the train killed him. And that's all we'll ever know about him.

This is how a man dies.

This is how a *man* . . . lives!

> "They shall not grow old
>   as we that are left grow old,
>   age shall not wither them
>   nor the years condemn;
> At the going down of the sun
>   and in the morning,
>   we shall remember them . . ."

> —Tomb of the
>   Scottish Unknown Soldier
>   Edinburgh

PAUL DIRAC, ANTIMATTER, AND YOU

A Riddle

What have these in common?

1. 1926: A graduate student, Cambridge University
2. Billions of years ago: Quasars exploding
3. 1908: A Siberian forest devastated
4. 10 million years ago: A galaxy exploding
5. 1932: A cloud-chamber track, Pasadena, Calif.

Answer: All may, and 1 and 5 *do* involve antimatter. (*ANTI* matter?)

Yes—like ordinary matter with electrical properties of particles reversed. Each atom of matter is one or more nucleons surrounded by one or more electrons; charges add up to zero. A hydrogen atom has a proton with positive charge as nucleus, surrounded by an electron with negative charge. A proton is 1836.11 times as massive as an electron, but their charges are equal and opposite: $+1 \ -1 \ = \ 0$. Uranium-235 (or $_{92}U^{235}$, meaning "an isotope of element 92, uranium, nuclear weight 235") has 235 nucleons: 143 neutrons of zero charge and 92 protons of positive charge ($143 + 92 = 235$; hence its name); these 235 are surrounded by 92 electrons (negative), so total charge is zero: 0

Portrait of Paul Dirac by Stephen Fabian.

$+92-92 = 0$. (Nuclear weight is never zero, being the mass of all the nucleons.)

Make electrons positive, protons negative: charges still balance; nuclear weight is unchanged—but it is *not* an atom of matter; it is an antiatom of antimatter.

"Touch Me Not!"

In an antimatter world, antimatter behaves like matter. Bread dough rises, weapons kill, kisses still taste sweet. You would be antimatter and not notice it.

WARNING! Since your body is matter (else you could not be reading this), *don't* kiss an antimatter girl. You both would explode with violence unbelievable.

But you'll never meet one, nor will your grandchildren. (I'm not sure about *their* grandchildren.)

$E = mc^2$

Antimatter is no science-fiction nightmare; it's as real as Texas. That Cambridge graduate student was Paul A. M. Dirac inventing new mathematics to merge Albert Einstein's special theory of relativity with Max Planck's quantum theory. Both theories worked—but conflicted. Dirac sought to merge them without conflict.

He succeeded.

His equations were published in 1928, and from them, in 1930, he made an incredible prediction: each sort of particle had antiparticles of opposite charge: "antimatter."

Scientists have their human foibles; a scientist can grow as fond of his world concept as a cat of its "own" chair. By 1930 the cozy 19th-century "world" of physics had been repeatedly outraged. This ridiculous new assault insulted all common sense.

But in 1932 at the California Institute of Technology, Carl D. Anderson photographed proof of the electron's antiparticle (named "positron" for its positive charge but otherwise twin to the electron). Radical theory has seldom been confirmed so quickly or re-

Courtesy California Institute of Technology and Carnegie Institution of Washington

A photograph taken in 1932 by Carl D. Anderson through the glass wall of a wilson cloud chamber at the California Institute of Technology, provided the first proof of the existence of an antiparticle. Using a lead plate (viewed edge on as the vertical band in photo) to slow down the rapidly moving particle and thereby increase the curvature (caused by an applied magnetic field of known strength and polarity) of its track, Anderson first determined from the leftward movement that the particle was positively charged like a proton. Calculations based on the degree of the track's arc and magnetic field strength, however, revealed the particle's mass to be that of an electron. The particle tracked was therefore a positively charged electron — an antiparticle, or "positron" as Anderson called.

warded so promptly: Dirac received the Nobel prize in 1933, Anderson in 1936—each barely 31 years of age when awarded it.

Since 1932 so many sorts of antiparticles have been detected that no doubt remains: antimatter matches matter in every sort of particle. Matching is not always as simple as electron (e-) and positron (e+). Photons are their own antiparticles. Neutrons and neutrinos (zero charges) are matched by antineutrons and antineutrinos, also of zero charge—this sounds like meaningless redundancy because English is not appropriate language; abstract mathematics is the language required for precise statements in physical theory. (Try writing the score of a symphony solely in words *with no musical symbols whatever*.)

But a hint lies in noting that there are reaction series in which protons and electrons yield neutrons—one example: the *soi-disant* "Solar Phoenix" (solar power theory, Hans Bethe); if we ignore details, the Solar Phoenix can be summarized as changing four hydrogen atoms (four of $_1H^1$) into one helium atom ($_2H^4$). We start with four protons and four electrons; we end up six stages later with two neutrons, two protons, and two electrons—and that is neither precise nor adequate and is not an equation and ignores other isotopes involved, creation of positrons, release of energy through mutual annihilations of positrons and free electrons, and several other features, plus the fact that this transformation can occur by a variety of routes.

(But such are the booby traps of English or *any* verbal language where abstract mathematics is the *only* correct language.)

A wide variety of other transformations permits antiprotons and positrons to yield antineutrons. The twin types of varieties of transformations mentioned above are simply samples; there are many other types being both predicted mathematically and detected in the laboratories almost daily—and many or most transformation series involve antiparticles of antimatter.

Nevertheless, antimatter is scarce in our corner of the universe—lucky for us because, when matter encounters antimatter, *both* explode in total annihilation. $E = mc^2$ is known to everyone since its awful truth was demonstrated at Hiroshima, Japan. It states that energy is equivalent to mass, mass to energy, in this relation: energy equals mass times the square of the velocity of light in empty space.

That velocity is almost inconceivable. In blasting for the moon our astronauts reached nearly 7 miles/second; light travels almost 27,000 times that speed—186,282.4 (± 0.1) miles or 299,792.5 (± 0.15) kilometers each second. Round off that last figure as 300,000; then use the compatible units of science (grams, centimeters, ergs) and write in centimeters 3×10^{10}, then square it: 9×10^{20}, or 900,000,000,000,000,000,000. (!!!)

This fantastic figure shouts that a tiny mass can become a monstrous blast of energy—grim proof: Hiroshima.

But maximum possible efficiency of U^{235} fission is about 1/10 of 1%; the Hiroshima bomb's actual efficiency was much lower, and H-bomb fusion has still lower maximum (H-bombs can be more powerful through having no limit on size; all fission bombs have sharp limits). But fission or fusion, almost all the reacting mass splits or combines into other elements; only a trifle becomes energy.

In matter-antimatter reaction, however, *all* of *both* become energy. An engineer might say "200% efficient" as antimatter undergoing annihilation converts into raw energy an equal mass of matter.

Mathematical Physicists

An experimental physicist uses expensive giant accelerators to shoot particles at 99.9%+ of the speed of light, or sometimes gadgets built on his own time with

The world's great theoretical physicist have included (left to right, top to bottom) Nicolaus Copernicus (1473–1543); Johannes Kepler (1571–1630); Sir Isaac Newton (1643–1727); James Clerk Maxwell (1831–1879); Max Planck (1858–1947); Albert Einstein (1879–1955); and Paul A.M. Dirac (1902–   ).

Left to right, top to bottom, courtesy of Yerkes Observatory and the University of Chicago Press; *Archiv für Kunst und Geschichte*; National Portrait Gallery, London; National Portrait Gallery, London; *EB Inc.*; German Information Center.

scrounged materials. Large or small, cheap or costly, he works with *things*.

A mathematical physicist uses pencil, paper, and brain. Not my brain or yours—unless you are of the rare few with "mathematical intuition."

That's a tag for an unexplainable. It is a gift, not a skill, and cannot be learned or taught. Even advanced mathematics ("advanced" to laymen) such as higher calculus, Fourier analysis, n-dimensional and non-Euclidean geometries are skills requiring only patience and normal intelligence . . . *after* they have been invented by persons having mathematical intuition.

The oft-heard plaint "I can't cope with math!" may mean subnormal intelligence (unlikely), laziness (more likely), or poor teaching (extremely likely). But that plaint usually refers to common arithmetic—a trivial skill in the eyes of a mathematician. (*Creating* it was not trivial. Zero, positional notation, decimal-or-base point all took genius; imagine doing a Form 1040 in Roman numerals.)

Of billions living and dead perhaps a few thousand have been gifted with mathematical intuition; a few hundred have lived in circumstances permitting use of it; a smaller fraction have been mathematical physicists. Of these a few dozen have left permanent marks on physics.

But without these few we would not have science. Mathematical physics is basic to *all* sciences. No exceptions. *None*.

Mathematical physicists sometimes hint that experimentalists are frustrated pipefitters; experimentalists mutter that theoreticians are so lost in fog they need guardians. But they are indispensable to each other. Piling up facts is not science—science is facts-*and*-theories. Facts alone have limited use and lack meaning; a valid theory organizes them into far greater usefulness. To be valid a theory must be confirmed by *all* relevant facts. A "natural law" is theory repeatedly confirmed and drops back to "approximation" when *one* fact contradicts it. Then search resumes for better theory to embrace old facts plus this stubborn new one.

No "natural law" of 500 years ago is "law" today; all our present laws are probably approximations, useful but not perfect. Some scientists, notably Paul Dirac, suspect that perfection is unattainable.

A powerful theory not only embraces old facts and new but also discloses unsuspected facts. These are landmarks of science: Nicolaus Copernicus' heliocentric theory, Johannes Kepler's refining it into conic-sections ballistics, Isaac Newton's laws of motion and theory of universal gravitation, James C. Maxwell's equations linking electricity with magnetism, Planck's quantum theory, Einstein's relativity, Dirac's synthesis of quantum theory and special relativity—a few more, not many.

Mathematical physicists strive to create a mathematical structure interrelating all space-time events, past and future, from infinitesimally small to inconceivably huge and remote in space and time, a "unified field theory" embracing 10 or 20 billion years and light-years, more likely 80 billion or so—or possibly eternity in an infinity of multiple universes.

Some order!

They try. Newton made great strides. So did Einstein. Nearly 50 years ago Dirac brought it closer, has steadily added to it, is working on it today.

Paul Dirac may be and probably is the greatest living theoretical scientist. Dirac, Newton, and Einstein are equals.

Paul A. M. Dirac

The experimentalists' slur about theoretical physicists holds a grain of truth. Newton apparently never noticed the lovely sex in all his years. Einstein ignored such trivialities as socks. One mathematical physicist who swayed World War II could not be trusted with a screwdriver.

Dirac is *not* that sort of man.

Other than genius, his only unusual trait is strong dislike for idle talk. (His Cambridge students coined a unit the *dirac*—one word per light-year.) But he lectures and writes with admirable clarity. Taciturn, he is not unsocial; in 1937 he married a most charming Hungarian lady. They have two daughters and a son.

He can be trusted with tools; he sometimes builds instruments and performs his own experiments. He graduated in engineering before he became a mathematical physicist; this influenced his life. Engineers find working solutions from incomplete data; approximations are close enough if they do the job—too fussy wastes man-hours. But when a job needs it, a true engineer gives his utmost to achieve as near perfection as possible.

Dirac brought this attitude to theoretical physics; his successes justify his approach.

He was born in Bristol, England, Aug. 8, 1902, and named Paul Adrien Maurice Dirac. His precocity in mathematics showed early; his father supplied books and encouraged him to study on his own. Solitary walks and study were the boy's notion of fun—and are of the man today. Dirac works (and plays) hardest by doing and saying *nothing* . . . while his mind roams the universe.

When barely 16 years old, he entered the University of Bristol. At 18 he graduated, bachelor of science in electrical engineering. In 1923 a grant enabled him to return to school at the foremost institution for mathematics, Cambridge University. In three years of study for a doctorate Dirac published 12 papers in mathematical physics, 5 in *The Proceedings of the Royal Society*. A cub with only an engineering degree from a minor university has trouble getting published in *any* journal of science; to appear at the age of 22 in the most highly respected of them all is amazing.

Dirac received his doctorate in May 1926, his dissertation being "Quantum Mechanics"—the stickiest subject in physical science. He tackled it his first year at Cambridge and has continued to unravel its paradoxes throughout his career; out of 123 publications over the last 50 years the word *quantum* can be found 45 times in his titles.

Dirac remained at Cambridge—taught, thought, published. In 1932, the year before his Nobel prize, he received an honor rarer than that prize, one formerly held by Newton: Lucasian professor of mathematics. Dirac kept it 37 years, until he resigned from Cambridge. He accepted other posts during his Cantabrigian years: member of the Institute for Advanced Study at Princeton, N.J., professor of the Dublin Institute for Advanced Studies, visiting professorships here and there.

Intuitive mathematicians often burn out young. Not Dirac!—he is a Michelangelo who started very young, never stopped, is still going strong. Antimatter is not necessarily his contribution most esteemed by colleagues, but his other major ones are so abstruse as to defy putting them into common words:

A mathematical attribute of particles dubbed "spin"; coinvention of the Fermi-Dirac statistics; an abstract mathematical replacement for the "pellucid aether" of classical mechanics. For centuries, ether was used and its "physical reality" generally accepted either as "axiomatic" or "proved" through various negative proofs. Both "axiom" and "negative proof" are treacherous; the 1887 Michelson-Morley experiment showed no physical reality behind the concept of ether, and many variations of that experiment over many years gave the same null results.

So Einstein omitted ether from his treatments of relativity—while less brilliant men ignored the observed facts and clung to classical ether for at least 40 years.

Dirac's ether (circa 1950) is solely abstract mathematics, more useful thereby than classical ether as it avoids the paradoxes of the earlier concepts. Dirac has consistently warned against treating mathematical equations as if they were pictures of something that could be visualized in the way one may visualize the Taj Mahal or a loaf of bread; his equations are *rules* concerning space-time events—*not* pictures.

(This may be the key to his extraordinary successes.)

One more example must represent a long list: Dirac's work on Georges Lemaître's "primeval egg"— later popularized as the "big bang."

Honors also are too many to list in full: fellow of the Royal Society, its Royal Medal, its Copley Medal, honorary degrees (always refused), foreign associate of the American Academy of Sciences, Oppenheimer Memorial Prize, and (most valued by Dirac) Great Britain's Order of Merit.

Dirac "retired" by accepting a research professorship at Florida State University, where he is now working on gravitation theory. In 1937 he had theorized that Newton's "constant of gravitation" was in fact a decreasing variable . . . but the amount of decrease he predicted was so small that it could not be verified in 1937.

Today the decrease can be measured. In July 1974 Thomas C. Van Flandern of the U.S. Naval Observatory reported measurements showing a decrease in gravitation of about a ten-billionth each year (1 per 10^{10} per annum). This amount seems trivial, but it is *very* large in astronomical and geological time. If these findings are confirmed and if they continue to support Dirac's mathematical theory, he will have upset physical science even more than he did in 1928 and 1930.

Here is an incomplete list of the sciences that would undergo radical revision: physics from micro- through astro-, astronomy, geology, paleontology, meteorology, chemistry, cosmology, cosmogony, geogony, ballistics. It is too early to speculate about effects on the life sciences, but we exist inside this physical world and gravitation is the most pervasive feature of our world.

Courtesy Kitt Peak National Observatory

The Nicholas U. Mayall 158-inch reflecting mirror telescope at Arizona's Kitt Peak National Observatory has the widest field of view of any single-mirror telescope, effectively reaching out to the edges of the universe.

Theory of biological evolution would certainly be affected. It is possible that understanding gravitation could result in changes in engineering technology too sweeping easily to be imagined.

Antimatter and You

Of cosmologies there is no end; astrophysicists enjoy "playing God." It's safe fun, too, as the questions are so sweeping, the data so confusing, that any cosmology is hard to prove or disprove. But since 1932 antimatter has been a necessary datum. Many cosmologists feel that the universe (universes?) has as much antimatter as matter—but they disagree over how to balance the two.

Some think that, on the average, every other star in our Milky Way galaxy is antimatter. Others find that setup dangerously crowded—make it every second galaxy. Still others prefer universe-and-antiuniverse with antimatter in ours only on rare occasions when energetic particles collide so violently that some of the energy forms antiparticles. And some like higher numbers of universes—even an unlimited number.

One advantage of light's finite speed is that we can see several eons of the universe in action, rather than just one frame of a *very* long moving picture. Today's instruments reach not only far out into space but also far back into time; this permits us to test in some degree a proposed cosmology. The LST (Large Space Telescope), to be placed in orbit by the Space Shuttle in 1983, will have 20 times the resolving power of the best ground-based and atmosphere-distorted conventional telescope—therefore 20 times the reach, or more than enough to see clear back to the "beginning" by one cosmology, the "big bang."

(Q: What happened *before* the beginning? A: *You* tell *me*.)

When we double that reach—someday we will— what will we see? Empty space? Or the backs of our necks?

(Q: What's this to *me*? A: Patience one moment. . . .)

Currently in the design stage, the LST (Large Space Telescope) is to be orbited in 1983 and is expected to be 20 times more powerful than any current ground-based telescope.

The star nearest ours is a triplet system; one of the three resembles our sun and may have an Earthlike planet—an inviting target for our first attempt to cross interstellar space. Suppose that system is antimatter—*BANG!* Scratch one starship.

(Hooray for Zero Population Growth! To hell with space-travel boondoggles!)

Then consider this: June 30, 1908, a meteor struck Siberia, so blindingly bright in broad daylight that people 1,000 miles away saw it. Its roar was "deafening" at 500 miles. Its ground quake brought a train to emergency stop 400 miles from impact. North of Vanavara its air blast killed a herd of 1,500 reindeer.

Trouble and war and revolution—investigation waited 19 years. But still devastated were many hundreds of square miles. How giant trees lay pinpointed impact.

A meteor from inside our Galaxy can strike Earth at 50 miles/second.

But could one hit us from *outside* our Galaxy?

Yes! The only unlikely (but not impossible) routes are those plowing edgewise or nearly so through the Milky Way; most of the sky is an open road—step outside tonight and *look*. An antimeteor from an antigalaxy could sneak in through hard vacuum—losing an antiatom whenever it encountered a random atom but nevertheless could strike us massing, say, one pound.

One pound of antimatter at any speed or none would raise as much hell as *28,000 tons* of matter striking at 50 miles/second.

Today no one knows how to amass even a gram of antimatter or how to handle and control it either for power or for weaponry. Experts assert that all three are impossible.

However . . .

Two relevant examples of "expert" predictions:

Robert A. Millikan, Nobel laureate in physics and distinguished second to none by a half-century of re-

Sovfoto

In 1908 the Tunguska region of Siberia was struck by a blast equivalent to 30 million tons of TNT, the impact of which was felt by residents 400 miles from the site and which left in its wake a 20-mile radius of charred forests. Numerous theories attempting to explain the occurrence have been suggested over the years, but none has gained consensus in the scientific community. Among the more recent theories to explain the blast is the proposal that an antimeteor, composed of antimatter, plunged through Earth's atmosphere and upon coming in contact with ordinary matter exploded with devastating force.

search into charges and properties of atomic particles, in quantum mechanics, and in several other areas, predicted that all the power that could ever be extracted from atoms would no more than blow the whistle on a peanut vendor's cart. (In fairness I must add that most of his colleagues agreed—and the same is true of the next example.)

Forest Ray Moulton, for many years top astronomer of the University of Chicago and foremost authority in ballistics, stated in print (1935) that there was "not the slightest possibility of such a journey" as the one the whole world watched 34 years later: Apollo 11 to the moon.

In 1938, when there was not a pinch of pure uranium-235 anywhere on Earth and no technology to amass or control it, Lise Meitner devised mathematics that pointed straight to atom bombs. Less than seven years after she did this, the first one blazed "like a thousand suns."

No *possible* way to amass antimatter?

Or *ever* to handle it?

Being smugly certain of *that* (but mistaken) could mean to *you* . . . and me and everyone . . .

The END

AFTERWORD

I am precluded from revising this article because Encyclopaedia Britannica owns the copyright; I wrote it under contract. But in truth it needs no revision but can use some late news flashes.

1) Jonathan V. Post reports (OMNI, May '79) that scientists in Geneva have announced containment of a beam of antiprotons in a circular storage ring for 85 hours. Further deponent sayeth not as today (Nov. '79) I have not yet traced down details. The total mass could not have been large (Geneva is still on the map) as the storage method used is not suited to large masses—or, as in this case, a massive sum total of very small masses.

But I am astonished at any containment even though with dead seriousness I predicted it in the section just above. I did not expect it in the near future but now I learn it happened at least 10 months ago, only 4 years after I wrote the above article.

Too frighteningly soon! A very small (anti) mass to be sure—but when Dr. Lise Meitner wrote the equations that implicitly predicted the A-bomb, there was not enough purified U-235 anywhere to cause a gnat's eye to water.

How soon will we face a LARGE mass—say about an ounce—planted in Manhattan by someone who doesn't like us very well? If he releases the magnetic container by an alarm-clock timer or nine other simple make-it-in-your-own-kitchen devices, he can be in Singapore when it goes off. Or in Trenton if he enjoys watching his own little practical jokes—he won't worry about witnesses; they will be dead.

Too big? Too cumbersome? Too expensive? I don't know—and neither does anyone else today. I am not proposing sneaking a CERN particle accelerator past Hoboken customs . . . but note that the first reacting atomic pile (University of Chicago) was massive—but it was not flown to Hiroshima. The bomb that did go was called "Fat Boy" for good reason. Now we can fire them from

8-inch guns. As for the "suitcase" bomb—change that to a large briefcase; all the other essentials can be bought off the shelf for cash in any medium-large city, no questions asked as they are commonplace items.

Antimatter, containment and all, might turn out to be even smaller, lighter, simpler.

2) That variable constant: Dr. Van Flandern is still plugging away at Dr. Dirac's 1937 prediction about the "Constant" of Gravitation. The latest figures I have seen show (by his measurements) that the "Constant" is decreasing by 3.6 ± 1.8 parts in 10^{11} years, a figure surprisingly close to Dirac's 1937 prediction (5.6) in view of the extreme difficulty of making the measurements and of excluding extraneous variables. But all this is based on a universe 18–20 billion years old since the "big bang"— an assumption on current best data but still an assumption. If the universe is actually materially older than that (there are reasons to think so, and all the revisions since Abbé Lemaître first formulated the theory have all been upward, never downward), then Dirac's prediction may turn out to be right on the nose of observed data to their limit of accuracy.

The data above are from an article by Dr. Herbert Friedman of Naval Research Laboratory. Our Baker Street Irregulars have just established a pipeline to Dr. Van Flandern; if major new data become available before this book is closed for press, I will add a line to this.

3) In Where To *see prediction number fourteen, page 341: At the Naval Academy I slept my way through the course in physics; nothing had changed since I had covered the same ground in high school. "Little did I dream" that a young man at Cambridge, less than five years older than I, was at that very moment turning the world upside down. This quiet, polite, soft-spoken gentleman was going to turn out to be the* enfant terrible *of physics. This has been the stormiest century in natural philosophy of all history and the storms are not over. We would not today have over 200 "elementary" particles (an open scandal) if Paul Dirac had not simplified the relation of spin and magnetism in an electron into one equation over fifty years ago, then shown that the equation implied antimatter.*

Many thousands of man-hours, many millions of dollars have been spent since then exploring the byways opened up by this one equation. And the end is not yet. The four forces (strong, weak, gravitic, electromagnetic) are still to be combined into one system. Einstein died with the work unfinished, Hawking (although young) is tragically ill, Dirac himself has reached the age when he really should not climb stepladders (as I know too well; I'm not that much younger).

$E = mc^2$ everybody knows; it's short and simple. But the Dirac equation, at least as important, is known only to professionals—not surprising; it's hairy and uses symbols a layman never sees.

I include it here just for record; I won't try to explain it. For explanations, get a late text on quantum mechanics and be prepared to learn some not-easy mathematics. Lotsa luck!

$$\int \int \int [|\Psi_1|^2 + |\Psi_2|^2 + |\Psi_3|^2 + |\Psi_4|^2] \, dxdydz = 1$$

LATE BULLETIN:

Newton's "Constant" of Gravitation is a decreasing variable.

Just as I was about to dispatch this book MS to New York, through the good offices of Dr. Yoji Kondo (astrophysicist NASA Goddard) I received from Dr. Thomas C. Van Flandern a preprint of his latest results. They tend to confirm Dr. Dirac's 1937 prediction even more closely AND ARE BACKED UP BY TWO OTHER APPROACHES; all three show Gravitation as a variable decreasing with time.

I have just telephoned Dr. Van Flandern. With caution proper to a scientist he does not say that he has "proved" Dr. Dirac's prediction . . . but that data to date support it; no data that he knows of contradict it—and adds that some of his colleagues disagree with him.

I don't have to be cautious; this man has established the fact beyond any reasonable doubt. Twenty-odd years of endless Lunar data, done by atomic (cesium) clock, electrically-automatically timed occultations of stars, backed by both triangulation and radar ranging, counterchecked by similar work done on the inner planets by other astronomers at other observatories— Certainly he could be wrong . . . and I could be elected President!

T. C. Van Flandern turns out to be the sort of Renaissance Man Dirac is, but a generation younger (38 years). B.S. mathematics, Xavier, Cincinnati; Ph.D. astronomy, Yale—he has three other disciplines: biochemistry, nutrition, psychiatry. (When does he sleep?)

Reread that list of sciences affected (p. 486), then batten down the hatches! Dirac has done it again, and the World will never be the same.

LARGER THAN LIFE
A Memoir in Tribute to
Dr. Edward E. Smith

August 1940—a back road near Jackson, Michigan—
a 1939 Chevrolet sedan:

"Doc" Smith is at the wheel; I am in the righthand
seat and trying hard to appear cool, calm, fearless—a
credit to the Patrol. Doc has the accelerator floor-
boarded . . . but has his head tilted over at ninety degrees so that he can rest his skull against the frame of
the open left window—in order to listen by bone con-
duction for body squeaks.

Were you to attempt this position yourself—car
parked and brakes set, by all means; I am not suggesting that you *drive*—you would find that your view of
the road ahead is between negligible and zero.

I must note that Doc was *not* wearing his Lens.

This leaves (by Occam's Razor) his sense of percep-
tion, his almost superhuman reflexes, and his ability
to integrate instantly all available data and act therefrom decisively and correctly.

Sounds a lot like the Gray Lensman, does it not?

It should, as no one more nearly resembled (in character and in ability—not necessarily in appearance)
the Gray Lensman than did the good gray doctor who
created him.

Doc could do almost anything and do it quickly and

well. In this case he was selecting and road-testing for me a secondhand car. After rejecting numberless other cars, he approved this one; I bought it. Note the date: August 1940. We entered World War Two the following year and quit making automobiles. I drove that car for twelve years. When I finally did replace it, the mechanic who took care of it asked to be permitted to buy it rather than have it be turned in on a trade . . . because, after more than thirteen years and hundreds of thousands of miles, it was *still* a good car. Doc Smith had not missed *anything*.

Its name? *Skylark Five*, of course.

So far as I know, Doc Smith could not play a dulcimer (but it would not surprise me to learn that he had been expert at it). Here are some of the skills I know he possessed:

Chemist & chemical engineer—and anyone who thinks these two professions are one and the same is neither a chemist nor an engineer. (My wife is a chemist and is also an aeronautical engineer—but she is not a chemical engineer. All clear? No? See me after class.)

Metallurgist—an arcane art at the Trojan Point of Black Magic and science.

Photographer—all metallurgists are expert photographers; the converse is not necessarily true.

Lumberjack

Cereal chemist

Cook

Explosives chemist—research, test, & development —product control

Blacksmith

Machinist (tool & diemaker grade)

Carpenter

Hardrock miner—see chapter 14 of FIRST LENSMAN, titled "Mining and Disaster." That chapter was written by a man who had *been* there. And it is a refutation of the silly notion that science fiction does not require knowledge of science. Did I hear someone say that there is no *science* in that chapter? Just a trick vocabulary—trade argot—plus description of some commonplace mechanical work—

So? The science (several sciences!) lies just below the surface of the paper . . . and permeates every word. In some fields I could be fooled, but not in this one. I've been in mining, off and on, for more than forty years.

Or see SPACEHOUNDS OF IPC, chapters 3 & 4, pp. 40–80 . . . and especially p.52 of the Fantasy Press hardcover edition. Page 52 is almost purely autobiographical in that it tells *why* the male lead, "Steve" Stevens, knows how to fabricate from the wreckage at hand everything necessary to rescue Nadia and himself. I once discussed with Doc these two chapters, in detail; he convinced me that his hero character could do these things by convincing me that he, Edward E. Smith, could do all of them . . . and, being myself an experienced mechanical engineer, it was not possible for him to give me a "snow job." (I think he lacked the circuitry to give a "snow job" in any case; incorruptible honesty was Dr. Smith's prime attribute—with courage to match it.)

What else could he do? He could call square dances. Surely, almost anyone can square-dance . . . but to become a caller takes longer and is much more difficult. When and how he found time for this I do not know— but, since he did everything about three times as fast as ordinary people, there is probably no mystery.

Both Doc and his beautiful Jeannie were endlessly hospitable. I stayed with them once when they had *nine* houseguests. They seemed to enjoy it.

But, above all, Doc Smith was the perfect, gallant knight, sans peur et sans reproche.

And all of the above are reflected in his stories.

It is customary today among self-styled "literary critics" to sneer at Doc's space epics—plot, characterization, dialog, motivations, values, moral attitudes, etc. "Hopelessly old-fashioned" is one of the milder disparagements.

As Al Smith used to say: "Let's take a look at the record."

Edward Elmer Smith was born in 1890, some forty years before the American language started to fall to pieces—long, long before the idiot notion of "restricted vocabulary" infected our schools, a half century before our language was corrupted by the fallacy that popular usage defines grammatical correctness.

In consequence Dr. Smith made full use of his huge vocabulary, preferring always the exact word over a more common but inexact word. He did not hesitate to use complex sentences. His syntactical constructions show that he understood and used with precision the conditional and the subjunctive modes as well as the indicative. He did not split infinitives. The difference between "like" and "as" was not a mystery to him. He limited barbarisms to quoted dialog used in characterization.

("Oh, but that dialog!") In each story Doc's male lead character is a very intelligent, highly educated, cheerful, emotional, enthusiastic, and genuinely modest man who talks exactly like Doc Smith who was a very intelligent, highly educated, cheerful, emotional, enthusiastic, and genuinely modest man.

In casual conversation Doc used a number of clichés . . . and his male lead characters used the same or similar ones. This is a literary fault? I think not. In casual speech most people tend to repeat each his own idiosyncratic pattern of clichés. Doc's repertory of clichés was quite colorful, especially so when compared with patterns heard today that draw heavily on "The Seven Words That Must Never Be Used in Television." A 7-word vocabulary offers little variety.

("But those embarrassing love scenes!") E. E. Smith's adolescence was during the Mauve Decade; we may assume tentatively that his attitudes toward women were formed mainly in those years. In 1914, a few weeks before the war in Europe started, he met his Jeannie—and I can testify of my own knowledge that, 47 years later (i.e., the last time I saw him before his death) he was still dazzled by the wonderful fact that this glorious creature had consented to spend her life with him.

Do you remember the cultural attitudes toward romantic love during the years before the European War? Too early for you? Never mind, you'll find them throughout Doc Smith's novels. Now we come to the important question. The Lensman novels are laid in the far future. Can you think of any reason why the attitudes between sexes today (ca. 1979) are more likely to prevail in the far future than are attitudes prevailing before 1914?

(I stipulate that there are many other possible patterns. But we are now comparing just these two.)

I suggest that the current pattern is contrasurvival, is necessarily most temporary, and is merely one symptom of the kaleidoscopic and possibly catastrophic rapid change our culture is passing through (or dying from?).

Contrariwise, the pre-1914 values, whatever faults they may have, are firmly anchored in the concept that a male's first duty is to protect women and children. *Pro*survival!

"Ah, but those hackneyed plots!" Yes, indeed!—and for excellent reason: The ideas, the cosmic concepts, the complex and sweeping plots, all were brand new when Doc invented them. But in the past half century dozens of other writers have taken his plots, his concepts, and rung the changes on them. The ink was barely dry on SKYLARK OF SPACE when the imitators started in. They have never stopped—pygmies, standing on the shoulders of a giant.

But all the complaints about "Skylark" Smith's alleged literary faults are as nothing to the (usually unvoiced) major grievance:

Doc Smith did not go along with *any* of the hogwash that passes for a system of social values today.

He believed in Good and Evil. He had no truck with the moral relativism of the neo- (cocktail-party) Freudians.

He refused to concede that "mediocre" is better than "superior."

He had no patience with self-pity.

He did not think that men and women are equal— he would as lief have equated oranges with apples. His stories assumed that men and women are *different*, with different functions, different responsibilities, different duties. Not equal but complementary. Neither complete without the other.

Worse yet, in his greatest and longest story, the 6-volume Lensman novel, he assumes that all humans are *un*equal (and, by implication, that the cult of the common man is pernicious nonsense), and bases his grand epic on the idea that a planned genetic breeding program thousands of years long can (and *must*) produce a new race superior to *h. sapiens* . . . supermen who will become the guardians of civilization.

The Lensman novel was left unfinished; there was to have been at least a seventh volume. As always, Doc had worked it out in great detail but never (so far as I know) wrote it down . . . because it was unpublishable—then. But he told me the ending, orally and in private.

I shan't repeat it; it is not my story. Possibly somewhere there is a manuscript—I *hope* so! All I will say is that the ending develops by inescapable logic from clues in CHILDREN OF THE LENS.

So work it out for yourself. The original Gray Lensman left us quite suddenly—urgent business a long way off, no time to spare to tell us more stories.

SPINOFF

On 2 July 1979 I received a letter calling me to testify July 19th before a joint session of the House Select Committee on Aging (Honorable Claude Pepper, M.C., Chairman) and the House Committee on Science and Technology (Honorable Don Fuqua, M.C., Chairman)—subject: Applications of Space Technology for the Elderly and the Handicapped.

I stared at that letter with all the enthusiasm of a bridegroom handed a summons for jury duty. Space technology? Yeah, sure, I was gung-ho for space technology, space travel, spaceships, space exploration, space colonies—anything about space, always have been.

But "applications of space technology for the elderly and the handicapped"? Why not bee culture? Or Estonian folk dancing? Or the three-toed salamander? Tantric Yoga?

I faced up to the problem the way any married man does: "Honey? How do I get out of this?"

"Come clean," she advised me. "Tell them bluntly that you know nothing about the subject. Shall I write a letter for you to sign?"

"It's not that simple."

"Certainly it is. We don't want to go to Washington. In *July*? Let's not be silly."

"You don't have to go."

"You don't think I'd let you go alone, do you? After

the time and trouble I've spent keeping you alive? Then let you drop dead on a Washington sidewalk? *Hmmph!* You go—*I* go."

Some hours later I said, "Let's sum it up. We both know that any Congressional committee hearing, no matter how the call reads, has as its real subject 'Money'—who gets it and how much. And we know that the space program is in bad trouble. This joint session may not help—it looks as if it would take a miracle to save the space program—but it *might* help. Some, maybe. The only trouble is that I don't know anything about the subject I'm supposed to discuss."

"So you've said, about twenty times."

"I don't know anything about it *today*. But on July 19th I'm going to be a fully-qualified Expert Witness."

"So I told you, two hours ago."

Ginny and I have our own Baker Street Irregulars. Whether the subject be Chaucer or chalk, pulsars or poisons, we either know the man who knows the most about it, or we know a man who knows the man who knows the most. Within twenty-four hours we had a couple of dozen ~~spaceflight fanatics~~ public-spirited citizens helping us. Seventy-two hours, and information started to trickle in—within a week it was a flood and I was starting to draft my written testimony.

I completed my draft and immediately discarded it; galley proofs had arrived of TECHNOLOGIES FOR THE HANDICAPPED AND THE AGED by Trudy E. Bell, NASA July 1979. This brochure was to be submitted by Dr. Frosch, Administrator of NASA, as his testimony at the same hearing. Trudy Bell had done a beautiful job—one that made 95% of what I had written totally unnecessary.

So I started over.

What follows is condensed and abridged from both my written presentation and my oral testimony:

"Honorable Chairman, ladies, and gentlemen—

"Happy New Year!

"Indeed a happy New Year beginning the 11th year in the Age of Space, greatest era of our race—the *greatest!*—despite gasoline shortages, pollution, overpopulation, inflation, wars and threats of war. 'These too shall pass'—but the stars abide.

"Our race will spread out through space—unlimited room, unlimited energy, unlimited wealth. This is certain.

"But I am not certain that the working language will be English. The people of the United States seem to have suffered a loss of nerve. However, I am limited by the call to a discussion of 'spinoffs' from our space program useful to the aged and the handicapped.

"In all scientific research, the researcher may or may not find what he is looking for—indeed, his hypothesis may be demolished—but he is *certain* to learn something new . . . which may be and often is more important than what he had hoped to learn.

"This is the Principle of Serendipity. It is so invariant that it can be considered an empirically established natural law.

"In space research we always try to do more with less, because today the pay load is tightly limited in size and in weight. This means endless research and development to make everything smaller, lighter, foolproof, and fail-proof. It works out that almost everything developed for space can be used in therapy . . . and thereby benefits both the elderly and the handicapped, the two groups requiring the most therapy of all sorts.

"When you reach old age—say 70 and up—it approaches certainty that you will be in some way handicapped. Not necessarily a wheelchair or crutches or a white cane—most handicaps do not show. So all of us are customers for space spinoffs—if not today, then soon."

Witness holds up NASA brochure. "There is no need

for me to discuss applications that NASA has already described. But this I must say: NASA's presentation is *extremely* modest; it cites only 46 applications—whereas there are hundreds. Often one bit of research results in 2nd, 3rd, and 4th generations; each generation usually has multiple applications—spinoffs have spinoffs, branching out like a tree. To get a feeling for this, think of the endless applications of Lee De-Forest's vacuum tube, Dr. Shockley's transistor.

"Here is a way to spot space-research spinoffs: If it involves microminiaturization of *any* sort, minicomputers, miniaturized long-life power sources, highly reliable microswitches, remotely-controlled manipulators, image enhancers, small and sophisticated robotics or cybernetics, then, *no matter where you find the item*, at a critical point in its development it was part of our space program.

"Examples:

"*Image enhancer:* This magic gadget runs an x-ray or fluoroscope picture through a special computer, does things to it, then puts it back onto the screen. Or stores it for replay. Or both. It can sharpen the contrast, take out 'noise,' remove part of the picture that gets in the way of what you need to see, and do other Wizard-of-Oz stunts.

"This is the wonder toy that took extremely weak digital code signals and turned them into those beautiful, sharp, true-color photographs from the surface of Mars in the Viking program and also brought us the Voyager photographs of Jupiter and its moons.

"I first saw one in 1977 at the Medical School of the University of Arizona—saw them put a long catheter up through a dog's body in order to inject an x-ray-opaque dye into its brain. This does not hurt the dog. More about this later—

"I did not know what an image enhancer was until I saw one demonstrated and did not learn until this year that it came from our space program. Possibly the doctor did not know. M.D.'s can use instruments with no notion that they derive from space research .... and a patient usually knows as little about it as did that dog.

"The most ironical thing about our space program is that there are thousands of people alive today who would be dead were it not for some item derived from space research—but are blissfully unaware of the fact—and complain about 'wasting all that money on stupid, useless space stunts when we have so many really important problems to solve right here on Earth.'

" '—all that money—'!

"That sort of thinking would have kept Columbus at home.

"NASA's annual budget wouldn't carry H.E.W. ten days. The entire 10 years of the Moon program works out to slightly *less than five cents per citizen per day*.

"Would you like to be a wheelchair case caught by a hurricane such as that one that failed to swing east and instead hit the Texas and Louisiana coast? That storm was tracked by weather satellite; there was ample warning for anyone who would heed it—plenty of time to evacuate not only wheelchair cases but bed patients.

"A similar storm hit Bangladesh a while back; it too was tracked by satellite. But Bangladesh lacks means to warn its people; many thousands were killed. Here in the United States it would take real effort to *miss* a hurricane warning; even houses with no plumbing have television.

"*Weather satellites* are not spinoff; they *are* space program. But they must be listed because bad weather of any sort is much rougher on the aged and the handicapped than it is on the young and able-bodied.

"*Portable kidney machine:* If a person's kidneys fail, he must 'go on the machine' or die. 'The machine' is a fate so grim that the suicide rate is high. Miniaturization has made it possible to build portable kidney machines. This not only lets the patient lead a fairly normal life, travel and so forth, but also his blood is cleaned steadily as with a normal kidney; he is no longer cumulatively poisoned by his own toxins between his assigned days or nights 'on the machine.'

"This is new. A few have already made the switch but all kidney victims can expect it soon. The suicide rate has dropped markedly—life is again worth living; hope has been restored.

"*Computerized-Axial Tomography*, or CAT, or 'brain scan': They strap you to a table, fasten your skull firmly, duck behind a barrier, and punch a button—then an automatic x-ray machine takes endless pictures, a tiny slice at a time. A special computer synthesizes each series of slices into a picture; a couple of dozen such pictures show the brain in three-dimensional, fine detail, a layer at a time.

"*Doppler Ultrasound Stethoscope:* another microminiaturization spinoff. This instrument is to an ordinary stethoscope as a Rolls Royce is to a Model-T Ford."

Witness stands up, turns from side to side. "Look at me, please! I'll never be Mr. America; I'll never take part in the Olympics. I've climbed my last mountain.

"But I'm here, I'm alive, I'm functioning.

"Fourteen months ago my brain was dull-normal and getting worse, slipping toward 'human vegetable.' I slept 16 hours a day and wasn't worth a hoot the other 8 hours.

"Were it not for the skill of Dr. Norman Chater, **plus certain spinoffs from the space program,** today I would either be a human vegetable or, if lucky, dead of cerebral stroke.

"My father was *not* lucky; from a similar disorder it took him years to die—*miserable* years. He died before the operation that saved me had been invented, long before there was medical spinoff from space technology.

"Am I elderly? I'm 72. I suffered from a disorder typical of old age, almost never found in the young.

"Am I handicapped? Yes, but my handicaps do not interfere with my work—or my joy in life. Over forty years ago the Navy handed me a piece of paper that pronounced me totally and permanently disabled. I never believed it. That piece of paper wore out; I did not.

"Mrs. Heinlein and I spent 1976 and -77 on blood drives all over this nation. We crisscrossed the country so many times we lost track. It was worthwhile; we recruited several thousand new blood donors—but it was *very* strenuous. By the end of '77 we badly needed a rest, so we took a sea voyage. She and I were walking the beach on Moorea, Tahiti, when I turned my head to look at a mountain peak—and something happened.

"I balanced on my left leg and said, 'Darling, I'm terribly sorry but I think I've had a stroke. Something happened inside my head and now I'm seeing double and my right side feels paralyzed.'

"Mrs. Heinlein half carried me, half dragged me, back to the landing—got me back aboard.

"A shipmate friend, Dr. Armando Fortuna, diagnosed what had happened: a transient ischemic attack, not a stroke. When we reached California, this was confirmed by tests. However a TIA is frequently a prelude to a stroke.

"Remember that spinoff, computerized-axial tomography? That was done to me to rule out brain tumor. No tumor. The neurologist my physician had called in started me on medication to thin my blood as the clinical picture indicated constriction in blood flow to my brain. This treatment was to continue for six months.

"But in only two months I was failing so rapidly that I was shipped to the University of California Medical School at San Francisco for further diagnosis. Remember the *image enhancer* and that dog at the University of Arizona? I said that dog was *not* hurt. They did it to me, with *no* anesthesia; it did *not* hurt.

"The catheter goes in down here"—witness points at his right groin—"and goes all the way up and into the aortal arch above the heart. There three very large arteries lead up toward the brain; the catheter was used to shoot x-ray-opaque dye into each, in succession. The procedure took over two hours . . . but I was never bored because the image enhancer included closed-circuit television of the fluoroscopy with the screen right up here"—witness indicates a spot just above and to the left of his head—"above me, where the radiologist and his team, and the patient—*I*—could see it.

"How many people ever get a chance to watch their own hearts beat? Utterly fascinating! I could see my heart beating, see my diaphragm rise and fall, see my lungs expand and contract, see the dye go up into my brain . . . see the network of blood vessels in my brain suddenly spring into sharp relief. It was worth the trip!

"They spotted what was wrong; my left internal carotid was totally blocked. So the left half of my brain was starved for oxygen, as it was receiving only what leaked over from the right side or from the vertebrals where the network interconnected, principally at the Circle of Willis under the brain.

"But this is your speech center"—witness touches left side of skull above ear—" your word processor, the place where a writer does all his work. No wonder I was dopey—could not write, could not study, could not read anything difficult.

"My left internal carotid is still blocked; the stoppage is too high up for surgery. So they sent me to Dr. Chater at Franklin Hospital, who moved my left superficial temporal artery to feed the left side of my brain. This operation is pictured on pages 62 and 63 of the April 1978 *Scientific American*, so I will omit grisly details; if surgery interests you, you can look them up there.

"The procedure is this: Scalp the patient from the

left eyebrow, going high and curving down to a spot behind the left ear back of the mastoid. Cut away from the scalp the temporal artery. Saw a circular hole in the skull above the ear. Go inside the brain into the Sylvian fissure, find its main artery, join the two arteries, end to side. The left anterior lobe of my brain is now served by the left *external* carotid via this roundabout bypass. Dr. Chater did the hookup under a microscope with sutures so fine the naked eye can't see them.

"Check by *Doppler ultrasound* to make sure the bypass works, then close the hole in the skull with a plate that has a groove in it for the moved artery. Sew back the scalp—go to lunch. The surgeon has been operating for four hours; he's hungry. (The patient is not.)

"They placed me in a cardiac intensive-care room. When I woke, I found in my room a big screen with dancing lights all over it. Those curves meant nothing to me but were clear as print to the I.C. nurses and to my doctors—such things as EKG, blood pressure, respiration, temperature, brain waves, I don't know what all. The thing was so sensitive that my slightest movement caused one of the curves to spike.

"I mention this gadget because I was *not* wired to it.

"Another space-technology spinoff: This is the way Dr. Berry monitored our astronauts whenever they were out in space.

"Colonel Berry had to have remote monitoring for his astronaut patients. For me it may not have been utterly necessary. But it did mean that I was not cluttered with dozens of wires like a fly caught in a web; the microminiaturized sensors were so small and unobtrusive that I never noticed them—yet the nurses had the full picture every minute, every second.

"Another advantage of telemetered remote monitoring is that more than one terminal can display the signals. My wife tells me that there was one at the nursing supervisor's station. Dr. Chater may have had

a terminal in his offices—I don't know. But there can't
be any difficulty in remoting a hundred yards or so
when the technology was developed for remoting from
Luna to Houston, almost a quarter of a million miles.

"*Space spinoff in postoperative care*: a *Doppler ultrasound* stethoscope is an impressive example of microminiaturization. It is enormously more sensitive
than an acoustic stethoscope; the gain can be controlled, and, because of its Doppler nature, fluid flow
volume and direction can be inferred by a skilled operator. Being ultrasound at extremely high frequency,
it is highly directional; an acoustic stethoscope is not.

"It generates a tight beam of ultrasound beyond the
range of the human ear. This beam strikes something
and bounces back, causing interference beats in the
audible range. It behaves much like Doppler radar
save that the radiation is ultrasound rather than electromagnetic. Thus it is a *noninvasive* way to explore
inside the body without the dangers of x-ray . . . and is
able to 'see' soft tissues that x-ray can't see.

"Both characteristics make it especially useful for
protecting pregnant mothers and unborn babies. I am
not departing from the call; babies unborn and newly
born, and mothers at term *must* be classed as 'temporarily but severely handicapped.'

"*Doppler ultrasound* was used on me *before, during*,
and *after* surgery.

"After my convalescence I was again examined by
computerized axial tomography. No abnormalities—
other than the new plate in my skull.

"This brain surgery is not itself a spinoff from space
technology . . . but note how repeatedly space spinoffs
were used on me before, during, and after surgery.
This operation is *very* touchy; in the whole world only
a handful of surgical teams dare attempt it. Of the
thousand-odd of these operations to date, worldwide,
Dr. Chater has performed more than 300. His mortality rate is far lower than that of any other team any-

where. This is a tribute to his skill but part of it comes from his attitude: he *always* uses the latest, most sophisticated tools available.

"I was far gone; I needed every edge possible. Several things that tipped the odds in my favor are spinoffs from space technology.

"Was it worthwhile? Yes, even if I had died at one of the four critical points—because sinking into senility while one is still bright enough to realize that one's mental powers are steadily failing is a miserable, nogood way to live. Early last year I was just smart enough to realize that I had *nothing* left to look forward to, nothing whatever. This caused me to be quite willing to 'Go-for-Broke'—get well or die.

"Did it work? I have been out of convalescence about one year, during which I've caught up on two years of technical journals, resumed studying—I have long been convinced that life-long learning helps to keep one young and happy. True or not, both my wife and I do this. At present I am reviewing symbolic logic, going on into more advanced n-dimensional, non-Euclidean geometries, plus another subject quite new to me: Chinese history.

"But I am working, too; I have completed writing a very long novel and am about halfway through another book.

"I feel that I have proved one of two things: either I have fully recovered . . . or a hole in the head is no handicap to a science-fiction author.

"I must note one spinoff especially important to the aged and the handicapped: *spiritual* spinoff.

" 'Man does not live by bread alone.' Any physician will tell you that the most important factor in getting well is the will to live—contrariwise, a terminal patient dies when he gives up the fight.

"I have been in death row three times. The unfailing support of my wife sustained my will to live . . . so here I am. In addition I have believed firmly in space flight for the past sixty-odd years; this has been a permanent incentive to *hang on, hang on!* My wife shares this; she decided years back to die on the Moon, not here in the smog and the crowds. Now that I am well again I intend to hang in there, lead a disciplined life, stay alive until we can *buy* commercial tickets to the Moon . . . and spend our last days in low-gravity comfort in the Luna Hilton, six levels down in Luna City.

"Foolishness? Everyone in this room is old enough to know by direct experience that today's foolishness is tomorrow's wisdom. I can remember when 'Get a horse!' was considered the height of wit. As may be, *anything* that gives one a strong incentive to live can't be *entirely* foolish.

"I get a flood of mail from my readers; a disproportionate part of it is from the very old and the handicapped. It is impossible to be a fan of my fiction and not be enthusiastic for space travel. Besides, they *tell* me so, explicitly, in writing.

"Examples:

"A college professor, blind from birth. He's never *seen* the the stars; he's never *seen* the Moon. The books he reads and rereads—has read to him by his secretary—are about space travel. He went to a lot of trouble to look me up . . . to discuss our space program.

"A teen-age boy, tied to a wheelchair, who wrote to ask me whether or not he could become an astronautical engineer—some 'friend' had told him that it was a silly ambition for a cripple. I assured him that an engineer did not need legs even on Earth surface, advised him in what courses to take, and referred him to a story by Arthur C. Clarke in which a double amputee, both legs, commands a space station.

"A housewife with epilepsy, *grand mal*, who doesn't expect ever to be able to go out into space . . . but finds her greatest interest in life, her major relief from the tedious routine she must follow, in our space program.

"A *very* large number of elderly people who wrote to me immediately after the first landing on the Moon, all saying, in effect, that they thanked the Lord that they had been spared long enough to see this great day.

"I could add examples endlessly. Just let me state flatly that my files hold proof that the aged retired, the shut-ins and the disabled of all ages get more spiritual lift out of space flight than does any other definable group of our citizens. For many of them the television screen is their only window on the world; something great and shining and wonderful went out of their lives when the Apollo Moon program ended.

"Even if a space program had no other spinoff, isn't *that* sort worth 5¢ a day?"

AFTERWORD

Later: No, to most citizens of the United States the entire space program plus all its spinoffs is not worth even 5¢ per day; the polls (and letters to Congress) plainly show it. And they won't believe that 5¢ figure even if you do the arithmetic right in front of their eyes. They will still think of it as "all that money" being "wasted" on "a few rocks."

It is easy to prove that the space program paid for itself several times over in terms of increased gross national product . . . and in new technology . . . and in saved lives. But they won't believe any of that, either.

NASA has two remarkable records: first, a space program far more successful than anyone had dared hope; and, second, the most incredibly bumbling, stupid, inept public relations of any government agency.

A Congressman's counsel pointed out to me that NASA and other government agencies were by law not permitted to advertise themselves. Oh, come off it!—it does not matter whether a man is called a "public information aide" or a flack; a press agent defines himself by what he does. The man who was NASA's boss flack all during the Moon program had the endearing manners of Dennis the Menace. He's gone now—but the damage he did lives on, while our space program is dying.

Still . . . if you aren't willing to give up and start studying Mandarin or possibly Japanese, you can write to your congressman and to both your senators and tell them how you feel about it. If you do, send copies to Don Fuqua (Democrat, Lower House) and to Barry Goldwater, Sr. (Republican, Upper House). A strong space program has many friends in both parties and in both houses— but it is necessary to let them know that they have friends.

One would think that a "prophet" unable to score higher than 66% after 30 years have elapsed on 50-year predictions would have the humility (or the caution) to refrain from repeating his folly. But I've never been very humble, and the motto of my prime vocation has always been: "L'audace! Toujours l'audace!"

So the culprit returns to his crime. Or see PROVERBS XXVI, 11. And hang on to your hats!

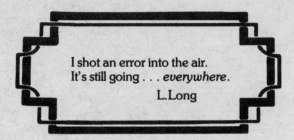

I shot an error into the air.
It's still going . . . *everywhere*.

L. Long

THE HAPPY DAYS AHEAD

"It does not pay a prophet to be too specific."
—L. Sprague de Camp
"You never get rich peddling gloom."
—William Lindsay Gresham

The late Bill Gresham was, before consumption forced him into fiction writing, a carnie mentalist of great skill. He could give a cold reading that would scare the pants off a marble statue. In six words he summarized the secret of success as a fortuneteller. Always tell the mark what he wants to hear. He will love you for it, happily pay you, then forgive and forget when your cheerful prediction fails to come true—and always come back for more.

Stockbrokers stay in business this way; their tips are no better than guesses but they are *not* peddling dividends; they are peddling happiness. Millions of priests and preachers have used this formula, promising eternal bliss in exchange for following, or at least giving lip service to, some short and tolerable rules, plus a variable cash fee not too steep for the customer's purse . . . and have continued to make this formula work *without ever in all the years producing even one client who had actually received the promised prize.*

Then how do churches stay in business? Because, in talking about "Pie in the Sky, By and By," they offer happiness and peace of mind *right here on Earth.* When

Karl Marx said, "Religion is the opium of the people," he was not being cynical or sarcastic; he was being correctly descriptive. In the middle nineteenth century opium was the *only* relief from intolerable pain; Karl Marx was stating that faith in a happy religion made the lives of the people of the abyss tolerable.

Sprague de Camp is Grand Master of practically everything and probably the most learned of all living practitioners of science fiction and fantasy. I heard those words of wisdom from him before I wrote the 1950 version of PANDORA'S BOX. So why didn't I listen? Three reasons: 1) money; 2) money; and 3) I thought I could get away with it during my lifetime for predictions attributed to 2000 A.D. I never expected to live that long; I had strong reasons to expect to die young. But I seem to have more lives than a cat; it may be necessary to kill me by driving a steak through my heart (sirloin by choice), then bury me at a crossroads.

Still, I could have gotten away with it if I had stuck to predictions that could not mature before 2000 A.D. Take the two where I *really* flopped, #5 and #16. *In both cases I named a specific year short of 2000 A.D.* Had I not ignored Mr. de Camp's warning, I could look bland and murmur, "Wait and see. Don't be impatient," on all in which the prediction does not look as promising in 1980 as it did in 1950.

Had I heeded a wise man on 2 out of 19 I could today, by sheer brass, claim to be batting a thousand.

I have made some successful predictions. One is "The Crazy Years." (Take a look out your window. Or at your morning paper.) Another is the water bed. Some joker tried to patent the water bed to shut out competition, and discovered that he could not because it was in the public domain, having been described in detail in STRANGER IN A STRANGE LAND. It had been mentioned in stories of mine as far back as 1941 and several times after that, but not until STRANGER did the mechanics of a scene require describing how it worked.

It was *not* the first man to build water beds who tried to patent it. The first man in the field knew where it came from; he sent me one, free and freight prepaid, with a telegram naming his firm as the "Share-Water Bed Company." Q.E.D.

Our house has no place to set up a water bed. None. So that bed is still in storage a couple of hundred yards from our main house. I've owned a water bed from the time they first came on market—but have never slept in one.

I designed the water bed during years as a bed patient in the middle thirties: a pump to control water-level, side supports to permit one to float rather than simply lying on a not-very-soft water-filled mattress, thermostatic control of temperature, safety interfaces to avoid all possibility of electrical shock, waterproof box to make a leak no more important than a leaky hot water bottle rather than a domestic disaster, calculation of floor loads (important!), internal rubber mattress, and lighting, reading, and eating arrangements—an attempt to design the perfect hospital bed by one who had spent too *damned* much time in hospital beds.

Nothing about it was eligible for patent—nothing new—unless a sharp patent lawyer could persuade the examiners that a working assemblage enabling a person to sleep on water involved that—how does the law describe it?—"flash of inspiration" transcending former art. But I never thought of trying; I simply wanted to build one—but at that time I could not have afforded a custom-made soapbox.

But I know exactly where I got the idea. In 1931, a few days after the radio-compass incident described in the afterword to SEARCHLIGHT, I was ordered to Fort Clayton, Canal Zone, to fire in Fleet Rifle & Pistol Matches. During that vacation-with-pay I often re-

turned from Panama City after taps, when all was
quiet. There was a large swimming pool near the post
gate used by the Navy and our camp was well separated from the Army regiment barracked there.

I would stop, strip naked, and have a swim—nonreg
(no life guards) but no one around, and regulations are
made to be broken.

Full moon occurred about the middle of Fleet
Matches—and I am one of those oddies who cannot
sink, even in fresh water (which this was). The water
was blood warm, there was no noise louder than night
jungle sounds, the Moon blazed overhead, and I would
lie back with every muscle relaxed and stare at it—fall
into it—wonder whether we would get there in my
lifetime. Sometimes I dozed off.

Eventually I would climb out, wipe my feet dry with
a hanky, pull on shoes, hang clothes over my arm, and
walk to my tent in the dark. I don't recall ever meeting
anyone but it couldn't matter—dark, all male, surrounded by armed sentries, and responsible myself
only to a Marine Corps officer junior to me but my TDY
boss as team captain—and he did not give a hoot what
I did as long as I racked a high score on the range (and
I did, largely because my coach was a small wiry Marine sergeant nicknamed "Deacon"—who reappears
as survival teacher in TUNNEL IN THE SKY).

Some years later, bothered by bed sores and with
every joint aching no matter what position I twisted
into, I thought often of the Sybaritic comfort of floating in blood-warm water at night in Panama—and
wished that it could be done for bed patients . . . and
eventually figured out how to do it, all details, long
before I was well enough to make working drawings.

But 1) I never expected one to be built; 2) never
thought of them (except for myself) other than as hospital beds; 3) never expected them to be widely used
by a fair percentage of the public; 4) and never
dreamed that they would someday be advertised by
motels for romantic-exotic-erotic weekends along
with X-rated films on closed-circuit TV.

By stacking the cards, I'm about to follow the advice of both Bill Gresham and Sprague de Camp. First, I will paint a gloomy picture of what our future may be. Second, I'll offer a cheerful scenario of how wonderful it *could* be. I can afford to be specific as each scenario will deny everything said in the other one (de Camp), and I can risk great gloom in the first because I'll play you out with music at the end (Gresham).

GLOOM, WOE, AND DISASTER—There are increasing pathological trends in our culture that show us headed down the chute to self-destruction. These trends do *not* require that we be conquered—wait a bit and we will fall into the lap of whichever power cares to occupy us. I'll list some of these trends and illustrate (rather than prove) what I mean. But it would be tediously depressing to pile up convincing proof—I'm not running for office. I *do have* proof, on file right in this room. I started clipping and filing by categories on trends as early as 1930 and my "youngest" file was started in 1945.

Span of time is important; the 3-legged stool of understanding is held up by **history, languages,** and **mathematics.** Equipped with these three you can learn anything you want to learn. But if you lack *any one* of them you are just another ignorant peasant with dung on your boots.

A few years ago I was visited by an astronomer, young and quite brilliant. He claimed to be a long-time reader of my fiction and his conversation proved it. I was telling him about a time I needed a synergistic orbit from Earth to a 24-hour station; I told him what story it was in, he was familiar with the scene, mentioned having read the book in grammar school.

This orbit is similar in appearance to cometary interplanet transfer but is in fact a series of compromises in order to arrive in step with the space station; elapsed time is an unsmooth integral not to be found in Hudson's Manual but it can be solved by the methods used on Siacci empiricals for atmosphere ballistics: numerical integration.

I'm married to a woman who knows more math, history, and languages than I do. This should teach me humility (and sometimes does, for a few minutes). Her brain is a great help to me professionally. I was telling this young scientist how we obtained yards of butcher paper, then each of us worked three days, independently, solved the problem and checked each other—then the answer disappeared into *one* line of *one* paragraph (SPACE CADET) but the effort had been worthwhile as it controlled what I could do dramatically in that sequence.

Doctor Whoosis said, "But *why* didn't you just shove it through a computer?"

I blinked at him. Then said slowly, gently, "My dear boy—" (I don't usually call Ph.D.'s in hardcore sciences "My dear boy"—they impress me. But this was a special case.)

"My dear boy . . . this was *1947*."

It took him some seconds to get it, then he blushed.

Age is not an accomplishment and youth is no sin. This young man was (is) brilliant, skilled in mathematics, had picked German and Russian for his doctorate. At the time I met him he seemed to lack feeling for historical span . . . but, if true, I suspect that it began to itch him and he made up that lack either formally or by reading. Come to think of it, much of my own knowledge of history derives not from history courses but from history of astronomy, of war and military art, and of mathematics, as my formal history study stopped with Alexander and resumed with Prince Henry the Navigator. But to understand the history of those three subjects, you *must* branch out into general history.

Span of time—the Decline of Education

My father never went to college. He attended high school in a southern Missouri town of 3000+, then attended a private 2-year academy roughly analogous to junior college today, except that it was *very* small—had to be; a day school, and Missouri had no paved roads.

Here are some of the subjects he studied in back-country 19th century schools: Latin, Greek, physics (natural philosophy), French, geometry, algebra, 1st year calculus, bookkeeping, American history, World history, chemistry, geology.

Twenty-eight years later I attended a much larger city high school. I took Latin and French but Greek was not offered; I took physics and chemistry but geology was not offered. I took geometry and algebra but calculus was not offered. I took American history and ancient history but no comprehensive history course was offered. Anyone wishing comprehensive history could take (each a one-year 5-hrs/wk course) ancient history, medieval history, modern European history, and American history—and note that the available courses ignored all of Asia, all of South America, all of Africa except ancient Egypt, and touched Canada and Mexico solely with respect to our wars with each.

I've had to repair what I missed with a combination of travel and private study . . . and must admit that I did not tackle Chinese history in depth until this year. My training in history was so spotty that it was not until I went to the Naval Academy and saw captured battle flags that I learned that we fought Korea some *eighty years* earlier than the mess we are still trying to clean up.

From my father's textbook I know that the world history course he studied was not detailed (how could it be?) but at least it treated the world as *round;* it did not ignore three fourths of our planet.

Now, let me report what I've seen, heard, looked up, clipped out of newspapers and elsewhere, and read in books such as WHY JOHNNY CAN'T READ, BLACK-BOARD JUNGLE, etc.

Colorado Springs, our home until 1965, in 1960 offered first-year Latin—but that was all. Caesar, Cicero, Virgil—Who dat?

Latin is not taught in the high schools of Santa Cruz County. From oral reports and clippings I note that it is not taught in most high schools across the country.

"Why this emphasis on Latin? It's a dead language!" Brother, as with jazz, in the words of a great artist, "If you have to ask, you ain't never goin' to find out." A person who knows *only* his own language does not even know his *own* language; epistemology necessitates knowing more than one human language. Besides that sharp edge, Latin is a giant help in *all* the sciences—and so is Greek, so I studied it on my own.

A friend of mine, now a dean in a state university, was a tenured professor of history—but got riffed when history was eliminated from the required subjects for a bachelor's degree. His courses (American history) are still offered but the one or two who sign up, he tutors; the overhead of a classroom cannot be justified.

A recent *Wall Street Journal* story described the bloodthirsty job hunting that goes on at the annual meeting of the Modern Languages Association; modern languages—even English—are being deemphasized right across the country; there are more professors in MLA than there are jobs.

I mentioned elsewhere the straight-A student on a scholarship who did not know the relations between weeks, months, and years. This is not uncommon; high school and college students in this country usually can't do simple arithmetic without using a pocket calculator. (I mean with pencil on paper; to ask one to do *mental* arithmetic causes jaws to drop—say 17×34, done mentally. How? Answer: Chuck away the 34 but remember it. $(10 + 7)^2$ is 289, obviously. Double it: $2(300 - 11)$, or 578.

But my father would have given the answer at once, as his country grammar school a century ago required *perfect* memorizing of multiplication tables *through 20 $\times$ 20 = 400* . . . so his ciphering the above would have been merely the doubling of a number already known (289)—or 578. He might have done it again by another route to check it: $(68 + 510)$—but his hesitation would not have been noticeable.

Was my father a mathematician? Not at all. Am I? Hell, no! This is the simplest sort of kitchen arithmetic, the sort *that high school students can no longer do*—at least in Santa Cruz.

If they don't study math and languages and history, what *do* they study? (**Nota Bene!** Any student can learn the truly tough subjects *on almost any campus if he/she wishes*—the professors and books and labs are there. But the student must *want* to.)

But if that student does not want to learn anything requiring brain sweat, most U.S. campuses will baby-sit him 4 years, then hand him a baccalaureate for not burning down the library. That girl in Colorado Springs who studied Latin—but no classic Latin—got a "general" bachelor's degree at the University of Colorado in 1964. I attended her graduation, asked what she had majored in. No major. What had she studied? Nothing, really, it turned out—and, sure enough, she's as ignorant today as she was in high school.

Santa Cruz has an enormous, lavish 2-year college and also a campus of the University of California, degree granting through Ph.D. level. But, since math and languages and history are not required, let's see how they fill the other classrooms.

The University of California (all campuses) is classed as a "tough school." It is paralleled by a State University system with lower entrance requirements, and this is paralleled by local junior colleges (*never* called "junior") that accept any warm body.

UCSC was planned as an elite school ("The Oxford of the West") but falling enrollment made it necessary to accept any applicant who can qualify for the University of California as a whole; therefore UCSC now typifies the "statewide campus." Entrance can be by examination (usually College Entrance Examination Boards) or by high school certificate. Either way, admission requires a certain spread—2 years of math, 2 of a modern language, 1 of a natural science, 1 of

American history, 3 years of English—and a level of performance that translates as B+. There are two additional requirements: English composition, and American History and Institutions. The second requirement acknowledges that some high schools do not require American history; UCSC permits an otherwise acceptable applicant to make up this deficiency (with credit) after admission.

The first additional requirement, English composition, can be met by written examination such as CEEB, or by transferring *college* credits considered equivalent, or, lacking either of these, by passing an examination given at UCSC at the start of each quarter.

The above looks middlin' good on the surface. College requirements from high school have been watered down somewhat (or more than somewhat) but that B+ average as a requirement looks good . . . *if* high schools are teaching what they taught two and three generations ago. The rules limit admission to the upper 8% of California high school graduates (out-of-state applicants must meet slightly higher requirements).

8%— So 92% fall by the wayside. These 8% are the intellectual elite of young adults of the biggest, richest, and most lavishly educated state in the Union.

Those examinations for the English-composition requirement: How can anyone fail who has had 3 years of high school English and averages B+ across the board?

If he fails to qualify, he may enter but must take at once (no credit) "Subject A"—better known as "Bonehead English."

"Bonehead English" must be repeated, if necessary, until passed. To be forced to take this no-credit course does *not* mean that the victim splits an occasional infinitive, sometimes has a dangling modifier, or a failure in agreement or case—he can even get away with such atrocities as "—like I say—."

It means that he has reached the Groves of Academe

unable to express himself by writing in the English language.

It means that his command of his native language does not equal that of a 12-year-old country grammar school graduate of ninety years ago. It means that he verges on subliterate but that his record is such in other ways that the University will tutor him (no credit and for a fee) rather than turn him away.

But, since these students are the upper 8% and each has had not less than three years of high school English, it follows that only the exceptionally unfortunate student needs "Bonehead English." That's right, isn't it? Each one is eighteen years old, old enough to vote, old enough to contract or to marry without consulting parents, old enough to hang for murder, old enough to have children (and some do); all have had 12 years of schooling including 11 years of English, 3 of them in high school.

(Stipulated: California has special cases to whom English is not native language. But such a person who winds up in that upper 8% is usually—I'm tempted to say "always"—fully literate in English.)

So here we have the cream of California's young adults; each has learned to read and write and spell and has been taught the basics of English during eight years in grammar school, and has polished this by not less than three years of English in high school—and also has had at least two years of a second language, a drill that vastly illuminates the subject of grammar even though grasp of the second language may be imperfect.

It stands to reason that *very* few applicants need "Bonehead English." Yes?

No!

I have just checked. The new class at UCSC is "about 50%" in Bonehead English—and this is normal—normal right across California—and California is no worse than most of the states.

8% off the top—

Half of this elite 8% must take "Bonehead English."

The prosecution rests.

This scandal must be charged to grammar and high
school teachers . . . many of whom are not themselves
literate (I know!)—but are not personally to blame, *as
we are now in the second generation of illiteracy*. The
blind lead the blind.

But what happens after this child (sorry—young
adult citizen) enters UCSC?

I TELL YOU THREE TIMES I TELL YOU THREE
TIMES I TELL YOU THREE TIMES: A student who
wants an education can get one at UCSC in a number
of very difficult subjects, plus a broad general education.

I ask you never to forget this while we see how one
can slide through, never do any real work, never learn
anything solid, and still receive a bachelor of arts degree from the prestigious University of California. Although I offer examples from the campus I know best,
I assume conclusively that this can be done throughout the state, as it is one statewide university operating under one set of rules.

Some guidelines apply to any campus: Don't pick a
medical school or an engineering school. Don't pick a
natural science that requires difficult mathematics. (A
subject called "science" that does *not* require difficult
mathematics usually is "science" in the sense that
"Christian Science" is science—in its widest sense
"science" simply means "knowledge" and anyone
may use the word for any subject . . . but shun the subjects that can't be understood without mind-stretching math.)

Try to get a stupid but good-natured adviser. There
are plenty around, especially in subjects in which to
get a no-sweat degree; Sturgeon's Law applies to professors as well as to other categories.

For a bachelor's degree:

1) You must spend the equivalent of one academic
year in acquiring "breadth"—but wait till you see the
goodies!

2) You must take the equivalent of one full academic year in your major subject in upper division courses, plus prerequisite lower division courses. Your 4-year program you must rationalize to your adviser as making sense for your major ("Doctor, I picked *that* course because it *is* so far from my major—for perspective. I was getting too narrow." He'll beam approvingly . . . or you had better look for a stupider adviser).

3) Quite a lot of time will be spent off campus but counted toward your degree. This should be fun, but it can range from hard labor at sea, to counting noses and asking snoopy questions of "ethnics" (excuse, please!), to time in Europe or Hong Kong, et al., where you are in danger of learning something new and useful even if you don't try.

4) You will be encouraged to take interdisciplinary majors and are invited (urged) to invent and justify unheard-of new lines of study. For this you need the talent of a used-car salesman as *any* aggregation of courses can be sold as a logical pattern if your "new" subject considers the many complex relationships between three or four or more old and orthodox fields. Careful here! If you are smart enough to put this over, you may find yourself not only *earning* a baccalaureate but in fact doing original work worthy of a Ph.D. (You won't get it.)

5) You must have at least one upper-division seminar. Pick one in which the staff leader likes your body odor and you like his. ("I do not like thee, Dr. Fell; the reason why I cannot tell—") But you've at least two years in which to learn which professors in your subject are simpatico, and which ones to avoid at any cost.

6) You must write a 10,000 word thesis on your chosen nonsubject and may have to defend it orally. If you can't write 10,000 words of bull on a bull subject, you've made a mistake—you may have to *work* for a living.

The rules above allow plenty of elbowroom; at least three out of four courses can be elective and the remainder elective in part, from a long menu. We are still talking *solely* about nonmathematical subjects. If you are after a Ph.D. in astronomy, UCSC is a wonderful place to get one . . . but you will start by getting a degree in physics including the toughest of mathematics, and will study also chemistry, geology, technical photography, computer science—and will resent any time not leading toward the ultra-interdisciplinary subject lumped under the deceptively simple word "astronomy."

Breadth—the humanities, natural science, and social science—1/3 in each, total 3/3 or one academic year, but spread as suits you over the years. Classically "the humanities" are defined as literature, philosophy, and art—but history has been added since it stopped being required in college and became "social studies" in secondary schools. "Natural science" does not necessarily mean what it says—it can be a "nonalcoholic gin"; see below. "Social science" means that grab bag of studies in which answers are matters of opinion.

Courses satisfying "breadth" requirements
Humanities

Literature and Politics—political & moral choices in literature

Philosophy of the Self

Philosophy of History in the Prose and Poetry of W. B. Yeats

Art and the Perceptual Process

The Fortunes of Faust

Science and the American Culture (satisfies both the Humanities requirement and the American History and Institutions requirement *without* teaching *any* science or *any* basic American History. A companion course, *Science and Pressure Politics,* satisfies both the Social Sciences requirement and the American History and Institutions requirement while teaching still less; it concentrates on post-World-War-II period and concerns scientists as lobbyists and their own interactions [rows] with Congress and the President. Highly recommended as a way to avoid learning American history or very much social "science.")

American Country Music—Whee! You don't play it, you listen.

Man and the Cosmos—philosophy, sorta. Not science.

Science Fiction (I refrain from comment.)

The Visual Arts—"What, if any, are the critical and artistic foundations for judgment in the visual arts?"—exact quotation from catalog.

Mysticism—that's what it says.

(The above list is incomplete.)

Natural Science requirement

General Astronomy—no mathematics required

Marine Biology—no mathematics required

Sound, Music, and Tonal Properties of Musical Instruments—neither math nor music required for this one!

Seminar: Darwin's Explanation

Mathematical Ideas—for nonmathematicians; requires only that high school math you must have to enter.

The Phenomenon of Man—"—examine the question of whether there remains any meaning to human values." (Oh, the pity of it all!)

Physical Geography: Climate

The Social "Sciences" requirement

Any course in Anthropology—many have no prereq.

Introduction to Art Education—You don't have to *make* art; you study how to teach it.

Music and the Enlightenment—no technical knowledge of music required. This is a discussion of the effect of music on philosophical, religious, and social ideas, late 18th–early 19th centuries. That is what it says—and it counts as "social science."

The Novel of Adultery—and this, too, counts as "so-

cial science." I don't mind anyone studying this subject or teaching it—but I object to its being done on
my (your, our) tax money. (P.S. The same bloke
teaches science fiction. He doesn't *write* science fiction; I don't know what his qualifications are in this
other field.)

Human Sexuality

Cultural Roots for Verbal and Visual Expression—a
fancy name of still another "creative writing" class
with frills—the students are taught how to draw out
"other culture" pupils. So it says.

All the 30-odd *"Community Studies"* courses qualify
as "social science," but I found myself awed by these
two: *Politics and Violence,* which studies, among other
things, "political assassination as sacrifice" and *Lei-
sure and Recreation in the Urban Community* ("Bread
and Circuses").

Again, listing must remain incomplete; I picked
those below as intriguing:

Seminar: Evil and the Devil in the Hindu Tradition.

Science and Pressure Politics—already mentioned on
page 529 as the course that qualifies both as social
"science" and as American History and Institutions
while teaching an utter minimum about each. The
blind man now has hold of the elephant's tail.

The Political Socialization of La Raza—another double header, social "science" and American History and
Institutions. It covers greater time span (from 1900
rather than from 1945) but it's like comparing cheese
and chalk to guess which one is narrower in scope in
either category.

The name of this game is to plan a course involving
minimum effort and minimum learning while "earning" a degree under the rules of the nation's largest
and most prestigious state university.

To take care of "breadth" and also the American history your high school did not require I recommend
Science and Pressure Politics, The Phenomenon of Man,

and *American Country Music*. These three get you home free without learning *any* math, history, or language that you did not already know . . . and without sullying your mind with science.

You must pick a major . . . but it must *not* involve mathematics, history, or actually being able to *read* a second language. This rules out *all* natural sciences (this campus's greatest strength).

Anthropology? You would learn something in spite of yourself; you'd get interested. Art? Better not major in it without major talent. Economics can be difficult, but also and worse, you may incline toward the Chicago or the Austrian school and not realize it until your (Keynesian or Marxist) instructor has failed you with a big black mark against your name. Philosophy? Easy and lots of fun and absolutely guaranteed not to teach you anything while loosening up your mind. In more than twenty-five centuries of effort *not one* basic problem of philosophy has *ever* been solved . . . but the efforts to solve them are most amusing. The same goes for comparative religion as a major: You won't actually *learn* anything you can sink your teeth into . . . but you'll be vastly entertained—if the Human Comedy entertains you. It does me.

Psychology, Sociology, Politics, and Community Studies involve not only risk of learning something— not much, but *something*—and each is likely to involve real work, tedious and lengthy.

To play this game and win, with the highest score, it's Hobson's choice: American literature. I assume that you did not have to take Bonehead English and that you can type. In a school that has no school of education (UCSC has none) majoring in English Literature is the obvious way to loaf through four years. It will be necessary to cater to the whims of professors who know no more than you do about anything that matters . . . but catering to your mentors is necessary in any subject not ruled by mathematics.

Have you noticed that professors of English and/or

American Literature are not expected to be proficient in the art they profess to teach? Medicine is taught by M.D.'s on living patients, civil engineering is taught by men who in fact have built bridges that did not fall; law is taught by lawyers; music is taught by musicians; mathematics is taught by mathematicians—and so on.

But is—for example—the American Novel taught by American novelists?

Yes. Occasionally. But so seldom that the exceptions stand out. John Barth. John Erskine fifty years ago. Several science-fiction writers almost all of whom were selling writers long before they took the King's Shilling. A corporal's guard in our whole country out of battalions of English profs.

For a Ph.D. in American/English literature a candidate is not expected to *write* literature; he is expected to *criticize* it.

Can you imagine a man being awarded an M.D. for writing a *criticism* of some great physician without ever himself having learned to remove an appendix or to diagnose *Herpes zoster*? And for that dissertation then be hired to *teach* therapy to medical students?

There is, of course, a reason for this nonsense. The rewards to a competent novelist are so much greater than the salaries of professors of English at even our top schools that once he/she learns this racket, teaching holds no charms.

There are exceptions—successful storytellers who *like* to teach so well that they keep their jobs and write only during summers, vacations, evenings, weekends, sabbaticals. I know a few—emphasis on "few." But most selling wordsmiths are lazy, contrary, and so opposed to any fixed regime that they will do *anything*—even meet a deadline—rather than accept a job.

Most professors of English *can't* write publishable novels . . . and many of them can't write nonfiction prose very well—certainly not with the style and distinction and grace—and content—of Professor of Biology Thomas H. Huxley. Or Professor of Astronomy

Sir Fred Hoyle. Or Professor of Physics John R. Pierce. Most Professors of English get published, when they do, by university presses or in professional quarterlies. But fight it out for cash against *Playboy* and Travis Magee? They can't and they don't!

But if you are careful not to rub their noses in this embarrassing fact and pay respectful attention to their opinions even about (ugh!) "creative writing," they will help you slide through to a painless baccalaureate.

You still have time for many electives and will need them for your required hours-units-courses; here are some fun-filled ones that will teach you almost nothing:

The Fortunes of Faust

Mysticism

The Search for a New Life Style

The American Dilemma—Are "all men equal"?

Enology—history, biology, and chemistry of winemaking and wine appreciation. This one will teach you something but it's too good to miss.

Western Occultism: Magic, Myth, and Heresy.

There is an entire college organized for fun and games ("aesthetic enrichment"). It offers courses for credit but you'll be able to afford noncredit activity as well in your lazyman's course—and *anything* can be turned into credit by some sincere selling to your adviser and/or Academic Committee. I have already listed nine of its courses but must add:

Popular Culture

—plus clubs or "guilds" for gardening, photography, filmmedia, printing, pottery, silkscreening, orchestra, jazz, etc.

Related are *Theater Arts*. These courses give credit, including:

Films of Fantasy and Imagination—fantasy, horror, SF, etc. (!)

Seminar on Films

Filmmaking

History and Aesthetics of Silent Cinema

History and Aesthetics of Cinema since Sound
Introduction to World Cinema
Sitting and looking at movies can surely be justified for an English major. Movies and television use writers—as little as possible, it's true. But somewhat; the linkage is there.

Enjoy yourself while it lasts. These dinosaurs are on their way to extinction.

The 2-year "warm body" campus is even more lavish than UCSC. It is a good trade school for some things—e.g., dental assistant. But it offers a smörgåsbord of fun—Symbolism of the Tarot, Intermediate Contract Bridge, Folk Guitar, Quilting, Horseshoeing, Chinese Cooking, Hearst Castle Tours, Modern Jazz, Taoism, Hatha Yoga Asanas, Aikido, Polarity Therapy, Mime, Raku, Bicycling, Belly Dancing, Shiatsu Massage, Armenian Cuisine, Revelation and Prophecy, Cake Art, Life Insurance Sales Techniques, Sexuality and Spirituality, Home Bread Baking, Ecuadorian Backstrap Weaving, The Tao of Physics, and lots, lots more! One of the newest courses is "The Anthropology of Science Fiction" and I'm still trying to figure that out.

I have no objection to any of this . . . but why should this kindergarten be paid for by *taxes?* "Bread and Circuses."

I first started noticing the decline of education through mail from readers. I have saved mail from readers for forty years. Shortly after World War Two I noticed that letters from the youngest were not written but hand-printed. By the middle fifties deterioration in handwriting and in spelling became very noticeable. By today a letter from a youngster in grammar school *or in high school* is usually difficult to read and sometimes illegible—penmanship atrocious (*pencil*manship—nine out of ten are in soft pencil, with well-smudged pages), spelling unique, grammar an arcane art.

Most youngsters have not been taught how to fold 8½″ × 11″ paper for the two standard sizes of envelopes intended for that standard sheet.

Then such defects began to show up among college students. Apparently "Bonehead English" (taught everywhere today, so I hear) is not sufficient to repair the failure of grammar and high school teachers *who themselves in most cases were not adequately taught*.

I saw sharply this progressive deterioration because part of my mail comes from abroad, especially Canada, the United Kingdom, the Scandinavian countries, and Japan. A letter from any part of the Commonwealth is invariably neat, legible, grammatical, correct in spelling, and polite. The same applies to letters from Scandinavian countries. (Teenagers of Copenhagen usually speak and write English better than most teenagers of Santa Cruz.) Letters from Japan are invariably neat—but the syntax is sometimes odd. I have one young correspondent in Tokyo who has been writing steadily these past four years. The handwriting in the first letter was almost stylebook perfect but I could hardly understand the phrasing; now, four years later, the handwriting looks the same but command of grammar, syntax, and rhetoric is excellent, with only an occasional odd choice in wording giving an exotic flavor.

Our public schools no longer give good value. We remain strong in science and engineering but even students in those subjects are handicapped by failures of our primary and secondary schools and by cutback in funding of research both public and private. Our great decline in education is alone enough to destroy this country . . . but I offer no solutions because the only solutions I think would work are so drastic as to be incredible.

Span of Time—Decline in Patriotism
and in the Quality of our Armed Forces

The high school I attended (1919–24) was an early experiment in the junior and senior high school method. The last year of grammar school was joined with the freshman class as "junior high" while the sophomores, juniors, and seniors were "senior high."

There was a company of junior ROTC in junior high and two companies in senior high. Military training gave no credit and was not compulsory; it was neither pushed nor discouraged. A boy took it or not, as suited him and his parents. Some of the subfreshman (aet. ca. 13 an.) were barely big enough to tote a Springfield rifle.

Kansas City had a regiment of Federalized National Guard, with one authorized drill per week, 3 hours each Wednesday evening. For this a private was paid 69¢, a PFC got a dollar, and a corporal got big money—$1.18.

The required & paid weekly drill was not all, as about half of the regiment showed up on Sundays at the "Military Country Club"—acres of raw wood lot until the regiment turned it into rifle range, club house, stables, etc. No pay for Sundays. Two weeks encampment per year, with pay. For most of the regiment, this was their only vacation, two weeks then being standard.

That regiment ran about 96% authorized strength.

About 1921 Congress authorized the CMTC, Citizens Military Training Corps. It proved very popular. A month of summer training in camp at an Army post, continued through 4 years, could (if a candidate's grades were satisfactory) result in certification for commission in the reserve. Civilians submitted to military discipline in CMTC but were not subject to court martial. Offenders could be sent home or turned over to civilian police, depending on the offense. There were few offenses.

CMTC candidates got 3¢ per mile to and from their homes, no other money.

In 1925 I was appointed midshipman. There were 51 qualified applicants trying for that one appointment.

240 of my class graduated; 130 fell by the wayside. *One* of that 130 resigned voluntarily; all the others resigned involuntarily, most of them plebe year for failure in academics (usually mathematics), the others were requested to resign over the next three years for academic, physical, or other reasons. A few resigned graduation day through having failed the final physical examination for commissioning. Three more served about one year in the Fleet, then resigned—but these three volunteered after the attack on Pearl Harbor. 28 of the 129 who left the service involuntarily managed to get back on active duty in World War Two.

So with four exceptions all of my class stayed in the Navy *as long as the Navy would have them*. About 25% were killed in line of duty or died later of wounds. Neither at the Academy nor in the Fleet did I ever hear a midshipman or officer talk about resigning. While it is likely that some thought about it, all discussion tacitly carried the assumption that the Navy was our life, the Fleet our home, and that we would leave only feet first or when put out to pasture as too old.

Enlisted men: When I entered the Fleet, *before* the Crash of '29 and about a year before unemployment became a problem, Navy recruiting offices were turning down 19 out of 20 volunteers; the Army was turning down 5 out of 6. The reenlistment rate was high; the desertion rate almost too small to count.

Span of Time—Today in the Armed Forces

I have said repeatedly that I am opposed to conscription at any time, peace or war, for moral reasons beyond argument. For the rest of this I will try to keep my personal feelings out of the discussion—as I did in the rosy picture painted above. I reported *facts*, not my emotions.

I will not review details showing that the USSR is today militarily stronger than we are as the matter has been discussed endlessly in news media, in Congress, and in professional journals. The public discussion today concedes the military superiority of the USSR and centers on *how much* they are ahead of us, and what should be done about it. The details of this debate are of supreme importance as **the most expensive thing in the world is a second-best military establishment**, good but not good enough to win. At the moment the three-cornered standoff is saving us from that silly way to die . . . but I cannot predict how long this stalemate will last as key factors are not under our control, and neither our government nor our citizens seem willing to accept guns instead of butter on the scale required to make us too strong for anyone to risk attacking us. Polls seem to show that a controlling number of voters think that we are already spending too much on our Armed Forces.

What I set forth below comes primarily from an article by Richard A. Gabriel, Associate Professor of Politics, St. Anselm's College, Manchester, New Hampshire, author of CRISIS IN COMMAND. I lack personal experience with Army conditions today but what Dr. Gabriel says about them matches what I have heard from other sources and what I have read (I belong to all three associations—Army, Navy, Air Force—plus the Naval Institute and the Retired Officers Association; I get much data secondhand but no longer see it with my own eyes, hear it with my own ears).

Readers with personal experience in Korea, Viet Nam, and in the Services anywhere since the end of the Viet Nam debacle, I urge to write and tell me what you know that I don't, especially on points in which I am seriously mistaken.

Summarized from "The Slow Dying of the Ameri-

can Army," Dr. Richard A. Gabriel in *Gallery* magazine, June 1979, p.41 et seq.:

Concerning the All Volunteer Force (AVF): Early
this year the Pentagon admitted that all services had
failed to meet quotas.

30% of all Army volunteers are discharged for offenses during first enlistment. Of the 70 per 100 left, 26
do not reenlist. The desertion rates are the highest in
history . . . and this fact is partly covered up by using
administrative discharges (—i.e., "You're fired!")
rather than courts martial and punishment—*if* the de-
serter turns up. But no effort is made to find him.

According to Dr. Gabriel, citing General George S.
Blanchard and others, hard-drug use (heroin, cocaine,
angel dust—not marijuana) is greater than ever, especially in Europe, with estimates from a low of 10%
to a high of 64%. Marijuana is ignored—but let me add
that a man stoned out of his mind on grass is not one I
want on my flank in combat.

Category 3B and 4 (ranging down from dull to mentally retarded) make up 59% of Army volunteers . . . in
a day when privates handle very complex and sophisticated weapons and machinery. Add to this that the
mix is changing so that a typical private might be Chi-
cano or Puerto Rican, the typical sergeant a Black, the
typical officer "Anglo." And that officers are transferred with great frequency and enlisted men with
considerable frequency and you have a situation in
which esprit de corps *cannot* be developed (an outfit
without esprit de corps is not an army unit; it is an
armed mob—R.A.H.).

Today we have more general officers than we did in
World War Two. Our ratio of officers to enlisted men
is more than twice as high as that of successful armies
in the past. But an officer is not with his troops long
enough to be "the Old Man"—he is a "manager," not
a leader of men.

Dr. Gabriel concludes: "The most basic aspect is the
need to reinstate the draft."

I disagree.

My disagreement is not on moral grounds. Forget that I ever voiced opposition to slave soldiers; think of me as Old Blood-and-Guts willing to use any means whatever to win.

Reinstating the draft would *not* get us out of trouble, even with the changes Dr. Gabriel suggests to make the draft "fair."

As everyone knows, we were in the frying pan; shifting to AVF, instead of producing an efficient professional army, put us into the fire. Dr. Gabriel urges that we climb back into the frying pan—but with improvements: a national lottery with no deferments whatever for any reason.

I can't disagree with the even-steven rule . . . but my reason for thinking that Dr. Gabriel's solution will not work is this:

A lottery, even meticulously fair, *cannot* make a man willing to charge a machine-gun nest in the face of almost certain death. That sort of drive comes from emotional sources. Esprit de corps and patriotism *cannot* be drawn in a lottery.

Conscription works (among free men) only when it is not needed. I have seen two world wars; we used the draft in each . . . but in each case it was a means of straightening out the manpower situation; it was *not* needed to make men fight. Both wars were popular.

Since then we have had two non-Wars—Korea and Nam—in "peacetime" and using conscript troops. **And each non-War was a scandalous disaster.**

I don't have a neat solution to offer. If the American people have lost their willingness to fight and die for their country, the defect cannot be cured by conscription. Unless this emotional condition changes (and I do not know how to change it), we are whipped no matter what weapons we build. It could be overnight, or it could continue to be a long slow slide downhill over many years—ten, twenty, thirty. But the outcome is the same. Unless *something* renews the spirit this country once had, we are in the terminal stages of decay; history is ending for us.

Our foreign masters might graciously let us keep our flag, even our national name. But "the Land of the Free and the Home of the Brave" will be dead.

Time Span—Inflation

The Winter of '23–'24 I paid a street vendor 5¢ for a five billion mark German note and I paid too much; 5,000,000,000 DM was worth a trifle over 1¢. A bit later it was worth nothing.

In 1955 at the foot of the Acropolis I bought a small marble replica of the Venus of Melos for 10,000 drachma. I wasn't cheated; that was 35¢ USA.

There are the British pound, the Turkish lira, the Italian lira, the Mexican peso, and several others; all mean one pound of silver. Look up "exchange" and "commodities" in your newspaper; grab your pocket calculator and see how much each is inflated.

When I was a child of four or five my brothers and I used great stacks of hundred-dollar bills as play money. Confederate—

After two centuries, "Not worth a continental," still means "worthless." Memory is long for the damage done by inflation.

Before paper "money" was invented, inflation was accomplished by adding base metal to silver and/or gold while retaining the name of the coin. By this means the Roman denarius was devalued to zero during the first three centuries A.D. But inflation did not start with Caesar Augustus. In the early days of the Republic before the Punic Wars the cash unit was the libra (libra = lb. — pound = 273 grams, or about 60% of our pound avoirdupois, 454 grams). That's too large a unit for daily retail use; it was divided into 12 unciae (ounces).

A "lb." of silver was called an "as." 1/12 of that, struck as coinage, made efficient currency. Now comes war and inflation—

Eventually the "as"—once a pound of silver—was so debased that it amounted to a penny, more or less. Augustus, by decree, went back on a silver/gold standard and created the denarius, 3.87 grams of fine silver. He made 25 denarii equal in value to one aureus (7.74 grams of gold), or a ratio of 12.5 to one. ("Free and unlimited coinage of silver at a ratio of sixteen to one!" The Great Commoner and the august Emperor had similar notions about hard currency.)

One Augustan denarius equalled in gold at today's London fix ($385/troy ounce) a nominal $3.83, or about $3/10$ of a gram of gold. This tells us nothing about purchasing power; it simply says that the Augustan denarius was a solid silver coin almost the size and weight of the solid silver quarter we used to have before the government foisted on us those sandwich things. How much olive oil or meal that would buy in Rome around 1 A.D. can be estimated from surviving records—but all the gold in Rome could not buy an aspirin tablet or a paper of matches. No way to compare. And hard money was not supplemented by printed money, bank checks, and transactions that take place entirely inside computers—but I can't go into how those phenomena affect purchasing power without writing a book twice as long as this one on fiscal theory (which I am quite willing to do but nobody would buy it).

What Augustus did was to stabilize Rome's money by defining it in terms of two commodities, each intrinsically valuable, each stable in supply, each almost indestructible, and he defined also the legal ratio between the two coinages—an effort to circumvent Gresham's Law, unknown then but Augustus appears to have had a gut feeling for it. (Not Bill Gresham—the other one. Thomas Gresham.) But a bimetallic standard has its problems; the free economy ratio tends to drift away from the legal ratio, and Gresham's Law begins to work. But this happens very slowly with hard money and is not the disaster that printing-press inflation is, or the debasing of hard money.

Caesar Augustus died in 14 A.D.

His corpse was hardly cold before the vultures got to work. Tiberius, Caligula, Claudius, Nero—even Claudius did nothing to stop the robbery. Titus attempted an Augustan return to honest money in 80 A.D. but he died in September the following year; his successor was a disaster even as Caesars go.

"Put not your trust in Princes." Debasement of the currency continued under every Caesar for the next two centuries. Diocletian (reign: 294–305) inherited a worthless denarius; he returned Rome to the bimetallic standard at a level barely below that of Augustus. But he increased enormously the bureaucracy, instituted the harshest of taxation to pay for his "reforms," and decreed price-fixing—which worked just as it always does.

On his retirement (not assassination[!]) debasement was resumed while taxes stayed high, and Rome was on the skids. The decline and fall of the denarius and of Rome paralleled each other.

I'm tempted to discuss France's incredible inflation and collapse thereof during the French Revolution (and three more French inflations since then), and the inflations of several other countries in other centuries. But they are monotonously alike and differ from debasement primarily in the fact that the invention of paper "money" permits the corruption of legal tender to get utterly out of hand before the people notice it. In Germany in the early twenties people used to take wheelbarrows to the grocery store—not to fetch back groceries but to carry money to the grocer. But the early stages of disastrous inflation feel like "prosperity." Wages and profits go up, old debts are easier to pay off, business booms.

It is not until later that most people notice that prices and taxes have gone up faster than wages and profits, and that it is getting harder and harder to make ends meet.

There is a strong emotional feeling that "a dollar is a dollar." (Hitler called it, "Mark is Mark!") But you can reexamine it in terms of prices on bread, or how many minutes to earn a dollar. And don't forget taxes! If you aren't working at least the first three months of each year to pay taxes before you can keep one dollar for yourself, then you are on welfare, one way or another. You may not think you are taxed that much—paycheck deductions and hidden taxes are extracted under anesthesia. Try dividing the Federal Budget by the number of wage earners *not on the public payroll*, then take a stab at where you fit in. Don't forget the same process for state, county, and city. There are Makers, Takers, and Fakers, no fourth category, and today the Takers and the Fakers outnumber (and outvote) the Makers.

Today it takes more dollars each year to service the National Debt than the total budget for the last and most expensive year of the Korean War. I am not going to state here the amount of our National Debt. If you have not heard it recently, you wouldn't believe me. If you don't know, telephone your Congressman and ask; he has a local office near you. If the telephone information service can't (won't) tell you, the city room of *any* newspaper does know his number.

Our National Debt will *never* be paid. We are beyond the point of no return. Inflation will continue and get worse . . . and the elderly on fixed incomes and the young adults trying to start families will continue to bear the brunt.

Every congressman, every senator, knows precisely what causes inflation . . . but can't (won't) support the drastic reforms to stop it because it could (and probably would) cost him his job. I have no solution and only once piece of advice:

Buy a wheelbarrow.

The Age of Unreason

Having been reared in the most bigoted of Bible Belt fundamentalism in which every word of the King James version of the Bible is the literal word of God— then having broken loose at thirteen when I first laid hands on THE ORIGIN OF SPECIES and THE DESCENT OF MAN—I should have been unsurprised by the anti-intellectual and anti-science ground swell in this country.

I knew that our American temperament, practical as sharp tools on one side, was never more than three quarters of an inch from mindless hysteria on the other side. I *knew* this—my first long story was IF THIS GOES ON—, a yarn based on the assumption that my compatriots were capable of throwing away their dearly-bought liberties to submit to a crude and ridiculous religious dictatorship.

(In forty years of letters about that story no one has ever criticized this assumption; I infer that I am not alone in believing it.)

I had read much about the Ku Klux Klan during the Tragic Era, talked with many who had experienced it, then experienced its nationwide recrudescence in the early 1920's. I had seen damfoolishness from dance marathons to flagpole sitters, and had made considerable study of crowd behavior and mass delusions. I had noted, rather casually, the initial slow growth of anti-science-&-intellect-ism.

Yet the durned thing shocked me.

Let me list some signs:

a) I CHING;

b) Back-to-nature cults;

c) The collapse of basic education;

d) The current respectability of natal horological astrology among "intelligentsia"—e.g. professors, N.Y. lit'rary people, etc.;

e) "Experts" on nuclear power and nuclear weapons who know nothing whatever of mathematical physics and are smug in admitting it;

f) "Experts" on the ecology of northern Alaska who have never been there and are not mathematically equipped to analyse a problem in ecology;

g) People who watch television several hours a day and derive all their opinions therefrom—and expound them;

h) People who watch television several hours a day;

i) The return of creationism — "Equal time for Yahweh;"

j) The return of witchcraft.

The mindless yahoos, people who think linearly like a savage instead of inductively or deductively, and people who used to be respectful to learned opinion or at least kept quiet, now are aggressively on the attack. Facts and logic don't count; their intuition is the source of "truth."

If any item on the above list strikes you as rational, I won't debate it with you; you are part of the problem.

But I will illustrate what I mean in categories where I think I might be misunderstood.

a) **I CHING**— easier than "reading the augurs" but with nothing else to recommend it. Chinese fortune cookies are just as as accurate—and you get to eat the cookie. Nevertheless this bit of oriental nonsense is treated with solemn seriousness by many "educated" people. It is popular enough to make profitable the sale of books, equipment, magazine articles, and personal instruction. Paralleling I CHING is the widespread use of Tarot cards. Fortunetelling by cards used to be a playful parlor game, a mating rite—a nubile girl limited by the vocabulary and public manners of the Mauve Decade could convey to a rutty young male almost any message by how she chose to "read his fortune"—with no impropriety. But neither he nor she took the cards seriously.

Tarot cards formerly were used only by Gypsy or

fake-Gypsy fortunetellers; they were not an article of commerce, were not easy to find. Today they are as easy to buy as liquor during prohibition, and also books on their "interpretation." Reading the Tarot is taken with deep seriousness by a dismaying number of people—having the Hanging Man turn up can cause great anguish.

b) **Back-to-nature cults:** I do *not* mean nudist resorts or "liberated" beaches. The growing realization that human bodies are not obscene is a sane, healthy counter trend in our crazy culture. By back-to-nature cults I mean people who band together to "return to the land" to grow their own food without pesticides, without artificial fertilizers, without power machinery, self-reliant in all ways . . . but with no comprehension that a spading fork implies coal mines, iron ore, blast furnaces, steel mills, factories, etc., that any building more complex than a log cabin or a sod house implies a building-materials industry, etc.

If all of us tried to go back-to-nature, most of us would starve rather quickly. These back-to-nature freaks can't do arithmetic.

c) **The collapse of basic education**—no need to repeat.

d) **Natal horological astrology**—Baseline: fifty-odd years ago astrology was commonly regarded as a ridiculous *former* superstition, one all but a tiny minority had outgrown. It is now the orthodoxy of many, possibly a majority. This pathological change parallels the decay of public education.

Stipulated: Ancient astrologers were scientists in being able to predict certain aspects of descriptive astronomy such as eclipses, positions of the sun, moon, and naked-eye planets, etc. Whether or not they believed the fortunetelling they supplied to their kings, patrons, or clients is irrelevant. The test of a science is its ability to predict; in the cited phenomena the Chaldean priests (for example) performed remarkable feats of prediction with handcrafted naked-eye instruments.

It has long been known that Sol is the heat engine that controls our weather. Recently, with the discovery of solar wind, the Van Allen belts, et al., we have become aware of previously unsuspected variables affecting us and our weather, and successful predictions are being made empirically—no satisfactory theory.

"What sign were you born under?"—I don't recall having heard that question until sometime after World War Two. Today it is almost impossible to attend a social gathering (including parties made up almost solely of university staff and spouses) without being asked that question or hearing it asked of someone else.

Today natal horological astrology is so widely accepted that those who believe in it take it for granted that anyone they meet believes in it, too—if you don't, you're some sort of a nut. I don't know what percentage of the population believe in natal horological astrology (sorry about that clumsy expression but I wish to limit this precisely to the notion that the exact time, date, latitude, and longitude of your birth and the pattern of the Sun, Moon, and planets with respect to the Zodiac at that exact time all constitute a factor affecting your life comparable in importance to your genetic inheritance and your rearing and education)—I don't know the percentage of True Believers but it is high enough that newspaper editors will omit any feature or secondary news rather than leave out the daily horoscope.

Or possibly *more* important than heredity and environment in the minds of True Believers since it is seriously alleged that this natal heavenly pattern *affects every day of your life*—good days for new business ventures—a bad day to start a trip—and so forth, endlessly.

The test of a science is its capacity to make correct predictions. Possibly the most respected astrologer in America is a lady who not only has her daily column in most of the largest newspapers but also annually publishes predictions for the coming year.

For ten years I clipped her annual predictions, filed them. She is highly recommended and I think she is sincere; I intended to give her every possible benefit of doubt.

I hold in my hand her predictions for 1974 dated Sunday January 13, 1974:

Here are some highlights: " . . . Nixon . . . will ride out the Watergate storm . . . will survive both the impeachment ordeal and the pressures to resign . . . will go down in history as a great president . . . will fix the responsibility for Pearl Harbor" (vindicating Kimmel and Short) . . . "in . . . 1978 . . . the cure for cancer will be acknowledged by the medical world . . . end the long search." (1974) "The dollar will be enormously strengthened as the balance of payments reflects the self-sufficiency in oil production." "The trouble in Ireland will continue to be a tragic situation *until 1978.*" (Italics added—R.A.H.) "Willy Brandt" (will be reelected) "and be in office for quite some time to come. He will go on to fantastic recognition about the middle of 1978." (On 6 May 1974 Brandt resigned during a spy scandal.) She makes many other predictions either too far in the future to check or too vaguely worded. I have omitted her many predictions about Gerald Ford because they all depend on his serving out the term as vice president.

You can check the above in the files of most large newspapers.

e) & f)—no comment needed.

g) & h) need no comment except to note that they are overlapping but not identical categories—and I should add "People who allow their children to watch television several hours a day." (Television, like the automobile, is a development widely predicted . . . but its major consequences *never* predicted.)

i) **The return of creationism**—If it suits you to believe that Yahweh created the universe in the fashion related in Genesis, I won't argue it. But I don't have to respect your belief and I do not think that legislation requiring that the Biblical version be included in public school textbooks is either constitutional or fair. How about Ormuzd? Ouranos? Odin? There is an unnumbered throng of religions, each with its creation myth—all different. Shall one of them be taught as having the status of a scientific hypothesis merely because the members of the religion subscribing to it can drum up a majority at the polls, or organize a pressure group at a state capital? This is tyranny by the mob inflicted on minorities in defiance of the Bill of Rights.

Revelation has no place in a science textbook; it belongs under religious studies. Cosmogony is the most difficult and least satisfactory branch of astronomy; cosmologists would be the first to agree. But, damn it; they're *trying!*—on the evidence as it becomes available, by logical methodology, and their hypotheses are constantly subjected to pitiless criticism by their informed equals.

They should not have to surrender time on their platform, space in their textbooks, to purveyors of ancient myths supported only by a claim of "divine revelation."

If almost everyone believed in Yahweh and Genesis, and less than one in a million U.S. citizens believe in Brahma the Creator, it would not change the constitutional aspect. *Neither* belongs in a science textbook in a tax-supported school. But if Yahweh is there, Brahma should be. And how about that Eskimo Creator with the unusually unsavory methods? We have a large number of Eskimo citizens.

j) **The return of witchcraft**—It used to be assumed that Southern California had almost a monopoly on cults. No longer. (Cult vs. religion—I am indebted to L. Sprague de Camp for this definition of the difference. A "religion" is a faith one is born into; a "cult" is a faith an adult joins voluntarily. "Cult" is often used as a slur by a member of an older faith to disparage a newer faith. But this quickly leads to contradictions. In the 1st century A.D. the Christians were an upstart cult both to the Sanhedrin and to the Roman priests.

"Cult" is also used as a slur on a faith with "weird ideas" and "weird practices." But this can cause you to bite your tail even more quickly than the other. "Weird" by whose standards?

(Mr. de Camp's distinction implies something about a mature and presumably sane adult becoming a prose-lyte in a major and long-established faith, such as Islam or Shintoism or the Church of England . . . but the important thing it implies is that a person born into, let us say, the Presbyterian Church is not being odd or unreasonable if he remains in it all his life despite having lost all faith; he's merely being pragmatic. His wife and kids are there; he feels that church is a good influence on the kids, many of his friends are there. It's a comfortable habit, one carrying with it a degree of prestige in the community.

(But if he changes into a saffron robe and shaves his pate, then goes dancing down the street, shouting, "Hare Krishna!" he won't keep his Chevrolet dealership very long. Theology has nothing to do with it.)

One of the symptoms of this Age of Unreason, anti-science and anti-intellect, in the United States is the very prominent increase in new cults. We've never been without them. 19th Century New England used to breed them like flies. Then it was Southern California's turn. Now they seem to spring up anywhere and also are readily imported from abroad. Zen Buddhism has been here so long that it is usually treated with respect . . . but still so short a time (1950) that few American adults not of Japanese ancestry can claim to have been born into it. Ancient in Japan, it is still a cult *here*—e.g., Alan Watts (1915 – 1973), who moved from Roman Catholic priest to Episcopal priest to Zen priest. I doubt that there is any count on American Zen Buddhists but it is significant that both "satori" and "koan" were assimilated words in all four standard U.S. dictionaries only 16 years after Zen Buddhism penetrated the non-Japanese population.

And there are the Moonies and the Church of Scientology and that strange group that went to South America and committed suicide en masse and the followers of that fat boy from India and—look around you. Check your telephone book. *I express no opinion on the tenets of any of these*; I simply note that, since World War Two, Americans have been leaving their "orthodox" churches in droves and joining churches new in this country.

Witchcraft is not new and never quite died out. But it is effectively new to most of its adherents here today because of the enormous increase in numbers of witches. ("Warlock" is insulting, "Wizard" barely acceptable and considered gauche, "Witch" is the correct term both male and female. The religion is usually called either "the Old Religion" or "the Craft" rather than witchcraft.)

The Craft is by its nature underground; witches cannot forget the hangings in Salem, the burnings in Germany, the fact that the injunction, "Thou shalt not suffer a witch to live" (Exodus XXII, 18) has usually been carried out whenever the Old Religion surfaced. Even during this resurgence only four covens have come to my attention and, not being a witch myself, I have never attended an esbat (easier to enter a tyled lodge!).

The Craft is *not* Devil worship and it is *not* Black Mass but both of the latter have enjoyed some increase in recent years.

If witchcraft has not come to your attention, search any large book store; note how very many new titles concern witchcraft. Most of these books are phony, not written by witches, mere exploitation books—but their very existence shows the change. Continue to show interest and a witch just might halfway reveal himself by saying, "Don't bother with that one. Try this one." Treat him with warm politeness and you may learn much more.

To my great surprise when I learned of it, there are over a dozen (how much over a dozen I have no way to guess) periodicals in this country devoted solely to the Old Religion.

Time Span—The Cancerous Explosion of Government

Will Rogers told us that we were lucky in that we didn't get as much government as we pay for. He was (and is) emphatically right . . . but he died 15 August 1935. The Federal government spent $6,400,000,000 in the last 12 months of his tragically short life. The year he was born (1879) the Federal government spent $274,000,000—an expensive year, as we resumed paying specie for the Greenback Inflation, $346,700,000 of fiat money.

What would Will Rogers think of a budget of $300 billion and up?

(Figures quoted from THE STATISTICAL HISTORY OF THE UNITED STATES,
Prepared by the U.S. Bureau of the Census)

Census Year	Population	Fed. Employees State & Local Total Pub. Emp.	Fed. Receipts Fed. Expenditure Surplus/Deficit	Fed. Public Debt
1910	91,972,266	388,708 ?	$675,512,000 693,617,000 (−)$18,105,000	$1,146,940,000
1920	105,710,620	655,265 ?	$6,648,898,000 6,357,677,000 $291,221,000	$24,299,321,000
1930	122,755,046	601,319 2,622,000 3,223,319	$4,057,884,000 3,320,211,000 $737,673,000	$16,185,310,000
1940	131,669,275	1,042,420 3,206,000 4,248,420	$6,900,000,000 9,600,000,000 (−)$2,700,000,000	$50,700,000,000
1950	150,697,361	1,960,708 4,098,000 6,058,708	$40,900,000,000 43,100,000,000 (−)$2,200,000,000	$256,900,000,000
1960	178,464,236	2,398,704 6,083,000 8,481,704	$92,500,000,000 92,200,000,000 $300,000,000	$290,900,000,000
1970	203,235,298	2,981,574 9,830,000 12,811,574	$193,700,000,000 196,600,000,000 (−)$2,900,000,000	$382,600,000,000
(1980)	(222,000,000)	(3,600,000) (14,500,000) (18,100,000)	($300,000,000,000) ($310,000,000,000) (−)($10,000,000,000)	($525,000,000,000)

(1980 figures are extrapolations = wild guesses)
(Too timid?) *Much* too timid!—as you knew when you
read them, as I knew when I prepared them. I plotted
all of the above figures on graph paper, faired the
curves, *suppressed what I knew by memory* (even
refrained from consulting World Almanacs to bridge
the 9 years since the close of compilation of THE
STATISTICAL HISTORY) and extrapolated to
1980 by the curves—*not* tangent, but on the indicated curve.

By the best figures I can get from Washington today
(20 Nov 1979) the budget is $547,600,000,000; the ex-
pected deficit is $29,800,000,000; and our current Fed-
eral Public Debt is estimated at $886,480,000,000.(!!!)

The end of the Federal fiscal year, September 30, is
still over ten months away. In ten months a lot of
things can happen. Unexpected events always cause
unexpected expense . . . but with great good luck the
deficit will not increase much and the National Public
Debt will stay under $900,000,000,000.

In case of war, all bets are off.

What is happening is what always happens in fiat-
currency inflation: After a certain point, unpredictable as to date because of uncountable human variables, it becomes uncontrollable and the currency
becomes worthless. Dictatorship usually follows.
From there on anything can happen—all bad.

The Greenback Inflation did *not* result in collapse of
the dollar and of constitutional government because
gold backing was not disavowed, simply postponed
for a relatively short time. The Greenback Party
wanted to go on printing paper money, never resume
specie payment—but eventually we toughed it out and
paid hard money for the Greenbacks that had financed
the Union side of the war. From 1862 to 1879 gold and
silver were not used internally. Our unfavorable balance of trade for 1861–65, which *had* to be met in gold,
was $296,000,000. Hard times and high taxes—but we
made it.

The French Revolution inflation was unsecured. Between April 1790 and February 1796, 40 billion livres or francs were issued. New paper money (Mandats) replaced them that year; the following year both sorts were declared no longer legal tender (waste paper!)— and 2 years later Napoleon took over "to save the Republic."(!)

We could still keep from going utterly bankrupt by going back on some hard standard (gold, silver, uranium, mercury, bushels of wheat—*something*). But it would not be easy, it would not be popular; it would mean hard times for everyone while we recovered from an almighty hangover. Do you think a Congress and a President can be elected on any such platform?

One chink in the armor of any democracy is that, when the Plebs discover that they can vote themselves Bread & Circuses, they usually do . . . right up to the day there is neither bread nor circuses. At that point they often start lynching the senators, congressmen, bankers, tax collectors, Jews, grocers, foreigners, any minority—take your choice. For they know that *they* didn't do it. The citizen is sovereign until it comes to accepting blame for his sovereign acts—then he demands a scapegoat.

I used official figures without comment to show where we have been the past 70 years . . . and how we got into the mess we are in. But, while I think our government is more nearly honest than some others (see INSIDE INTOURIST Afterword, page 439), there is a lot of hanky-panky in those official figures. Example: Social Security taxes go into the general fund and are spent. If Social Security were *in fact* insurance (the basis on which the gimmick was sold to us by FDR's "New Deal"), the receipts would be segregated and invested and not shown as income . . . *OR* a competent insurance actuary with staff would calculate the commitment and it would show in the National Public Debt.

(The fact that a debt is amortized over the years

doesn't stop it from being a debt. It was an amortized mortgage that got me into this racket. The prospect of years and years of future monthly payments spoiled my sleep.)

The only way the Government can go on paying Social "Security" to my generation is by taxing you young people more and more heavily . . . and each year there are more and more old people and fewer and fewer young people. It won't help to run the printing presses faster; that causes food to rise in price, rents to go up, etc.—and people over 65 start putting pressure on Congress . . . and there's an election coming up. (There's *always* an election coming up.)

One thing I learned as a wardheeler was that (with scarce exceptions) people in my age group want one of two things: 1) They want to keep on clipping those coupons and collecting those rents and they don't give a damn what it does to the country, or 2) they want that raise in Social Security (Townsend Plan) ("Ham & Eggs") (you name one) and they don't give a damn what it does to the country.

(I don't claim to be altruistic. Just this pragmatic difference: I am sharply aware that, if the United States goes down the chute, *I* go down with it.)

I use the term "*Federal* Public Debt" because what is usually termed the "Public Debt" is by no means our total public debt. There are also state, county, city, and special-district debts. It is difficult to get accurate figures on these public debts but the total appears to be larger than the Federal Public Debt. I can't make even a wild guess at the Social Security commitment . . . but our *total* public promises-to-pay have to exceed two trillion dollars. How much is a trillion? Well, it means that a baby born today owes at least $4,347.83 to the Federal Government alone before his eyes open. (No wonder he yells). It means that the Zero Population Growth family (who was going to save us all—remember?) of father, mother, and 2.1 children owes $17,826 in addition to private debts (mortgage, automobile, college for 2.1 children).

Of course papa won't pay it off; that debt will grow larger. But it will cost him $2000 a year (and rising) just to "service" his pro-rata; any taxes for which he gets *anything at all*—even more laws—is on top of that.

A trillion seconds is 31,688 years, 9 months, 5 days, 8 hours, 6 minutes, and 42 seconds—long enough for the precession of the equinoxes to make Vega the Pole Star, swing back again to Polaris, and go on past to Alpha Cephei. Or counting the other way it would take us to 29,708 B.C. . . . or more than 25 thousand years before Creation by Bishop Usher's chronology for creationism.

I don't understand a trillion dollars any better than I do a trillion seconds. I simply know that we had better stop spending money we don't have if we want to avoid that Man on Horseback.

But I don't think we will stop "deficit financing," the euphemism that sounds so much better than "kiting checks."

You may have noticed that 1970 figure for public employees (not my extrapolation for 1980, but the official 1970 figures straight from the United States Bureau of the Census).

That figure does not include the Armed Forces. It does not include some special categories. It is easier to learn the number of slaves imported in 1769 (6,736) than it is to find out exactly how many people are on public payrolls in this country. And it is not simply difficult but *impossible* to determine how many people receive Federal checks for which they perform no services. (Or food stamps. Are food stamps money?) But one thing is certain: the number of people eligible to vote who *do* receive money from some unit of government (aid to dependent children, Supreme Court justices, not growing wheat, removing garbage, governors of states, whoever) exceeds the number eligible to vote but receiving no pay or subsidy of any sort from any unit of government.

Have you read the Federal Register lately? Have you *ever* read the Federal Register? Under powers delegated by Congress certain *appointed* officials can publish a new regulation in the Federal Register and, if Congress does not stop it, after a prescribed waiting time, that regulation has the force of law—it *is* law, to you and to me, although a lawyer sees nuances. I have vastly oversimplified this description, but my only purpose is to point out that "administrative law" reaches into every corner of our lives, and is the major factor in the enormous and strangling invasion of the Federal Government into our private affairs.

I can't see anything in the Constitution that permits the Congress to delegate its power to pass laws . . . but the Supreme Court says it's okay and that makes my opinion worthless.

I'm stopping. There are endless other gloomy things to discuss—the oil shortage, the power shortage (not the same thing), pollution, population pressure, a projected change in climate that can and probably will turn the problems of population and food into sudden and extreme crisis, crime in the streets and bankrupt cities, our incredible plunge from the most respected nation on Earth to the most despised (but we are nonetheless expected to pick up the tab). Bill Gresham was right but he told only half of it: you not only don't get rich peddling gloom; it isn't any fun.

So now come with me—

"OVER THE RAINBOW—"

The new President had not been in office ten days before it became clear to his own party as well as to the "loyal opposition" that he was even more of a disaster than the defeated candidate had predicted. Nevertheless the country was shocked when he served even fewer days than the ninth President—killed in a crash, his private plane, himself at the controls; dying with him his three top aides: White House chief of staff, press secretary, appointments secretary.

No U.S. or Canadian news medium said a word about alcohol or incidents in the dead President's past; they treated it as a tragic accident. Papers and TV reporters elsewhere were not as reticent.

The Speaker of the new House saw the ex-Vice President first (even before the oath of office) as the Speaker's seniority in line of succession enabled him to do. He came right to the point. "I am ready to take this load off your shoulders. We both know that you were picked simply to support the ticket; no one ever expected to load you down with *this*. Here's how we'll do it: You resign at once, then we'll meet the press together—after I'm sworn in. I'll do most of the talking. I promise you, it won't be a strain on you."

"I'm sure that it won't be. You're excused."

"*Huh!*"

"You may leave. In fact I am telling you to leave. I thought you had come to stand beside me as I take the oath . . . but you have something entirely different in mind. You would not enjoy staying; I would not enjoy having you stay."

"You'll regret this! You're making a mistake!"

"If a mistake was made, it was made at the Convention. By you and five others, I believe; I was not present. Yes, I may regret it but this is what I undertook to do when I accepted the nomination for the Vice-Presidency. Now get out. *Pronto!*"

The new President sent for the Director of the Budget forty minutes after the swearing in. "Explain this to me."

The Director hemmed and hawed and tried to say that the budget was too technical for anyone not in public life before—

—and was answered, "I'm accepting your resignation. Send in your deputy."

It was almost a week before this call was made: "Admiral? This is the President. If I come to your home, do you feel well enough to see me?"

There was a tussle of wills that the Admiral won only through pointing out that it was never proper to subject the President of the United States to unnecessary risk of assassination . . . and that with his new car, fitted for his wheelchair, he still went to the Pentagon twice a week. "I'm old, I admit; I was born in 1900. But I'm not dead and I'm quite able to report to my Commander in Chief. And we both know that threats have been made."

The President won the next argument. On being wheeled in the Admiral started to get out of his chair. "Do please sit down!"

The old man continued to try to rise, leaning on the arm of his nurse. The President said quickly, "That was expressed as a request but was an order. Sit down."

The Admiral promptly sat back down, caught his breath and said formally, "Ma'am, I report—with great pleasure!—to the President of the United States."

"Thank you for coming, sir. In view of our respective ages . . . and your health, I felt that it was a time to dispense with protocol. But you are right; there are indeed a flood of threats, many more than get into the news. I don't intend to be a target . . . at least until we have a new Vice President sworn in."

"*Never* be a target, Madam. You would be mourned by everyone, both parties. Uh, if I may say so, you are even more beautiful in person than you are on the screen."

"Not mourned by everyone, I'm certain, or I would not have to be cautious about assassination. As for that other, I'm not beautiful and you know it. I know what

I have. I project. But it's not physical beauty. It's something that a pro—a professionally competent actress—does with her whole being. Her voice, her expression, her hands, her body. A gestalt, with regular features the least important factor. Or not present, as with me."

The President smiled, got up and went around the big desk, leaned over the Admiral, kissed his forehead. "But you are an old dear to have said it."

He cleared his throat, noisily. "Ma'am, what is your opinion in the matter against that of millions of men?"

"We've dropped that subject. Now to work! Admiral, why is it that there has been so much difficulty with nuclear power plants ashore but never any trouble with your nuclear submarines?"

The President slapped her desk, glared at the leader of the delegation. "Stop that! Han'kerchief head, you've come to the wrong church. In this office there are *no* Blacks—or Blues, Whites, Greens, or Yellows—just Americans. Besides that, you claim to be a Black representing Blacks. Hmmph! That's a phony claim if I ever—"

"I resent that, Mrs. Ni—"

"*Pipe down!* 'Madam President,' if you please. And one does *not* interrupt the President. I said your claim was phony. It is. I'm at least three shades darker than you are . . . yet I'm smooth brown, not black." She looked around. "I don't see a real sooty black in your whole delegation. Mmm, I see just one darker than I am. Mr. Green, isn't it? That is your name?"

"Yes, Madam President. From Brooklyn."

"Any white blood, Mr. Green? Perhaps I should say 'Any Caucasian ancestry?' "

"Possibly. But none that I know of, Ma'am."

"We're all in that boat . . . including all whites. A person who claims to be absolutely certain of his ancestry more than three generations back is accepting the short end of a bet. But since you are from Brooklyn, you can help me pass a word. An important word, one that I'll be emphasizing on the networks tonight but I'll need help from a lot of people to let *all* the people know that I mean it. A Black who gets elected from Brooklyn has lots of Jewish friends, people who trust him."

"That's right, Madam President."

"Listen to my talk tonight, then pass it on in your own words. This nation has split itself into at least a hundred splinter groups, pressure groups, each trying for a bigger bite of the pie. That's got to *stop!*—before it kills us. No more Black Americans. No more Japanese Americans. Israel is not our country and neither is Ireland. A group calling itself La Raza had better mean the human race—the *whole* human race—or they'll get the same treatment from me as the Ku Klux Klan. Amerindians looking for special favors will have just two choices: Either come out and *be* Americans and accept the responsibilities of citizenship . . . or go back to the reservation and shut up. Some of their ancestors got a rough deal. But so did yours and so did mine. There are no Anglos left alive who were at Wounded Knee or Little Big Horn, so it's time to shut up about it.

"But race and skin color and national ancestry isn't all that I mean. I intend to refuse to see *any* splinter group claiming to deserve special treatment not accorded other citizens and I will veto any legislation perverted to that end. Wheat farmers. Bankrupt corporations. Bankrupt cities. Labor leaders claiming to represent 'the workers' . . . when most of the people they claim to represent repudiate any such leadership. Business leaders just as phony. *Any*one who wants the deck stacked in his favor because, somehow, he's 'special.' "

The President took a deep breath, went on: "Any such group gets thrown out. But two groups will get thrown out so hard they'll bounce! I'm a woman and I'm Negro. We've wiped the Jim-Crow laws off the books; I'll veto any Crow-Jim bill that reaches this office. Discrimination? Certainly there is still discrimination—but you can't kill prejudice by passing a law. We'll make it by how we behave and what we produce—not by trick laws.

"I feel even more strongly about women. We women are a majority, by so many millions that in an election it would be called a landslide. And *will* be a landslide, on *anything*, any time women really want it to be. So women don't need favors; they just need to make up their minds what they want—then take it." The President stood up again. "That's all. I'm going to devote this term to those 'unalienable rights'—for *everybody*. No splinter groups. Go tell people so. Now git . . . and don't come back! Not as a splinter group. Come back as *Americans*."

They moved toward the door. Their erstwhile leader muttered something. The President demanded, "Mr. Chairman, what did you say?"

"I said," he answered loudly, "you aren't going to have a second term."

She laughed at him. "I thought that's what I heard. Burr head, I'm not worrying about being reelected; I worry only about how much I can do in four years."

(Editorial in the Springfield *Eagle*)

LIFE INSURANCE?

The President's surprise nomination of the House Minority Leader for the vacant vice-presidency has produced some snide theories, one of the nastiest being the idea that she fears a plot on her life by the wheeler-dealers who put the late President into office, so she is spiking their guns (literally!) by rigging things to turn the presidency over to the opposition party should anything happen to her. . . .

. . . prefer to take her at her word, that her objective is to get the country unified again, and that a woman and a man, a Republican and a Democrat, a White and a Black, could be the team to do it.

The Speaker of the House has still not commented, but his floor leader and the nominated minority leader appeared with the President when she announced her choice. The Senate President Pro Tempore said, "I see no reason why confirmation should not go through quickly. I've known Don for thirty years; I trust that I am not so narrow-minded that I can't recognize presidential caliber in a man of another party . . . .

. . . customary to be of the same party, there is a custom just as long standing (and more important) that a President have a Vice President he (she) trusts to carry out his (her) policies.

Let's back them to the limit! Let's all be *Americans* again!

"Thanks for coming."

"Madam President, any time you send a car for me, then scoot me across the country in a hypersonic military jet, thanks should be the other way. My first experience above the speed of sound—and my first time in the Oval Office. I never expected to be in it."

She chuckled. "Nor did I. Especially on this side of this desk. Let's get to work." She held up a book. "Recognize this?"

"Eh?" He looked startled. "Yes, Ma'am, I do. I should."

"You should, yes." She opened to a marked page, read aloud: " '—I have learned this about engineers. When something *must* be done, engineers can find a way that is economically feasible.' Is that true?"

"*I* think so, Ma'am."

"You're an engineer."

"I am an *obsolete* engineer, Ma'am."

"I don't expect you to do the job yourself. You know what I did about fusion power plants."

"You sent for the one man with a perfect record. I've seen the power ship moored off Point Sur. Brilliant. Solved an engineering and a public relations problem simultaneously."

"Not quite what I mean. I consulted the Admiral, yes. But the job was done by his first deputy, the officer he has groomed to replace him. And by some other Navy people. Now we're working on ways to make the key fission-power people—safety control especially—all former Navy nuclear submariners. But we have to do it without stripping the Navy of their Blue and Gold crews. On things I know nothing about—most things, for this job! I consult someone who *does*—and that leads me to the person who can do it. Since I know very little about how to be President, I look for advice on almost everything."

"Ma'am, it seems to me—and a lot of other people—that you were born for the job."

"Hardly. Oh, politics isn't strange to me; my father held office when I was still a girl at home. But I did my first television commercial at fourteen and I was hooked. If I hadn't been 'resting' between contracts, I would not have had accepted the Governor's appointment—I was just his 'exhibit coon' but the Commission's work did interest me. Then I was still an 'exhibit coon' when he saw to it that I was on his favorite-son slate. Then, when the three leading candidates deadlocked, my late predecessor broke the deadlock in his favor by naming me as the other half of his ticket. I went along with it with a wry grin inside, figuring, first, that the ploy wouldn't work, and second, that, if he *did* get nominated, he would find some way to wiggle out—ask me to withdraw in favor of his leading rival or some such."

She shrugged. "But he didn't—or couldn't. I don't know which; he rarely talked to me. Real talk, I mean. Not just, 'Good morning,' and, 'Did you have a comfortable flight' and not wait for an answer.

"I didn't care. I relished every minute of the campaign. An actress sometimes plays a queen . . . but for four months I got to *be* one. Never dreaming that our ticket would win. I knew what a—No, *de mortuis nil nisi bonum*, and we must get back to work. What would you do about pollution of streams?"

"Eh? But that one has already been solved. By one of the Scandinavian countries, I believe. You simply require every user to place his intake immediately downstream from his discharge of effluent into the stream. In self-protection the user cleans up his discharge. It's self-enforcing. No need to test the water until someone downstream complains. Seldom. Because it has negative feedback. Ma'am, complying with a law should be more rewarding than breaking it—or you get positive feedback."

She made a note. "We could clean up the Mississippi that way. But I'm fretted about streams inside states, too. For example, the Missouri, where it is largest, is entirely inside the State of Missouri."

"Ma'am, I think you'll find that you have jurisdiction over *all* navigable streams."

"I do?"

"Ma'am, you have powers you may never have dreamed existed. A 'navigable stream' is one only three feet deep, I think. You may right now have the power to order this under law already on the books. If there is a paragraph or even a clause on placement of inlets and outlets, you almost certainly can issue an executive order right away. Today. The boss of the U.S. Engineers would know. General Somebody. A French name."

She touched a switch. "Get me the head of the U.S. Engineers. How would you dispose of nuclear power plant wastes? Rocket them onto the Moon as someone urged last week? Why wouldn't the Sun be better? We may want to go back to the Moon someday."

"Oh, my, no! Neither one, Ma'am."

"Why not? Some of those byproducts are poisonous for hundreds of years, so I've heard. No?"

"You heard correctly. But the really rough ones have short half-lives. The ones with long half-lives— hundreds, even thousands of years, or longer—are simple to handle. But don't throw away *any* of it, Ma'am. Not where you can't recover it easily."

"Why not? We're speaking of *wastes*. I assume that we have extracted anything we can use."

"Yes, Ma'am, anything *we* can use. But our great grandchildren are going to hate you. Do you know the only use the ancient Romans had for petroleum? Medicine, that's all. *I* don't know how those isotopic wastes will be used next century . . . any more than those old Romans could guess how *very* important oil would become. But I certainly wouldn't throw those so-called wastes into the Sun! Besides, rockets do fail . . . and who wants to scatter radioactives over a couple of states? And there's the matter of the fuel and steel and a dozen other expensive things for the rockets. You could easily wind up spending more money to get rid of the ashes than you ever got from selling the power."

"Then what *do* you do? They say we mustn't sink it into the ocean. Or put it on the Antarctic ice cap. Salt mines?"

"Madam President, honest so help me, this is one of those nonproblems that the antitechnology nuts delight in. Radioactive wastes aren't any harder to handle than garbage. Or hot ashes. Or anything else you don't want to pick up in your bare hands. The quantity isn't much, not at all like garbage, or coal ashes. There are at least a half dozen easy ways. One of the easiest is to mix them with sand and gravel and cement into concrete bricks, then stack them in any unused piece of desert.

"Or glass bricks. Or let the stuff dry and store it in steel barrels such as oil drums and use those old salt mines you mentioned—the bricks you could leave in the open. All by remote manipulation, of course; that's the way a radioactives engineer does everything. Waldoes. That's old stuff. No trouble."

"I thought you said you were obsolete."

He grinned sheepishly. "Ma'am, it's easy to talk. As long as I know that young fellows will have to do the tedious drudgery that goes into making anything new work. But the solutions I've offered *are* practical. No new discoveries needed."

"How about air pollution?"

"What sorts, Ma'am? The two main sources are internal combustion engines—trucks and autos—and industrial smokes. Quite different problems."

"Pick one."

"Transportation pollution is going to solve itself soon—either the hard way or the easy way. Oil, whether it's our own or from the OPEC, is too valuable to be burned in cars and trucks; it's the backbone of the chemical engineering industry—fertilizers, plastics, pesticides, lubricants, and so forth. So, quite aside from the energy problem, we need to stop burning it. We can either wait until it's forced on us catastrophically . . . or we can turn to other transportation power voluntarily, and thereby become self-sufficient in oil for peace or for war. Either way, transportation pollution is ended."

"But *what* other transportation power, Doctor?"

"Oh. Half a dozen ways, at least. Get rid of the I.C. engine completely, both Otto cycle and Diesel cycle, and go back to the external combustion engine and steam. The I.C. engine never did make sense; starting and stopping combustion every split second is a guarantee of incomplete combustion, wasted fuel, and smog. Air pollution. External combustion has no such built-in stupidity; no matter what fuel, it burns continuously and can be adjusted for complete combustion. The Stanley Steamer used kerosene. But that's petroleum again. I would use wood alcohol as a starter—it hurts me every time I pass a sawmill and see them burning chips and slash.

"But wood alcohol has its drawbacks. We may burn hydrogen someday. Or learn to store electricity in less weight and less space. Or store energy in a flywheel. But all of those, even hydrogen, are simply ways to store energy. It still leaves an energy problem."

"Hydrogen, too? But you said we would burn it. No?"

"We'll burn it for some purposes; in some ways it's the ideal fuel; its only ash is water vapor. But, Ma'am, we don't *have* hydrogen; we have *water*—and even with perfect efficiency—never achieved—the energy you get out of hydrogen by burning it cannot exceed the energy you must use in getting that hydrogen by electrolysis of water. So you must generate electricity first."

"I see. No free lunch."

"Never a free lunch. But the energy problem can be solved several ways . . . through renewable resources. We've been using nonrenewable resources—coal and oil and cutting trees faster than they grow."

"Renewable resources—Windmills and water power and sun power?"

"Wind and water power are fine but limited. I mean effectively unlimited power. Such as this new wrinkle of thermoelectric power from the temperature difference of deep ocean and surface ocean. But there aren't too many really convenient places to do that. You named the one energy that is unlimited and convenient anywhere. Sun power."

"So? What desert is convenient to the Gary steel mills?"

"Not desert, Ma'am; the Sierra Club wouldn't like it."

"I plan to tell the Sierra Club that they are *not* the government of the United States. But in stronger language."

"I look forward to hearing you, Madam President. The Sierra Club loves deserts and hates people. But our deserts aren't sufficient. Sun power, yes—but *unlimited* sun power. In orbit."

South Africa Enraged

United States Surprise Return to Gold Standard at $350 per Troy Ounce of Fine Gold Has Bourses in Turmoil

"New Policy Obvious Concommitant of Return to Balanced Budget," Says Treasury Secretary Spokesman

"The Way to Resume is to Resume."

By ADAM SMITH
Finance Editor

WASHINGTON—The Treasury Secretary, after reading aloud to the Press the President's brief announcement of resumption of specie payments immediately at $350/oz., emphasized that this was not a tactical maneuver to "strengthen the dollar," not an auction of bullion such as those in the past, but a permanent policy consistent with the administration's total policy. "A return to our traditional policy, I must add. A century ago, for 15 years, war caused us to suspend specie payments—but never with any intent to accept the vice of fiat money. Since 1971, as sequelae to 3 wars, we have had a similar problem. By letting the dollar float until the world price of gold in terms of dollars settled down, we have determined what could be called the natural price. So we have resumed specie payment at a firm gold standard. God willing, we will never leave it."

This was in answer to the London *Times* correspondent's

frosty inquiry as to whether or not the Secretary thought anyone would want our gold at that price. The Treasury Secretary told him that we were not "selling gold" but promising
to redeem our paper money at a gold-standard price. The
Times' question was inspired by the fact that at the close of
market Friday the London fix was $423.195 per troy ounce,
with the Zurich fix, the Winnipeg fix, and the Hong Kong fix
(the last only hours before the Washington announcement)
all within a dollar of the London fix.

PRAVDA: "—capitalistic trickery—"

Moscow has not had a free market in gold since pre-1914
but, as a gold-producing country, its response to our resumption policy has been even more acid than the shrill complaints
from Johannesburg. The Zurich gold market did not open
today. London opened on time but the price dropped at once,
with the first purchase at $397.127, which slowed but did not
stop the decline. Winnipeg opened an hour late; the reason
became clear when the Prime Minister announced the tying
of the Canadian dollar to the U.S. dollar at one-to-one—a
fait accompli as the two currencies have hunted up and down,
never more than 1% apart, for the past several months.

The timing of the announcement gave the world a weekend
in which to think things over, the purpose being presumably
to reduce oscillations. The New York Stock Market responded with an upward surge. The Dow-Jones Industrials
closed at . . . .

"Mr. Chairman, are these unofficial figures I have in
front of me—that each of you has in front of you—correct? Or have my informants been leading me down
the garden path? The figures on the use of hard drugs,
for example?"

"Madam President, I don't know quite how to answer that."

"You don't, eh? You're Chairman of the Joint Chiefs
and for four years before that chief of staff of your service. If these figures are not right, how far are they off
and which way?"

"Ma'am, that is a question that should be put to
each of the Services, not to me."

"So? General, you are relieved of active duty. A request for retirement will be acted on favorably, later today. You are excused. General Smith, take the chair."

The President waited until the door closed behind the ex-Chairman. Then she said soberly, "Gentlemen, it gives me no pleasure to put an end to the career of a man with a long and brilliant record. But I cannot keep in a top spot in my official family a military officer who can't or won't answer questions that, in my opinion, must be answered if I am to carry out my duties as Commander in Chief. If he had answered, 'I don't know now but I'll start digging at once and won't stop until'—but he said nothing of the sort. I gave him two chances; he brushed me off." She sighed. "I suppose he dislikes taking orders from one with no military experience; I do not assume that my sex and skin color had anything to do with it. General Smith, you are in the chair by default; I can't ask you about the other Services. How about your own? Hard drugs."

"I suspect that this figure is conservative, Ma'am. I've been trying to get hard data on hard drugs since I was appointed to this job a year ago. In most cases we need evidence from medical officers to make it stick . . . and all our doctors are overworked; we don't have nearly enough of them. Worse yet, some of the doctors are pushers themselves; two were caught."

"What happened to them? Making little ones out of big ones?"

"No, Ma'am. Discharged. In civilian practice, I suppose."

"For God's sake, *why?* Has the Army forgotten how to hold a court martial? Two drug pushers, simply sent home and still licensed to practice medicine— and to prescribe drugs. General, I'm shocked."

"Ma'am, may I say something in my own defense? Then you can have my request for retirement, if you wish it."

"Please. Go ahead."

"These cases occurred before I became Chief of Staff. At the time these two were caught, I was Superintendent of the War College; drugs are not a problem there. When last I had troop duty, I *did* have a policy of treating use of hard drugs as a criminal offense, as permitted and required by regulations. But the very most I ever managed was to get some sent to the V.A. for hospital cure and rehabilitation. Under the present rules, if a man has a good lawyer—and they do, usually—he can get away from courts martial and appeal to a civilian judge. That usually ends it."

"Madam President, may I add something?"

"Certainly, Admiral."

"Have you heard of the mutiny in the *Somers* about a century and a half back?"

"I— Yes, I think I have! A novel. *Voyage to the—Voyage to the First of December.* Right?"

"There was a novel some years back; I think that was the book's title. I haven't read it. Then you are aware that it was a tragic scandal, with mutineers hanged at the yardarms. What I wanted to say was this: I think the figures on drugs in the Navy are about right—lower than in the Army, of course; the circumstances are different. But what is killing the Navy—aside from a shortage of career officer material—is that both mutiny and sabotage are out of hand . . . because offenses that used to rate hanging from the yardarm are now treated as 'Boys will be boys.' A great deal of it does derive from a change in the legal structure, as the General said. I would rather have five ships properly maintained, properly manned, shipshape and Bristol style, than ten ships undermanned and shot through with men who should never have been accepted in the first place. A stupid and sullen seaman is worse than no one at all."

The President said, "Judges, chapter seven."

The Admiral looked puzzled. The Marine Commandant suddenly said, "Gideon's Band!"

"Exactly. I suspect that we have been trying to meet

quotas—numbers of men—rather than placing quality first. I'm sure it's not as simple as that, but that does seem to be part of it. General, does the Air Force have any different slant on this?"

"No, Ma'am, I think the Navy and the Corps both speak for me. And the Army . . . although Smitty's problems are different from ours. Our worst problem is hanging on to trained men . . . because what we teach them, flying and electronics especially, are very salable on the outside. I want to add something, though. Marijuana is not on the list of drugs. It may very well be true that grass is no worse than liquor. But neither one mixes with driving a flying machine. Or anything in an airplane. But grass is harder to cope with. A stash is easier to hide than a bottle, and it is harder to tell when a man is stoned than when he is drunk. And much harder to prove. I welcome suggestions."

"I think we all do. Although I think we've pinpointed one essential. Quality before quantity. Gentlemen, we'll let this marinate about ten days while all of us try to spot all of the basic things that are wrong . . . then meet again and exchange ideas. In writing. Call the shots as you see them, don't be afraid of hurting feelings, pay no attention to sacred cows. Admiral, you found things wrong with the military legal system; please analyse the matter, with specific recommendations. If you truly feel that we need to go back to keelhauling and hanging at the yardarm, say so."

"I do not, Ma'am. But I do think the present rules are more suited to a Scout camp than to a fighting force. Punishment should be swift and certain; mutineers should not be coddled. We need a new code."

"Work on it. I assume that you have legal aides. Mr. Secretary of Defense, I have not intended to monopolize the floor. Before we adjourn, I want you to give us your opinions on problems of discipline. I would like to hear comment on those figures I supplied, all categories. But you aren't limited to that. Feel free to bring up anything. I think that discipline in the Armed Forces is as serious a problem as I face . . . and the most difficult."

"Discipline is not one of the duties of the Secretary of Defense."

"So? What are your duties?"

"To manage my department. Discipline belongs to these gentlemen. Not to me. And certainly not to *you*. You are way out of line."

"You forgot something, sir. The President is in the direct line of command, at the top, and cannot avoid responsibility for any aspect of her command. The Secretary of Defense is *not* in the line of command; he is an executive secretary for the President. However, since you see your job as merely managerial, and not concerned with morale and discipline, I won't press you about it. I have your signed resignation in my desk, inherited from my predecessor. I'm accepting it. At once."

The ex-Secretary leaned back and laughed. "How just like a woman! Ruffle her feathers and she flies off the handle. But it's okay, Shortie; I didn't intend to stay this long. After the Chief died I was ready to quit. But Charlie asked me to stick around a little longer, keep an eye on you. I know what you did to him the day of the tragedy, standing in his way when he was entitled to the job. You never were anything but an election poster. Didn't anybody ever tell you that?"

"You may leave now. You're excused."

"Oh, I'm leaving; I've got a press conference in ten minutes. Just one thing: You said Joe probably disliked taking orders from you because you've had no military experience. Nonsense. Any top brass expects to take orders from a civilian. But no real man will take orders from a nigger, much less a nigger wench."

The Marine was out of his chair so fast that it overturned, snatched the ex-Secretary out of his chair and got a hammerlock on him—but beat the others to it only by being closest.

"Down on your knees and apologize, you jerk! That's the *President of the United States* you're talking to!" The Marine General's Deep South accent, ordinarily carefully corrected, came out in full force, thick as gumbo.

"Make him take his hands off me!"

"Keep him secure, General. And thank you, sir. But don't rough him up more than necessary. Admiral, if you will be so kind as to check, I think you will find two Marines and two Secret Service men just outside that door. Please ask one of them to telephone for two White House Police. I want this person removed from the building and not allowed back in. Nor back into the Pentagon, ever. Most especially not into his former office."

"A pleasure, Ma'am!"

"Thank you, sir. I hope to see you all here at the same time a week from Thursday. General Smith, I ask you to remain chairman pro tem, in addition to your regular duties. Adjourn when it suits you. I'm withdrawing now; I want to lie down. I find that I am a bit shaky. . . . "

CND 4Ø6CRH
CHEYENNE—LEGISLATURE BOTH HOUSES PASSED OVER-WHELMINGLY FIRST AND SECOND READING EMERGENCY MEA-SURE RESTORING PAUPERS OATH FOR RECIPIENTS OF ANY PUBLIC ASSISTANCE OF ANY SORT REPEAT ANY SORT IN RESPONSE TO GOVERNOR'S IMPASSIONED CLAIM THAT THERE WOULD BE NO MONEY FOR THE BLIND AND THE TOTALLY HELPLESS UNLESS STATE RETURNED TO NINETEENTH CENTURY TEST OF ELIGIBIL-ITY MORE MORE
CND4Ø9CRH
CHEYENNE—AMERICAN CIVIL LIBERTIES UNION WILL FILE CLASS ACTION IN FEDERAL COURT TO STOP RESTORATION OF PAUPERS OATH AS PREREQUISITE FOR PUBLIC ASSISTANCE.

"Come in, Senator! Thank you for doing me this favor!"

"Madam President, it would be a pleasure to call on you at any time even if you were not President. Perhaps more."

"Uncle Sam, I don't know what that means but I like it. Now to work! Would it suit you to work for me?"

"You know it would, my dear—but I have a constituency."

"I don't mean resign and take a job here. But can't you pair votes, or something? I need a lot of help from you right now and more later."

"Anything the President wants, the President gets. Yes, I can always arrange a pair . . . even when I'm only nominally out of the District." He looked down at her. "Trouble?"

"Work I don't know how to handle. I've got to appoint twenty-three judges and I can't put it off much longer. And I don't know how to tell a knucklehead from an Oliver Wendell Holmes. See that tall stack? And that one? Those are the written opinions—or other legal writings if they are not already judges— from the candidates for judgeships. No names on them, and other identifications blacked out. Just identification numbers. I thought I could read this mess and tell which ones had their heads screwed on tight. I can't. I don't understand legalese, I'm not a lawyer."

"I'm not a lawyer either, bright eyes."

"No, but you're the world's leading semanticist. I figured that, if you couldn't understand something, then it was really nonsense."

"It's a good approach. If a person of normal intelligence, and a reasonably full education, cannot understand a piece of prose, then it *is* gibberish. But you shouldn't be doing it; you have a country to worry about. I don't have time, either, but I'll take time; my staff are quite competent to wipe the noses and hold the hands of my constituents for a while. I'll arrange it."

"Then you'll do it! Uncle Sam, you're a dear!"

"But I want a bribe."

"You do? I thought *I* was supposed to be offered bribes, not have to pay them."

"I'm eccentric. I take bribes only from pretty little girls I've known a long time."

"You're eccentric, all right. What is that thing you wear on your head? A cow pat?"

"My dear, you're colorblind. Madam President, I have a proposed amendment to the Constitution I want you to sponsor . . . and by great good luck I just happen to have a copy of it on me."

"I'll bet you sleep with a copy of it on you. No, just put it on the desk. Now tell me what it is supposed to accomplish."

"It permits a citizen to challenge the Constitutionality of any law or regulation, Federal or any lesser authority, on the grounds that it is ambivalent, equivocal, or cannot be understood by a person of average intelligence. Paragraph two defines 'average intelligence.' Paragraph three defines and limits the tests that may be used to test the challenged law. The fourth paragraph excludes law students, law school graduates, lawyers, judges, and uncertified j.p.'s from being test subjects. I call it 'the Semantic Amendment.'"

"No, you don't; you call it 'the Plain English Amendment.' Show biz, Uncle Sam. Senator, under this amendment could a person challenge the income tax law on the grounds that he has to hire an expert to make out his form 1040?"

"He certainly could. And he would win, too, as no three I.R.S men can get the same answers out of identical data if the picture is at all complex."

"Hmm— What if he's bright enough but can't read?"

"Paragraph three."

"How about the Federal Budget? It isn't law in the usual meaning but Congress votes on it and it has the force of law, where it applies."

"First paragraph. It quacks like a duck, waddles like a duck—it's a duck."

"I'll try to study this before I fall asleep tonight. Senator, this one we're going to put over!"

"Don't be too certain, Madam President. Lawyers are going to hate this . . . and the Congress and all the state legislatures have a majority of lawyers."

"And every one of them not anxious to lose his job. That's their weakness . . . because it's awfully easy to work up hate against lawyers. Senator, this bill will be introduced by lawyers. Both Houses. Both parties. Not by you, you're not a lawyer. Uncle Sam, I'm an amateur president but I'm a pro in show biz. It'll play in Paducah."

The two Presidents were seated alone at the front of the crowded grandstand. Two kilometers in front of them a spaceship, small compared with the Shuttle assemblage, but close to the size of the Shuttle alone, stood upright in the bright Mexican mountain sunshine. A voice from everywhere was counting: "—sixty-one seconds . . . . . one minute . . . . fifty-nine . . . fifty-eight—"

She said, "How are you coming with Spanglish, Señor el Presidente?"

He shrugged and smiled, "As before, Doña la Presidenta. I know it is simple; I hear your people and ours talking in it . . . and I understand them. But I don't have time to study. When I leave office—" He spread his hands.

"I know. Perhaps two years from now—I can't believe I've been in office only six years. It feels like sixty."

"You've accomplished sixty years of statecraft; the whole world is awestruck."

"—forty-one . . . forty . . . thirty-nine—"

"There never was anything really seriously wrong with my country, Mr. President. We made some silly mistakes, then compounded them by being stubborn. The Fence, for example. What's the point in a Fence that doesn't work? So I had it torn down."

"Madam, your most creative act of statesmanship! Without that act of faith you and I could never have put over our Treaty of Mutual Assistance. And the dozen major advances we have started under it. This. You and I would not be sitting here."

"Yes. No more wetbacks and *this*. Mr. President, I *still* don't understand how a beam of light can put a spaceship into orbit."

"Neither do I, Madam President, neither do I. But I believe your engineers."

"So do I but it frightens me."

"—fifteen . . . The Binational Solar Power Zone is now on standby power . . . nine . . . eight—"

"*Oh!* Will you hold my hand? *Please!*"

"—four! . . . three! . . . two! . . . one! . . . *LIGHT!*"

A single inhalation by thousands, then came the everywhere voice in soft, reverent tones: "Look at that bastard *go!*"

☆ ☆ ☆

"—direct from O'Neill Village, Ell-Five. It's a beautiful day here, it's *always* a beautiful day here. But today is our happiest fiesta ever; little Ariel Henson Jones, first baby born in space, is one year old today. All four of her grandparents are here, her father's parents having traveled all the way from Over-the-Rainbow, Ell-Four, via Luna City Complex, just to be here on this great day. Don't repeat this but a little bird, a parrot, told me that one of Ariel's grandmothers is pregnant again. I won't say which one but it's *personal* good news for *all* of us here in the sky because, if true and I can assure you it is, it is one more and very important datum in the rapidly growing list to show that youthfulness in all ways is markedly extended simply by living in free-fall. Correction: the mild acceleration we experience at the skin of our Village . . . but which we can leave behind completely at any time for free-fall sports at the axis.

"And *you* can enjoy them, too. This newscast comes to you sponsored by O'Neill Village Chamber of Commerce. Visitors welcome. You <u>haven't</u> *lived* until you ride the Light Beam, the cheapest way to travel per thousand kilometers ever invented by a factor of at least one hundred . . . and not uncomfortable even the first few seconds since the installation of the new total-support hydraulic couches. Also you haven't lived until you've seen our free-fall ballet! You think Las Vegas has shows? Wait till you see a Coriolis torch dance. Or what free-fall does for a hundred-centimeter bust. Oh, boy! Or if you like to gamble we'll take your money with brand-new games as happily as Monte Carlo or Atlantic City. See your travel agent for a variety of package vacations.

"Or more than a vacation. Buying a share in the Village is cheaper than buying a house in most cities down heavyside. But if you are young and healthy and possess certain needed skills your migration into the sky can be subsidized. Phone the placement office here for details, same rates as from San Francisco to New York. Wups! Almost forgot to tell you: knowledge of industrial Spanglish required, plus some Brownie points for any other language you know. . . . "

☆ ☆ ☆

It *could* be that way, over the Rainbow. As Madam President said, there never has been anything incurably wrong with our country and our world—just a horrid accumulation of silly mistakes that could be corrected with horse sense and the will to do it.

We have a lot of healthy, intelligent people with a wide spread of useful skills, trades, and professions. We have a wonderful big country not yet too crowded and still wealthy in real wealth—oh, bankrupt on paper but that can always be corrected with real wealth, will, and work. Actually it's easier to be happy and get rich than it is to go down the chute. This country has so much going for it that it takes a lot of work combined with wrong-headed stubbornness to ruin this country. It's not easy.

☆ ☆ ☆

In the meantime don't go away. There are still a lot of sacred cows I haven't kicked but plan to . . . someday. So, unless I'm hit by a taxicab while swiveling on my cane to ogle pretty girls, I'll be back.

The End.